Naked *in* Mayfair

The Secret Socialite

First published in 2023 by The Secret Socialite,
in partnership with Whitefox Publishing

This paperback edition published in 2024

www.wearewhitefox.com

Copyright © The Secret Socialite, 2023

ISBN 978-1-916797-00-0
Also available as an ebook
ISBN 978-1-915635-24-2

The Secret Socialite asserts the moral right to be identified as the author of this work.

All rights reserved. No part of this publication may be reproduced, stored in a retrieval system or transmitted in any form or by any means, electronic, mechanical, photocopying, recording or otherwise, without prior written permission of the author.

While every effort has been made to trace the owners of copyright material reproduced herein, the author would like to apologise for any omissions and will be pleased to incorporate missing acknowledgements in any future editions.

Designed and typeset by Typo•glyphix, Burton-on-Trent, DE14 3HE
Cover design by Heike Schüssler
Project management by Whitefox Publishing

Printed and bound by CPI Group (UK) Ltd, Croydon, CR0 4YY

This novel is based on true events. The identifying features of people and places have been changed in order to protect their privacy, and the descriptions of certain individuals and situations have been altered to further protect their identity. Any similarities are purely coincidental.

The truth that we hide is naked,
the one that we flaunt is so well dressed.
    Abhijit Kar Gupta, computational physicist

To my children, who carry the light.

To H, the man of my dreams.

And to you, dear reader.
Never give up on love.

Contents

Prologue: Be More Woman	vii
1. A Study in Alternate Reality	1
2. What Doesn't Kill You Makes You Stronger	19
3. Love Is Not Enough	33
4. His Lordship's View: Keeping the British End Up	49
5. Paradise Lost	61
6. Stepping into the Same River Twice	77
7. The Lieutenant Colonel's View: The Empire Strikes Back	91
8. Some Like It Hot	97
9. If I Dream of You, Do You Dream of Me Too?	109
10. It's in the Kiss	117
11. Déjà Vu All Over Again	131
12. The Etonian's View: Life in the Slow Lane	143
13. Basic Instinct	151
14. Justice? What Justice?	163
15. The Circle of Enlightenment, Mayfair Style	167
16. A First Time for Everything	175
17. An Angel's View: Everything, All the Time	189

CONTENTS

18.	Three Blondes Waiting for Godot	195
19.	Mind the Gap	205
20.	Mayfair Marriage: Uncomfortably Numb	217
21.	In Another Time, Another Life	231
22.	Beware Fog	239
23.	The California Boy's View: Cosmic Karma	253
24.	Why Can't Love Be More Like Maths?	259
25.	Pop Goes the Weasel	265
26.	View from the Grouse Moors: What's Under the Kilt?	277
27.	Don't You Want Me, Baby?	279
28.	The Hero's View: The Delicate Dance of Mortality	299
29.	Now You See Me, Now You Don't	309
30.	Life: Don't Cock It Up	323
31.	The Course of True Love Never Did Run Smooth	331

Prologue: Be More Woman

Love is the answer. Love is always the answer, whatever the question. Ava knew that, to her core. But she was failing in love: failing to find love, failing to feel love, failing to live love. She was out every night, in a fog of loneliness.

While Ava was not into the darker arts, she decided to see a celebrity psychic. Ostensibly, it was for fun, but in reality, it was to give her hope that maybe, one fine day, she might find Real Love and feel a little less alone in the world.

Like all good psychics, she wore a big black kaftan, with silver chains clattering around her neck and coloured rings sparkling on her fingers. She was a tiny woman with a huge life force, and she spoke with a strong Greek accent and a twinkle in her eye. She scrutinised Ava, then pulled out her tarot cards, half closing her eyes to enhance her concentration. She sucked her breath in, and then breathed out slowly.

'I see you, Ava. I see you *verrrrry* well. You have many, many men. You like men, eh! You like men verrrrry, verrrrry much. There ees many men around you, always. But I see one. He has blue eyes. I like him.' Her dark eyes went straight through Ava. 'You're gonna meet a tall man. He works in finance. He has kind eyes. I like him. I like him a lot.'

Ava laughed, confident that this was the psychic's favourite line. What single woman would not want to meet a tall man in finance with kind eyes?

'Thees man, he's gonna take his time to appear. There's gonna be three or four other men in your life. But he's the one, Ava. He's gonna be the man of your dreams. Your cards are amaaaaaazing. I never see cards like thees. Amaaaaaazing!'

Ava thought of the many times the psychic must have uttered those same reassuring words.

'But, Ava, stop being such a smart-arse. Be more feminine. Be more woman. Let the man be the man,' the psychic said with a smile.

Ava bit her lip.

The psychic nodded and continued. 'Thees man, his name, it begin with the letter "H". He's a grrrrrreat guy. Believe me. You're gonna be verrrrry, verrrrry happy.'

Ava racked her brains. She did not know any 'H' men that she could think of. And in the days and weeks that followed, Ava often thought about those happy words. They reassured her: yes, she would, finally, fall in love and she would also be loved back. But as the weeks became months, and the search for 'H' failed to bear fruit, she realised the words were less of a blessing, and more of a curse.

1.

A Study in Alternate Reality

O nce upon a time, there was a lonely woman who was beautiful on the outside but sad on the inside. Solitary in her Mayfair pad, she dreamt of the day her Prince Charming would find her and awaken her with the kiss of True Love, and then whisk her off on his fine white charger, galloping into the golden sunset.

Ava reclined on her grey velvet sofa, gazing wistfully into the flames that roared in the marble fireplace. The clock struck midnight. In her endless search for her soulmate, she sighed and picked up her iPhone. It was time for her to embrace the modern world and look for love online. She logged on to Tinder.

No. No. Definitely no. Are you kidding? Oh, no. No. Another no. Crikey, no. Those teeth? Urgh. Ava continued to swipe. *For sure, no. I never knew there were so many roofers in London. No, not on your life.*

Love in the twenty-first century is like everything else that can be ordered up with a couple of clicks and swipes: a dating app with a secret algorithm that conjures up the perfect match on the basis of alleged age, location and a set of alluring snaps. Theoretically, it was as good a place to start as any. After all, where else could you find all that choice and the ease and speed of access to so many single men? In reality, it was tedious and utterly soul-destroying. Ava swiped a hundred times, and a hundred nos.

She almost missed him. Hugo. Forty-seven. Blond, sad blue eyes, Etonian, financier, dog-lover. She swiped right, then forgot about him until Hugo messaged her a few days later. They exchanged the usual banter. After a couple of texts, they realised they came from similar worlds: both bankers, bruised but somehow still hopeful and looking for love, or some version of it.

The texts started banally enough.

How are you?

How was your day?

How's life in the fast lane?

Then:

You look vaguely familiar. I know it sounds like a line, but haven't I seen you somewhere before, perhaps in one of the fleshpots of Mayfair?

Now I remember where I've seen you. Our children went to the same prep school. Odd we should meet on Tinder, when we could have met at the school gates.

Somehow, they had still not met in person, but the texts shifted seamlessly to:

I'm feeling bouncy.

That's promising. I'm feeling perky.

Bouncy and perky is a winning combination. Like strawberries and cream, gin and tonic, hard and wet...

In the space of a few days, they had graduated to:

You're electrifying. I want to smell you, to taste you.

Such are the mysterious workings of the hope serum that is a promising Tinder connection. All that desire, distilled into a set of tantalising text messages. Then came hours and hours of longing, verging on the lyrical.

There's no emoji to express how much I want you. I want to be deep inside you, to feel you, to look deep into your eyes and kiss you. You make me hard, just getting a text from you.

And then the late-night bedtime variants, more colourful still.

I want to fuck you very hard, and then very, very tenderly.

Ava was enthralled. How could she not be? Hugo's texts were both sexy and witty. And he was exactly her type, or at least, so he appeared in his photos. With his Nordic good looks, he was refined, even in scruffy jeans and a plain white T-shirt. And his soulful blue eyes that were tinged with pain melted her heart. When they spoke on the phone, Ava was even more mesmerised. Hugo's voice was low and upper class, and Ava swooned, like the eighteenth-century romantic heroine that she clearly was not. They had not even met, but they both felt a strong connection. Every text was a jolt of electricity, and every voicemail made her heart race. Ava could not wait for the big reveal.

After what felt like months but was in fact two weeks, Hugo asked Ava on a date. She aspired to be a modern woman, but Ava always waited for the man to make the first move. Despite her fancy education and her professional successes, Ava still operated on the basis that the man was Tarzan and she was Jane, and never the other way round. A female Tarzan was undignified. In her Mayfair jungle, the man was the hunter and if he wanted her, he should be man enough to come and get her.

On the appointed day, Ava sat listlessly on the trading floor. Her eyes glazed over as she scanned her hedge fund's key positions, now just blurs of blinking neon on the three computer screens and the two trading terminals at her desk. She rifled through the latest Fed Monetary Policy Report and then attempted to read the *Financial Times*. She was unable to eat and she felt a pressing need to visit the loo every couple of hours. All she could think about was the moment when she would look into Hugo's eyes, and smell and feel him. Even the thought of holding his hand was arousing.

Still recovering from her first relationship post-divorce, Ava had already been on many first dates. She knew the drill: don't get your hopes up, wear something feminine but not overtly sexy, let the man do most of the talking, engage him in intense eye contact, and whatever you do, don't ever say you're looking for a serious relationship, let alone a new husband. Above all, be light, playful and uncomplicated: the epitome of feminine sweetness.

She bathed every nook and cranny, even though she knew she would never go beyond first base on a first date. She appraised herself in the mirror as she slathered on her Chanel N° 5 body oil. She might be on the wrong side of thirty-five, but she was still beautiful: slender, hard body; full breasts; silky-smooth olive skin. A body made for loving. Those green eyes were shining; her pupils dilated with anticipation, her full lips waiting, wanting to be kissed. She tossed her long blonde hair back and tonight, for a change, she was able to smile at her reflection.

'Would you want to fuck you?' she asked herself, with a self-mocking giggle.

This was the ultimate litmus test of desirability; Ava was her harshest critic and she never felt remotely as stunning as she wanted to.

'Fuck me? Tonight? Hell, yes.' Ava laughed out loud.

Date dress was a tight taupe sleeveless leather sheath that embraced her curves, worn with preposterously high heels, naturally. And bare legs, of course. A tiny spritz of Guerlain perfume, not too much. She wanted to smell Hugo and she wanted him to smell her, not her scent. She was so giddy with excitement that she tripped on the pavement, and only just regained her balance in the nick of time. Still, she was laughing. She was happy that even at this age, she was not immune to the butterflies that accompany a first date.

As she skipped into the candlelit Connaught Bar, her heart was beating so fast that at first she did not see him.

'Ava?'

A familiar voice. The voice of seduction. Hugo stood up. Yes, he was, beyond doubt, six feet tall; he had not inflated his height on his dating profile. She drew breath. He was even more handsome in the flesh than in the photos.

Bullseye, she thought. *Call off the search. Where do I sign? This is it. I've found Him.*

Like Jane Eyre before her, Ava was ready to pronounce, 'Reader, I married him', right there and then.

They sipped a few lychee martinis at the bar, then stayed on and had dinner. Lost in Hugo's eyes, Ava fought the overwhelming urge to reach out and squeeze his hand at the table. She was falling deeper into the whirlwind of her romantic fantasies. She could already picture herself, Sleeping Beauty awakened, standing next to her very own Mr H at the altar, in a diaphanous bridal gown, radiant with love.

Ava shook herself out of her reverie and forced herself to listen to what Hugo was saying. There were a couple of minor snags. Obviously. No one gets to forty-seven without them. Hugo had not had sex in almost two years, which was marginally disturbing for a woman like Ava, with her turbo-charged libido, but understandable within the context of a failing marriage and the intention to go slowly next time around. If anything, it confirmed his status as a serious, discriminating person, rather than the player type Ava was normally drawn to.

More perplexingly, he was not quite the carefree, sophisticated figure from his messaging. His aristocratic background was more a burden than a badge of honour. His understated dress sense was not that curiously patrician English affectation of wanting to look impoverished, but rather a way of passing unnoticed. Stunning as he was, he displayed a startling diffidence, uncannily mirroring Ava's own. They just expressed their insecurity in opposite ways: Ava, by hiding under her sexy leathers, and Hugo, by hiding under his inconspicuous T-shirt and jeans. His bashful style was not amusing posturing *à la* Hugh Grant. His lack of confidence was sincere, and it reflected his genuine doubts about himself and his place in the world.

When Ava looked at Hugo, she noticed the cracks. But she adored him all the more for them. All she saw was his light.

'I had an idyllic childhood on the estate,' Hugo said. 'We were always riding and hunting and fishing. In my memory, it was always summer, and we were always eating scrumptious picnics, stretched out on a tartan blanket on the grass. But it all went a bit pear-shaped after I turned thirteen and I was packed off to board at Eton. I was a painfully lonely child, and I was rubbish at sports, so it was hard to fit in. I felt like I didn't belong.'

Ava's eyes widened. She knew all about not belonging, except she had been at the other end of the socio-economic spectrum.

'Then my father died young. His chopper fell out of the sky. Engine failure, they said. I had three older brothers, but somehow, being the youngest, I was the one who spent a lot of time looking after Mum, who wasn't coping terribly well.'

The conversation turned to the present day.

'So, Ava, why did you get divorced, if I may ask?' Hugo blinked.

It was such a simple, obvious and innocent question. It yielded a complex, nuanced and multi-layered answer. Ava should, by now, have a short and snappy reply ready. But she didn't. And she always struggled to respond. She wanted to be truthful, and yet she knew how difficult it was to explain the idiosyncratic nuances of her marriage to herself, let alone to another person.

'Well,' Ava said, running her finger along the rim of her glass, 'I guess, um, the marriage had run its course.'

She tried to speak as evenly as possible. This was her stock non-answer.

She thought Hugo deserved a bit better, so she paused and added, 'We had a highly functioning marriage, and most women would probably have stayed. We were an ultra-glamorous couple, jetting around the world and, you know, living the dream.'

Hugo raised his left eyebrow.

'Ironically, we were the least likely of all our friends to get divorced.' Ava fiddled with her hair. 'But my former husband, well, he was not quite husband of the year. He spent many years misbehaving and generally buggering about.' Ava cleared her throat. 'This is so boring, Hugo. Do you really want to hear all this stuff?'

Hugo nodded.

'Well, when I found out about all his affairs, I was shell-shocked. I literally felt the ground fall from under me,' said Ava, biting her lip. 'It was the classic infidelity stereotype: I was so busy with my full-on trading job and raising my daughters, I had absolutely no idea. I was the last person to know.' Her eyes misted over. 'We saw a couple of marriage therapists, but they were useless. Let's face it: it's more or less impossible to keep a couple together after such a massive betrayal, and they couldn't heal the rift between us. How could I ever trust him again? Even so, I made a conscious decision to sweep everything under the carpet. My husband was faithful after that, I think, and we rolled along for another few years. But deep inside, I was broken. When my daughters were older, I could justify leaving him. And here we are. Anyway, that's more than enough about me.' Ava forced a smile. 'What about you, Hugo, why did you leave your wife?'

'Well, actually, my wife left me,' Hugo replied.

Ava was stunned at his honesty. And bewildered. Who in their right mind would ever want to leave this man?

'It was not altogether the most blissful of unions. By the time I turned thirty, I guess I was, er, lonely and I really wanted my own family. My cousin set me up with Hettie, a tall, luscious blonde – well, she was back then – and we sort of fell into marriage.' Hugo gave a ghost of a smile. 'Ah, the innocence of youth. Then we had our two boys, and Hettie somehow forgot I even existed. And the years passed, as they do. Turned out, Hettie was the kind of woman who's never happy. She was very focused on the boys. And when she remembered that I was still around, she just complained. All the time. Non-stop. It was exhausting never being, er, good enough.' Hugo coughed and looked away. 'Well, that's my little story. I think we've both had our dose of pop psychology for one night. Let's get out of here. I'll walk you home.'

It was pouring with rain. So much for Ava's lovely strappy sandals. But Ava was not thinking about her footwear as they huddled together under the umbrella, with Hugo's arm wrapped protectively around her shoulders. They arrived at her house and the door was barely closed behind them when he took her face in his hands, looked deep into her eyes and kissed her.

It was not a kiss; it was The Kiss. His tongue brushed over her lips, she stroked the back of his neck and drew his head to hers, electrified by his smell and taste. She moved her body instinctively into his. They were an exact fit. They were wet and fully clothed, but she could feel his huge erection. Perfect. It had been a while since she had felt such a massive cock. She wanted to go down on her knees, unzip his jeans and give him the best head he'd ever had. But she restrained herself. In any event, the kissing was so exquisite, it was enough, for now. They both savoured it and lost themselves in it. They were their very own golden Gustav Klimt, their own marble Carrara Rodin; and all the better for being real flesh and blood.

It was late. Very late. So late, it was now early morning.

'I should probably head home,' Hugo said. 'I've got an investment debrief with the team first thing.'

He stumbled out into the cold morning air. As soon as he left her house, he texted her. He told her what a lovely evening he had spent with her, how marvellous she felt in his arms, and how their tongues and lips and bodies meshed so well together.

Date number two: more of the same. Date three: much more of the same. Date four: the mutual intensity of their desire was now running at fever pitch, and they decided it was time to fuck for real, not in the safety of text messages hurtling through cyberspace.

They had fantasised about it a hundred times. They had visualised it and described it to themselves, and to each other, on WhatsApp, in many multiple variations. They had gone to sleep dreaming about it and woken up stirred by it. And the thrilling buzz of desire accompanied them throughout the day.

They had dinner at 34, a discreet Mayfair restaurant. Quietly chic and, crucially, local; from there, they could fall straight into Ava's bed. Her thoughts were far from food, but she chose her meal with care. No onion (she didn't want bad breath), no spinach (fear of green bits stuck to her teeth), no sashimi (too smelly) and limited alcohol (just enough to lubricate, but not enough to dull the senses). Hugo managed half a steak tartare; he seemed rather less anxious than Ava about any lingering odours.

They rushed home and, at last, they sat on Ava's bed. They were both nervous. Hugo unzipped Ava's dress and then pulled off his jeans and T-shirt. He blinked as he stared at Ava in her carefully chosen nude La Perla silk-and-lace underwear. It was tasteful and classy, nothing too racy at this point. She did not want to surprise Hugo with her full-on bondage-style lingerie quite yet. Underwear was the last thing on Hugo's mind. Or rather, his thoughts were of getting it off. He managed to unhook her bra, even though his hands were shaking.

Hugo cupped Ava's breast and bent down to lick her nipples, precisely as Ava loved, as though he had read her very own personal sex instruction manual. He stroked her neck and shoulders, gazing into her eyes. For all the differences in their backgrounds and in their outward styles, there was no denying their sexual compatibility and the white heat of their desire.

Ava was so overwhelmed to have Hugo in her bed, she was unusually slow to take action. She experienced sensory overload. In the mouth-watering buffet that was Hugo's body, she did not know where to start. There was so much tempting fare on offer: a bounty of deliciousness she had only dreamt about. She wanted to relish and savour every second.

As Hugo slipped off his pants, the buffet became even more appetising. Ava was transfixed. She had never seen such a beautiful cock. And she had seen many cocks. Hugo's was definitely *primus inter pares*. Long and thick, Hugo's cock was perfectly formed and rock hard. No erectile dysfunction here. No 'I'm so sorry, but this has *never* happened to me before' sad excuses for wilting tumescence.

Ava wanted to take all of Hugo in, physically and emotionally. She wanted to remember every detail of his body, his touch, his kiss. Most of all, she wanted to be in the moment and in the flow; she wanted to feel, not think. She admired his creamy, muscular body, practically hairless bar his strawberry-blond pubic hair. She had never seen such peerless proportions before. She could not believe her luck. Maybe it was a numbers game after all: the law of large numbers. Very large. Perhaps, if you kiss enough toads, odds are you'll eventually kiss your Prince Charming. And he'll have an impressive big sword too.

'Hugo,' she said, caressing his chest, 'how come you never hinted at how big and beautiful your cock is? All those thousands of texts you sent me, and you didn't breathe a word. Any other man would have boasted or at least mentioned it in some way. But you didn't say anything at all. Not a whisper.'

'Oh, you know,' Hugo mumbled.

Ava did not know.

Hugo's hand trembled as he stroked her face. 'It's not my style to brag. I prefer to surprise on the upside. One of the tricks of the trade I learnt from the world of investing. Best to under-promise and over-deliver,' he stammered.

'But, Hugo,' Ava persevered, not wanting this to veer off into a discussion on investment philosophy, 'you do have a spectacular cock.'

Hugo wondered if Ava said that to all the boys. Truth be told, she had been unusually lucky in the spectacular cock department. But even with her exceptionally high standards in that area, as in so many others, Hugo's cock was an outlier. The cock of cocks.

Hugo kissed her again. Soft and sweet and wet. Their mouths melded together just as their bodies were about to. He drew her long blonde hair off her face. Ava's senses were fully awakened and aroused, and she could not resist anymore. She decided to take charge, and pushed him back onto the pillow, then straddled him. She teased Hugo's cock with her wet pussy, sliding it over her swollen clit, as she thrust her hips back and forth, feeling him. They moaned with pleasure, turned on and tuned in to each other.

Both Hugo and Ava wanted to prolong that perfect moment of peak desire, just before his cock would be deep inside her. Hugo looked up into Ava's eyes as he caressed the curves of her breasts and hips. She felt so close and connected to him. She never imagined that a stuffy Etonian could be this sensual. He pulled her down, rolled her onto her back and manoeuvred his massive cock into her, very slowly.

Ava gasped. It was beyond exquisite. Deeper than deep. She felt him moving inside her. He felt enveloped by her warm, tight, wet pussy. She arched her back to feel him deeper still. They held each other tightly as they kissed. Rapture.

But not quite yet.

Now she wanted to taste him. Repositioning herself, she nestled between his thighs. She smiled: she could barely fit him into her mouth, which was itself on the large side. She took his shaft in her fist and gently played with his circumcised head with her lips and tongue. Losing herself in the moment, she was practically orgasming from the flicker of her tongue over the tip of his cock. Hugo lay back and watched her, not knowing which he preferred: watching her enjoying sucking him or feeling her suck his cock. Gently, he moved her away, afraid to come too soon, and he pushed her back down on the bed. He parted her smooth, golden legs and her hairless vulva, and slowly inserted two fingers into her wet pussy. With a flat tongue, he licked her clit, feeling her body tense, taking his time, until she exploded in his mouth with a loud groan. Then he came on top and thrust hard into her. She kissed him passionately and tasted herself on his lips.

'Tell me when you're coming,' said Ava, 'I want to feel you.'

Ava loved the weight of Hugo's body on top of her. He filled her completely. After all those racy texts, Ava knew that Hugo was even more tightly wrapped than she was, but she had succeeded in peeling away some of the layers, just as he had. He had penetrated and reached her inner core. And now she wanted to unleash him, and in so doing, unleash herself.

'I'm coming again,' Ava whispered. 'Come with me, Hugo.' She thrust her pelvis forwards and pulled him closer, wanting to feel every inch of him. They gripped each other as they came together, strongly, so strongly that Ava was utterly silent.

Afterwards, she wiped away a tear and hoped Hugo did not notice. She was wrong. Hugo had a finely trained eye for small details. He saw it all right, but said nothing.

They tried to sleep but did not succeed. She clung to his beautiful body, inhaling and memorising his intoxicating smell, the softness of his skin, the sweet milkiness of his taste, the Apollo-esque visual. That night, Ava had the vaguest of intimations that she was not quite so alone in the world after all. Hugo had seen her for who she really was, and with him she was naked, inside and out.

Ava luxuriated in that post-coital euphoria, where all was well with the world. She was bursting with happiness and the simple joy of being alive. It had been a long time since she had felt this whole. And calm. The flood of hormones brought her a sense of peace and oneness with the universe and her place in it.

Now, safely enveloped in Hugo's warmth and tenderness, it all started to make sense. Just as the psychic had predicted, here he was, her dream

'H' man, Hugo. It had to be Hugo. Of course it was Hugo. There was no doubt about it whatsoever. He was tall, he worked in finance and his eyes were most definitely kind. Ava felt a sense of poetic justice and perseverance rewarded, all rolled into one sumptuous, blue-eyed package. At long last.

After Hugo left, Ava could barely focus on anything more taxing than staring into space. She smiled as she thought only Hugo thoughts. She relived all the best Hugo moments from the night before, remembering them all in exquisite detail. She could still taste and smell him. She heard the buzz of a new WhatsApp message and snatched her phone, eagerly anticipating what Hugo would say about their wonderful time together.

Thank you, Hugo texted.

Thank you? Ava was flummoxed. Who writes 'thank you' after a night of fucking? Perhaps it was an Etonian thing, extreme politeness and good manners, though usually the famous Etonian charm offensive did not misfire.

Last night was amazing, he added.

There was an excruciating pause in the text messaging. Heart hammering, Ava waited for Hugo to continue texting.

But I don't think I can be in a relationship with you.

These were the words that he wrote to her, mere hours after their heavenly love-making. Ava could barely breathe.

Being with you has highlighted my sense of inadequacy.

Ava laughed. It was a nervous laugh. What? *Què*?

She reread Hugo's text. Surely there was a typo in there, a word she had misread on first cursory glance. Perhaps the entire sentence was a typo, one of those annoying autocorrect glitches. Ava wondered if she had been in the same bed as Hugo last night. Was she operating in cloud cuckoo land? Had she hallucinated the whole beautiful affair? Did she exist in her own parallel reality metaverse?

Ava blinked.

She cast her mind back to the protracted dance, the deliciously drawn-out developments that had led her to believe she had, finally, found someone with whom she could connect, someone with whom she thought she had indeed connected. She had taken things slowly. She had got to know him before going to bed with him. And she had hoped that, like all the dating books said, this would reinforce his knowing and wanting the real Ava, not just Ava the sexy blonde. She was baffled, and angry.

Why had he waited two months to tell her that he did not think he was ready to be in a relationship? Why did he realise this only *after* going to bed with her? Ha bloody ha. She tried to weave some form of narrative to explain this painful and bewildering kick in the heart.

To think of all the things Ava had tried to do, over so many lonely years, for some meagre crumbs of warmth and intimacy, for the vaguest feeling of closeness and for some semblance of a connection, maybe something possibly resembling L-O-V-E. At least some of the men from her past had the good manners to be cads from the start. That was helpful, as they saved her considerable time and heartache. And then there were the sweet men who had adored her, or at least, who had tried to. She got rid of them fast. It was unfamiliar terrain.

In her heart of hearts, Ava wondered if she deserved to be treated with kindness. After all, that was not how the men in her past had ever treated her, starting with her father and her stepfather. She felt uncomfortable with the decent men. She told herself that they did not challenge and excite her, but in reality, the kindness they offered scared her, and she dumped them. It was far easier to follow the usual script of unrequited love. It was Ava's very own Proustian *madeleine* of non-love.

But Hugo fell into neither category: he was neither a bastard nor a boring 'nice' guy. How did she get him so wrong? How did she fail to recognise the signs? She set her brain to playback mode and reviewed the last couple of months objectively, taking her ego out of the equation. She looked for clues. Self-delusion was, to her, one of the seven deadly sins, and one in which she hoped never to indulge.

What had she done wrong? Had she been too cool and distant? No. With Hugo, she had been uncharacteristically candid about how she felt about him.

Had she, on the other hand, been too keen and overwhelmed him? Yes, quite possibly. It had been such a long time since she had met anyone she liked this much. She had decided to listen to her heart and open it for a change. Maybe that was the problem: her unappealing over-enthusiasm? A moment of nakedness gone horribly wrong?

Or perhaps it was that hoary old chestnut: Hugo was just not as into Ava as she was into him. No, that wasn't it either. His body responded instantaneously to her touch. He'd told her several times he had never felt so attracted and so connected to any woman before, and no one had got to his core like she did. Ever. And he told her, over and over again, how she was a 'sensational and irresistible kisser' and how 'sexy, head-turning, funny and intelligent' he found her. These were the exact words Hugo had used. Multiple times. In person and on text. Ava still had the evidence from the reams and reams of his messages.

Maybe Hugo did not want to be in a relationship. The fact he was on a dating app did not necessarily mean he was interested in getting tied down again. It could be he just wanted a quick and easy hook-up with no strings. No. That was not Hugo's style at all. He had told her that when they would eventually go to bed together, he wanted it to 'mean something'. Fucking and running did not seem to be Hugo's modus operandi at all.

Or was it simply that hurt people hurt people? Did Ava fail to appreciate quite how damaged Hugo was? Maybe he needed to see a good shrink, and while he was at it, his relationship etiquette could do with a decent upgrade too.

Or could it be that Hugo changed his mind about being with Ava, *ex post facto*, and had summoned up that most irritating and cowardly of all fake excuses: the banal, 'It's not you, it's me.' Yeah, right. Not.

Maybe Ava was confusing sex with love. She was letting the quality of the sex be her guide to the quality of the man. Just because the sex had been sensational didn't necessarily mean that Hugo was a sensational match. Or something.

Ava's brain whirred. She was guilty of analysis paralysis. Hugo simply didn't want to be with her. Because. It happens. Too bad. One of life's great mysteries. Move on.

Whatever it was, Hugo's brush-off was all the more painful because it was so unexpected. Ava did not know whether she was more upset or more furious; quite possibly both. She sobbed for an hour. His rejection was magnified by reverberating like all the previous rejections she encountered through the course of what passed for her love life. As Bryan Ferry sang of the torments of being a 'Slave to Love', Ava could only agree. She reached for the Baileys with alarming regularity, liquidating its entire contents straight from the bottle. At this point, Ava was a blubbering slave to nothing but her own delusional fantasies.

The next morning, she woke to the sweet aftertaste of yesterday's Baileys. She decided that was quite enough snivelling self-pity, and she pulled herself together. She did what she had learnt to do whenever something unpleasant happened for which she could find neither a decent explanation nor unearth some useful pearls of wisdom. She pretended that the bad bits never happened.

Ava activated her own personal control+alt+delete function and erased Hugo from her memory bank. She started by removing his contact details, all his beautiful photos, his many funny and sexy voicemails and thousands of his exquisite text messages. It was a painful moment. All Ava's hopes and dreams of The Big Love were obliterated with a couple of clicks and wiped out, without trace, in the black hole of WhatsApp end-to-end encrypted nothingness.

And in that moment, rather satisfying it was too. No more Hugo. It was a full reset to default factory settings, pre-Hugo. No vestige of him remained; that is, except in Ava's head and heart, and hopefully that too would soon disappear. She knew from past experience that her phone could become a dangerous weapon of self-destruction, and she wanted to be one hundred per cent sure that she could not embarrass herself any more than she had already done, by contacting him in a moment of late-night vodka-fuelled longing.

And Ava moved on, as fast as was humanly possible. She went out even more than usual. She met new people, or more precisely, new men. And she got on with her lovely life. After all, everyone knows that the best way to get over one man is to get under a new one. She tried to forgive herself for the fiasco that was the gloriously underwhelming Hugo experience.

Sometimes you just get it wrong. And Ava found comfort in the words of that great post-modern philosopher, Ariana Grande, as she sang, 'Thank U, Next'.

2.

What Doesn't Kill You Makes You Stronger

'Your father wanted to get rid of you,' Ava's mother, Maman, said, as she pounded the iron on the ironing board, working through a pile of jumbled clothes.

Ava had just turned five. She sat at Maman's feet, clutching her favourite teddy bear, *Gros*, Fat. He wasn't actually fat, just warm and cuddly, with one of his button-eyes on the verge of falling off. It had been a big mistake to name such a lovely teddy bear Gros, but it was impossible to change it. As Ava grew older, and as she came to understand the world a little better, she deeply regretted her error. It made her love her Gros even more.

'It's not as if we married because I fell pregnant. No, not at all. We were married for a year. But the marriage was already rotten. It was rotten from day one. Your father just didn't want you. He made all the arrangements for an abortion. All I had to do was show up. It wasn't easy, back then, to get an abortion. But he found a little clinic outside

Zurich that would do it. Five hundred Swiss francs. That was a lot of money, back then. But I put my foot down and said no. I wasn't going to abort you.'

Ava never forgot that her Papa did not want her. And, through the decades, Maman reminded her how grateful she should be that she was still alive. True to form, Papa didn't change his mind about wanting Ava around, once she survived the carefully laid abortion plans.

'Of course I wanted to abort you,' Papa bellowed during one of his usual tirades. 'You think I wanted to have a child with that crazy witch of a mother of yours?' Ava could practically write his lines; she had heard them so many times through her parents' long and bitter divorce.

He would cast a wild glance in her direction, never looking her in the eye, but always ten centimetres above her forehead, as though she was not really there. Then he would change the conversation to his favourite of all topics.

'Look at your beautiful sister,' he would say, as he stared with admiration at Eliana, Ava's cherubic younger sister, sitting next to her.

Eliana, Hebrew for 'god has answered', smiled back, an angel on earth.

'She's going to look just like Grace Kelly in a few years' time,' Papa said. 'Grace Kelly. The perfect woman. A complete woman. So elegant. So refined. Look at Eliana's profile: that little upturned nose and those blue, blue eyes, like her Papa. Yes. Exactly like Grace Kelly. Come here, Eliana. Come and give your Papa a kiss.'

Eliana came and sat on her father's knee. Ava sat bereft at the table, odd daughter out. She studied her sister, with her translucent fair skin, her platinum-blonde hair and her athletic build. They barely looked like sisters at all. Ava could see why her father adored her. Eliana was as joyful and carefree as Ava was brooding and troubled. She was the ugly duckling: a chubby, awkward child, with long, bushy brown hair and big white teeth, who felt the weight of her darkness.

As Papa cuddled Eliana, Ava sought comfort by devouring books. She went to the public library every week and took out eight books at a time – the maximum that was allowed. She lost herself in the entire Penguin Classics collection: the grand balls and fierce battles of *War and Peace*, the injustice of *Animal Farm* and the restrained passions of *Pride and Prejudice*. Books were her escape and her friends. Books helped Ava win a scholarship to an exclusive private girls' school. Her studies were fully paid for, but the grant did not cover her school uniform, which was never quite right. The official school supplies store was far too expensive, so the skirts at H&M had to make do. In any event, they were 'perfectly fine', or so Maman assured her. It was obvious that her brown corduroy skirt was too short and an entirely different colour and fabric from the other girls', in their smart, pleated gabardine. The teachers must have known about her family's financial situation, because they never once complained.

Ava pretended not to hear the sniggers and the whispers as she waddled into class, always by herself. Her loneliness bred more loneliness. She had no talent for sports and there was a collective groan whenever she dropped the ball, which she invariably did, whatever the game. She was always the last girl to be picked for netball, hockey, lacrosse and even tennis doubles, and she would stand alone, shivering, waiting to be allocated by the games teacher to one of the hostile groups of girls that didn't want such a deadweight on their team. Her only consolation was that she was usually the first to be picked by the teachers in class to give the right answer. Her classmates would also groan then, and she was even more universally loathed.

She rarely saw her Papa, who lived high up in the remote purity of the

Swiss alps. She dreaded the three weeks over the summer when she would fly over to Switzerland with Eliana, as Unaccompanied Minors, for their annual visit. While he was a meticulous and caring eye doctor, he was a troubled and unhappy man with a raging temper. He helped others see. Pity he was unable to see himself.

Papa was the type of man who believed that every waitress, every secretary, every nurse, every patient even, was fair game. He married late, at fifty, and he started the marriage as he meant to go on, by cheating on Ava's mother on their honeymoon on the Bulgarian Riviera, otherwise known as the Black Sea. She was their blue-eyed tour guide, as it happened. And Ava imagined she gave him an extensive and in-depth tour of all the best sights.

The rules by which Papa lived were opposite to the ones he preached to his young daughters. Ava, with her olive skin and sultry eyes, was the image of his hated ex-wife, and she bore the brunt of his criticisms, with which he was not altogether sparing.

'Tie your hair back, Ava. It's vulgar to wear it loose like that,' he said, pointing his finger at her, his own white mane flying wildly.

Ava was twelve. Wearing her hair loose was the height of rebellion. Most of the time, it was easier to say nothing, to comply with his house rules and to scrape her abundant locks back into a demure bun or a neat ponytail. Then there were the few items of clothing which her mother bought her, and which were always wrong.

'Your jeans are too tight. I can see your entire anatomy. Go and put a skirt or a dress on.'

Ava could still hear her father's words ringing in her ears whenever she wriggled into a tight dress, decades later.

Papa even criticised Ava's walk.

'Stop walking so provocatively. Can't you see all the men in the street are staring at you? You're walking like a professional.'

By 'professional', her father meant prostitute. Ava noticed the men watching her. It was only through their gaze that she felt half alive.

When she turned seventeen, Papa introduced Eliana and her to his latest girlfriend, Maria. She was a self-effacing girl of twenty-one, the daughter of a priest. By then, Papa was, at sixty-six, clearly not yet ready for his pipe and slippers. The quintessential wandering Jew who spoke and wrote fluently in ten languages had fallen for a sweet God-fearing Catholic who had never left her local village.

Their improbable love was profound. Maria was tall and slim, with her long, mousy hair pinned up in a modest chignon. She did not wear a scrap of make-up, and she dressed in floaty paisley-patterned Laura Ashley dresses and ballet flats, though she could just as easily have been wearing a nun's habit. Like all Papa's former girlfriends, Maria devoted herself to trying to make him happy. This was a Sisyphean task. Ava never saw Papa happy. Even when he appeared to be laughing, she sensed the fissure of pain that ran through him. He died of a heart attack a few years later, in Maria's arms. He had been suffering from heart disease, silently, for decades. No wonder. His own heart was irreparably broken since the murder of his entire family by the Nazis when he was eighteen. In a gesture of perfect denial, the great doctor had refused to take any of the medication that his own doctor prescribed him. He knew that no drug could ever cure his kind of heartbreak.

Ava's mother's parents were also Holocaust survivors. It was astonishing how much her father and her beloved grandparents hated each other, given that all three had suffered similar unspeakable horrors during the war. They each inhabited their own separate universe of pain. The camps; the gas chambers; the massacre of their families, friends and communities; the incomprehensible decimation of six million human beings. In each of their homes lingered a smell that never cleared: the smell of death. The despair, the terror, they were somehow known. They were felt. But they were never, ever spoken of. Ava carried that pain; it coursed through her veins from birth.

Ava's most treasured childhood memory was sitting in her grandparents' kitchen, with its sticky linoleum floor and fluorescent strip lighting, eating mountains of pasta dripping in melted butter. It was not pasta she was eating. It was love, and she gobbled it up hungrily. Too much was never enough.

'Eat, my *bubeles*,' her grandmother, Mémé, would say to Eliana and her. She spoke a unique mix of broken Yiddish, French and German. 'Eat! *C'est bon*. It's good for you. Make you big and strong. *Es is gut. Du musst essen*. Don't leave anything. Just think of all those poor starving children in Africa with nothing to eat.'

Ava would always finish her plate, and usually go for seconds. She wondered how finishing her own plate might help the hungry African children, but she never dared ask. Once dinner had been devoured, she would be rewarded with the warmest, longest hugs and wet kisses from her bosomy grandmother. Her grandfather would then bring out dessert: a bar of supermarket milk chocolate that tasted of heaven. The visit would always end with her grandfather, Pépé, taking out his *kippah*, his skull cap, and gathering both his granddaughters close by his side. He would say the Hebrew prayer for Ava and Eliana's protection, with his hands tenderly resting over their bowed heads. The blessing finished with the words '*Gesund, Mazel und Bracha*': health, luck and benediction. Then he would cough, too choked up to speak, too distraught to cry.

Life back in the place Ava struggled to call home was bleak and joyless. After her acrimonious divorce, her mother married an Englishman, and she was dragged away from the picture-postcard alpine peaks to one of the dingier suburbs of North London. The heating was permanently switched off, even in the harshest winters. It was so cold, Ava struggled to study.

'Put another jumper on,' Maman would say. 'It's perfectly fine.' That was her signature line.

But it was even colder in Ava's frozen heart. Neither her mother nor her father cuddled her, even as a small child. She knew it was because she was an ugly, awkward and pained young girl. The lack of touch made her even more detached, and she withdrew further into her own world. She was irrelevant. It was easier to disappear into the wallpaper than to seek solace by somehow trying to become lovable. She longed to be hugged, even just to have her hand held. But that never happened, and she never managed to work out what she needed to do to merit the warmth of a parental embrace. But Gros, now only one-eyed, was always there for her.

When Ava turned thirteen, she realised she could not control her parents' hatred of each other, nor her mother's cold indifference, nor her father's neglect, nor the grimy little apartment in which she lived. But what she could control was what she put into her mouth and the grades she got in school. One day, she stopped scoffing the packets of Sainsbury's shortbread biscuits and slice after slice of processed white bread with lashings of butter and jam. From that moment, she ate only carrots, apples and cottage cheese, with the odd Twix bar, which she would cut into very small pieces, to draw out the pleasure. Her weight plummeted and somehow her grades soared. She was living off the heady fumes of discipline and self-control. She might not be able to control where she came from, but she sure could control where she was heading.

The summer when Ava turned fifteen, friends lent their mother a tiny flat outside Cannes in the South of France. Ava could not wait to see the ocean, to hear the cicadas and to feel the caress of the sun's rays.

Eliana's fair skin did not tolerate the sun well so she stayed at the apartment, napping, while Ava's skinny body turned the colour of dark honey. She could not afford the swanky beach clubs where the beautiful people hung out, so she spent her days covered in baby oil, sunbathing on the rocks by the moored yachts in the marina. Ava wondered what it might be like to lounge on the deck of one of those sleek boats with an ice-cold drink, watching the world go by. She was happy to observe at a distance, and dream.

One hazy afternoon after a sunbathing session while reading Dostoyevsky's *The Idiot*, Ava was wrapped up in her thoughts of Prince Myshkin's doomed innocence. It was a long walk back to the apartment, as she trudged uphill in the searing heat. A nice-looking middle-aged man pulled up next to her in his immaculate, black convertible Porsche 911.

'*Bonjour, ma belle gazelle*,' he said in an elegant Parisian accent. 'You want I give you a ride?'

Ava smiled and replied that she was happy to walk, even though she wasn't.

'Jump in, *ma cherie*. I drive you home. Don't worry. I have daughter. She your age too.' The man took off his sunglasses and smiled at Ava. He had warm hazel eyes and a slightly greying beard. 'You come in car,' he said, flipping his hair out of his eyes. 'You home fast. Is too hot for walk. I take you.'

Ava had not eaten or drunk all day. Thirsty as she was, she couldn't face drinking the warm liquid from the old bottle her mother had instructed her to fill with tap water that morning. So perhaps she was suffering a little heatstroke when she replied, 'Really? Are you sure? Thank you, that's so kind of you.'

Ava climbed in. She had never been in a Porsche before. Michael Jackson's 'P.Y.T. (Pretty Young Thing)' was pounding on the stereo as they spun around La Croisette. They made a detour to his luxury apartment building, where the man said he needed to pick up a document. As she entered his flat, the man took her hand and smiled kindly at her. Ava was too weak to think. He poured her a cold lemonade and led her to his bedroom. Ava felt a lurch in her stomach.

'Look! Is excited! You make this,' the man said, as he took her hand and put it on his small erect penis. 'Is you. You do this. Now you need take care of me.'

He kissed her, his beard bristling on her soft skin. He pushed her down onto his bed. Ava stiffened and recoiled. He smelled of oud and seawater.

'Stop, don't,' Ava protested. 'Please don't. I'm a virgin. Please. Think of your daughter.'

'Ha,' the man said as he yanked her Tampax out. 'I no have daughter.'

He spat on his hand, quickly rubbed his penis with it and then rammed it hard inside her.

'You like this. I know you like this,' he grunted. '*Putain, que c'est bon.* You tell me how much is you like this. I is good for you. Very good for me. Very good for you. *Oh, la vache!*' As Ava began to whimper, he covered her mouth with his sweaty hand.

Ava looked up at the ceiling. The sunlight hit the crystal chandelier and refracted the white beam of light into a beautiful rainbow. Ava floated high above and watched the colours dance. They were clear and bright and she counted them: one red, two orange, three yellow, four green, five blue, six indigo, seven violet. She observed herself on the bed, where she saw a slim, tanned, dazed teenager called Ava spreadeagled, her long brown hair fanned out on the white pillow, her green eyes vacant. Like particles and antiparticles of electrons, protons, neutrons and photons bouncing around in a boundless infinity of electromagnetic fields, she existed and she disappeared into nothingness, all at the same time. She was there, but she was not there.

She felt slime running down her thighs as the man pulled out with a loud cry, and she rushed to the ensuite bathroom to retch.

'I drive you home now,' the man said, shuffling his shorts back on. 'Is okay.'

Ava was too numb to speak. She curled up in the car seat with her arms crossed over her, and she suddenly felt very cold. When she got home, Eliana was dozing on the couch and her mother barely looked up as she darned one of her old, ripped sundresses in the kitchen. Ava crouched, trembling in the shower for a long time, watching the red-tinged water trickle down between her legs and exit through the plughole.

She always hated the smell of oud.

When the family returned to London, Ava became more withdrawn than ever. She spent ten hours a day studying, huddled over her books and shivering. But it was not a sacrifice; it was a joy. She was hungrier than ever to escape her situation and take charge of her life. Her 'incident' in Cannes was like a paradox of consciousness: simultaneously an objective reality and a subjective non-event. She knew her thoughts could not erase the deed; they would only compound her self-disgust, her shame and her pain. Instead, she willed herself into never thinking of it ever again. She decided to vote life.

Ava discovered that she loved numbers. She didn't simply calculate with numbers: she felt numbers, she dreamt numbers. Mathematical symbols, variables, expressions, formulae, the perfect beauty of symmetry and infinity: this was a precise and beautiful language with its own impeccable logic, and it was one in which she excelled. The right answer was always blindingly obvious to her. In maths, there were no doubts and half-truths, just perfect clarity and certainty.

When Ava was seventeen, she won a scholarship to read pure and applied mathematics at Cambridge. University opened up a whole new world and it was Ava's one-way ticket to independence. She need never rely on anyone for anything, and from that moment on, she felt free. In the city of lofty, golden spires and punting on the River Cam, freedom tasted good. The years of hard work paid off and she abandoned herself to a life of controlled dissipation; she became a highly disciplined hedonist. After years of sitting in ugly municipal public libraries with piles of books, she was now sitting in beautiful men's laps and revelling in the attention. Through sex, she finally received the touch on her body that she always yearned for. She discovered the power she had over the endless supply of gorgeous and attentive young suitors. For the first time, she felt wanted. She drank her first lychee martinis and danced the night away at decadent parties, but still she studied for ten hours a day, every day. And while she knew that sex had nothing to do with love, she could at least fool herself into believing she was an emancipated, empowered young woman that men might even desire. For now, that was sufficient to sustain her, more or less. After all, she didn't know any better.

Because her own experiences of family left her feeling so unloved, Ava longed to fill the void by becoming a mother and giving love. By her early twenties, when Ava was already making waves in her banking career, she could not wait any longer. She was less keen on the marriage part. She struggled to meet anyone with whom she felt connected, let alone anyone who might understand her. Never mind. At least Jake, her husband, was blond, blue-eyed and handsome. Ava's maternal dream materialised in the form of two beautiful daughters: Sasha and Khassya, the lights of her life. She cherished them with the fiercest love and devotion, and they rewarded her with the purest, most unconditional love.

Ava was a natural at juggling motherhood and her work as a trader in a hedge fund. She operated with a rigour and discipline that marked all aspects of her life. She never once complained about how hard it was to climb the ladder, nor how difficult it was to be taken seriously as an attractive young woman in the male-dominated world of finance. She just got on with it and worked twice as hard.

When they were old enough, Sasha and Khassya set their alarm clocks to wake up with their mother at 6:00 every morning, even though school didn't start until 9:00. They would help their mother pick out her outfits for the day and find the matching shoes and handbag. It was their special daily sunrise ritual and all three loved to cuddle tight. Ava struggled not to cry as the girls, looking so tiny and forlorn, waved at the balcony with their nanny, watching their mother drive away. Jake, meanwhile, was still fast asleep in bed.

One night at dinner with a group of friends, Ava innocently picked up Jake's phone to check the time, and inadvertently saw a saucy photograph that was clearly not destined for her eyes. The little self-confidence that she had crumbled completely once she found out about the full extent of her husband's multiple infidelities. She felt uglier and more worthless than ever, and she sloped around in a daze for months. It took Ava a few more years to cast aside her guilt about destroying the family unit, just as her own mother had done, and to leave Jake.

This was when she decided to go deep undercover and dye her hair golden. Becoming blonde was, quite possibly, one of the best decisions she ever made. Blonde was light, fun and sexy instead of the brunette she was underneath: deep, heavy and serious. Blonde was not a hair colour; it was a state of being. Blondes had more fun, clearly. Having made the transformation, Ava was inclined to agree, and she was never tempted to return to the dark side.

I'm blonde, therefore I am was the slogan which, henceforth, informed her modus operandi. Like Cary Grant, born Archibald Leach, who pretended to be suave and sophisticated until he became that person, Ava faked it until she became the embodiment of the blonde feminine archetype. She wanted to be the blondest, most luminous version of herself, the most atomic of Atomic Blonde Bombshells. Well, that was the plan at least.

To the outside world, she was a beautiful, thin, vivacious blonde woman. Inside she was still the ugly, fat, shy and dark little girl whom no man could ever love. Yet, as her private life unravelled, and as Ava felt deader and deader inside, her professional career took off, and she started to make the big bucks. Ava went from bank employee to partner in a leading hedge fund in record time. Trading was her ticket to financial freedom: she bought and sold money in multiple permutations, and she did it well. She enjoyed poring over the latest economic updates and wading through stacks of annual reports, paying special attention to the footnotes. The raw numbers spoke to her, and she specialised in constructing, sequencing and ceaselessly fine-tuning algorithmic trading models, simulations and risk analyses, all of which took the emotion out of making decisions. The ability to keep a cool head was her real edge, and that was when the big money was made: at times of crisis. Ava began to make serious money. Serious, serious money. She celebrated by buying herself her first Ferrari, a GTS convertible, in flaming red, of course.

It was not a car. It was the realisation of a dream.

3.

Love Is Not Enough

Children are generally a good indicator as to the values and well-being of their parents. On that basis, Ava was doing a pretty decent job. Both Sasha and Khassya were excelling, even though it had been harder than they cared to admit when their mother and father divorced.

Attending her daughters' parents' evening, Ava beamed with pride as she heard how well Sasha was progressing in her Russian, her fifth language, and Khassya was, as usual, top of her advanced maths stream. Ava never overcame her remorse at eventually finding the courage to leave Jake and for breaking up the family. But she gave her precious girls oceans and oceans of what she never had: deep, unconditional love and tenderness, and the confidence to believe in themselves and to fly.

She put her phone on the table. She had just put on a large trade in a biotech company that was developing proprietary CRISPR gene-editing technology, which would potentially help millions of people. She needed to monitor the share's progress on Nasdaq.

Her phone beeped. Ava squinted. It was not a stock-price update. It was not a text from her assistant, confirming her slew of meetings tomorrow. It was not even a message from Ocado about her next delivery.

It was a dick pic. Full-blown and in glorious technicolour. Ava blushed and grabbed the phone off the table, hoping Khassya's maths tutor had not seen it.

The news of Ava's divorce had spread like wildfire. Jake was fresh and appetising meat on the hungry dating market. And Ava? Well, Ava was incredibly blonde. Dick pics now entered her inbox with alarming regularity, like the wrong kind of magic, from the most unexpected of sources and at the worst possible time. Half flaccid or fully tumescent; proudly naked or semi-covered and bursting through designer underpants; deepest black, dark pink, pale pink, a worrying shade of very deep purple; pre-, mid- and post-ejaculation; with and without fist; circumcised and uncircumcised. All possible permutations. A cornucopia of cocks. The only constant was that they were uniformly uninteresting, unsolicited and unerotic.

Ava was a hardcore phallus worshipper. She loved the taste, the smell, the feel, the power and the sheer masculinity of cock. But devoid of their owner's face and some semblance of a connection, a photo of genitalia was an unwelcome exercise in biology, and not exactly the pinnacle of good taste.

Dick pics aside, Ava's post-divorce freedom was dizzying. For the first few months, she thought she would never want to marry again. She enjoyed a brief spell of wild emancipation and unbridled fun, fun, fun. But back in the real world: who was she kidding? After a few nights out on the town with her more liberated girlfriends, she realised that while dancing on tables with random men might be moderately amusing, riotous debauchery was not all it was cracked up to be.

Ava calmed down and realised that what she wanted, what she always wanted, was good old-fashioned love; love, pure and simple. She went in search of a Real Man, The Man.

As it happened, a man found her. Or rather, he tracked her down.

Ava's first lover post-divorce was Harry, who could not have been more different from Jake. While Jake came from nowhere, classless and rootless, Harry was a blue-blooded aristocrat, with an ancestral line that he could proudly trace back to the Battle of Hastings on one side and prosperous Austro-Hungarian industrialists on the other. And just as Jake was penniless when she met him, Harry was steeped in an abundance of the shiny trappings and privileges of his class and pedigree.

Harry had been Ava's client, back when she was a lowly bank employee in a conservative navy suit and a string of fake pearls, diligently working her way up the career ladder. And there was a long way to go. One day, her boss asked her to prepare for a meeting with their largest and most important client, whom he always addressed, with a clearing of his throat and a flourish, as 'His Lordship'. Ava had read all of his files and his Google search results, making copious notes on his portfolio's performance through the decades, and the changes she would make to the current asset allocation and currency mix. She grinned as she wrote out 'His Lordship's' full triple-barrelled name: Harry, the Earl of Huntington-von-Königsstadt-Saxe. Why, even his name had sex in it. As she ploughed through the information to hand, she read that his family was the bank's second-oldest client, after Her Majesty, Queen Elizabeth II, and the House of Windsor. She had not even met him yet, but she imagined how debonair His Lordship would look and how fascinating he would be.

Bang on the dot, Ava's assistant notified her of His Lordship's arrival. She adjusted her hair and straightened her skirt as she and her boss marched into the mahogany-panelled boardroom, with its genuine gold-leaf Georgian furniture and a splendid Van Dyck portrait of King Charles I, looking particularly dashing on his white horse. Only the most distinguished clients were received there.

His Lordship had his back to the room and was looking out of the window as they filed in. Ava's boss coughed and His Lordship turned around.

'How do you do?' he drawled, looking Ava up and down.

Ava did not believe in love at first sight. Lust, yes, of course, in the blink of an eye. But love at first sight? No. Love takes time to grow, obviously. That is, until she set eyes on Harry. He was tall and elegant in a grey pinstriped suit, and he stood very straight, effortlessly superior. Ava melted as soon as she looked into his blue eyes. He shook Ava's hand and greeted her formally, but she was sure she could detect a faint curl of the upper lip, as though he could already tell precisely what she was thinking.

His Lordship was an easy man to fall for. He was the ultimate fantasy figure: James Bond handsome, a fabled polo player, a skilled pilot of both planes and choppers, and a fearless Olympic skier. The fact that he was already on his third wife, and that he had bedded every glamorous blue-stocking beauty within a thousand-kilometre radius, only attested to his sexual prowess and added to his erotic mystique. His code name at the bank was 'Triple', in reference to his tongue-twister of a triple-barrelled surname and in tribute to his three wives. But Ava fantasised it was because he was such a legendary lover that he could make his conquests orgasm three times on the trot, as well as ejaculate three times himself, in rapid succession.

It was clear His Lordship was totally out of her league and that made him infinitely more desirable. Every email he sent her, every telephone conversation, whether it was to enquire as to the performance of his trust fund or to discuss buying gold as an inflation hedge, seemed to betray an underlying sexual subtext. He would catch her eye during long portfolio review meetings, and wink at her across the polished cherrywood boardroom table. Ava would half-smile back and then look away, embarrassed. His smallest of movements – the way he looked at her over his bone-china teacup, how he fondled his silver pen, the habit he had of running his hand through his blond hair with half-closed eyes – all betrayed hidden depths of meaning. Or so Ava imagined.

Now, years later, he contacted Ava out of the blue and invited his 'favourite and most competent banker' to lunch. Ava was perplexed. What could he possibly want? She assumed he was looking for investment advice, or to change his current banking arrangements. So she came to lunch armed with a full battalion of opinions as to the direction of sterling, the benefits of an allocation to alternative assets, and the geopolitical threats that might destabilise financial markets. By now, she could afford to upgrade her wardrobe. She wore a set of real pearls and a classic black Chanel suit, whose skirt was too short to be classed as elegant but was short enough to highlight her toned legs. Although not dressed to kill, she was definitely dressed to thrill a very special former client.

They met at Bellamy's, an unpretentious Mayfair gem frequented by those in the real know. It was suitably discreet, and the maître d' was also an Etonian, naturally. Ava caught her breath when she spotted Harry, already seated, ram-rod straight, refined as ever. He had aged: his hair was just as full but now grey, and his face was distinctly more lined. If anything, he looked sexier and more unattainable than ever. His Arctic-blue eyes blazed as brilliantly as she remembered, and he reeked of privilege and power. He was tanned and trim and looked as if he had just jetted in from the slopes of St Moritz or a yacht moored off the coast of Mustique. In fact, it transpired he had flown in from Jo'burg that morning. He had been somewhere in deepest, darkest Africa on some obscure government mission, about which he preferred to remain rather vague.

It soon became apparent that Harry was not remotely interested in discussing banking or anything else to do with finance or current affairs. Instead, with his characteristic understated humour, he regaled her with gossip from his latest supper with HRH; the recent official luncheon he hosted for former president Bill Clinton at Castle Huntington; and a state dinner in honour of President Vladimir Putin at BP, otherwise known as Buckingham Palace. The true nature of Harry's intentions became apparent when he passed her the salt shaker and, ever so briefly, let his hand rest on hers. It was the most minute of micro-contacts, but Ava felt the earth turn on its axis. Harry looked her straight in the eyes, and in those three seconds, she knew she was toast.

It emerged that Harry was, regrettably, still married, and rather miserably so. Araminta made a plausible and presentable third wife. Pre-marriage, she had managed to hide her acute addiction to a cocktail of uppers and downers, but this was a dependence which only grew over time. Theirs was a childless, joyless union. The beautiful countess began to add increasingly large amounts of alcohol to the toxic mix of narcotics, and she would hound Harry around the castle, brandishing a bottle of whisky and threatening to cut open her veins and ruin his reputation if he ever dared leave her. She slept in the east wing, and he slept in the west wing, bolting the door firmly behind him. It had been six years since they last had sex together.

So Harry said.

By now it was almost four in the afternoon, and they were the only diners still in the restaurant. Harry called his chauffeur and his midnight-blue Bentley arrived. They wafted over to the Connaught hotel. It was in that car that he kissed her for the first time. For a languid aristocrat he was unexpectedly passionate and his desire was palpable. The bulge in his trousers certainly was. It was a cliché, but they both felt a magnetism that defied their different backgrounds. Or was it their otherness that pulled them together?

They arrived at the Connaught and Ava made a quick dash for the loos. She needed time to think. Finally, Harry, the man of her dreams, appeared to want her. But he was married, and she loathed the idea of being with a man who belonged to another woman. After all, she knew first-hand how painful it was to have your husband cheat on you. What the Lord giveth, the Lord taketh away... Ava took a deep breath, pulled herself together and washed her face to remove all traces of her mini meltdown. She emerged fresh-faced, to meet Harry back at reception.

'Is everything all right?' he asked.

'Perfectly,' Ava answered with a wan smile.

In those few moments in the bathroom, she decided to go for it. After all, she reasoned, she was not the one being unfaithful. She was divorced and single. Her conscience was clear-ish. If Harry chose to transgress, that was his decision. And she knew full well that no man ever left his wife until he had secured himself another warm bed to fall into.

Harry squeezed her hand as they stepped into the lift and were whisked up to one of the palatial suites. It was decorated like an interior designer's vision of an English stately home, only too shiny and new, complete with ornate gilded mirrors, a couple of reproduction Constable-esque oil paintings, two matching anthracite-coloured velvet sofas and plumped-up aubergine cushions, embroidered with a gold crest of a unicorn entwined with a lion. A gas fire roared in the marble fireplace.

'Mr, Your Lordship, er, Sir and Mrs, er, Lord Harry Hunting-von-Cuntingstadt-Sex,' stammered the butler with a strong Polish accent, bowing and scraping. 'This is your sveet. The Presidential Connaught Sveet. Is very best in house.'

Ava tried to suppress her laughter. Even Harry raised an eyebrow.

'Not too shabby,' Harry muttered under his breath. 'Shame about the faux-Georgian antique tat.'

As the owner of not one but two castles, he could spot, in an instant, real antique furniture from fake. His own heirlooms were in impeccable taste; they had been passed down through eight generations before him and they would be handed down to at least eight more generations to come. Ava chose to ignore his remark. At this point, she wasn't interested in discussing the finer points of luxury hotel interior design.

'Mr, Your Lordship, 'ere we 'ave the five mood settings. We 'ave intelligent light system. And 'ere smart audio and television system.'

As the butler continued to show them the room amenities, Ava suspected there was zero chance they would be switching on the television. Harry was too polite to cut him short, so he smiled and discreetly slipped him a twenty-pound note. The butler bowed low and slipped out.

Ava sat back on the sofa, watching Harry. After all these years, the unattainable was now within arm's reach. She sat perfectly still, but her heart was thumping and she could scarcely breathe.

Harry took off his Savile Row jacket and set it on the back of the chair, then came to sit next to Ava. 'Come closer, my darling,' he said.

He stroked the back of her head, then drew her face to his and kissed her. The burning urgency that marked their kiss in the Bentley had changed into one of heart-melting sensuality. Now, they were tasting, sensing and feeling each other.

'I always remembered those sparkling eyes of yours,' Harry said, as he gazed into them. 'Like a lighthouse, beaming out. You could light oceans with your eyes. They always saw right into me.'

They sank deeper into the sofa. Ava was longing to feel Harry's skin next to hers. She whipped his trousers off and felt Harry wince, ever so slightly. He was meticulous in all his habits and fastidiously tidy. Knowing him as she did, she knew that he was fighting the urge to fold his trousers properly and have them pressed. Ava had other, more pressing ideas in mind, and she forged ahead, pretending not to notice. She fiddled with his onyx cufflinks, eased his shirt off and then fell to her knees.

Slowly, she started to stroke Harry's balls and his unexpectedly enormous cock. His smell was intoxicating. Leaning forward, she teased his head with her tongue, then took his entire cock in her mouth and started to suck more vigorously. She looked straight up into those blue eyes. He groaned, his whole body suffused with pleasure. Ava felt as though it had been a long time since any woman had adored his phallus.

'Do you like this? Do you like how I suck your cock?' Ava whispered, rhetorically.

'Good grief, Ava. You're incredible,' Harry gasped. 'Stop or I'll come too fast. I also want to taste you. I want to feel you, darling. Let's move into the bedroom.'

There are landmark moments in life that one remembers forever. Achieving straight As at GCSE and A-level; getting a scholarship to Cambridge; your first ever orgasm; the birth of your children; the death of a parent. The moment when Ava, straddling Harry and looking into his beautiful eyes, slid down and let his divine cook penetrate her, was one of those moments. There was a before and there was an after, and absolutely no looking back. It felt like the start of the ultimate voyage of discovery. Exploring the other, and in so doing, gaining a heightened knowledge of self.

That was how an English earl and the granddaughter of a Ukrainian vegetable market-stall seller fell in love. Head over heels. They may, ostensibly, have had nothing in common. But Harry touched Ava to her deepest core, and Ava touched Harry to his deepest core, as no one else ever had done before.

Ava knew all about the art of being nude. It was part of the dance of desire. But never before had she been naked. Early on, Ava realised that the only way for her to be naked was to limit it to the realm of the physical, by being sexual and in control. That meant you got to have lots of sex and orgasms, but no uncomfortable feelings. There was no upside to being emotionally naked: you just got hurt.

But with Harry, for the first time in her life, it was different. Ava no longer confused sex with intimacy. Sex was her path to intimacy and now, Ava wanted to bare all. She wanted to reveal her real self, her vulnerabilities, her inner core. She wanted to be penetrated, not only by Harry's cock, but by his eyes. She wanted to feel, and she wanted to be known. She knew all about how to undress physically; now she wanted to undress emotionally. Naked was the only way to be. After all these years she felt truly free, and a little less alone in the world. She had found her twin flame.

They spent the next few months together, seeing each other most weekdays. Now that Ava took to trading from home, Harry would swing by her house at eleven o'clock in the morning and leave at six o'clock at night, before her girls came home. He still needed to maintain the pretence of his marriage to Araminta, and he did not want to be seen out and about town with his mistress. After all, he was in the public eye, and he could not risk being exposed until the time was right. He would arrive and they would head straight to bed, where they would talk, laugh, cry, devour each other and then drink champagne, lunch hungrily and soak in the Calacatta white marble tub. Ava thought that these must be some of the happiest hours of her life.

Like mating dogs on heat, they loved each other's smell and taste.

They could not wait to kiss and lie in each other's arms. They were both damaged goods, and it was that, together with their sexual attraction, that bound them together. Harry recognised parts of himself in Ava, and Ava saw parts of herself in Harry. It was as though, with every thrust of his cock, Harry touched Ava's soul. Through sex, he gave her a sense of belonging. Most of all, Harry saw and loved Ava for Ava: her femininity, her fragility, her pain. He reached the little girl buried deep inside. And Ava saw Harry for Harry: not for his moated castles, nor his gleaming medals of past bravery and services to the Crown, nor his alluring playboy facade. Yet, what Ava saw before her, as she peeled away the handmade suits and penetrated the cool demeanour, was in many ways a mirror of herself: a man who was lost, a man who was sad, a man who was alone and a man who had never fully recovered from being the survivor of a boating accident that had claimed the life of his six-year-old twin brother.

'I see you,' Harry would say, his eyes brimming with pain and joy. 'I feel you.'

Harry knew Ava. He knew her sexually, he had carnal knowledge of her. But he also knew what made her heart beat and her soul sing. He knew her biblically, the way Adam knew Eve.

'Let's have a child together,' Harry said one day as they lay in bed, limbs entwined.

'Darling, I would love to have your baby inside me. A little Harry. Our little baby boy. Harry, my love, yes.'

Harry, the man of action, detached and aloof, wiped a tear off his face.

'You're such a wonderful, warm and caring woman. You're a marvellous mother. It would be so special to have a child with you.'

Ava leaned forwards and kissed away Harry's tear drop.

'You complete me,' he said, stroking her face. 'You fill that void. You take away my pain and you fill me with a love and a warmth I never knew existed.'

February in London was biting cold. He spirited her off to St Barts, and they took a white cube of a villa, with full-size windows for walls, overlooking the turquoise waters of Gouverneur Bay. They would wake early, Harry pressed against her, his hard cock pushing against her buttocks, kissing her neck and shoulders as he penetrated her and whispered her name.

'Ava, my love. I've never felt such bliss. Bliss is your middle name. I want to stay by your side forever.'

Ava never felt so loved and accepted. She was bathed in love, and she treasured and savoured every drop. And she never felt such desire. Her own, and Harry's. The more she fucked, the more she wanted to fuck, in an endlessly pleasurable loop of desire. The sex in itself was, quite possibly, the most traditional Ava had ever experienced. But it was the most powerful, the most intimate and the most deeply orgasmic. It was both hard and soft, urgent and timeless. She desired him by his smell, by the gaze of his blue eyes, by the touch of his fingertips. They moved together, breathed together, came together. Two became one.

They would lie in the sun all day, plunge into the sea to cool off, drink rosé and eat plates of grilled fish and fries, before retiring to the villa to make love again. The evenings were spent enjoying candlelit dinners overlooking the sea, listening to an eclectic mix of Mozart, bossa nova and Frank Sinatra, in a state of perfect joy. No phone calls to lawyers, stockbrokers, business partners, current wives, ex-wives or ex-husbands. For the first time ever, Ava spent the entire week barefoot, make-up free and with her long, blonde hair wilder and curlier than ever. Harry adored her even more au naturel. Here, she was pure and real. And Ava adored Harry in his cute white polo shirt, his navy twill shorts and his espadrilles. It was as though, by taking off that Savile Row suit and the starched Gieves & Hawkes shirt, and by untying the Huntsman tie, and by kicking off those solid John Lobb shoes, he became unburdened. He was softer, funnier, lighter and nicer. The weight of his ancestors and the responsibilities he felt to his descendants were lifted.

They fucked three or four times a day. Harry's stamina was the stuff of legend. With one kiss, one caress, he would spring to life and Ava would hunger for him all over again. They loved it all: kissing, teasing, licking, stroking, caressing, fondling, smelling, tasting, deep fucking. Together they were both playful and light, serious and deep.

They returned to rainy London, closer than ever. A full year had passed since their first lunch date. And still, Harry had not left Araminta. Thrilling as their affair was, it was not sustainable, at least not for Ava, for whom intimacy without commitment was a sham. Real life began to encroach more and more into their love-bubble. Ava spent hours counselling Harry about his wayward, drug-addled son, Leopold. He was twenty-seven, living a life of unadulterated privilege, yet unfit to inherit the title and the many responsibilities that went with it. He was sent to rehab, again, only to disappear a few weeks later and re-emerge, after an extensive and expensive manhunt led by Kroll Associates, semi-comatose, in the Temple of the Way of Light, an ayahuasca retreat in Iquitos, deep in the Peruvian Amazon. Harry's daughter, Lucinda, was awfully sweet. Regrettably, she was kicked out of Cheltenham Ladies' College for snorting coke, and then suffered a similar fate at an elite finishing school on Lake Geneva. She spent her time wining and dining on super-yachts, private jets and in the smartest dining rooms of Europe in the company of the great and the good. She was artistic, so Harry said, and she designed exclusive eco-friendly, socially conscious jewellery made of recycled metal. Her father had even managed to wangle an exclusive four-page spread for her in *Tatler*, yet somehow she never managed to sell a single piece, which appealed only to a unique type of woman.

As for Harry, he was only hazily aware of any concrete details of Ava's everyday life. For all his daily declarations of love over that magical year, Ava wondered if he even remembered the names of her two daughters.

The things you do for love.

Ava said nothing, but her patience was tested. She waited every day for him to announce that, after all her waiting, he had left his wife. She wanted him to tell her that, like her, he could not bear to live a lie for one minute longer, and that all he wanted to do was be with her and to make their love official.

Harry was good with his cock. And he was good with his words too.

'I love you,' he would say. 'I will always love you, Ava. I would climb K2 for you with no oxygen, carrying an elephant.'

Then, 'You, together with my two children, are my everything.'

And, 'Our love is too special and strong to die.'

Curiously, action did not follow the words. Ava was baffled. How could someone who professed so much love wait? How could someone who had so many financial resources wait? How could someone who could give away half his fortune and still be rich as Croesus wait? How could someone whose marriage was so broken, and had been for many years, wait? How could someone not want to fight tooth and claw for the rare and precious love they shared?

Yet Harry waited. And Ava waited for him. She waited so long, she thought she might die from waiting. Her love for him was so strong that it sustained her. But her internal voice of reason grew a little louder. She failed to understand why a winner like Harry, who held all the aces in the pack, could allow himself to be trapped, like a loser. Why did he not share her sense of urgency? Marcel Proust might have gone on a journey in search of lost time, but Harry was not even aware that time had passed.

Ava entered an Alice in Wonderland universe where time seemed to telescope out endlessly. Soon, she thought, Harry might ask her to believe six impossible things before breakfast. He kept her suspended in a holding pattern, held aloft by the sheer thrust of his beautiful, airy words.

'I love you, my darling. We are twinned. We are two peas in a pod. Inseparable. Just give me a bit more time, my sweet.'

He presented Ava with an impressive range of excuses and justifications for the delay, from:

'Araminta is being particularly frightful right now. She tells me she's suicidal. I caught her wandering around the gardens at midnight with a bottle of pills. Imagine the scandal if she did anything silly to herself.'

to:

'I've been through a divorce before. Two, in fact. Have you any idea, my love, of the utter devastation that a divorce sets in motion? Pure carnage,' Harry would drawl with his chilling nonchalance.

He conveniently forgot that Ava had, herself, divorced only a few months earlier. And was not without her own dramas.

Then would come the altruistic rationalisation for procrastination:

'Can one countenance causing so much unhappiness, for one's own selfish happiness?' he would say.

Harry's voice sounded more clipped and aristo-cold than ever. Ava imagined Prince Charles uttering something similar to Camilla Parker Bowles, until, even he, the future King of the United Kingdom of Great Britain and Northern Ireland and Head of the Commonwealth, Defender of the Faith, found the courage to follow his heart. What Harry conveniently ignored, in his stirring monologues, were the ravages he wreaked in Ava's life and the pain he unleashed in her heart. Where was her soulmate now? For a man who prided himself on his honour, a man whose word was his bond, Harry did not appear unduly troubled by the need to follow through with actions what he so eloquently expressed in words.

～ 4. ～

His Lordship's View: Keeping the British End Up

It was a sunny spring morning at Huntington Castle and Harry was seated at his great-great-grandfather's walnut and rosewood marquetry desk. Five generations of Huntington-von-Königsstadt-Saxes had sat on that very chair before him. The room was laden with treasures: here a series of Leonardo da Vinci anatomical ink drawings, there a grand Uccello battle scene, an exquisite gold-leaf Masaccio crucifixion, a set of deep-blue and bronze Sèvres vases, and a couple of green onyx-and-gilt console tables that had once belonged to King George III.

Harry's liquid-blue eyes stared out at the deer, grazing peacefully on the rolling green fields, as his two whippets, Sherlock and Watson, frolicked on the lawn under the French windows. For centuries, the family domain stretched out as far as the eye could see, all the way to the horizon: a bucolic idyll. In that seat, Harry felt that time was an endless continuum, and his sole, overriding purpose in life was to guard and steer the estate safely to the next generation. He sat straighter in his chair and smoothed out the creases in his trousers, even though there were none. He put his tortoiseshell glasses back on and forced himself to focus on his papers. He was trying to analyse a glossy proposal from an aggressive set of investment bankers. They wanted him to turn some of his vast expanses of farmland over to solar energy panels made by a radical new start-up called Sun4ward. For this they would earn a massive fee and recurring annuity income. Ava had advised him to be wary as the numbers did not stack up. His eyes went blank, and he took his glasses off again.

His lapsang souchong tea grew cold in the Meissen porcelain cup as he thought about Ava. She was all he could think about these days: Ava and how he could ever manage to leave Araminta and start a new life with her. He had known hundreds of women, but none had touched him to his core like Ava did. She turned him on and lit him up with the beam of her eyes, with a visceral force and an energy he had never experienced before. It was not supposed to be like this, not at fifty. He was ashamed of the breakdown of all three of his marriages: three wives, three failures. He shuddered as he visualised the entry for the 9th Earl of Huntington-von-Königsstadt-Saxe and his wife number four, as recorded in *Debrett's* for eternity. How would posterity judge him? He would be a total laughing stock. The Richard Burton of the British aristocracy.

And yet, Harry had never felt so loved and he had never loved so deeply. How complete and whole Ava made him feel, like something from another solar system.

A knock at the library door roused him from his interplanetary reveries, and his butler entered silently, immaculate in his black morning coat and bearing a silver tray with a fresh pot of tea and the morning's post.

'Thank you, Montague. How terribly kind of you,' Harry said.

Wearily, he took his crested silver letter opener and started to go through the mail. There was an abundance of gold-edged, embossed invitation cards to dreary dinners and tiresome cocktail parties, and a couple of obsequious requests for him to speak at various functions. He saw his life proceeding colourlessly before him. More of the same. Harry had spent a lifetime perfecting his cool, impassive exterior, irrespective of what he might be feeling, thinking or doing. After all, what else was Eton for? But as he contemplated his future, he thought about the next thirty years of cold and empty lovelessness that awaited him. It was even more intolerable, now that he had drunk from the warm cup of Ava's love. Ava made him feel. And she made him feel that his life was worth living.

His gaze passed over the bronze obelisk on his desk, given to him by former president Bill Clinton, when Harry had last hosted him here at Huntington. *Keep it up!* was engraved on it. Harry smiled. He was grateful that he was still able to get it up, let alone keep it up, and all Viagra-free. All those decades of competitive sports and that iron discipline of his were clearly paying off. Ava was so sexually voracious; she was always in the mood, practically insatiable. He was not used to that, and he worried that he might not be able to perform so well in the future.

There was another knock on the door, and Mrs Imogen Smythe-Osbourne, his flawless private secretary who had worked for him for the last twenty years, slipped in noiselessly, notebook and pen in hand.

'Good morning, Your Lordship,' she said cheerfully.

Harry stopped staring at the bronze phallus and turned to Mrs Smythe-Osbourne. 'Oh, good morning, Imogen. How are you today? And how's that lovely daughter of yours? Tell me, has she fully recovered from her appendicitis operation?'

'Oh, Your Lordship,' said Mrs Smythe-Osbourne with a big smile, 'thank you for asking after her. Yes. All in order now. So good of you to remember.' She took a seat on the yellow brocade chair next to Harry's desk, ready to discuss his upcoming engagements.

'Imogen, be a dear and draft a response to the Prince of Wales's trustees confirming that one would be honoured to stay on as a trustee of the Clarence and Carmarthen trusts for another five years. It's a colossal amount of work, but one does feel it's one's duty to serve one's country and one's royal family. And of course' – he coughed – 'to help one's dearest friend.'

Mrs Smythe-Osbourne nodded. She knew that there had never been a shadow of a doubt that His Lordship would continue in his role, like his father before him, and no doubt his son after him.

'Oh, and then there's another luncheon address I've been asked to make to the Confederation of British Industry next month. Jolly inconvenient: on the day I fly back from Doha on that ghastly early morning flight. The main director there serves on one of my boards, so I suppose it's only good form to agree. But what a wretched nuisance. Please write and tell them I'd be delighted to accept. Ask them what particular aspect they want me to cover.'

Harry flipped through the rest of the morning's post.

'And please ask Giles to fix that wrought-iron gate; the one that goes from the walled garden onto the deer park. I do worry that Sherlock and Watson will run off one day and never return. They're so naughty.' Harry perked up as he thought of his beloved whippets.

'Yes, Your Lordship. Of course,' said Mrs Smythe-Osbourne. 'Will that be all?'

'Er, one more thing, Imogen.' Harry took his glasses off, sucked the end of one of the arms, and shifted in his seat. 'Ahem.' He cleared his throat and continued, as casually as possible. 'Her Ladyship had, er, an unfortunate little accident last night. Regrettably, she, er, made a trifling rip on the Gobelins tapestry hanging by the main staircase. Quite a bore, really.'

That was Harry expressing how livid he was. During a drunken episode over the weekend, Araminta had managed to lacerate the valuable sixteenth-century French tapestry. She'd whacked her elbow into it as she hounded Harry all the way up the staircase, demanding to know why he was spending so much time down in London.

Mrs Smythe-Osbourne's eyes flickered imperceptibly. She said nothing and nodded. It was not the first time Her Ladyship had damaged some of the priceless works of art in Huntington.

'Be a dear, Imogen, and call Sotheby's,' Harry continued. 'Send a few photographs and ask them to get their best man onto it, pronto. It once belonged to Louis XIV, you know, and he presented it as a gift to my great-great-great-great-grandfather on my maternal side.'

Mrs Smythe-Osbourne blinked.

'These things are sent to try us, I suppose,' Harry sighed.

Mrs Smythe-Osbourne smiled respectfully, then retreated to her own study down the hallway.

Harry tried to bat away his anger about Araminta's latest act of destruction. It would be a boring expense to have it repaired, and such an unnecessary expense at that.

Glasses back on, he leafed through his large leather-bound desk agenda. He noticed it was the 15th of March. Beware the Ides of March, the day Julius Caesar was assassinated. And the day his beloved twin brother Harvey had drowned. How could he possibly have forgotten? He tossed his glasses aside, grabbed his Barbour jacket and marched over to the conservatory. There he cut the most beautiful white roses he could find and bound them together with a white silk ribbon. He slipped into his immaculate wellies and dashed outside. Sherlock and Watson came yapping by his side and Harry bent down and patted them. At least they were always happy to see him. He strode through the walled garden, with its manicured lollipop trees and landscaped lawns. The whippets bounced along as Harry pushed open the gate and sped through to the wild meadows. Sherlock and Watson knew where he was headed: to his brother's tombstone. There he bowed, careful not to let his trousers touch the wet grass, and laid the bouquet of roses down. He closed his eyes and smiled, conjuring memories of playing cricket on this very field with his brother before devouring Mars bars as a special treat. Those were enchanted, carefree days. How different his life was now, heavy with duties and responsibilities.

Harry stood tall again and trudged on. He had always been the one who would inherit the title, born, as he was, a full two minutes before Harvey. Why had he, rather than Harvey, not succumbed to the boating accident? How could he possibly ever be happy when Harvey was dead?

He looked at his watch. Already eleven o'clock. He had a call with his lawyer in half an hour. Sherlock and Watson scampered along next to him.

Back at his desk, Harry composed himself. How typical of Montague to have anticipated his needs before he was even aware of them. A fresh pot of lapsang souchong tea awaited him. The phone rang at precisely eleven-thirty.

'Crispin, old sport,' Harry said. 'How are you? So good of you to call. How's the family? Is that fragrant wife of yours keeping you on the straight and narrow?'

Harry had known Crispin from the playgrounds of Eton, and he was the only lawyer in London with the brains and the discretion to be trusted to manage his complex financial matters, his Byzantine family trusts, and sundry other ticklish issues.

Harry coughed. 'I'm in a spot of bother, Crispin. It's, ahem, terribly dull, I'm afraid.'

'Mmm,' Crispin said. Terribly dull was code for rather serious. 'Well, that's what I'm here for, Harry. How can I help?'

'To be perfectly candid, Crispin, I've been, er, playing away,' Harry said, clearing his throat. 'Not my finest hour, but there it is. One has one's needs. Turns out my, ahem, friend, well, she's got an ex-husband who's being rather unreasonable about it all. He says he wants to get back with his former wife and he's told me, in no uncertain terms, to back off and stay the hell away from her. And now he's threatening to expose my, err, little indiscretion to the *Daily Mail*. He's even said he's got a way to get to HRH, and he will send him a letter exposing me. So not exactly pistols at dawn, but the whole thing is a tiresome inconvenience. The fellow's called Jack or John, or something. No, Jake. That's it, Jake.'

'Mmm,' Crispin repeated.

'Well, Crispin, what can one do about it?' Harry said. 'Should one pay him off? Make him sign a non-disclosure agreement? Serve him with an injunction?'

'Mmm...' Crispin sighed. 'Things are a bit trickier nowadays, Harry. It's not like the good old days. Injunctions and NDAs don't work anymore. Stuff leaks out on the internet and social media.'

Harry crossed his legs and ran his hand through his hair.

'The question is, Harry, can you plausibly deny the whole affair? Does this Jake fellow have any proof?'

'Well, apparently, the scoundrel claims he got into his ex-wife's phone and downloaded a copy of our entire WhatsApp conversation.' Harry blushed as he recalled some of the more compelling exchanges, which could, at best, be described as 'fruity'. He imagined the readers of the *Daily Mail* might find them rather compelling too.

'Mmm...' Crispin said. 'My advice is to sit this one out, my friend. In my experience, these things tend to blow over. Lots of bluff and bluster, but when it comes down to it, not much else. That's if you're lucky.'

'I hope to God you're right,' Harry mumbled, displaying considerably less of the sangfroid for which he was famous.

'And a word of advice, old bean, from someone who's known you longer than most,' Crispin added. 'Perhaps you want to think about keeping your pecker zipped up in future.'

Keeping his pecker zipped up was not something Harry was particularly good at doing. He had, historically, maintained a low profile. And he had been somewhat fortunate that his little dalliances with that voluptuous contessa in Bergamo, with the official royal photographer on her ancestral sugar plantation in Antigua and with one of his nubile former secretaries, a dead ringer for the young Princess Diana, had, somehow, all slipped through unnoticed by the press. He did have to make some rather inconvenient payments to those women, and also to the different women he was married to at the time, but, mercifully, there had been no dispiriting press exposure.

Harry sipped his tea and surveyed the room, trying to imagine how his life might be with Ava in it. The jade Buddha statue on his desk caught his eye. It was so incongruous, nestled between the Georgian antiques and Florentine treasures. Harry had held off-the-record meetings with the government in Yangon last month, where he had met a wise old Buddhist monk who had given him the statue. The monk had seen straight through him. He knew all about Harvey's death and Harry's three loveless marriages. He had even seen Ava and the deep love he bore her. He had described her perfectly: her energy, her blazing eyes, her coltish legs, even down to the way she jauntily swung her Hermès bag when she walked down the street. Harry bit his lip as he replayed in his mind the exact words the monk had used.

'It is better to conquer yourself than to win a thousand battles. Do not dwell in the past. Do not dream of the future. Concentrate your mind on the present moment. What we think, we become. Open up your heart and give yourself to it. Ava is your soulmate. She is your fire, and she is your refuge. She will be your wife.'

Harry thought about Araminta. He knew it would create quite the fracas if he left her. She was still a beauty, despite all the pills and booze, and she would remarry well, though she might struggle to find another earl. Perhaps she might settle for a baron or a life peer. Harry noticed she had recently rifled through his desk, no doubt to take copies of his latest bank statements. They would come in handy for those meetings she held with her divorce lawyers. It was regrettable that she had seen those photographs of Ava hidden in Harry's drawer. There was Ava in a silver bikini, stretched out on the sand in the Maldives; Ava emerging from the sea in St Barts, topless and hair slicked back; Ava on fire, dancing on tables in St Tropez; there was even one of Ava from fifteen years back, wearing a conservative navy suit, a string of pearls and a shy smile.

Harry felt a pain in his chest and decided to FaceTime her.

'Hello you,' he said, his glasses perched on his head. 'Gosh, you look well, as usual. How are you, my sweet?'

Ava was also at her desk at home, bent over the financial accounts of the solar energy company: Sun4ward. 'Good morning, darling. I was just thinking about you.' Ava beamed. Harry was all she could think about these days.

'I'm awfully sorry, my sweet, but I can't make it to London tonight,' Harry said. 'We had a wearisome accident on the grounds over the weekend. One of the horses broke his femur and my foreman had a bad head injury. Then I had a call late last night from you-know-who in Balmoral. He wants me to go over there for the weekend and discuss one of his special projects. It's all a bit challenging. But such is my life, darling.'

'Oh. That's a shame,' murmured Ava. It was not the first time he'd cancelled plans at the last minute. What she meant to say was, 'You're letting me down, again, Harry. I need you by my side. When are we going to be properly and openly together?' Instead, she bit her tongue. She was not in the mood for another one of those discussions.

'I'm so sorry, my love,' Harry continued. 'It's completely beyond my control. The powers that be have requested an emergency audience. State affairs. You know the drill. I simply couldn't refuse. *Lèse-majesté* and all that. All a bit inconvenient. But you know that you are always with me, darling, in my head and my heart.'

He paused to take a better look at Ava.

'You look adorable today. I see you haven't straightened your hair; it looks marvellously leonine. I wish I was there with you. You have no idea how painful it is to love you. And how scary. Even for me as a man. But it's even more scary not to feel your love. I feel you, my love. That's about all I feel at the moment. It's a horrid mixture of cold and chaos here.'

Ava smiled. The words were standard operating procedure.

'My precious one. I am more inside you than I have ever experienced. I cannot not love you. My heart longs for you and belongs to you,' Harry said. 'I live in hope.'

'Mmm,' Ava said dryly. 'Hope is not a strategy, Harry.'

Ava wondered if Harry would ever leave Araminta. Predicting what Harry might do next was like an exercise in advanced quantum physics, minus the electromagnetic particle accelerator. With Harry, nothing was accelerated. Like a free atom travelling in wave function, Harry was simultaneously present and absent. His love was there, and it was not there. His words were exhilarating and empty. Anticipating Harry's movements was a variation on Heisenberg's uncertainty principle; there was, in essence, a limit to the possibility of prediction. All one could hope to do was infer a wide range of possibilities and assign their likely probability. Harry was many things, but binary and clear-cut he was not. With him, it was never an unequivocal 'yes' or a straightforward 'no'. More like fifty shades of grey, but in all the wrong ways.

'I know you need and want more,' Harry said. 'Araminta is being quite horrid at the moment, even by her standards. The low point was when she tore through one of my Gobelins tapestries with her elbow. It's going to be quite a bore getting it repaired.' He closed his eyes and took a deep breath. 'Ava, my love. I'm battling on so many fronts, you have no idea. It's not fair to you. Knowing my appalling track record, I will just exhaust you. Do you really think I can make you happy? I always mess everything up.'

'I'm here for you, Harry,' Ava said. 'I always will be. You know that. I love you. I love you with every cell in my body.'

'You are my champion and I love you for it,' Harry said. 'You are everywhere and everything. You always will be. It's so hard to explain and so painful to feel, darling. I bleed for life and for you. You are in my bloodstream. I love you so completely and more. My heart will always be yours, whatever happens. We belong together. We will find a way to make it work. I can't think of life ahead without loving you, my darling. Our love is too strong to fade and die.'

Harry stared at his phone long after Ava had hung up. He took a sip of his lapsang souchong tea, now cold, and put his glasses back on. He made another feeble attempt at getting to grips with Sun4ward's projected profit and loss, but his eyes blurred when he tried to understand those fiendishly complex spreadsheets. He would have to ask Ava again.

Several weeks later, the Gobelins tapestry had been removed, repaired and returned. Harry grimaced every time he walked past it on the way to his bedroom in the west wing. The Sotheby's restorers had done a splendid job, but Harry was sure he could see the ghost of an indent where Araminta's elbow had punctured through the priceless artefact that had withstood fires, floods, plagues and at least five European wars.

5.

Paradise Lost

'Harry, my love. You know how much I love you.'

Ava sat next to Harry on the velvet banquette, back at Bellamy's, the same Mayfair restaurant where they first had lunch just over a year ago. She squeezed his hand under the table.

'I will always love you. I would do anything for you, Harry. Anything. But I can't live like this anymore. I've had enough of skulking around. It's not fair on anyone. It's not fair on me, it's not fair on you. It's not even fair on Araminta. It's not a tenable situation. I want to walk down the street with you and hold your hand, out in the open. I can't go on. I've come to a decision, Harry. I don't want to share you: I love you too much. I want all of you, or nothing,' Ava said evenly. She had rehearsed these words over and over in her head. 'It's over. Please don't contact me anymore unless you leave your wife. I love you. You are my love. I will always love you.'

Ava wondered how many times she could use the word 'love' in a ten-second declaration.

Harry trembled. Truth be told, he had been expecting this moment for some time, and he was amazed at how patient Ava had been.

'I love you too, my sweet,' he said, squeezing her hand back. 'My love for you knows no bounds. But I need more time. You have to understand, Araminta's in such an appalling state, more appalling than ever. Now her mother's dying. She's got stage four pancreatic cancer and the poor woman's only got a few more weeks to live. It's all so terribly fraught.' He took a sip of tea and wiped his mouth on the napkin. 'Really, you have no idea how vile life is up at Huntington. It's thrown a dreadful spanner in the works. I simply can't leave now.' He paused and looked more closely at Ava. 'I need you, Ava. I want you. I love you. But my hands are tied. Give me a bit more time.' He squeezed her hand more tightly.

'Harry...' Ava's voice faltered. She took Harry's hand to her lips and kissed it softly. 'Time is passing.' She tossed her hair back and sat up straight. Her mind was made up. 'I will always love you, Harry. But it's over.'

It took a lot of strength for Ava to walk away from Harry. It was the ultimate marshmallow test: forsaking short-term satisfaction with the man she loved now, for a possible bigger, long-term win with the man she loved and wanted for life. It was not a clever tactic, nor a calculated ruse. Ava knew she had to do it for her own well-being, her self-respect and her sanity. She still had just about enough dignity and pride left to know that. Much as she loved Harry, much as she felt his love like she had never felt any man's love before, and much as she needed that love like she needed oxygen, she could not live as the shadow woman anymore.

When she got home, she poured herself a generous triple vodka in honour of Harry's old nickname, with one ice cube, no tonic. It was not vodka she was seeking, but oblivion. She sat on her sofa, shaking, and she made a ceremony of deleting Harry's contact details from her phone. The fact that they were indelibly imprinted on her mind was irrelevant.

Leaving Harry was the hardest thing she had ever done. Yet she knew it was the right decision. It was time to start to stop loving Harry.

And the mourning began.

Ava plummeted into a vortex of pain and deeper pain. She was a prisoner of her grief. She missed Harry viscerally. He had lived in her body, heart and soul for a year. His love for her and her love for him gushed through her veins. There was nothing left now save a desert of lovelessness. The man she loved did not choose her. The fantasy of love was over. Paradise lost.

Khassya and Sasha looked on, alarmed. They barely recognised their strong, positive mother with her indomitable energy, a woman for whom everything and anything was possible. She stopped eating and she hardly slept. She could barely function anymore.

The girls tiptoed into the darkened living room, as Ava lay on the couch.

'I made you a cup of Earl Grey tea, Mama,' Sasha said softly. 'And we got you some of your favourite Swiss chocolate.'

The mug of tea had the words 'The universe delivers!' written on it. It was a gift from the fortune teller.

The universe delivers? You don't say, Ava thought. She sat up and held each of her girls close. Now, she could begin to breathe again.

'Mama, Sasha and I did some research,' Khassya said. 'We found you a therapist who specialises in trauma. Apparently, his parents are Holocaust survivors too, so you have that in common.'

'Thank you, angels, but I don't want to talk to anyone,' Ava said. 'How can talking help? Waste of time.' But she was ashamed that her daughters saw her in such a state, and that alone made her agree to seek help.

Tall and imposing, with a beard and a full head of grey locks, Ava's therapist immediately reminded her of Moses, imperious on Mount Sinai, gripping the stone tablets engraved with the Ten Commandments. Perhaps he could also lead her out of her desolate wilderness and into the Promised Land?

For a split second, she lost her nerve and almost headed straight back down the path of his charming, leafy Hampstead home to hail a taxi. But Moses pulled her in with a firm handshake and she stumbled into his office.

She sat on the worn leather sofa in his den, cosy and womb-like. Books spilled out everywhere, piled on the floor, on the desk and in the densely packed wooden bookcases. Ava spotted a couple of surreal Dalí prints and a blood-red Rothko poster from the Tate Modern.

'It's good to meet you, Ava,' Moses said. His voice was deep and warm. 'Please make yourself comfortable.'

Ava huddled, as small as she could make herself, on the enormous brown couch.

'Now tell me a bit about yourself. Maybe you could start with why you've come here today.'

Ava's grief was so close to the surface that Moses simply asking about her well-being, with kindness and compassion, made her burst into tears before she was able to utter a single word. He handed her a box of Kleenex and waited patiently for her to compose herself.

'I'm so sorry. I'm really sorry. I couldn't control myself. Sorry,' Ava sniffed, wiping away her tears.

She was barely audible. The tears removed all traces of make-up from her face. She looked the way she felt: like a sad young girl.

'I feel so broken. I'm so ashamed to be here. But I'm in such pain,' Ava murmured. 'I found it hard to justify coming to see you, but my girls made me. I think I should be able to sort myself out without your help.'

'I see,' said Moses, rubbing his chin with his hand. 'And how's that working out for you?'

'Well, er, it's not working out so well. Looks like I might need some help after all.' She blew her nose.

'Well, you made it here, so well done,' said Moses.

Ava smiled weakly. They say that ninety per cent of success is showing up. If only it were that easy.

'So, tell me, Ava, what's been going on?'

'Well, there's been quite a lot going on, and plenty going wrong. And recent events have sort of brought matters to a head.' Ava fiddled with her bracelet. 'The main reason I'm here is because I fell deeply in love. But it didn't work out. Just a banal love story without a happy ending. You must see that every day.'

Moses gave a micro-nod.

'But for me, well, it was the first time I was ever truly in love. I've never loved a man so much. And I've never felt so loved and accepted. Harry, that's his name, he was my dream man. I know he loved me. I know he did. I could feel it. But there was one little problem: he happens to be married to someone else. I spent a whole year waiting for him to leave his wife. It was agony. He procrastinated and procrastinated, and he gave me a hundred reasons why I should wait for him. And I waited until I just couldn't take it anymore, and then I left him. I'm embarrassed to be sitting here. It feels like I'm wasting your time. But the truth is' – Ava looked away – 'I, well, I don't know. How do I put this? I'm falling apart.'

Moses stretched out his long legs and scratched his head. Ava wondered if he was already bored.

'Ah,' he said with authority and then paused. 'You're in pain, obviously. The end of a relationship is a loss; it's like a death. And like a death, it takes time to accept.' He leaned forwards. 'Maybe, Ava, it could be helpful for you to think of the five different stages that we see in the classic grieving process: denial, anger, bargaining, sadness and, ultimately, you get to a point of acceptance. That's when the healing can properly begin.'

'Mmm... I'm stuck deep in denial and sadness,' Ava whispered. 'Sometimes I wake up in the middle of the night and I think it was all a bad dream. Until I remember that this is my life.'

'It's normal to feel several emotions simultaneously,' Moses said. 'Grief is not linear. There's a lot for you to process.' Then he added, more softly, 'Ava, it's okay to feel pain. You can only move forward if you accept your pain. Your pain is telling you something. You need to feel and to understand your pain. Remember, our wounds are the openings to the best and the most beautiful parts of ourselves. What do you think your pain is telling you?'

The answer was so obvious, it required no thought. 'My pain? It's telling me that Harry didn't love me enough to leave his wife. I wasn't worth the upheaval that a third divorce would create in his life. The pain is telling me that I'm worthless. I don't deserve Harry's love. I'm just not good enough for him.'

Ava clenched both her fists and dug her long nails into the palms of her hands. She did not want to cry again. Moses watched her as she fought to regain control of her emotions.

'I feel like such a failure,' Ava said at last, unable to look Moses in the eye. 'I loathe myself. I feel revolting and alone. So alone. You know, my father wanted to abort me before I was born, and I've felt unwanted all through my life.'

Ava could barely get the words out. She felt so insignificant. She even felt guilty about seeing a shrink about how meaningless she felt. She loathed herself for not having the strength to simply get over herself and move on. So, a man whom she loved didn't love her back? Was that it? Couldn't she pull herself together and stop snivelling? It was all so self-indulgent.

'Ah.' Moses stroked his chin again. 'Feeling alone is part of the human condition. We're all alone, Ava. That's why we value connection. It's a way of feeling less alone. Connection makes us feel understood. Connection allows us to share life's rich tapestry with another human being.' He sat up and peered a bit more closely at Ava. She looked so tiny and lost on that large sofa, sitting with her legs curled under her. 'You have a strong inner critic, Ava. You've internalised those disapproving parental messages. And it sounds like your inner critic is sabotaging you, and probably has done for a long time.'

'Possibly,' Ava said, though she knew Moses' analysis was accurate. 'I even feel bad about being here. I don't feel my pain is worthy of closer examination. But you're right, I've felt bad for such a long, long time. Only I am, or at least I was, highly functional. I've got two marvellous daughters, Sasha and Khassya, whom I love and adore more than anything. They're the life of my life, the loves of my life, the heart of my heart. I guess everyone says that about their children.' She paused. 'Though come to think of it, well, I guess that's not exactly how my parents would talk about me. Anyway, I don't want to talk about my parents. I'm thirty-nine years old and I should have dealt with all that childhood baggage by now.' Ava shook her head. 'I've got a great career. I'm financially independent. I've got a full life and my role is to make sure my girls and everyone else in the family and around me is happy. When I was married, I didn't have time to notice how awful I felt inside. I was so busy working, running a full-on business and trading, and taking care of Sasha and Khassya and my husband – all that masked my pain. And my professional success, well, it was a way of proving to myself that I wasn't sad and ugly, underneath the glossy exterior.'

Moses cocked his head to one side, and then the other side, as though he had a stiff neck. He said nothing. He waited for Ava to say more. His patients usually said the more interesting things when he kept quiet, to fill the void.

'But now, everything feels so empty. Sometimes I wonder: what's the point of carrying on? I've had enough.' She choked up and looked away, her eyes drawn back to the red Rothko on the wall.

'I hear you, Ava. I feel your pain.'

Ava's eyes widened. She was not used to being heard, let alone understood.

'But perhaps, Ava, you could try allowing yourself to feel your pain. That will help you get in touch with your inner child. There are stories that we tell ourselves, the relationship patterns we follow from birth. Even if they're painful and self-destructive, they're familiar, so we follow the same old script. Am I right in thinking you suffered a traumatic childhood?'

Ava nodded, her eyes fixed on the Rothko.

'The pain you're suffering now is taking you right back to that time. It's taking you straight to the rejection you felt way back when you were a little girl. It's just amplified, by being repeated throughout your life. Let's look at the psychodynamics here.'

Ava didn't know what psychodynamics were, but she continued to speak in a stream of consciousness. 'I don't want to... carry on. It all feels so meaningless. Pointless, really. It hurts too much. I, er, I, can't anymore.' She took a couple of deep breaths in and out. She thought she might be about to hyperventilate. 'If I'm honest, my girls are the only meaning in my life. They bring me so much love and joy. Because of them, I could never end my life. I could never do that to them. They would be distraught. It would ruin their lives. They need me. But if my girls didn't need me, well, er, I wouldn't, um, I wouldn't know why I was here.'

Moses stared more intently at Ava. She wiped away a tear with the back of her hand and sat wordlessly running a finger along her lips, lost in her thoughts.

Suddenly, she sat up very straight. 'In any event, failure is not an option,' Ava said, her voice now loud and clear. 'I need to be strong for my children. I need to set an example. I need to show my daughters that it's important to fight adversity, and win, whatever "winning" means. After all, my father and my grandparents were Holocaust survivors and their blood runs through my veins. I could never end my life. It's disgraceful and absurd of me to compare the triviality of my suffering to the enormity of what my family went through. It's odd, but I also feel the guilt of being a survivor. Somehow, I feel the collective suffering of all those other six million people who didn't make it through the Holocaust. I can't end my life. No. I could never, ever, do that.'

'I get it,' said Moses. 'But bear in mind, Ava, that trauma is absolute, not relative. Just because you didn't personally go through the Holocaust doesn't mean you don't feel real pain. There's a lot of double negatives there, so let's unpack that. What I'm saying is, it's okay for you to feel pain. Don't put a value judgement on it. Pain is not relative. Pain is pain.'

Ava nodded. She appreciated what Moses was saying, but inside she felt deeply ashamed.

Moses scratched his head. 'What you're saying about the Holocaust reminds me of what Viktor Frankl wrote about freedom, after he survived the concentration camp in Auschwitz. He said that you can take everything away from a man, but you can still choose how you feel, and you can choose what you think. You have that choice. You have that freedom. You can decide.'

'Mmm,' Ava said, tapping her foot. 'I've read a lot of Frankl and Bettelheim and Levi and all those Holocaust writers. They're almost too agonising to read. But they're also incredibly humbling and uplifting. Because those Holocaust survivors saw unspeakable things. And yet, they had the strength and the courage to fight for happiness, for freedom. They looked beyond themselves and helped others. I can't even talk about myself in the same breath. I'm nothing. I'm insignificant. But I'm trying to be positive. I know that my thoughts are optional. I'm trying to control what I think and what I feel. But it's not easy. Maybe I should try meditating.'

'Yes,' said Moses, 'that could work for you. It could help you find an inner stillness. Tune in to your inner self and listen to what your heart is telling you.'

The only thing Ava's heart was telling her right now was that her heart was bleeding pain, raw like the haemorrhaging red Rothko.

'Why don't you tell me about your relationship history, Ava?' Moses said softly.

'Pretty bog-standard, I guess,' Ava said.

Moses knew that there was no such thing as bog-standard in his line of work and he smiled.

'Well, perhaps not,' Ava said, recognising the fallacy. 'Happiness, from the outside at least, is boring and looks much the same for everyone. Wasn't it de Montherlant who said that happiness writes in white ink on a white page? But everyone's unhappiness is so different. There is no bog-standard unhappiness, just many various shades of black.' She frowned. 'As to my relationship history, well, it started with my playboy of a father whom I rarely saw. He disapproved of me, and he never showed me any love at all. I also had a stepfather, who did the same, and I was basically ignored. I concluded two things, early on: one, that men aren't to be trusted and two, that I'm not lovable. I don't think my opinions changed as life went on; in fact, they were reinforced by my experiences.'

Ava sounded very matter-of-fact, as if she was talking about another person.

'At around thirteen, I got very thin, and I became less of an ugly duckling. I went to Cambridge, where I discovered men and sex. All I wanted was to love and to be loved back. From the outside, I was bubbly and fun, but inside, I was totally lost. I thought sex was the gateway to love. That was another thing I got wrong. I spent years looking for love in all the wrong places. My romantic experiences were like a perfect mirror to my early childhood of non-love, of feeling unwanted. The inexorable pull of the familiar, or something. I didn't know any better. Anyway, by my early twenties, I was desperate to have children and to build my own loving family unit, something I'd never really had. There were some good times, but essentially, my ex-husband, Jake, lied and cheated his way through our marriage. When I eventually found out, he said it was my fault he cheated, since I made him feel insecure.'

Ava shook her head and sniggered at the irony. 'Quite an imaginative excuse, really, I'll give Jake that. I was super-busy being the breadwinner, as well as raising my girls, and running a few homes around the world. I never so much as touched another man's hand in all those years. My sex life with Jake was always active, but that was a smokescreen because it was mechanical and unsatisfying. I've always felt alone, in and outside the bedroom. I guess I never properly connected to Jake, neither emotionally nor sexually. It's hard to connect to a man you don't trust.'

Ava paused and cleared her throat. 'Do you know, in all my years of marriage, my husband never looked me in the eye. Have you got any idea how that feels? It was like he didn't want to see me, the real me. Or maybe he was so ashamed of his behaviour, he didn't want to be seen. Anyway, it was not the "happily ever after" ending I used to dream about. I ultimately found the courage to get divorced and I started seeing Harry. I fell madly in love. Finally, I found the Big Love, and I thought that was it. Transpired that was yet another thing I got wrong. And here we are.'

Ava twisted her hair up into a bun, pulling it off her face. Her so-called love life, as she recounted it, was a pathetic joke: a love life devoid of love.

'Woody Allen was right. Sooner or later, everything turns to shit,' Ava said. 'Sorry for the swear word. I hate swearing. But it's the only word that summarises my situation perfectly.'

Moses smiled. 'Don't worry about swearing. It's important that you express yourself freely here. It's a safe space for you.' Moses leaned back and stretched out. 'Now tell me: how does your relationship history make you feel?'

'Well, if you really want to know, it makes me feel *fucking* awful.' She laughed out loud for the first time in a long while. 'Sorry.'

Moses grinned, then, looking more serious, said, 'I think it's interesting how you've sexualised your need for love.'

Ava nodded. 'Yes, I know. I did it consciously. I guess with sex, I'm in control. Sex is empowering. It feels good when a man wants me. But that's not love. Even I can see that. Sex hasn't led to love, more like the opposite. I guess I'm, er, good at sex and bad at love.'

Ava bit her lower lip. It was not a boast. It was a cry for help.

'I think that maybe,' she said, with a self-mocking lightness of tone, 'it could, quite possibly, be time for a little rethink.'

She noticed Moses trying, discreetly, to scratch his groin area and loosen the pull of his trousers. Why was she even looking there? Moses spread his long legs out again.

'Mmm,' he said. 'It sounds like your sexual activity hasn't led to real love and happiness.'

Ava flinched.

'Have you thought, Ava,' Moses said gently, 'that perhaps you could reframe your past? Rewrite your narrative. Change your limiting belief system. I don't think what you've been telling yourself all these years has served you that well. Maybe experience is a better name we should give to the mistakes that we all make going through life. Bear in mind that the only real mistakes are the ones you don't learn from. Defeat is not falling down. Defeat is not being able to stand up again.'

Ava nodded. 'I guess my failed relationship with Harry has grown into a full-blown existential crisis.' She hated sounding like a mid-life cliché. 'It's all linked, obviously. I'm trying to find some sense of purpose. I'm trying to understand what life is about. You know, the meaning of life and all that. But I'm stuck. I'm asking myself some fundamental questions. What is a good life? What makes life purposeful and worthwhile? You know, those big, universal questions that are so hard to answer. Did you know we live an average of four thousand weeks? Put that way, life is shockingly short, isn't it?'

Her comments sounded so glib; she felt ridiculous. Perhaps it wasn't a shrink she should be speaking to, but a rabbi or a moral philosopher.

'Ava, we're all trying to answer these questions as best we can. You're not alone,' Moses said. 'I don't have the answers either. What is happiness? What brings meaning to life? I guess meaning, like happiness, is not something you find. It's a process, a lifetime's journey of discovery. You might find that happiness is not something you look for. Perhaps purpose, like happiness, like love even, lies inside of you? Have you thought that it's not about finding the meaning of life? Perhaps it's the other way round: it's about the meaning that you bring to your life.'

Ava walked out into the cold air. As she stepped into the taxi, she was surprised to realise she felt better. The session had been cathartic, even if Moses had also given her a whole new set of problems to think about.

As she leaned back into the soft leather car seat, her mind automatically flipped back to Harry. It felt like she had taken two tentative steps forward and three giant steps back.

She visualised the neon Tracey Emin graffiti piece she had bought in the White Cube gallery after they broke up, with the words *When I go to sleep I dream of you inside of me* emblazoned in fluorescent-pink cursive. She had it mounted above her bed, in memory of never, ever wanting to feel that bitter-sweet yearning again. The strategy had not been a resounding success. What she really wanted was to live that feeling, not dream of it.

Had she pushed Harry too hard? Should she have been more patient and given him more time? After all, doesn't love conquer all?

Ava took a deep breath. She knew that she had done the right thing to leave Harry. She'd had enough of her little pity party. Now she didn't just want to survive. Surviving was not enough. She needed to thrive. Onwards and upwards. Onwards and downwards, or even onwards and sideways was not a viable option. Her new and unexpected sense of freedom was dizzying. She could have a complete reset. She could redefine herself and make new choices. She was free to do what she wanted, when she wanted and with whom she wanted. And for that freedom, she was incredibly grateful.

Ava had said goodbye to Harry. She knew it would be a long, painful goodbye. But she also said hello to her new life, which was where the psychic and her new 'H' man came in.

6.

Stepping into the Same River Twice

Once Ava had had enough of being curled up in a ball under her duvet, feeling sorry for herself, she slipped into her Lycra and hit the gym. Her marriage had failed, she had failed to win over Harry, and she had failed to get into some semblance of a proper relationship with Hugo. She concluded that it was perhaps time to press pause and take a little break from men. There had to be more to life than looking for Prince Charming. She threw herself into her charity work in education, where she could make a real difference to disadvantaged children's lives. She went out to the theatre, the opera and art galleries to broaden her mind. And she travelled to the bright blue glaciers of Antarctica, to the lush green forests of the Amazon and the burnished golds of the African bush. She pursued her passions and interests with renewed zeal. And she stopped focusing on finding a man.

Except life doesn't work that way.

Ava met the next man in her life in the street. It was a Mayfair street, but a street, nonetheless. She spent her whole life going to the right hotspots, being seen with the right people in the right restaurants, having the right kind of fun. But Ava, who liked to believe she could control everything in her life, succumbed to the hand of fate.

She sashayed down Grosvenor Street in her dark sunglasses, tight black leggings and a black leather jacket, flooded with post-Pilates endorphins. Led Zeppelin's 'Whole Lotta Love' pumped through her AirPods. Robert Plant, for one, knew that was exactly what Ava needed.

Eventually, Ava noticed a tall, slim man, also in dark glasses, circling around her. He was dressed in the smart-casual uniform of successful men in finance: jeans, a tailored shirt and a dark blazer. He stopped right in front of her. What on earth was he doing, standing in her way?

'Do you know the way to the Connaught Hotel?' he asked.

Ava cocked an eyebrow. Was this man really asking for directions as a way to talk to her? That was what she thought he was saying, because she couldn't hear him. The music was still pounding in her ears. He mouthed a few more words and she removed her AirPods.

'Do you know the way to the Connaught hotel?' he repeated in a thick Israeli accent.

It was such a corny line, he had to stop himself from laughing out loud as he said it. He removed his sunglasses, and Ava did the same. She wanted to take a closer look at his face. Judging by his impeccable posture and the whiff of arrogance, she suspected he might be stunningly handsome. She suspected right. Warm, dark eyes. High cheekbones. Chiselled jaw. He was hot, and he knew it.

Seamlessly, Ava found herself sitting with Sami, the silky-smooth Israeli, at a corner table in the Connaught Bar, drinking her favourite lychee martini. As he gesticulated to emphasise an amusing anecdote, she noticed Sami's thin gold wedding band. How come she had not spotted it before? Her cardinal rule, post Harry, was never to waste her precious time with married men, especially over lychee martinis. It appeared that rule had now lapsed, or at least, it was temporarily on hold.

'What made you stop me in the street, Sami?' Ava asked.

It was pretty obvious why Sami had intercepted Ava. The question was more: why had Ava stopped to speak to a man in the street, and what on earth was she doing flirting with a married man over cocktails in the middle of the day?

'I caught your vibe. Your energy. You looked so happy and confident. I couldn't resist. I don't usually stop women in the street.'

Ava almost believed him.

Three lychee martinis later...

'You're so beautiful. You're strong and intelligent. But what I like the most about you is the hint of fragility underneath, and what I sense is your tender side; it's there, big time.' Sami had known her for all of two hours. 'If I wasn't married, what I'd like to do right now is take you upstairs and fuck you.'

Ava laughed at his cheek, but she found his self-assurance compelling.

'I wouldn't take my pants off until I'd made you come at least twice,' he added.

They stared at each other, Ava melting like the ice cubes in her glass.

'Life is now,' Sami proclaimed, apropos of nothing, eerily echoing her thoughts.

This was the line Ava used to justify more or less any course of action, especially action of a more questionable kind.

'I need to go to a meeting now. In fact, I'm already three-quarters of an hour late. But let's meet soon,' Sami said with a wink. 'How about tonight? Come back here, at this spot, at six.'

Sami made Ava an offer she did not care to refuse. After all, she reasoned, it was just a friendly drink between a man and a woman who shared a similar view of life, wasn't it?

She dressed carefully for the second rendezvous of the day. Tight, low-cut navy Hervé Léger dress, absurdly high heels and a long, dramatic black coat. It was a look that was possibly past its sell-by date for the avant-garde fashionista, but it suited her. Sami was already waiting for her at the same table when she flounced in. She was floating on air, but she was falling, falling, falling. They smiled knowingly at each other. They were both old and experienced enough to know better. But this was something that they were both old and experienced enough to know was way too powerful to resist.

'You look ravishing,' Sami said approvingly. 'Good enough to eat.'

Ava felt him undressing her with his eyes, and she spent a delicious moment imagining exactly how he was going to eat her.

'I despise men who cheat on their wives,' he said, interrupting her reverie.

Ava frowned, uncertain if he was addressing her, or voicing out loud what he might be thinking about adulterers and, by extension, himself.

'If a man doesn't want to be with his wife, he should leave. I don't cheat on my wife. I couldn't look at myself, let alone my children, if I did.'

It transpired Sami was a devoted and caring father of four. The youngest was only seven. Ava did the maths. That meant another nine or so years until Sami might allow himself to escape the family nest. She sighed internally. Aside from the futility of seeing yet another married man, she just did not have eight years to sit around and wait. Being with a married man was one of the greatest acts of self-sabotage. Was this how she wanted to live out the rest of her years? Had she learnt nothing from her time with Harry?

'I tell my wife every year, on our wedding anniversary, that marriages don't last a lifetime,' Sami said dryly.

Ava raised an eyebrow.

'A long marriage is not necessarily a mark of success. What really counts as success is still wanting to fuck your wife, after all those years.'

Ava wondered how much Sami wanted to fuck his wife. And how much he wanted to fuck the woman he had just met on Grosvenor Street. She found all this wife and family talk more than mildly distasteful. And her own behaviour was inconsistent, at best. After all, she herself had been cheated on by her ex-husband, and she had suffered from the aftermath of total pain and humiliation. Then she had fallen in love with a married man, and suffered, again, from total pain and humiliation. Did she want to embark on an affair with another married man, and suffer yet more total pain and humiliation? The intellectual somersaults required to justify such an absurd course of action were beyond even her. She should have been jolted back to reality and got up and left. Nothing had even begun, and yet it felt too late to leave. She was already on the edge of surrender. Ava resigned herself to cosmic inevitability. It was déjà vu all over again.

Sami had only known her for a few hours, but he caught the subtle shift in her mood, and sensed the shadow behind her smile. He took her hand and kissed it softly. 'You're utterly delicious, Ava,' he said. 'Everything about you is off-the-charts amazing on every level.'

Ava had heard these lines before and, every time, she could not resist their gravitational pull. She was like a vase with a big hole at the bottom. The compliments came pouring in, but they flowed straight out again. She heard the words, but she never, ever felt either delicious or amazing.

'I can't resist you,' he said. 'You're ultra-special. Kissing you would be like kissing the Pope. I get a special dispensation. It's allowed because you're exceptional. It's okay for me to kiss the Pope.'

He had found the perfect way to justify his transgression, and he cast aside any scruples he might have had with some handy self-serving lateral thinking. He also knew that when he wanted something, he would stop at nothing until he got it. Saying this, and oblivious to the other guests in the bar, Sami took Ava's face in both his hands and kissed her, slowly at first, then more passionately. It was a kiss that stopped time. A kiss that Ava wanted to last forever.

Eventually, Ava sensed a presence hovering over them. The waiter, standing tall in his black tuxedo and bow tie, gave a polite cough.

'I'm sorry, sir,' he began in hushed tones, 'but we've, er, had a complaint from one of our regulars. Please could you kindly refrain from, er, overt displays of, er, affection in public.'

Ava and Sami came back down to earth with a jolt and laughed, embarrassed.

Ava met Sami several more times over decadent daytime cocktails, always at the Connaught. One fateful autumnal afternoon, Sami took charge. Before she knew it, they'd moved from the bar to one of the suites upstairs. It was a swift one-two manoeuvre, like another trick Sami had perfected in the Israeli army. They kissed voraciously. Sami ripped off her clothes and he began to mount his attack. Every cell in Ava's body was aroused by Sami's expert touch and kiss.

'Oh my God,' Sami said, stopping to take her in, 'those breasts, those nipples. I want to bite that arse. Turn over. You look even better naked.'

He pushed her down on the bed and spread her legs, then went down on her expertly. Slowly, patiently, he savoured every lick. He felt every muscle and every twitch of her body. He was so in tune with her, it was as if he desired what she desired, he felt what she felt, he was aroused by what aroused her, he breathed what she breathed. Ava lost all sense of self. She no longer knew where her breath stopped and Sami's began.

Eternity in the lips and eyes. She came twice, in his mouth, and cried out his name. Then, just when she thought she could not come any more, he stopped.

Sami got up from the bed and paused, taking a sip from the glass of iced water on the antique cherry-wood table. Ava wondered why he was taking so long to drink. He turned back to her. Now she knew. As he bent down to lick her clit, Ava felt a frisson of iciness, and the irresistible flicks of his tongue. She moaned, and came again, shuddering. She lay in Sami's arms as he gently massaged her shoulders and caressed the side of her breasts. For a moment, she allowed herself to feel wanted and safe.

'When I was a lieutenant colonel in the Israeli army,' Sami said, 'they made us memorise the typography of enemy territory, so that we could operate, even in the dark, without any GPS. I've memorised the typography of your pussy. I know exactly what I need to do to make you come hard. Flat tongue here, quick tongue flicks there, my fingers inside you. I would be able to identify your pussy immediately in a photographic line up. I know just what you love. But I want to find new ways of making you come.'

Ava decided to suspend reality. Like Sami, she gave herself special papal dispensation. She could not and did not want to resist him. He was way too special to pass up. She consciously switched her brain off and became all senses and feeling. She found it disturbingly easy to be herself with Sami, precisely because he was married with four young children. She was able to let all her barriers down because she knew the 'relationship' would go nowhere. If there was no future, there was no need to be anything but her authentic, vulnerable, loving self.

No games.

No pretence.

Sami did the same. She excited him and awakened in him a dominant sexuality he never knew he had. And with her, he was honest and real. The sex was electrifying because they were so intimate, and they were so intimate because the sex was so electrifying.

'Sami,' Ava whispered, 'you have the most perfect cock I've ever seen.'

Sami smiled proudly. Part of his appeal was his unswerving self-belief. He was definitely cocksure.

'And do you want to know why your cock is so perfect?' Ava continued, smiling, stroking him.

Sami thought it was because of his cock's length and girth, and the way he could grow so hard again within minutes of orgasm.

'Your cock is perfect,' Ava said, 'because it's *yours*.'

Ava worshipped Sami's cock. She sucked him with abandon, savouring every inch.

Ava and Sami saw each other twice a week in the afternoon for the next few months. In an attempt to save her heart from breaking, Ava introduced her 'two-centimetre rule': Sami was not allowed to penetrate her beyond two centimetres. She could pretend she was not having an affair with a married man because full penetration was off the menu. The Clintonian defence. She could make-believe she was fully in control of the situation and of her emotions. And Sami, who was wracked with guilt, could also pretend that he was not cheating on his wife if he was only barely two centimetres inside Ava.

But even penetration turned out to be a relatively elastic concept. Sami and Ava kissed and almost-fucked in a hundred different ways: in front of the three-way mirror in her dressing room; perched on the kitchen counter; on the velvet dining-room chair; balancing off the windowsill; against the marble tiles in the shower... They were inventive, imaginative, uninhibited and utterly insatiable. But what

Sami wanted most of all, of course, was to fully penetrate Ava and to be deep inside her. And what Ava wanted most of all was the exact complement of that: to be penetrated by Sami and to feel his cock moving deep inside her. If anything, the two-centimetre rule only served to heighten their desire.

Having tasted what two centimetres felt like, both wanted and needed more. Deeper, harder, stronger. Inside. They lay on Ava's grey velvet couch, talking, kissing, laughing, licking, stroking, caressing, biting. They had both come twice already that afternoon. Suddenly, without warning, Sami eased himself on top of her and thrust fully into her, deep, hard and strong. Past the two centimetres. Ava gasped and caught her breath. There had been no discussion. Just action. She knew that they had now broken the only cardinal rule they had. Two centimetres went out the window. But by now they were beyond caring. It had been a short-lived exercise in self-control. And they had both failed.

Ava arched her back to let him penetrate her deeper still. They were now fully animal. He pulled her hair hard, and they balanced on the edge of the sofa as she threw her head back. Then he put his hands around her neck in a strong grip. It was a moment carefully balanced between lust and trust, perfectly suspended between agony and ecstasy, fear and tenderness. Only Sami could have pulled it off. Only Sami could get it so right. It hurt, but Ava said nothing; she enjoyed being submissive for a change, and she was totally under his spell. Entwined, they fell to the floor and onto the gold silk Persian rug. Sami penetrated her hard from behind, as she cried out, wanting him more than ever. He was deep inside her. He drove further and further into her until they both came together, loudly, breathless and, finally, spent.

Ava suspected this was quite different from anything Sami got at home.

'I would never let anyone else but you circle my throat like that,' she said, still gasping, as they lay on the carpet, limbs interlaced.

'I know. But you love it. I know you do.'

'Yeah, maybe,' Ava said. 'It's because I trust you; I trust you completely.'

The truth is, Ava didn't know any other man who had it in him to be so fully masculine. And she only allowed it because she knew how tender he was to his core.

'You really love to fuck, don't you?' Sami said with approval, running his hand down her hips and thighs. He stroked her inner thighs and then kept his hand between her legs. 'Some women go through the motions of sex, but you, you love it. And you need it.'

'Yes,' Ava said simply. 'Fucking to me is like oxygen. Like breathing. I can't live without it.'

Sami had just come, strongly and loudly, but Ava saw that he was already hard again. She looked at his smooth, long-limbed and hairless swimmer's body with admiration.

'You're utterly irrepressible. You're unique. I've never seen a man who can grow so hard, so fast, after coming so hard. How old are you? Forty-five?'

Effortlessly, Sami picked Ava up from the floor and carried her up the flight of stairs and into her bedroom.

'Put me down,' Ava squealed. 'I'm too heavy, Sami. We're both going to fall down the stairs.'

Ava's words only served to encourage him more. Sami continued up the stairs until he reached the bed and laid her down with the softest of kisses.

By the next time they made love, they had fallen in love. They clung to each other tenderly, achingly. Ava sobbed as she came. She looked into Sami's dark eyes and saw he also had tears in his eyes.

'Darling. We both know this is not fucking. I wish it was,' he said. 'The fucking is just an excuse to lie next to you and to be close to you. I want to lie by your side and make love to you all the time. I want to inhale you. I want to breathe you. I want to taste and explore you. No boundaries. I want to be inside you forever and never leave.'

Ava felt her eyes well up. Why had she allowed herself to lose control? She had known from the start, before anything had happened, that it would be like this. She knew there was no such thing as a zipless fuck. There was no sex without strings. How to get around those inconvenient feelings? With Sami, she had allowed herself to feel. She was naked and he was under her skin.

They both knew this must end.

'We need to draw a line in the sand,' Sami said one afternoon, after they had shared a particularly powerful orgasm.

A line in the sand? Another oxymoron. A line in the sand was erasable. A line in the sand was no line at all. It would disappear with a little gust of wind.

'We can't do this anymore,' Sami said. 'I can't leave my family, my children. Not now. The more time we spend together, the harder it's going to be to stop. I'm not going down that rabbit hole.'

Ava knew more about rabbit holes than she cared to remember. And she never wanted to go back there, ever again. Much as she would have liked to live the dream for a bit longer, she knew this must end. What she wanted was reality, not suspended reality.

'I love you, Sami,' Ava whispered. She could barely utter the words.

'I love you, Ava,' Sami responded, stroking her face. 'You make me feel so alive. You make me want to shine. You unleashed something in me. You awakened me. But this needs to stop.'

Sami loved Ava. She had refreshed and renewed his sexuality, and he could now go back to his wife, refuelled, and unleash himself on her with new vigour. The law of unintended consequences.

Ava was not a jealous woman, but now, for the first time in her life, she experienced the opposite of *schadenfreude*. She felt a deep pain at someone else's pleasure. She was envious of Sami's wife, as she thought of Sami fucking her with renewed passion. Of course, Ava wanted to be that wife. But the biggest irony of all was that Sami's wife did everything to avoid sex. She gave her husband a hundred and one reasons why she did not want to fuck him: the famous headache; the children running ragged and needing to be fed; the onset of the menopause, low libido and vaginal dryness; the dishwasher that needed unpacking; the spice rack that had to be rearranged in alphabetical order ... And all Ava could think of were the hundred and one reasons why all she wanted to do was to fuck Sami and be fucked by him.

They lay close and Sami held Ava tightly, as though he never wanted to let her go.

'You know, Ava, I'm your benchmark man. I'm the man against whom you will measure all other men. The men after me,' he said.

It was like a curse.

'Fuck you!' Ava pulled away from him.

She was furious. How dare he say that? It was as though if he could not have her, he did not want anyone else, least of all someone 'better' than him, to have her.

'You're saying "Fuck you" because you know it's true,' Sami said. 'You're going to compare all the other men in your life to me.'

'Fuck you, Sami,' Ava repeated.

Ava knew that Sami was right. She knew how childish it was to compare and contrast all the men in her life. But she could not help it. Sami was not only the tenderest, he was also the most masculine. He understood her and he knew her at her most naked.

She escaped to the Eden Roc, a paradise in the South of France that blended hedonism with zen, and she pretended she was absolutely fine. But Sami had got to her. He had reached deep inside her, in all ways. And now, Ava needed time and space, and sun and sea. Most of all, she needed to regain her sense of self and to feel whole again. As she walked into her beautiful hotel suite, she breathed in the salty sea air and gasped as she looked out at the glassy blue sea and the cobalt sky that met in a haze of gold at the horizon. An extravagant bouquet of flowers, bigger and wider than she was, awaited her on the glass coffee table.

To the love of life! Sami wrote on the accompanying card.

Ava smiled. Trust Sami. He did not want to be forgotten, as much as she did not want to forget him. She immediately understood the pun on the Hebrew toast, *L'chaim*, meaning 'To life'. She hoped the woman in the florist shop had missed out one critical little word in the note, and that what Sami had surely wanted to write was, *To the love of* my *life!* Was it deliberate or an unfortunate oversight? Net-net, it changed nothing. Ava was still single and alone.

7.

The Lieutenant Colonel's View: The Empire Strikes Back

Sami sprawled on the carpet with his four children: Talia, Isaac, Gad and Doron. It was their usual Friday-night Sabbath ritual: enacting the latest instalment of *Star Wars* in Lego. They were recreating Darth Vader's rescue mission in *Return of the Jedi*, and they fired off the dual shooters to repel the dark forces of evil.

'Dudududududu,' Gad sputtered, imitating the sound of gunfire and spinning the command shuttle.

For a brief moment, Sami was back in the hot armoured tank near the Gaza border. He felt the searing heat of the scorched Negev desert, and smelled the fear mixed with sweat that oozed from him and his fellow soldiers in the tank. A droplet dribbled down his back. Sami loosened the collar of his shirt and blinked hard to bring himself back to his children's playroom in the large Hampstead mansion that was now his home.

'*Abba*,' said Isaac, addressing his father in Hebrew. 'You've gotta let the Millennium Falcon through. Close the docking ports, switch on the sub-light engines. Come on. Hurry. Put the quad laser cannons on standby. Han Solo's gotta escape with Chewbacca and fly off into inter-galactic freedom.'

Sami grinned. He had enjoyed some pretty captivating inter-galactic freedom with Ava that afternoon. He could still taste her, even now. He thought about how he had kissed her under her rain-shower, her hair slicked back, as he pinned her against the wall, and how strongly he came inside her, with her legs wrapped around his hips. She had felt so tight and wet. Sami felt himself grow hard, just reliving the moment. He adjusted the front of his underpants through his jeans.

'*Abba*,' Isaac repeated, 'you gotta focus. Come on. It's a fight to the death. We gotta attack the resistance fleet. We need to fly in reinforcements from across the solar system.'

'Yes, buddy, you're absolutely right,' Sami said, forcing himself to take his mind back to lightsabers and the Sith wayfinder. 'Luke Skywalker is leading the Imperial Fleet to planet Exegol,' he said, slipping back into role play.

He loved this precious time with his children. But right now, he longed for peace and quiet, to reflect on what had happened that afternoon. He chased away his thoughts of tight and wet, as he resumed launching probe droids across the galaxy.

'Talia' – he turned to his beloved daughter – 'tell me. How did your maths test go? Did you do the long division, like I showed you the other night?'

'It was so hard, *Abba*,' Talia said, as she came over and slid into her father's lap. 'But I think I nailed it.'

'Of course you nailed it. You're *Abba*'s best girl, aren't you?' he said, as he cuddled her and patted down her curly brown hair pensively.

'*Shalom ahuvi*, Sami,' said Sami's wife, walking into the room, smiling. Sharon was wearing jeans and ballet flats, but she had not found the time to brush her hair and wear it wild and open, like Sami liked. 'Dinner's ready. Come on, kids. Come and sit down and eat before it gets cold. Sami, help me get the kids to the table.'

Sharon regarded Sami. He was looking particularly handsome and happy these days. She knew how lucky she was to have such a wonderful, loving husband.

'Sami, *habibi*, did you ask the plumber to deal with the time settings on the boiler?' she asked. 'There was no hot water again this morning after you showered.'

Sami had forgotten. He had other things on his mind, but he made a mental note to call the plumber first thing on Monday morning.

'Oh, and we need to talk about Isaac's orthodontist appointment,' Sharon continued. 'I'm not sure whether he should go for those ugly train tracks or Invisalign.' She brought a large, steaming bowl of spaghetti bolognese, the children's favourite, to the table. 'Hey, what's that's cut on your lip, Sami? Looks like you're bleeding. Here, take my napkin.'

Sami licked his lips and dabbed his mouth. He remembered that Ava had bitten him roughly that afternoon.

'Oh, it's nothing,' he improvised. 'I must have cut myself drinking from that can of Diet Coke.'

Dinner was the usual tumult of cheerful banter. Friday night was the family's special time together, when they would talk about the highlights of the past week and what they would get up to over the weekend. Sharon looked around the table at the smiling faces. She was blessed to have four beautiful healthy children and a marvellous husband.

'Don't wait up for me, Sharon,' Sami told his wife, after he had helped her clear the table. He kissed her gently on the top of her head. 'I've got a few things I need to take care of after today's meeting with that demanding new client.'

He retreated into his study. It was the only room in the house that was not strewn with football kit, broken gaming consoles and Ottolenghi cookery books that Solomon, their golden retriever, liked to chew up. He sat and stretched his long legs out under the big glass desk, struggling to focus on his client's financial statements. He stroked his pen and then traced his lips with it. It was a limited edition, from the Montblanc StarWalker 'Racing Spirit' collection, and a birthday present from Ava.

As he gazed around the room, his eyes alighted on two framed photographs on his desk. One was a picture of the whole family, taken last year in Jerusalem, at Doron's bar mitzvah. How joyous and happy the whole family looked: such an unbreakable unit. He looked at the other picture. It was one of him in a silver helmet, grinning from ear to ear, in a yellow vintage Ferrari on the racing track in Maranello. The two pictures were a perfect representation of the two contrasting sides of his personality: a need for security versus a love of freedom. It was an equation for which he had yet to find the perfect point of equilibrium.

Absentmindedly, he picked up the solid-gold bullion bar which he used as a paperweight for his documents. It had been a gift from his father-in-law for his fortieth birthday. A gift? A permanent reminder, more like, of the financial hold he had over Sami. When Sami started his asset management business, his father-in-law had sent his first $300 million for him to manage, and then introduced him to a couple of multi-millionaires who also became clients. Sami owed him everything. He hated being in his debt. There was a lot at stake here. If he ever left Sharon, he'd be done for. It would be a total *balagan*, a complete fiasco. Reputational and commercial suicide. He couldn't do it. Not now. Not ever. It was madness. Only *fauda*, chaos, could possibly ensue.

And then there were his children. How could he ever look them in the eye if he left? Especially his beautiful little Talia: it would ruin her world. She would never love him in the same way, with that innocence and purity. Sami loved how she looked at her *Abba* with those big brown trusting eyes of hers. Freedom? Security? Security? Freedom? What to choose? Could he not have both? It was a catch-22. Sami knew that if he ever mustered up the courage to leave, he would be a disappointment to his children, to his wife, and ultimately, to himself. And probably to Ava too.

Sami swung his legs off the desk and tidied his papers into a neat pile, ready for tomorrow morning. He thought of the underlying message of *Star Wars*, of the moral imperative to choose good over evil, and he remembered Obi-Wan Kenobi's iconic comment, 'May the force be with you.' He smiled as he shuffled out of his office and climbed the stairs. He brought Talia's maths book into her bedroom and tucked her in with a loving kiss.

8.

Some Like It Hot

'**H**ow come you're *still* single?'

It was the insertion of the seemingly innocuous little adverb *still* that was the most irritating part of that question, and one which Ava had to fend off with painful regularity.

The question was not the slightly more delicate, 'Do you have a boyfriend?'

Or even the vaguely romantic, 'Is someone looking after you?'

Ava tried to imagine what having someone looking after her might feel like. It was an alien concept and not one she had ever experienced, however vaguely. Something for the relationship bucket list, maybe?

No doubt, most of the people who asked Ava if she was *still* single were just making polite conversation. It was much like discussing the weather. A bit of idle tittle-tattle. The smallest of small talk. But not all those who asked had innocent intentions, that was clear. Some women took pleasure in watching the usually inscrutable Ava squirm, as she struggled to answer. Failure is fascinating, especially when it is attached to someone else.

To Ava, it was a question that went straight to the jugular of all her self-doubts. As a woman who believed that real meaning could only be found in loving and being loved, it hit the bullseye of all her deepest insecurities. It was bang on target, with an immaculate and cruel precision. Being *still* single signalled that she was unworthy of being loved. What was she, who was she, if a man did not love her? What was the value of her existence, as a woman and as a human being, if she was unloved and unpaired? What did any of her achievements amount to, if she still had not managed to acquire that most vital of all accoutrements, a loving life partner?

'I am single, therefore I am not,' was Ava's painful logical conclusion.

She was steeped in shame. The real reason the question was so agonising was obvious. What was wrong with her? Why the hell was she *still* single? She had absolutely no idea.

Of course, for a man, being *still* single was an altogether different proposition. Being *still* single meant being an eligible bachelor, a dashing young man about town. As a man, he was always young, irrespective of his real biological age. Being *still* single, a man revelled in his freedom. He lived a life of many sybaritic pleasures. He was the envy of all his male friends and an appetising target for all those desperate *still* single females.

For a woman, being *still* single meant waiting patiently for a man to find her and whisk her away from a life of M&S chicken masala TV dinners for one. Or worse, it meant spending her time on permanent red alert in all the usual hotspots, in full make-up and fake high spirits, desperately waiting for The One to materialise out of the ether.

Aside from the humiliating existential crisis that being *still* single triggered in Ava, she asked herself why she might *not* want to be *still* single. After all, she could have sex with more or less anyone she chose. She could fix her fuse box when it blew, and she learnt how to change her lightbulbs, even those delicate halogen ones. She could even fiddle around with her dreaded Wi-Fi router and get it to work. So why did she *not* want to be *still* single? Was life really so much better going to sleep with 'him', with a smile on her face, and waking up next to 'him', with a smile on her face? Or was it because M&S chicken masala TV dinners tasted so much better shared?

The question of why she was *still* single, along with another non-favourite, 'Why did you get divorced?' were the two questions that came up all the time. People were curious as to why a vivacious blonde who met men all the time was mysteriously *still* unattached. So Ava developed a full armoury of staple answers, depending on who was asking and how bold she was feeling at the time.

To the smug marrieds, her classic answer was, 'Yes, I'm *still* single. Plenty of nice men around though.' Big broad smile and cheeky wink.

That usually elicited two stock responses, clearly differentiated by gender.

'Oh, isn't that what you said last time?'

Her smile faltered a little.

'It must be so hard to be alone. Ava, how do you manage?' was the passive-aggressive, fake commiseration offered by the wives who, above all, were projecting their horror at the thought of losing their own respectable married status.

What these women were really thinking was, 'Crikey! I hope I never, ever have to face the indignity of soldiering on through life on my own again. I remember so well what it was like first time around. It was so hard to find a man, any man, to marry me at twenty-five. God knows how hard it must be when you're pushing forty. Oh, that reminds me, I must book another appointment with Dr Magic for some more laser skin rejuvenation, new-gen Botox and a spot of cheek filler. Perhaps redo the lip collagen while I'm at it.'

And then there was the opposite response from their husbands.

'You're one lucky lady, Ava. Ah, the joys of fresh and regular sex,' they would say, going misty-eyed. 'Young nubile bodies... Freedom... Liberty...'

The conversation could practically take a metaphysical turn.

What these men were really saying was, 'Oh, yes! All those exciting, young women I could be banging, night after night. Maybe I should lay off that big bowl of truffle fries with my extra-large cheeseburger. Now might be a good time to lose a few pounds and do something about my dad bod, for when I'm single again.'

Ava's less flippant answer to the dreaded question could sometimes veer off into a declaration of human rights.

'Yes, I'm *still* single. I love my new-found freedom. I was in a serious marriage for many long, monogamous years. I'm having a great time. Why on earth should I hurry to settle down? This is a great opportunity for me to go on a voyage of self-discovery, to have fun, and to choose carefully who I want and what I want for the second part of my life.'

Then there was its feminist post-modern variant.

'Yes, I'm *still* single. Marriage is a worthy institution, but who the hell wants to live in an institution? It's so last century. It's an unnatural construct to control female sexuality and to shackle women within the confines of a monogamous relationship. Why does society frown on single, sexually active women let loose on the world? Why shouldn't women enjoy sex for the sake of sex, in the same way men do?'

Ava would then pause for breath. She would mutter, 'Phew,' at end of her long monologue, smile and toss her long blonde hair. Militant feminine emancipation was not quite the vibe she was going for. For a start, she did not have the right wardrobe, and it would be such a pity to have to burn all her beautiful silk La Perla bras.

Then there was the more truthful answer.

'Yes, I'm *still* single. I'm not afraid of commitment. I just want to find a man that I want to be committed to.' So much wanting: two 'wants' in one sentence.

And then, perhaps the truest reply of all, which Ava never voiced, and which she could barely admit, even to herself.

'Yes, I'm *still* single. I always fall for exactly those men who, by definition, can't give me what I crave: true love. As my therapist said, it's an act of pure self-sabotage. It's my script. I'm subconsciously doing everything to prove what I secretly believe: that I don't deserve to be loved.'

Then Ava would either yawn, have another lychee martini, or find the nearest metaphorical cliff to hurl herself over.

Ava was in Scott's, her favourite, perennially fashionable Mayfair canteen. She scanned the room, which was buzzing. There was Charles Saatchi, in his usual dark suit, sitting at his corner table with his perky long-term squeeze, Trinny. And wasn't that a rather hunky-looking George Osborne with his pretty new girlfriend? Hadn't he just got divorced and had a baby? He had a major glow-up: was it because he left his former wife, or left Number 11, Downing Street, or because he found himself a beautiful, adoring young woman to take to bed every night?

Ava sat at the bar counter, waiting for her sister to arrive. She was excited as she had spent all morning discussing the establishment of a new programme for Arab and Israeli schoolchildren to learn science together at one of Tel Aviv's top research institutes. Young people, education, science, conflict-resolution, cross-cultural bonding: all issues that Ava was passionate about.

She looked up and saw Eliana stumble in, late again.

'You need to get your hair done,' Ava whispered, as she embraced Eliana. 'The roots have gone dark and there's some grey coming through.' That was a classic greeting between the two sisters who loved each other deeply.

'Oh, really? I didn't notice. I haven't had time to think about my hair.'

'But your eyes, they're looking great.'

'Yes, I'm over the moon. Thank you; thank you so much, Ava, for paying for the op. Money's a bit tight, and Saul's start-up is taking a bit longer to get up and running. Round two teething problems with the network protocol interface, or something. I can't tell you how grateful I am that you're paying the boys' school fees: it's such a weight off my mind. I'm working all hours. But you know, working as a psychotherapist, it's not like being a trader. No money in saving souls. But tons of money in what you do: making rich people richer.'

Ava still bristled when she heard those familiar words, but she chose to let it pass. 'I'm happy to help, you know that. I'm always here for you. I think the surgeon did a fabulous job. Great symmetry and no visible scars at all.'

'Yes. Transformative. I didn't realise how droopy my lids had become and how bad those bags under my eyes were until you made me look in the mirror.'

The sisters sat side by side, polar opposites. Ava: blonde, slim, radiant in a sleek grey Oscar de la Renta sheath dress. Eliana: flustered, chubby, not a scrap of make-up in a puffy dress with large yellow flowers. Who was Grace Kelly now?

'So, how's the love life?'

'Oh, don't start, Eliana. I can't take it. Not today.' Ava bit her lip. 'There's a lot of life. Not much love. You know how it is.'

Eliana, as it happens, did not know how it was. In love, as in everything else, the sisters' paths had been so different. Eliana, basking in her father's unfailing love and attention, was now blissfully married to her childhood sweetheart, who also nourished her with unfailing love and attention, and revered the real Eliana, grey hair and all.

'I'm not exactly short of admirers. There's always about five new guys circling. Nothing desperately serious. I'm *still* single,' Ava said, toying with her food. 'I should probably do a Marie Kondo on my men and only keep the ones that spark joy. I don't want five men. I only want one.'

'It's ironic, isn't it? It's easier than ever to meet men, and yet it's never been harder for two humans to connect. Or at least that's what it feels like, talking to my patients.'

'Maybe it's always been hard to connect, but now we talk about it.'

'People are so much more demanding; there are so many boxes we expect to be ticked.'

'Yes. It's all very boring.' Ava nodded. Boring was shorthand for utterly frustrating. 'The last time I properly connected with a man was with Hugo. Well, apart from Sami and Harry. But they don't count because they're both married and perfectly unavailable. Yes. Hugo. Remember him?'

How could Eliana forget? She had sat through endless hours of discussing what Hugo had or had not done, and what Ava should or should not do.

'Of course. Hugo. The blue-eyed Etonian. Another one. Why do you keep going for men who are either married or emotionally unavailable? What on earth did you ever see in Hugo anyway?'

'I felt connected to him. But I guess he wasn't that interested in connecting with me.' She winced. It still hurt. 'Maybe I've got some daddy and relationship issues I need to work through.'

'Well, that's great: almost forty and you're both fucked up *and* self-aware,' Eliana said, her eyes narrowing. 'I'm worried about you, darling. You're either going to end up with the most amazing guy. A real alpha, the kind of guy you dream of and deserve. And I hope to God you do. Or you'll go the other way and end up sad, old and alone.'

Ava cowered. She felt an overwhelming urge for another lychee martini.

'Oh, Eliana. I know. And you of all people, you know me so well. I simply can't be with just anyone unless I'm totally and deeply in love.'

Eliana raised her left eyebrow. 'What *are* you looking for, Ava?'

'You know: my soulmate. My twin flame. I need the Real Thing. I can't go through the motions and fool myself into feeling something I'm not feeling. I can't do lukewarm. I can only do sizzling hot. I need a man who challenges and excites me. A man who sets my mind and body on fire. A union of mind, body and soul. One breath.'

Eliana's right eyebrow lifted to meet her left one.

'One breath? Well, let me break it to you. That's not real life. Life isn't like those fairy-tale Disney cartoons we used to watch.'

'Maybe not. But I can't settle for the next nice, semi-plausible guy who rocks up and live mediocrely ever after. I'd rather be alone.'

'Ava, I love you. But come off it; you're totally unrealistic. You're looking for a superhero. You want 007 with a big golden heart and a big golden phallus. Back in the real world, your dream man simply doesn't exist. Even if he did, do you think he'd want you?'

Ava blanched. Why would a great guy want her? What could she possibly offer such a magnificent man in return?

'You're going to have to compromise. You're way too demanding. Remember what Pépé used to say? "You're farting higher than your arse." Or, in *Downtown Abbey*-speak, "You've got ideas above your station."'

Ava softened at the mention of her beloved Pépé. 'I don't mind compromising. But I can't settle. I haven't gone through all the agony and upheaval of divorce to end up in another bad relationship. Alone is grim, but I can't lie to myself. I can't pretend to be in love when I'm not.'

'Be honest with me. Aren't you afraid of ending up alone?'

Ava flinched. 'I'm not actually,' she replied weakly. Her voice was strangely squeaky. 'Well, not really.' Perhaps if she repeated it enough times, she might even start to believe it. Fake it until you make it?

Ava's eyes watered: surely the effect of three lychee martinis on an empty stomach. 'I'm struggling. It's hard.' She blinked, forcing herself not to tear up. 'I know what you're thinking: that I keep repeating the same pattern of behaviour, over and over again, falling for the wrong guys, always the identical unavailable type, and somehow expecting a different result. It's like I'm exhibit A in Einstein's definition of insanity.' She sighed. 'I know I need to change. But it's difficult.'

'Perhaps you might try something different,' Eliana said. 'Stop focusing on finding a man. Stop chasing all the time. Like a dog chasing his own tail: it doesn't work. Start attracting. Start receiving. Live your life and be happy. On your own. And a man will find you. Being needy is not attractive. You need to feel abundance, not lack. Think about radiating luminous joy and happiness. That will send a message out to the universe.'

Ava flashed a wry smile at the mumbo jumbo she had heard so many times before. But in her heart of hearts, she knew Eliana was right. 'Believing is half the battle, I know. I've tried meditating and manifesting and visualising. It feels so airy fairy.'

'I think part of your problem,' Eliana said, now fully in shrink mode, 'is that you're choosing a man like you might conduct a business deal. You think that if you work hard enough, you'll get your dream guy. Well, newsflash: love doesn't work like that. Finding love is not about ticking boxes. Why aren't you a bit more flexible? Find a man who's free and available and capable of love for a change, and give him a chance. Why don't you open up your heart?'

'Because every time I open up my heart,' Ava stammered, 'it only gets a little more broken.'

Luckily, the waiter arrived, just in time, with a mountain of champagne truffles and both sisters perked up. Chocolate: food of the gods. Ava needed to think about reducing her alcohol and chocolate intake. At some point. Not now, evidently. But at some point, in the future.

'I think you might find it easier to connect with a man if you were more connected with yourself,' Eliana said. 'And you might want to reveal a bit more of the real you. Show your feminine side. Not the hyper-sexualised blonde, but the sweet and sensitive brunette hiding underneath. Vulnerability, you know, it's different to being needy. Needy is ugly. Vulnerability is strength. It takes courage to show your authentic self. It's the only way to properly connect with a man, to let him in, and to be intimate and close.'

Ava gobbled up all the chocolate truffles and ordered another plate.

'I'm not remotely surprised you can't connect with a man. How do you expect any man to connect with you? You keep giving off those invincible Wonder Woman vibes. Men feel they can't offer you anything that you don't already have, except for their hard dicks. And even that wilts, if you emasculate them. Remember what happened with that hotshot CEO? Even he couldn't get it up with you.' Eliana had an uncanny way of remembering all of Ava's dating fiascos. 'Look, Ava, I don't mean to be harsh. I love you. You're my sister. I want you to be happy. I want to see you thriving in a great relationship. I love you because I know the real you. You should be the same person with these men as you are with me. Show them who you are underneath. You've got to get properly naked.'

Ava was ashamed. Not only did she bore Eliana, but she bored herself with the infinite regress of these repetitive conversations. And if you're bored, you're most definitely boring. It was about time she picked up her game.

She knew what she had to do. She just needed to do it.

9.

If I Dream of You, Do You Dream of Me Too?

Ava thought of the men with whom she had been to bed, in what she liked to refer to as her 'experimental' phase, who meant absolutely nothing to her. She could easily conjure up memories of some of the more exciting scenarios and moves, and the tantalising smells and tastes and visuals of her sexual conquests. But she struggled to remember the names of all her past lovers. During that wild time, she imagined she was exploring the Glorious Universe of Men. But in reality, she was lost and looking for love in all the wrong places, in the only way she knew how: through sex.

'I fuck, therefore I am' was her guiding motto.

Only through sex could she be truly herself, truly naked. She could give herself with abandon. She knew that in the bedroom, at least, no man would turn her down. She was driven by a longing for the touch she had never had as a child, the physical and emotional contact she never received, and the closeness and intimacy she had never felt.

But instead of the truth and intimacy she craved, what Ava found were too many sexual encounters that left no trace whatsoever. Sometimes, she had a purple bruise from a friendly bite on the shoulder, or an inner thigh ache, but that too would disappear in a couple of days. She went through all the motions, longing to feel, but she felt nothing at all. And in her search for meaning, Ava found only a desert of emptiness.

Bad sex was definitely worse than no sex. It left her feeling even more alone and it perpetuated a vicious cycle of self-loathing. It took Ava many years to realise that what she was searching for was not another orgasm, or even the orgasm of orgasms. She could achieve that all by herself. What she wanted was to touch and be touched, to know and be known, to see and be seen, to understand and be understood. To her, these were synonyms for loving and being loved. After all, what else was there?

There were the perfectly forgettable fucks of Ava's life. And then there was a man with whom she spent only a few hours, fully clothed, and that one kiss which she would never forget.

Darius spotted Ava immediately, at a private equity investor conference. She was hard to miss, with her long blonde hair, her cream Chanel dress and pearls, and her extravagantly high heels. She was a beacon of light in a sea of grey suits. He managed to work his way through the group of men who had gathered around her. That was not saying much, as there were no other women there. He introduced himself and gallantly offered to bring her a fresh glass of champagne. He flashed his dazzling smile. Ava wondered which of the two of them had better teeth. Darius did, for sure.

It took them only a couple of minutes to sniff each other out. They both came from the same world: humble beginnings that they had fought hard to transcend; Oxbridge; several years' penance in investment banking; financial payback and, eventually, a charmed new life, far, far away from their early years. Ava appraised this glorious alpha male – a rare specimen. She could practically see him as the dominant gorilla in the mists of the African rainforest, beating his chest to assert his dominance. Confident, bordering on arrogant, he was articulate and funny with it too. Tall, gym-honed body; fair, faintly freckled face that belied his Persian origins; bewitching green eyes.

As they talked of their mutual love of dancing, he grabbed her by the waist to demonstrate a fancy move. Ava felt a jolt of electricity. There was a greater erotic charge, even through the layers of tweed and silk, than with many of the men with whom she had been fully naked.

Darius invited Ava for drinks later that week. She was unusually excited. Darius was hot, he was masculine and he seemed into her. Best of all, he did not wear a wedding band. They sat outside on a sunny terrace, on a perfect summer's evening, sipping chilled Ruinart. Darius was checking her out, like a hungry lion might evaluate a passing zebra, wondering if she might make a tasty lunch and how long it would take for her to capitulate and surrender to him. The topic of conversation moved seamlessly from why ninety per cent of venture capital start-ups fail, to sex. Obviously. It transpired that Darius was indeed married, for the second time, but unhappily so. Sob. Ava's usually foolproof gut instincts as to Darius's marital status had let her down. No wonder. Darius gave off the air of a man who had more or less checked out of his marriage.

'Sex,' whispered Ava, with a bat of her long eyelashes. 'How sex with that person makes you feel; how often you want it; how and where you touch; how and where your partner touches you; how you kiss; what's on the menu; what's strictly off limits. They're all such great markers of the health of a relationship.'

'Mmm,' Darius said. 'Maybe. But most of us are too busy with the daily grind to find the time or energy to analyse our relationships like that.'

Ava knew full well that a strong-willed male like Darius would always make the time for something he wanted. 'We all lead busy lives,' she replied. 'But if you don't nurture your relationship and spend time with your partner, making time for play, things just fall apart. And by then, the damage is done and it's almost impossible to get back on track.' Ava took a sip of her champagne and looked straight into Darius's green eyes. 'Somehow, we imagine that relationships should flow naturally, but relationships take work. Like everything else in life.'

Ava had put a lot of work into her marriage. As it happened, even 'putting in work' had not been enough to guarantee success.

'I went to couples therapy with my ex,' she continued. 'It's a thankless job, if you ask me. It takes a lot to repair a marriage, let alone make it good again. No wonder fifty per cent of marriages end in divorce.'

Darius nodded.

'Our therapist didn't help at all. It was very painful, and ultimately it just confirmed my decision to leave,' Ava said. What on earth was she doing talking about her former husband to this stunning man? 'But our therapist did say something interesting about love that I'll never forget.' She looked more intently at Darius. 'She said that love is an active verb. Love is an action, not a state. It's about doing, not saying. And there are seven verbs that you need to engage in, to keep that love alive, in and out of the bedroom: to give, to take, to receive, to ask, to share, to play and to refuse. In a great relationship, you should be doing all of those.'

Darius ran his fingers through his dark hair and moved his head sensually from side to side. 'Your list of verbs is, um, interesting.' He paused. 'I guess I haven't been doing much receiving in the last few years.'

He leaned forward and let his hand lightly graze Ava's bronzed, bare legs. It was almost accidental, except they both knew it was a premeditated killer move. Who knew legs could be such an erogenous zone? Darius did, clearly.

'Oh,' Ava ventured, pretending not to understand, but understanding perfectly well. 'What haven't you been receiving?'

'I'd rather not talk about it. Too boring.'

Ouch. Darius was touchy about that. Ava knew precisely which raw nerve she had hit. It was obvious he was no longer having sex with his wife. She waited for him to lament that his wife didn't understand him, that his sex life had ground to a halt, that he hadn't had sex in years and so forth. Ava had heard that story so many times. It was such a cliché, it had to be true in bedrooms in Mayfair and all around the world.

'My first wife went a bit loopy after the birth of our twins. She had a breakdown and then completely shut down. She never fully recovered. I tried to help, but it didn't work. We had no relationship whatsoever, beyond discussing the children. Life became unbearable and I left when the children were five.'

Ava looked shocked.

'And before you ask, no, there was no one else involved.'

Ava smiled. Darius had correctly anticipated the exact question that was on her mind.

'I was single for quite a while after that,' he continued. 'Then I met my second wife and we had twins, again. They're five now. And it looks like I'm in the exact same movie all over again.'

'Sorry to hear that,' Ava said.

Her heart beat a little faster. She wanted to say that, statistically, more second marriages fail than first marriages. She thought better of it and kept her mouth shut. The setting sun threw a lustrous glow on both of them. In the golden light, Ava looked even softer and more feminine. Darius may not be receiving at home, but he wanted to receive Ava right now. And Ava wanted to be received.

They continued to dance the dance.

'What are you most afraid of?' he asked, out of the blue.

It was one of the famous set of thirty-six questions that were scientifically proven to make anyone fall in love with you.

'I'm not afraid of anything,' Ava said boldly. But then she decided she had nothing to lose by being candid. She had, by now, drunk three glasses of Ruinart. 'Maybe there is one thing I'm afraid of: that I will never love deeply and be loved just as deeply back.'

Ava's voice trembled and faltered, and her eyes watered.

'Same,' said Darius. 'That's what I fear, and it's what I want the most. To love and be loved.'

Darius mirrored her honesty with his own. She had been a little naked. He responded by being a little naked too. She had slightly opened her kimono. He had slightly opened his. It was a whole new world of semi-nakedness.

But tonight, neither Darius nor Ava had expected their drinks to be that interesting and they had both made dinner plans. It was time to leave and to wrap those kimonos tightly closed again.

Darius guided her out onto the unusually quiet Mayfair street. 'Let's continue this discussion after the holidays. I'm going to my place in the South of France for the whole summer. But I want to take you to dinner when I get back.' Darius smiled.

Ava smiled back, dazzled. The time with him had been so intense, it had been like staring into the sun.

'I love the process of discovery. So mutually pleasurable,' he said, his eyes full of promise.

'What an amazing coincidence,' Ava said archly. 'I love the process of discovery too.'

She stared back into those shining eyes and felt a rush of desire. Darius drew her body close to his and, clasping her by the waist with both hands, he kissed her. His kiss was sweet and lingering and utterly exquisite. More intimate and erotic than too many fucks she did not care to remember and others she had completely forgotten. Why so memorable? Because in those moments together, he had touched her soul and she had touched his. It had been one of the best encounters of her life.

Darius never rang Ava. Perhaps he had started to receive. She hoped so.

10.

It's in the Kiss

When Ava was a child, she was rarely allowed to watch television. Sometimes, if she had exceptionally good grades at school, she might be allowed to watch a David Attenborough animal programme, or a historical documentary, because it was 'educational'. Hosting a modest play date at home, with a slice of her favourite Sainsbury's walnut and coffee cream cake, a glass of Ribena and a round of Monopoly was never an option.

'It's a total waste of time,' her mother would say, 'and a waste of money too.'

Ava stopped asking.

However, as a very special treat, Ava was sometimes allowed to go to the cinema. She would seek refuge in the enchanted world of *Sleeping Beauty* and *Cinderella*. She would root for the handsome prince, in his tireless search for his One and Only, and lose herself in the dramatic irony of Snow White's sweet innocence, and her stepmother's scheming wickedness. Her favourite part was the kiss, of course, when Prince Charming awakens his beautiful princess from her death-like slumbers. It was not just a kiss, it was THE kiss: the kiss of love, the kiss of life. Even as a young girl, Ava dreamt of that kiss. She suspected that some of the more regrettable issues she experienced with men in her later life stemmed from years and years of watching fairy tales that bore absolutely no resemblance to her own reality, let alone any other reality for that matter. And it might explain why she was willing to kiss quite a few frogs.

Ava was introduced to Roger at a glossy dinner party hosted by her glamorous friend Chantal. Chantal herself was plodding through a 'perfectly happy' thirty-year marriage, whose monthly sexual zenith was 'stick-it in Saturday', and whose annual pinnacle was 'birthday blow job'. She lived vicariously through her newly divorced girlfriends' thrilling sex lives. What that meant was that she listened with bated breath, as they recounted their tales of sexual highs. And she was also there to hold their hand through the crashing lows that inevitably followed.

Chantal was convinced she 'had someone' for Ava, in the way that one might have the perfect ointment to treat an acute case of toenail fungus. Ava's *still* single status was a dreadful affliction that required urgent attention. Chantal decided that Roger was Ava's cure. She regaled her with his multiple attributes. He was a successful property developer, newly widowed, with no troublesome ex-wives or expensive alimony to contend with, and two well-adjusted, grown-up sons. Wonder of wonders, he was six foot four, far above Ava's preposterous minimum height requirement. As though tall men did it better. Well, for Ava, they did.

'He's a real catch,' Chantal told Ava. 'He's got a massive house on Eaton Square. Extensive lateral footprint, of course. And on the more prestigious north side, naturally. There's an underground swimming pool that converts into a ballroom at the flick of a switch. Then the water drains out and the floor moves up. It's like something out of a James Bond movie.'

Ava vaguely recognised Roger's name and nodded listlessly.

'And then there's his amazing Grade I listed Georgian estate in Oxfordshire,' Chantal went on. 'It's right bang next to the Clooneys. He's actually friends with them. Apparently, George is a real charmer, just like in his movies, and Amal, she's sooooooo skinny and really quite lovely too.'

Ava started to tap her foot; she had never been wildly interested in the contents of *Hello!* magazine.

'Oh, and did I mention, he's got an i-n-c-r-e-d-i-b-l-e villa in St Tropez? Right on the sea, next to his yacht.' Chantal gripped Ava's arm and looked her in the eye. 'Ava. You know I want the best for you. You need to stop wasting time now. Enough of your fun little dalliances. It's high time you found a proper man: someone who's real husband material. Realistically, I give you eighteen months to find a husband to put a ring on your finger. Roger's your man.'

Ava flinched. Deep down, she knew Chantal was right. She had a shelf life, and she was in danger of being stuck on it, way past her sell-by date. But she yearned to fall madly, truly, deeply in love, not complete a delicate business transaction within a tight timeframe.

'Roger's perfect for you,' Chantal continued. 'He's single. He's successful. He's a great catch. And he isn't going to be on the market for long. You're going to have to move fast, darling.'

Chantal sounded more excited about the project than Ava. Ava had some vague inkling that Chantal might secretly be lusting after Roger herself. In any event, Ava was more interested in who Roger was, rather than what he owned. She had a vague memory that their paths had crossed briefly, many years back, and she did not have to wait long, as Chantal kindly threw a large dinner party that very weekend. Time was clearly of the essence.

Ava had been to Chantal's home before, so she was somewhat prepared for a night of unapologetic opulence, in the very best possible taste. Still, she gasped as she strode through the cold luxury of the embassy-grade security at the entrance and floated up to the top penthouse of the Four Seasons Private Residences on Grosvenor Square. The pad was a splurge of subtle excess, with its own specially curated lifestyle that included a creamy Carrara marble-clad spa, an aquamarine infinity pool and a state-of-the-art gym, complete with its own celebrity trainer and reiki healer, who, it was whispered, had helped Kate Middleton bounce back so fast after the births of all three of her children. As if that was not enticing enough, there was also a five-hundred-bottle wine cellar and a cinema with ivory leather recliners fitted with a heated massage function to soothe and pamper the perfect bodies of those who led such a stressful existence. The furnishings were sustainably organic rather than harshly minimalistic, and the accents were antique bronze rather than shiny gold. The vibe was less 'money shouts', more 'wealth whispers'.

Ava drew breath as she saw the expanse of Hyde Park stretched out below. The handsome young butler glided over and offered her a welcome glass of chilled Krug and a foie gras canapé topped with a warm fig. She looked around the dining room, now feeling like the David Attenborough of the exotic species of *homo sapiens* that populated Mayfair. There was the usual mix of thin, photogenic blondes bragging about their punishing fitness regimes and their uber-gifted children, and some prosperous-looking men who signalled their success in navy blazers and Patek Philippe watches, boasting loudly about their golf handicaps and the killing they had recently made in tech VC.

Ava stifled a yawn and decided to focus on the sensational artwork. The pieces were instantly recognisable: four Warhol *Marilyns* in different primary colours; one of the larger, more valuable, iconic Damien Hirst spot paintings; and the show-stopper, a large Gerhard Richter diptych in varying tones of orange and grey, ironically titled, *I have nothing to say and I'm saying it*. It was a magnificent blaze of colour, ostensibly about nothing, but it was an accurate metaphor for the conversations currently going on in the room.

Chantal introduced Ava to the other guests, and she smiled graciously as she made the obligatory small talk. They proceeded into the candlelit dining room, with its dropped copper ceiling, lined with dark grey raw silk wallpaper and distressed mirrors in silver and weathered gold leaf. The long glass table appeared to be suspended in thin air, and it was groaning under heaving clusters of crimson roses and shimmering crystal. Ella Fitzgerald's 'It Don't Mean a Thing (If It Ain't Got That Swing)' streamed through the room.

Ava was eagerly anticipating meeting Roger and now, finally, she was seated next to him. He was, indeed, everything that Chantal had promised. He was six foot four, though he seemed like a short six foot four, and he was charismatic, rather than handsome, with a rough-hewn masculinity. He exuded the air – and, unabashedly, he displayed the paunch – of a man with multiple lusty appetites. Ava wondered, idly, if his attachment to the pleasures of the table was matched by an attachment to the pleasures of the flesh. Chantal had, alas, not said anything about that.

The dinner party guests sat straight-backed, talking politely, here twenty minutes to the neighbour on the left with the grilled Maine lobster, there twenty minutes to the right with the wagyu beef topped with gold flakes. Roger pulled his chair back from the table and spread his long legs wide apart. It was a position which heightened Ava's natural focus on his crotch area. She could not help but notice, indeed admire, the prominent bulge in his trousers. It provided a pleasant distraction from the highly civilised but predictable prattle, and she found herself momentarily floating far, far away, out of the candlelit dining room into quite another place altogether.

It transpired that Ava and Roger had indeed met some twenty years ago, when he was in his final year of law at Cambridge. The encounter had taken all of five minutes. Roger, slim and athletic back then, was sauntering off the tennis court in pristine whites and they were briefly introduced. It was a scene straight out of *Brideshead Revisited*: rolling green meadows, the bucolic charms of the River Cam and an atmosphere heavy with studied cool. They both looked a bit different back then: Roger with his dark romantic Byronic curls and Ava with her long dark-brown curls too. But the intensity, warmth and intelligence in Roger's eyes remained the same. The chance encounter years ago added a sense of destiny, like a foreshadowing of what was meant to be. It was all looking rather promising.

'The last few months before my wife died were bad,' Roger said. 'It was so painful to watch her shut down. No one should have to go through that. I felt so helpless.' He coughed. 'I know I need to look forwards, for my boys,' he stammered.

Ava nodded sympathetically.

'Let's not talk about that anymore,' Roger said, as he looked away, then back to Ava. 'I've talked way too much. Tell me about you. Chantal tells me you're a big art lover. We should go to the British Museum together sometime. There's an interesting Munch exhibition. Apparently, they've got two versions of *The Scream*. That resonates with me, on some profound level, especially now.'

Ava understood perfectly. *The Scream* resonated with her too. Sheer angst about life and the inexorable passage of time were part of the universal existential condition.

She was pleased that Roger was doing most of the talking. She listened attentively, trying to get a measure of him and his essence. He was kind and clever, just as Chantal had described him. But Ava tuned into her gut instincts and realised she was, annoyingly, not physically attracted to him. She wondered if, as Mémé had once told her, she could become attracted to him once they got to know each other better.

Roger took Ava's number. He wanted to take her out for dinner, but he had to be in New York for the next couple of weeks, working on a large deal. So, inevitably, the texting began.

It was remarkable what two people who barely knew each other shared over WhatsApp. Within a few days, their texting grew to several hours a day, all through the day. It was as if Roger was next to her, all the time.

The evolution of their texts followed a familiar path.

From:

Isn't it amazing that we both remembered meeting each other all those years ago, even though we barely spoke to each other.

To:

It's hard to believe you're single. You're beautiful and desirable and insightful and successful and fun. I don't want you in my bed only for sex. I want you for life.

Ava always longed to hear those exact words.

And then, of course, came the spicier multiple variations on:

You're thrilling and scintillating and so sexy. I want to lick you for hours and make you come, over and over again. Not just in my mouth, but all over my mouth. I'm rock hard. My cock is throbbing under my desk. I can't wait to feel your clit on my tongue.

But between some of the fruitier texts, usually first thing in the morning and last thing at night, Roger showed a genuine interest in Ava the person, rather than Ava the potential new playmate. Ava was used to being prodded and poked sexually. But being prodded and poked intellectually and emotionally was a new thing. Roger wanted to know all about her childhood, her suffering, what made her happy, what she wanted from life now. She realised that Roger was quite possibly a Real Man who wanted a Real Woman by his side, not a pneumatic Barbie doll. He wanted a woman with whom he could discuss geopolitics and books and art and financial markets. He craved intimacy and closeness and he longed to bare his soul and touch Ava's. He wanted and needed to get naked as much as Ava did.

The intensity of their connection and the sexual charge of their texting escalated. It was astonishing what they achieved in cyberspace.

Every time I get a text message from you, I get excited, Roger typed. *But it's going to be so long until we see each other. I'm not sure I can wait that long. I want to hear you come.*

Ava was surprised at how easily she agreed. Roger made her feel both desired and comfortable being who she really was.

I'm so hard, Ava. I want you all the time.

She had heard those words before.

I'm so wet, she texted back.

Ava had written those words a few times before too. She knew that playbook well. The hard-to-wet ratio in the conversation was pretty even, which was encouraging. The one begot the other and vice versa, in a constant positive feedback loop. They set up a phone call for ten o'clock that night. Ava got undressed and lay on her bed, her soft skin on soft silk sheets, heart racing.

Roger called Ava on the dot. 'What are you wearing?' he asked, even though he already knew the answer.

'I'm naked. Totally naked.' Ava's voice was deep and breathless, even though she was lying quite still.

'I can just picture you. Start stroking your breasts, your nipples,' he told her.

Roger was in charge. Ava loved that.

'Now move down to your hips. Slowly. Put your hands between your legs. Caress your thighs and start rubbing your clit. Take your time. Now put your fingers inside. Tell me how wet you are. What are you feeling? What are you thinking?'

Ava complied, obediently. She was spellbound. She closed her eyes as she touched herself, listening to Roger's detailed instructions and following his every command. She moaned deeply, as she felt herself getting closer and closer to orgasm.

'I'm so hard, you have no idea,' Roger said.

As it happens, Ava did have a pretty good idea, as she heard him breathing heavily.

'I'm thinking about you naked, your legs wide open, so I can see all your pussy. I want to kiss every inch of you. I want to enter you deep and hard, with your legs on my shoulders. I want to feel you. I'm thinking about you licking and sucking the head of my cock. It's making me so hard. Tell me when you're close to coming. I want to come with you,' he said.

'I'm very close now... I'm imagining you deep inside me... I'm coming... Now!' Ava threw her head back and felt herself climax. Simultaneously, she heard Roger gasping.

Even though they were separated by the whole of the Atlantic Ocean and had yet to exchange a first kiss, they felt exhilarated and close. Technology had changed the world and the way people love, or the way they try to love, at least.

Roger rushed back from the Big Apple earlier than planned. He couldn't wait one more day to be with Ava in the flesh, so he took the red eye and invited her to dinner that very night. A couple of hours before their much-anticipated first date, Ava received an enormous white orchid planter with a card saying, *I want to get to know you. The more I know you, the more I want to know you.* X-rated texts and phone calls aside, Roger was a gentleman of the old school. Old school was usually the best school and Ava enjoyed how this gentleman made her feel.

He insisted on picking her up from her house, and he arrived punctually in his black chauffeur-driven Mercedes. He commented on her white Hervé Léger dress, whose colour and cut highlighted her golden limbs and large breasts to perfection. Roger wore a grey Zegna suit, no tie, and Ava could not help but notice, again, the appreciative protrusion in his trousers as he sat next to her. He took her hand as they wafted off to the River Cafe, a perfect choice for a romantic first date. There were no jolts of electricity as their flesh touched for the first time, but these were early days and Ava was dizzy with the promise of things to come. And she hoped they would.

Conversation flowed effortlessly, even about tricky topics.

'What are the qualities you're looking for in a woman?' Ava asked. Standard-issue date talk. Not terribly original, but interesting, nonetheless.

'The ability to forgive,' he answered.

Ava was perplexed.

Roger spoke about his wife's illness. 'It was a happy union, but the last five years were tough. My wife was too ill to have sex, so I had a few Russian girlfriends. Made jolly sure none of them fell pregnant. My wife found out, of course, but she said nothing.' He looked pained. 'She knew I would never leave her.'

Ability to forgive? Now Ava understood.

The chauffeur drove them back to Ava's house. They stood awkwardly in the entrance hall. The conversation dried up and they both fell silent. Roger fidgeted with his watch, then leaned into Ava's mouth.

The first kiss.

It was Ava's litmus test of sexual compatibility. The moment of truth. Ava dreamt of being transported, of melting into Roger, a moment transcending time and space. Roger's lips touched Ava's and his tongue began to probe her mouth. Ava felt nothing: *nada, non, rien de rien.*

It was not a re-enactment of Prince Charming awakening Sleeping Beauty with That Kiss. Prince Charmless more like.

Ava pushed her body into Roger. She wanted to feel the big bulge in his pants, if nothing else. It was there, all right. But still, she felt nothing. She reached up and took his face tenderly in her hands, as she kissed him more deeply. She knew this man to be kind and good and very much deserving of her love and admiration.

Please, for fuck's sake! Ava sent out a quick prayer. *Let me feel something, a stirring of lust. Make me want to rip Roger's clothes off and devour him.*

God was not listening. She felt nothing.

This kiss is so lacking in chemistry, you could use the vacuum for a physics experiment, Ava thought, mixing all her scientific metaphors.

She remembered her other recent first kisses: Harry, Sami, Hugo, Darius. She remembered how effortlessly desire had pumped through her veins. She felt herself getting wet just at their memory. Usually, the physical connection was the easy part; it was the intellectual and spiritual connection that posed more of a challenge. With Roger, Ava faced the opposite problem. She wanted to will herself into being turned on by him. He was definitely too lovely to pass up. After all, beauty is only skin deep. And you should never judge a book by its cover. Ava invoked those and every other tedious platitude she could think of.

There was no doubt, on the other hand, about Roger's attraction to Ava. It was refreshing to be with a man who was not only clear about how much he wanted her, but also how ready, willing and able he was to act on it. There were no impediments whatsoever to them being together. Roger was perfectly single. He did not need more time to enjoy his freedom and play the field. He was not emotionally damaged by his previous relationships. His children did not need all his time and attention. His business was not faltering. He was not recovering from the body blow of having his net worth halved. And there were no other excuses that Ava was used to hearing for not embarking on a proper relationship.

With characteristic kindness and generosity, Roger decided to whisk Ava off.

'Let's get out of London. It's so cold here. I want to take you to Marrakesh. It's one of my favourite places. We'll spend a week in the sun. Get to know each other better. No distractions. A week of fuck, talk, sleep, repeat. Just pack a couple of bikinis, a few evening dresses and some heels, of course,' Roger said.

They arrived at the first-class desk at Heathrow and were escorted rapidly through the airport security checks. They sat in the lounge, waiting to board. Roger smiled at Ava, as he munched through a mountain of Cheddar cheese sandwiches. Ava brushed off a piece of cheese that had found its way onto the sleeve of Roger's Harris tweed jacket.

'Roger,' Ava said, 'don't you think it would be lovely to have lunch when we arrive at the hotel?'

'Of course, honey bun,' Roger replied. 'I need a little something to tide me over. I only had a plate of eggs and bacon for breakfast.'

Ava sipped her Earl Grey tea.

They sped through the medinas and the crowded squares of Marrakesh and into their opulent villa. It was a lavish profusion of purple and orange, with silk and velvet cushions and a deep, sunken green onyx bath. Every surface was made for sex. And after exhausting all the possibilities inside, they could explore outside, and indulge by their very own private pool, or in the shaded gazebo, or the outside shower, or the sun loungers, as they relaxed to the soothing patter of the running water from the fountains.

As they settled in their villa, Roger ordered a bottle of ice-cold Cristal. Even then, kind as he was, Ava was irritated because she knew she needed the buzz of alcohol to get her juices flowing. Her preference was for making love with little alcohol in her blood, so that all her sensations were fully aroused and awakened, and every cell in her body could experience the pleasures of touch and taste. But now, she needed the booze simply to feel turned on.

Roger tore off his clothes and threw them in a pile on the floor. He lay expectantly on the bed in his underpants and socks, already fully erect. Ava made a show of getting undressed, as much for Roger's titillation as for her own. She peeled off her long gold Missoni crochet dress and wiggled out of it. She stood in her heels, popping out of her nude Agent Provocateur bra and matching silk thong, like a succulent peach ready to be enjoyed, then she strutted over to the bed and playfully tossed her hair back. Roger grabbed her by the waist and pulled her down.

Now the mystery of his bulging crotch unfurled. His cock was practically as wide as it was long. He kissed her. Ava tried to switch her brain off, with its incessant internal chatter. She wanted to get wet and in the mood. She hated herself for having to think of Hugo, or Harry, or the sexy chauffeur who had picked them up at the airport – anyone else but Roger. Technically, he was flawless. He manoeuvred himself on top of Ava, in the coital alignment position, grinding into her, rocking up and down on his haunches. He was deep and hard inside her and she felt her clit being rubbed as he moved. It was not completely unpleasant. He came hard and fast and grunted loudly. Three minutes later, he was ready for round two.

He now turned his focus on her. Or at least, that's what he thought he was doing. He sat up and started to rub between Ava's legs, roughly and with a careless rhythm. He was sweating profusely, from every pore in his body. Ava was sure she could even see his eyeballs sweat. She closed her eyes tight and clenched her jaw as she endured a waterfall of his sweat cascading liberally all over her freshly blow-dried hair and face. The earth was most definitely not moving.

'Just give me one little second, Roger,' Ava said faintly, escaping out of the bed. 'I'm going to go and turn up the air conditioning before you pass out.'

Ava was glad for any excuse to get up and towel off his sweat. As a lover of all things wet, she had to admit, this was a low point. She should have known from the very first kiss that Roger was not her man. He was certainly large and in charge, which was most definitely her thing. He was kind and he was crazy about her, which was also a good thing. But it was not enough. Ava could not make herself feel what she didn't feel. Roger was right, on paper, but so wrong in real life.

Ava ended her short liaison with Roger as soon as they got back to London. Sure enough, Roger was married six months later. His new wife bore an uncanny resemblance to his first one; she was the motherly type, with short brown hair and flat shoes, and she cooked a great Sunday roast with all the trimmings. She was everything Ava was not, and everything Roger needed. Ava was thrilled to hear that they formed a happy couple. He deserved to be loved. Ava, who was always very discreet about such matters, never told Chantal what had happened with Roger. To this day, Chantal likes to believe that, contrary to all appearances, Ava must be utterly useless in bed.

11.

Déjà Vu All Over Again

In the extremely unlikely circumstance that you don't have any better offers and are free tomorrow night, may I take you out for dinner?

Ava's heart thumped. She had deleted his contact details three months ago, so the unexpected text message just came up as a telephone number together with the profile photo of a rather adorable sad-eyed beagle. But she recognised that distinctive syntax anywhere.

Hugo.

Nine months had elapsed without any contact whatsoever, not even a lustful midnight text. She was shaking and elated. Maybe he did like her after all? She couldn't wait to respond but she wanted to act cool. Most of all, she wanted to be cool. She waited ten seconds. She waited a minute. She restrained herself for all of four and a half minutes, and after what felt like a massive exercise in self-control, she responded.

Hello, stranger. Nice to hear from you. How are you?

It was a suitably neutral but friendly response.

Good, thanks, Hugo wrote back. *I thought dinner with a sexy, funny and intelligent woman would make it even better.*

Their conversation flowed effortlessly, instantaneously. It was as if there had never been a nine-month hiatus since they stopped seeing each other. Ava wondered if Hugo getting back in touch meant that he was now ready for a 'proper relationship'. She decided it was best not to ask. That would not be cool at all. Ava operated on the principle of Occam's razor: what you see is usually what you get, and the simplest explanation is usually the right one. In any event, she preferred to err on the side of being positive. Given how chirpy Hugo appeared in these messages, Ava thought he seemed happier, and she very much wanted to believe that he was now ready to be in a real relationship with her.

Ava thought of the psychic she had seen. Perhaps she was right after all. It had been a slow, rough start, but she could now vividly see Mr H, galloping masterfully on his black stallion, his shirt slashed open to the waist, blond hair flying in the wind, rushing to be with Ava, his One True Love. She imagined him scooping her up effortlessly with one hand and then they would ride off, locked together as one, inseparable, into the sunset. Happily ever after.

Ava shook herself out of her daydream. Perhaps Hugo got in touch with her because he was feeling horny and fancied a high-quality shag with someone who would say yes immediately and deliver a decent blow job to boot.

Not in town, darling, Ava typed, then deleted 'darling' and wrote 'H' instead. *I'm in the land of milk and honey. Another time?*

Sasha, an expert in the dos and don'ts of dating in the twenty-first century, had once looked at some of Ava's more wholesome WhatsApp text exchanges. She was horrified to see how overly keen Ava sounded in her messages. And the ratio of text length between Ava and her men was all wrong; her texts were about three times as long as the responses she elicited. Ava henceforth tried to keep her communication as short and dry as possible. So she resisted the urge to text Hugo that she was in Israel because of her exciting new charity project that finally bore fruit: a joint Arab-Israeli science education programme for young kids. She could tell him in person.

In any event, Ava was happy to be away and busy for a few days. She wanted to regain her equilibrium before seeing Hugo again. As it was, they immediately slipped back into their old routine of incessant texting. There was something about his wit, his boyish self-deprecation and the way he expressed his desire for her that Ava found utterly irresistible.

How's my favourite blonde bombshell trader? he texted the next day, as Ava rushed from meeting to meeting under the blazing Israeli sun.

Ava laughed, as she deconstructed the message. She knew perfectly well that Hugo had no other blondes in his little black book. She was not his favourite; she was his *only* blonde. She wondered why he addressed her as 'my'. She was not his, even though she wanted to be. But still, it was always nice to be called a bombshell.

Happy and well. My default setting. How's my favourite sexy hedge funder? she responded, though Hugo was certainly not 'hers' either. Ava had a few hedge funders circling around her at the moment. But he was, by far, her favourite. No contest. She thought about her use of the word 'sexy'. She found Hugo sexy because he was so cool he did not care about being cool. That was the ultimate in cool. And then there was that spectacular cock of his... An anatomical royal flush.

Hugo responded immediately, as he always did.

The elixir of a positive mental attitude. I'm well. A bit harder than I was before reading your message. Whatever text message I get from you, I get hard.

Good to hear I still reach the parts. If it's any consolation, I have a similar Pavlovian response to your texts, Ava replied. She was in danger of forgetting all of Sasha's 101 texting rules.

Yes, it's a consolation. I take pleasure from knowing I have an impact on you.

Yes, Hugo. You have an impact. You make me feel. Doesn't happen often.

Me too. Never had it with anyone but you.

Coming from Hugo, that was quite an admission. She reread the text three times, to make sure she had read it properly.

What she really wanted to ask was, 'If you've never felt like this before, why the hell aren't you doing anything about it? Like us being in a proper relationship?'

Instead, she texted, *Has anything changed in your life since we last saw each other?*

After a few Flaming Ferraris, I came round to your way of thinking. I realised I have to switch things up a bit. I'm not sure yet how. You remind me that I could be a better version of myself.

Hugo was starting to unlearn four decades of the stiff upper lip.

Ava wanted to tell him that she loved him exactly as he was, that he did not need to change anything at all. She just wanted him by her side, always and forever. She longed to make him happy. But she decided to run with the classic therapist's question, *How does that make you feel?*

Our texting has practically taken on a metaphysical quality. I think I preferred our hard/wet chats, Hugo texted back. This was not an answer to her question, but was probably a true indication of his present frame of mind.

There was no doubt, Hugo's texts were mesmerising. And much as she enjoyed philosophical WhatsApp banter, nothing beat reading, *I want to feel you and be very deep inside you.*

Ava returned from Israel tired and happy to get an early night at home, after a week of relentless early starts and late nights. She lay in bed, listening to BBC Radio 4. She felt her phone vibrate on her night table. She had tried sleeping without her phone next to her. Mission impossible. There was too much she might miss, such as this latest text from Hugo.

I'm having dinner at the Guinea Grill with five middle-aged men. Not one of his most riveting texts. But as usual, it was great to hear from him.

Have fun! Ava responded. The exclamation mark was code for *Well, fuck off, then.*

Ava knew that fun was not exactly Hugo's thing, and if he was going to be having any, she hoped it would be with her, not with five middle-aged clients.

I will try, in your spirit.

At least he was thinking about her. *Hugo, in my spirit, you don't try, you succeed.*

Ava wondered how much fun Hugo might indeed be having, as the texts streamed in throughout the night with pleasing regularity. At 1 a.m., Ava forced herself to put her phone down. The texts had given her plenty of material with which to have some very sweet dreams.

She woke up at 5 a.m., her usual wake-up time, to another text from Hugo.

Are you awake at ridiculous o'clock?

And then ten minutes later:

I just got rid of my last client. I'm in Mayfair, around the corner from you. I was tempted to press your buzzer, as it were.

Why don't you? Ava wrote back. *Swing by. You can test your buzzer-pressing skills.*

She had precisely three minutes flat to shower, run a razor over her legs, brush her teeth and decide what to wear. The latter took the longest.

She decided to go for grey cashmere leggings and a cream cashmere V-neck jumper with no bra, which she knew Hugo would love.

Precisely three minutes later, the doorbell rang, and Ava was shaking as she opened the front door.

Hugo looked as sexy as ever. No, he looked sexier. He was losing his hair, but it only highlighted his soulful blue eyes, his high cheekbones and his kissable mouth. It must have been cold out there because for once he was wearing a coat, a navy wool pea coat, with suede Chelsea boots. For a man who had pulled an all-nighter, he looked spectacularly fuckable.

Ava threw her arms around him, and they kissed.

'You look great,' Hugo said, smiling. 'You always look great.'

Ava loved it when he smiled, which was rare.

'I want to kiss you all over,' Hugo said, 'but let me jump in the shower first and grab a toothbrush and then I can take you to bed.'

As Hugo showered, Ava lay in bed waiting for him. Her heart was palpitating, and her mind was racing. She was already wet just thinking about how much she wanted him. She tried to calibrate her anticipation. After all, she was a woman of the world. She thought about how much coitus she had enjoyed in her life. She did the maths quickly in her head. Over twenty years of sex. Was it already that many years? An average of three hundred couplings a year. She arrived at a figure of six thousand, give or take a few hundred, given the outlier university years of extreme activity, the months of semi-abstinence during her two pregnancies, and an adherence to the strict technical definition of what constituted 'a fuck', namely full penetration. Six thousand. That was quite a number. And yet, as she eagerly waited for Hugo to jump into bed with her, she had as much enthusiasm and desire as ever.

Is there anything better than great sex?

Hugo emerged from the bathroom, fresh and ready for action. Ava admired his massive erection as he slipped under the cream silk sheets. She was electrified by the touch of his skin. If anything, Hugo was even more appetising than Ava remembered. He looked deep into her eyes, and they kissed. Hugo took control. He pulled off the bedclothes so he could see her entire tanned, naked body, and he started to caress and kiss and lick and arouse every inch of her. Ava followed his lead and mirrored his slow, sensual rhythm. She kissed his thighs, then ran her fingers over his broad, hairless chest and shoulders and his strong, muscular legs. She lightly grazed his cock with her fingertips. He groaned softly as his hard cock stirred. She felt a few drops of precum and inhaled deeply as she licked his inner thighs and then moved to his balls and cock.

'I want you up here, Ava,' said Hugo as he pulled her from his crotch and up to his face.

He kissed her again, and Ava felt herself melt; she always did when he kissed her. His kiss was like a drug, and she was his addict. She wanted only his kiss, more and more, all the time. More was never enough. He licked her breasts and hard nipples, and started rubbing her clit with one finger and slipped another in her wet pussy.

Ava felt a flash of panic. She usually came easily, but it took longer when a man fingered her because it was difficult to get it just right. She need not have worried. Hugo knew exactly how to stimulate her: he was sensual, and patient, and her body responded effortlessly to his touch. He sensed exactly where to stroke, when to press harder, when to move faster, and she was simultaneously melting and pulsating with desire for him. She lay back and enjoyed the rising waves in her whole body, and that exquisite moment when she knew she would go over the edge, in a whoosh of total release and bliss. She came hard, twice.

Hugo went on top and teased her clit, still engorged from her orgasms, with his cock. It was even bigger in the flesh than when she used to dream about it. How could she have forgotten? Hugo had never looked better than in that early morning light, with his smooth, milky skin, his stubble and his massive cock. Ava was close to coming again. He thrust hard inside her.

'Fuck,' he murmured. 'You make me so hard. I want you.' Then more softly, almost inaudibly, 'I need you.'

'Come, darling, deeper. I want to feel you, Hugo. I want to feel you coming.'

She held Hugo tightly. She wanted to hold him and never let him go. He came fast, with a gasp.

'I'm sorry,' Hugo stammered. 'Not my best performance. It's been so long. I just couldn't stop myself.'

'Hugo,' Ava whispered. 'You're amazing. I don't know what you do to me. You turn me on so much. You have no idea. I find you irresistible. Intoxicating. I can't keep my hands off you. Your body, your cock... You drive me wild.'

It was her attempt at a Brené Brown moment: a terrifying experiment in revealing her true vulnerability and opening up about her feelings for a change. Vulnerability was, according to the experts, a display of real strength. She wanted to tell Hugo that she was madly in love with him, that he touched her heart and soul, and that she wanted to bring oceans of love and joy into his life. All she wanted was to take away his pain and make him happy.

Instead, Ava told him he had a fabulous cock.

'I love your cock,' she said.

Hugo looked embarrassed. 'You have such a beautiful body,' he replied. 'And a great mind, of course.'

He didn't tell her that he loved and adored her. He didn't tell her that he wanted to spend the rest of his life with her. He didn't tell her that what he wanted to share with her was so much more than just their bodily fluids.

And Ava continued with the sex talk. The Brené Brown moment of authentic vulnerability might have to wait for another day.

'Hugo, may I say something? Sometimes I sense you get a bit nervous when I'm giving you head.'

'Er, yes,' Hugo said. 'I guess I worry about how I look, how I taste, and feel and smell. I, er, haven't, er, been with that many women. I've got low self-esteem. Um, always have done.'

Ava was taken aback by Hugo's candour. She knew his insecurities by now, but still, he was so far from the classic Etonian prototype, oozing with self-confidence.

'For the record, I think your cock is spectacular. Beautiful. And it looks and tastes and feels and smells divine.' Ava waxed lyrical again. How many times had she already told him that?

Hugo smiled. 'Well, er, thank you.'

'I know you must be tired, and I should let you catch up on some sleep. I can't resist caressing you all the time. Sorry.'

'I've got a ten o'clock meet, but I'll be fine. If anything, I feel, er, quite energised.'

He was holding her close from behind now and she could feel the energised stirring of his cock on her buttocks. She reached back and slipped him very slightly into her wet pussy, a couple of centimetres in. She felt the tip of his cock sliding back and forth over her clit and they both groaned in pleasure. He nuzzled the back of her neck and kissed it. Then he entered her, slowly and deeply. She felt him moving inside her and she thought, for a moment, that this was exactly where he belonged. The body never lies.

'Hugo, you feel *so* good. I can really feel you, my love.'

Ava was in heaven.

'What did you say?' Hugo whispered.

'You feel so good. I can really feel you.'

Ava did not want to drop the 'love' bomb again. Cock, fuck, pussy, clit: all these words were fine. But Ava tried hard never, ever to use the word 'love', in any context whatsoever. That is, not until the man had said it first. Hugo let it go, but he knew precisely what he had heard.

They came together, as one. Hugo was in Ava, and she was in him.

She lay in his arms and, for a brief moment, she felt safe. Or rather, she deluded herself into thinking she felt safe. Love is an involuntary reflex and Ava's neural pathways were powerless to stop the uncontrolled arcs of tenderness and deep connectedness that flooded her body, and which surged straight to her heart. Her love was completely beyond her control.

She knew she was in love with Hugo, but she knew he was incapable of properly loving her back. She knew that Hugo was struggling to get his divorce finalised. She knew that his soon-to-be ex-wife's divorce lawyers were being as greedy as they were being paid to be. She knew that his eldest son, Mungo, was about to be expelled from his prep school and that he needed therapy to address his rebellious behaviour. She knew that one of his biggest fund positions had turned sour and needed to be sold. She knew that Hugo was trying to find a new four-bed des res with garden in Kensington. She knew how Hugo liked his tea: PG Tips builders' tea, milky, two sugars. She even knew how he liked to sleep: on his front, arms up, like a newborn baby.

Ava wondered if Hugo knew anything about her, except that she worshipped his cock and that she knew exactly how to make him come. Did Hugo even realise that Ava also had a life made up of complex moving parts? He never asked, funnily enough.

'Right,' said Hugo, breaking Ava's reverie. 'I better go grab a shower and put my game face on. I've got a meeting with a company I'm about to buy in precisely fifty minutes and even I can't be late for that.'

As they kissed a long, lingering goodbye in the hall, Ava leaned close into Hugo's body and felt his huge erection.

'I think we'd better stop now,' Hugo said, 'or else we'll never leave the house.'

Ava slipped on a cream chiffon dress, knee-high suede boots and a tan suede coat. She grabbed her Hermès bag and dashed to her breakfast meeting at Claridge's. She was slightly early, as usual, and as she took her seat, the grey-haired, blue-eyed man in a slim-cut pin-stripe suit at the next table caught her eye.

'Cold out there, isn't it?' he said with a smile, and a faint Scandinavian accent.

It was not the most original of opening gambits.

'Yes. It does feel rather nippy,' Ava said, smiling back. 'I got in from Tel Aviv yesterday. Great weather there. Thirty-two degrees.' *Why, oh why, am I talking about the weather?* she thought. *Intellectual plankton.* Yet much as she hated idle chatter, she couldn't resist a handsome blue-eyed male.

'Oh, how wonderful. That's global warming for you,' the Viking said.

His name was Magnus. Ava's mind boggled, wondering if his name reflected his size. She had always had a thing for Nordics: all that cool aloofness and raw, marauding masculinity. That plus Big? Wow: that was practically a hole in one, as it were.

'So now I see why you're looking so radiant,' Magnus said. 'Must have been perfect weather for sunbathing.'

Ava smiled again. She knew her radiance had nothing to do with the hot Israeli weather and everything to do with having just enjoyed one of the best fucks of her life.

Magnus was the exact opposite to Hugo. Smooth and sophisticated, he looked like a man about town, and he exuded self-assurance. Ava wondered if she could be in love with Hugo, if, in the twinkling of an eye, she could so easily have taken Magnus's hand and slipped upstairs with him to one of the suites. Was she really that lost and hungry for love that any semi-possible man would do?

'Hello, Ava. I'm so sorry to keep you waiting. Such bad traffic this morning,' said her breakfast date, arriving flustered and late. 'I'm famished. Shall we order eggs and crumpets? They're so good here.'

'Oh, yes. Great idea. The crumpet at Claridge's is first rate,' said Ava loudly, winking at Magnus.

Magnus winked back.

12.

The Etonian's View: Life in the Slow Lane

Hugo and his sad-eyed beagle, Nelson, were out for a long walk along the beach. Hugo had his earphones in, and he was listening to Coldplay as he looked for glossy white stones for his two sons; apparently it was a 'thing'. The bracing sea air worked wonders to clear his mind. He needed it.

After years of humdrum blandness, there was a lot going on in his life right now. There always was these days, ever since Hettie had booted him out of their sprawling Wiltshire manor house. The blustery weather mirrored the uncertainty he felt about his future. It was biting cold, but he wore no coat, as usual. He trudged on, heedless to the elements.

He banged the brass lion-head door knocker and stood, like a stranger, shivering outside the family home that had been his for fifteen years, waiting for someone, anyone, to let him in. His younger son, Matt, eventually opened the front door. He was wearing large headphones and playing on his game console.

'Hello, my boy, how's it going? How was that football match? Score any goals?' Hugo said cheerfully, ruffling his son's hair.

Matt grunted without looking up and shuffled back to the sofa, where his brother Mungo lay slumped, also playing *Final Fantasy VII Remake*.

'Hey, Mungo,' Hugo said. 'How's Daddy's boy?'

Mungo ignored him.

Hugo wandered into the kitchen. It was strewn with the usual schoolboy paraphernalia: a cricket bat; a pair of old, tattered trainers; an elementary biology textbook and a couple of half-empty cheese-and-onion crisp packets. Hettie was blending herself a coconut cream, vodka and açai berry concoction, which she was sure was practically a health drink, and the noise from the food mixer was excruciating.

'Hello, Hettie,' Hugo shouted above the din. 'How are you? All good? The boys look like they're power chilling.'

Hettie nodded hazily in his direction. Hugo assumed that it was not her first drink of the day. Once a stunning English rose, she had lost that fresh bloom many years ago and she had not cared to replace it with even a vague attempt at making the best of herself. She was wearing her old jeans with a shapeless navy jumper and an olive quilted Barbour vest on top. Her hair was scraped back with a black hairband and even Hugo noted the grey roots coming through. The house was cold. It was apparently too expensive to have the heating on in October. Eventually, she switched the blender off and poured herself another long drink.

'I'm going to make a pot of tea. Jolly cold outside. Can I pour you a cup?' Hugo asked.

'Don't bother,' Hettie said. 'I just made myself a little afternoon pick-me-up.'

Hugo could smell the alcohol on her breath even though she was standing next to the AGA cooker some way off. It did not occur to her to offer Hugo some of her liquid refreshment.

'I thought I might take the boys out for some fresh air, play a bit of football with them, and then maybe a lads' night in, back at my house, with Domino's pizza,' Hugo said.

'Yah, great. I'm totally worn out. Do take them off my hands,' Hettie answered. 'Mungo and Matt flew into a bate because I confiscated their gaming consoles earlier. They've been fighting incessantly. They're totally insufferable. I had to capitulate and give them their PlayStations back after a few minutes; the shouting was simply unbearable. And now I feel my migraine coming on. Hugo, for once,' Hettie took a long sip of her drink, 'could you fulfil your fatherly duties and go and speak to them about their unruly behaviour.'

Hugo winced. He could sense Hettie about to go off on one of her rants and he switched off. He went into his happy space and thought about how Ava had looked into his eyes when she gave him a blow job earlier that week. He became hard and hoped Hettie did not notice. He need not have worried.

'Oh and, Hugo, will you do something about those bramble bushes that have totally overgrown in the back garden?' Hettie continued. Hugo's eyes glazed over. 'The gardener gave me the most exorbitant quote for the job. I'm sure you could dash it off in a couple of hours.'

Hugo shook himself out of his reverie and nodded automatically. He suspected it would take at least four days' solid hard work to wrest back control from the advancing sprawl of weeds and brambles, but he did not mind: he enjoyed his time outdoors. All that wood chopping and physical exercise brought out his inner Mellors, and he could readily identify with the earthy gamekeeper in *Lady Chatterley's Lover*. That had been his chief source of sex education, way back when he was a horny schoolboy, in the days before Pornhub. Gardening remained an activity which he always subliminally associated with sex. And gardening was also a welcome escape from Hettie's incessant nagging, and a money-saver to boot.

'Sure,' Hugo said wearily. 'I'll do the gardening next weekend, Hettie.'

Hettie went over to lie on the couch and closed her eyes with a sigh. It had been such a tiresome day.

'By the way, Hettie, I dropped in to see Mungo's therapist earlier,' Hugo said. 'He diagnosed acute anger management issues. He said something about his traumatised, bi-directional, co-creative intersubjective field. I think that means he's got problems talking to us, to his teachers and even to his mates at school. He thought it might be a good idea for us to stop letting him spend all day on his PlayStation. And now that he's been suspended from school, perhaps we could get him a tutor, so he doesn't fall behind completely.'

'Yah,' answered Hettie, absent-mindedly, savouring her long drink. 'Be a dear, Hugo, and organise a tutor, will you? You've got an army of people in your office running around at your beck and call. It's so easy for you. I'm all alone here and I've got a hideously busy day tomorrow, what with the school run and then that women's golf tournament. You've really got no idea what hard work it is running a large house in the country.'

Hugo got up and fiddled around making his tea, as Hettie stretched out on the sofa. He let her running commentary wash over him, as he remembered something his wise uncle had once told him, and which he wished he had heeded when he married Hettie: that all men secretly want to marry their mother, but because all women eventually become just like their own mother, men end up with their mother-in-law instead. Why had he not paid closer attention to the dried-up harridan that was his mother-in-law, rather than the voluptuous, creamy-skinned siren that Hettie had been fifteen years ago? They were now one and the same.

'Yes, Hettie. Of course. Leave it with me,' Hugo said.

Taking charge of all the stuff that needed doing, be it in the house or the garden, the upkeep of the boys' bicycles and the cars, the house electrics, the Wi-Fi, the plumbing, the bins, the summer holidays, and the boys, their school, their multiple tutors, their football training and their matches: that was Hugo's world. Hettie forgot, somehow, that Hugo had a challenging day job of his own, involving an office of over forty people, demanding clients and their billions of pounds under management.

'I was not untroubled by what the shrink said,' Hugo said. That was his way of saying he was very concerned. 'Mungo's like me in so many ways.'

He petted Nelson's back as he lay next to him, wagging his tail.

Hettie picked up a copy of *Country Life* and started flipping through the pages.

'He's hypersensitive, and I think his behaviour is a way of masking his anger and his pain,' Hugo continued, even though he knew Hettie was not listening. 'I also caused a lot of headaches at Eton. I got caned a lot, but mainly because my headmaster enjoyed it. Then I was drinking and smoking, even shoplifting, to change it up a bit. I behaved like a rebel without a clue for many years. I guess my bad behaviour was a way of hiding my shyness. Actually, it made me even more detached. Not a great way of dealing with things, but then again, detachment is how we deal with things in our family. No one ever listened to me, so I stopped sharing. History seems to be repeating itself. Even now.'

Hugo sipped his tea. Of course, Hettie wasn't listening; she never did. He looked out at the large expanse of lawn. The grass needed mowing too.

'Hugo,' Hettie said, 'fetch me those wasabi nuts, would you? They're on the kitchen island.'

Hugo got up and went to get the bowl. He picked out a couple of nuts and ate them. He realised he had not eaten all day. He brought the bowl over to Hettie. She did not look up as she dived into the nuts.

'Right,' Hugo said decisively. 'I'm off. I'll bring the boys back here on Sunday night, around five. And I'm leaving their gaming consoles here with you.'

Hugo easily removed the boys' headphones that had seemed surgically clamped around their ears a couple of hours earlier. Neither Mungo nor Matt said a word in protest. He bundled them into the Land Rover, and he remembered to pack Matt's bedraggled comfort blanket and Mungo's fluorescent squidgy stress ball. The boys were excited to spend the weekend with their father. As soon as they arrived at Hugo's new place, they rushed off to change into their football kit and they played in the garden. All three kicked the ball around with squeals of laughter. Hugo noticed that Mungo was much more talkative when he had a ball at his feet, and he didn't have to make eye contact.

'Dad,' Mungo blurted out, 'you know, sometimes I feel, like, alone.'

'You're never alone, my son,' Hugo said, his eyes watering. 'I carry you in my heart. Always.'

'Oh, Dad, yuck.' Mungo laughed as he dribbled the ball down the lawn.

'Just hang on in there, Mungo, my boy,' Hugo said. It was good to hear his son laughing for a change. 'Things will get easier as you get older.'

Hugo wondered if that was, strictly speaking, the case. He himself felt more alone than ever, though now he did have his boys.

It was getting cold and dark, and Hugo managed to get the boys into the bathtub for a good soak and a scrub. All three sat around the kitchen table, tired but happy. Hugo ordered an extra-large pizza, with sweetcorn and mushroom on one half for Mungo, who was going through a vegan phase, and spicy sausage on the other half for Matt, who was more carnivorous than ever. The gluten-free chocolate cake was a hit with both boys. Then they all piled onto the sofa, with Hugo sandwiched between his sons, and Nelson nestled at his feet, as they watched *The Terminator*. They must have seen it five times already, but their enjoyment grew with the watching.

Hugo nuzzled Mungo's freshly washed hair and let his mind wander. He was glad that he had finished rewriting his letter of wishes and that, after some deliberation, the trustees had amended the list of beneficiaries and removed Hettie. She had certainly made quite enough already from the divorce settlement. He had also taken out a new life insurance policy, and his life was now insured for practically more than his net worth. Isn't that how all murder mysteries start? Perhaps not that mysterious.

Hugo acknowledged he needed to keep himself on a tighter leash. He was worried he was drinking too much, and he planned to go cold turkey for a month, to prove he could. He wanted to start eating better, to go to the gym more, to take better care of himself and to generally slap himself around the face. He felt a buzz from the phone in his back pocket.

Hello H. Fancy a drink at 5H? I'm here with friends. Thought you might need uplifting.

5H – Five Hertford Street – was Ava's favourite haunt, and also a favourite with the glamorous denizens of Mayfair. Hugo had only been a couple of times. He hated having to put on a blazer and shirt to get in. He felt so much more comfortable in a T-shirt and a cashmere jumper, even if it did have a couple of holes in it. Ava accompanied the text with a photo of herself in a tight sleeveless red dress, blowing him a kiss. Hugo couldn't help but smile.

Saturday night and, as always, he was sprawled on his sofa with two boys and one dog, a long way from lychee martini land. Ava was on fire, as usual, vodka-ing away. He thought how different his life was from hers. He remembered a sweatshirt he had bought with the words 'Same, same, but different' written across the front. That was back in the day, when he still had lots of hair and an almost-six-pack. Now he was in limbo. What could he possibly offer any woman today, let alone a woman like Ava? She had such high expectations of everything. He did not feel remotely ready for a proper relationship. Ava always said that feeling was everything to her and that she wanted to feel more. Hugo found it hard to feel anything at all. His past suggested there was very little upside to feelings.

'*Hasta la vista*, baby,' said the Terminator, booming from the quadraphonic sound system. 'I'll be back!'

Hugo wanted to be back too: he just didn't know how. He took his boys to bed, tucked them in, and slumped in front of the television with another large gin and tonic.

13.

Basic Instinct

The rain was beating down hard and the damp air hung heavy above the glistening streets of W1. Ava was happy to be home, warm and snug in her cashmere, doing a spot of light reading – von Neumann's *Mathematical Foundations of Quantum Mechanics* – and furiously scribbling in the margin as she drank Earl Grey in her kitchen. It was an old Cambridge set text and she wanted to brush up on her knowledge of quantum computers and qubits, as substitutes for the classic '1' and '0' binary computers, for a potential new investment for her fund. She was 'between boyfriends'. What that meant was that she did not have a date that Saturday and she could not face a fun, wild night out on the town with a group of women pretending to have a fun, wild night out.

She had not had sex in eight weeks. Eight weeks! Her body ached to be touched and held. Sometimes masturbation just did not cut it, though it was helpful that one did not need to look one's best. Some of Ava's girlfriends developed deep relationships with their Rampant Rabbit and their Pocket Rocket clit vibrator. But Ava was not a fan of sex toys: she found them cold, mechanical and utterly joyless. Rather than help her reach the biggest of big 'O's, they had the opposite effect; they left her feeling disappointed, alone and pining more than ever for the Real Thing. Was that really the best she could do? A vibrating lump of pink silicone with twelve speeds and ten different settings to take her to the end of the rainbow at the flick of a switch? Or the ultimate experience of a blended clitoral and vaginal orgasm through optimised dual stimulation, gentle suction and personalised pulsations, with a feather-light caress? The only magic wand Ava was interested in was a large, live flesh-and-blood one, attached to a large, live flesh-and-blood male.

Ava took a little break from the position-space Schrödinger equation for a non-single relativistic particle in one dimension:

$$i\hbar \frac{\partial}{\partial t} \psi(\mathbf{r}, t) = \left(\frac{-\hbar^2}{2m} \nabla^2 + V(r) \right) \psi(\mathbf{r}, t)$$

She was startled from her slightly more compelling daydream of bigger, stronger, enhanced, blended and multiple orgasms by her oldest daughter, Sasha, who came bounding into the kitchen.

'Good night, Mama,' she said. Sasha was a dark, sultry brunette, and she reminded Ava of herself when she was young. 'Alex and I are heading out to a birthday dinner at Sexy Fish. Thank you for lending me your YSL biker jacket. It works well with this dress, don't you think? Gives it an edge.'

She gave her mother a long hug and kiss. Ava lived for those hugs and kisses.

'We're going to this new club afterwards; I'm totally gassed. We won't be late. I need to work on my anthropology dissertation in the morning.'

'Oh, hello, Alex,' Ava said to Sasha's boyfriend, who walked in and grabbed Sasha by the waist. 'How've you been? How's life at Eton? Are they working you hard enough?'

Alex laughed. He was the classic Etonian type, confident and charming, but with an unusual twist: he was sweet and caring. If anything, he was more in love with Sasha than she was with him.

'Er, yes,' Alex said with a grin. 'My Oxbridge entrance exams are looming. Dad's going to be furious if I fluff it. He's a Balliol man, and so was his dad. So, no pressure...'

'I see,' said Ava, recalling how hard she had to work to get her scholarship to Cambridge. 'Those entrance exams are no walk in the park.'

'Yup, I'm on it. And about tonight, don't worry, Ava. We're not going to have a late night. I'll take good care of your daughter. I'm going to make sure she wraps up warmly and I'll have her tucked up and in bed by one, latest.'

Alex smiled lovingly at Sasha and squeezed her hand. She looked back adoringly. He was tall and slim, and his dark good looks were a perfect match for Sasha's smouldering beauty. They made a striking couple. Ava imagined the gorgeous, smart, olive-skinned babies they might have together.

'Well, have a nice quiet evening in, Mama,' Sasha said. 'I love you so much.' She gave her mother another kiss and floated off, arm in arm with Alex.

Then Khassya, Ava's younger daughter, bounced in with her boyfriend, Ilia, in tow. Khassya was blonde and blue-eyed, a younger version of Ava in her blonde iteration. Like her sister, she radiated warmth and sunshine. She too gave her mother a big hug and a kiss.

'Goodnight, Mama,' Khassya said. 'I'm going over to Ilia's house. His family are having a little house-warming party. Actually, do you want to come?'

'Oh, yes,' Ilia said. 'Sorry, I should have asked you earlier. My parents would love to meet you. We've just moved into a new place on Berkeley

Square. It's pretty neat. There's going to be some interesting people there. More your age group than ours, really.'

Ava flinched. She knew that she was officially middle-aged, even if inside she still felt as young as her own daughters, most of the time. 'That's very sweet of you, Ilia,' Ava said, 'but I'm going to stay in tonight. I need to catch up on some reading and do a spot of work. But I'd love to meet your parents. Let's do that another time.'

'I'll stay at Ilia's tonight, Mama,' Khassya said, 'if that's okay with you.'

'Sure,' Ava answered, 'but don't forget we've got that lunch I'm hosting at Scott's tomorrow with a few of the wonderful young women we've sponsored through university. They're going to be giving a little talk about female empowerment through education.'

'Of course. I haven't forgotten.' Khassya smiled. 'I remember meeting a few of those girls last year. I was blown away by their passion and commitment.'

'I'm glad you remember, darling. It's so important to work in an area you believe in. And always keep your financial independence, Khassya, always.'

'I know, Mama, I know. You've told me that since I was about five years old. Don't worry. I won't let you down.'

Mother and daughter laughed. Though the girls grew up in Mayfair, Ava raised them to work hard and to make their own money, without ever relying on a man. The girls never once forgot that their great-grandparents sold fruit and veg in the market, and they knew how hard their mother had worked to get to where she was.

Ava sighed. She thought of Alex and Ilia, and the other lovely young men who came traipsing in and out of her kitchen, courting her beautiful girls. They came in all shapes and sizes, but they were all uniformly sweet and kind. All of them. How different they were to the older, colder, harder men that Ava knew. It was baffling. What happened? Where did those sweet, sensitive and kind young men go? Where were they in midlife? Was that sweetness still there somewhere, buried deep underneath? Could you reach it, if you managed to peel off all those protective layers acquired through the battering journey of life?

Ava was proud to see her girls flourishing, enjoying life, and in loving relationships. Love begets love, clearly. By contrast, she was ashamed that Sasha and Khassya saw her like this, alone, *still* single and struggling to find love. Even at their age, Ava dated men who sexualised her and enjoyed her skinny body, but who were not terribly interested in knowing who she was and what she might be feeling. It was a pattern that had not changed through the years, and the dance of superficiality continued. Had she consistently chosen the wrong men? Or was there something intrinsically wrong with her that made even good men behave badly? Maybe. Definitely.

Ava snapped into action. She was not interested in going down memory lane yet again. Suddenly, she did not want to be alone on a Saturday night. She took out her phone and opened up her contacts. It was time to liven up her evening. She started scrolling through the names.

What about Karl? A black leather jacket and artfully distressed jeans dude who did something unfathomable in *meedja*. He was definitely cool. Cool Karl. Actually, he was way too cool for Ava, whose own musical tastes oscillated between nineteenth-century opera and eighties vintage disco. He never stopped talking about all the celebs he regularly snorted coke with, in the beach clubs of Ibiza and the loos of Soho House. But while being seen out on the town with Karl might do wonders for her street cred, Ava was not sure street cred was something she wanted. Although some of Ava's behaviour might be labelled 'transgressive', she was, at heart, an unreconstructed schoolgirl swot, and she was incapable of being cool. It didn't help that she once caught a whiff of a rather unfortunate odour that emanated from Karl's armpit, one hot summer's night. For someone for whom smell was one of the most important defining sexual characteristics, Karl's pheromones telegraphed 'no go' zone in no uncertain terms. She thought Cool Karl might be cooler if he started using a deodorant stick.

How about Frédérique? He was a dashing Belgian, and as such, a walking, talking oxymoron fluent in four languages. He was certainly tall and handsome, but he did not have an ounce of sensuality, and Ava suspected it would make for a particularly joyless coupling. He had all the erotic appeal of a Brussels sprout, and, come to think of it, he smelled a bit like one too, detectable even under the Eau Sauvage cologne that he habitually doused himself in. Ava wished her nose was a little less finely tuned, and her gut instinct for nice men more so. Frédérique was another *non*. He registered *nul points*.

Rex? What about that devilishly charming Rex the Sex? True to his self-styled nickname, he was sexy as hell, with his razor-sharp brain and ironic wit, his steely-blue eyes and that promising bulge in his pants that Ava could not help but zoom in on every time she saw him. Yes, Rex. He was definitely interesting. But he was not the most discreet of chaps and she did not care to be another notch on his bedpost. Men of the conquering kind, men who 'come and run', men who 'blow their load and hit the road', were typically mediocre in the sack. Their game was scoring, not satisfying. It might be amazing, for five seconds. But no, the equation did not stack up, however you did the maths. Ava thought she might be worth a little more than a five-second wonder.

What about Caspar? Tall, elegant, effetely good-looking. Unfortunately, there was absolutely no flicker of sexual fire, however horny she might be feeling, and she was. She suspected that Caspar was a man who found sex slightly distasteful, a bit like a wet fart. While he might make a great date to take to the opera, a man who knew his Verdi from his Wagner and his Netrebko from his Kaufmann, she doubted he could tell her G-spot from her C-spot. And more troublingly, he did not seem remotely interested to find out.

They were all lovely men, but Ava felt nothing for any of them. She wondered, with remorse, what those men might say about her. She imagined the comments:

'Ava's a decent piece of arse. But she's a piece of work. She collects men. She devours them and spits them out when she's done. She's got a beautiful house, which she keeps immaculately tidy. Her fridge is empty aside from a few bottles of Ruinart, some Konik's Tail vodka, and freshly pressed lychee juice. She's interesting, and she can talk about many things, but you never know what she's thinking. She always wears high heels, always. And she smells amazing. Ava in a word: she's a nympho-bitch.'

Ava winced. She was relieved that she would never know for sure what those men really thought of her. She cast those uncomfortable thoughts aside and went back to the contacts on her phone. What about Damian? Yes. Damian. Why hadn't she thought of him sooner?

Of course.

Dangerously delicious Damian. Or was that deliciously dangerous Damian? Quite possibly, it amounted to one and the same thing: trouble. Tall, aristocratic, slightly louche, blue eyes, of course. A man who prided himself on his swordsmanship. He looked as though he could fuck for England, and then some.

Ava was attracted to Damian because he was physically and intellectually her type. He was also single and, in theory, available. Emotionally, too, he was Ava's type: dark and damaged, which only added to his allure and brought out the rescuer in Ava. Ava was a great rescuer. But sometimes, just sometimes, she wondered if there was anyone out there to rescue her.

Hello, sexy! How's His Naughtiness? Ava texted Damian. She knew that who dares wins. Usually.

I've been boringly well-behaved actually, he responded immediately.

I don't believe that for one minute. You breathe naughtiness. Fancy a glass of champagne at my place tonight?

Miraculously, Damian was also free on a Saturday night.

Ava's preparations were fast but meticulous. She knew the drill: low lights, Sade, Fleetwood Mac and Eagles playlist, oldies but goodies, Diptyque amber-scented candles, with champagne perfectly chilled in the ice box. She quickly washed her hair and shaved her body hair until she was as sleek as a dolphin. Outfit? Something casual yet sexy and chic; she did not want to look as though she had tried too hard. She slipped on a pair of skin-tight black leather pants, a deep V-neck cashmere jumper, no bra. No dangly earrings or long necklaces; she knew from past experience how easy it was to break her jewellery in the throes of passion.

Damian arrived, bang on time, with a bouquet of white roses. It was a nice touch.

'Wow,' he said, as she opened the front door, 'you look edible.'

Ava glowed. 'That's the general idea,' she said with a wink.

As the fire roared, they settled on Ava's grey velvet sofa, savouring the crisp, dry champagne and the intense sexual tension. Ava relished the excitement, the minutes before anything happens, before the touch, before the kiss, before any physical contact, before the Moment of Truth.

She gazed into Damian's eyes, listening only hazily, as he held forth on his latest investment in an ecologically sustainable rubber plantation in Indonesia. It was hardly the most erotic of foreplay topics. She was more mesmerised by the tiny flecks of gold in his blue eyes, surprised that she had never noticed them before. Now they were close, and he looked deep into her own green eyes. They both knew that they would kiss very, very soon. Their mouths were a few centimetres away from each other. Damian finally stopped talking. He leaned forwards and pulled her head gently to him. And they kissed, slowly, tongues licking and exploring. They savoured the exquisiteness of taste and touch, two beings about to come together.

Ava pushed Damian down on the sofa and straddled him, feeling his erection through his trousers. She unzipped his jeans. He was not wearing underwear, and she slipped her hand onto his cock, stroking it as they continued to kiss hungrily. She continued to caress him as she seamlessly whipped off his pants. He tugged awkwardly at her leathers, not making much headway. Ava squirmed, then took over, and pulled and wriggled until, finally, she managed to yank them off.

Note to self: never wear stiff, tight trousers on a hot assignation, thought Ava, now fully focused on other stiff matters in hand.

She could feel his throbbing cock and he felt her wet pussy, even through her silk panties. She wanted to dominate him, knowing that he was a difficult man to control. Most of all, she wanted to eke out that crowning moment when all of her skin would touch all of his skin.

Damian couldn't wait anymore and he ripped her knickers, first on one side, then the other. Ava winced at the thought of her beautiful £200 La Perla silk thong, now destroyed, but she appreciated the intensity and the desire that drove Damian to do it. Or did he think they were £10 panties in a special three-for-one discount pack from H&M? Ava suspected he was not thinking at all.

They were now both naked, and Ava inhaled their mingled scents. She lay on the sofa and arched her back, moaning as he licked her breasts and gently held her hair back off her face. He took his large cock and slid it back and forth across her glistening inner lips. Their desire was heightened as they watched themselves, reduced to cock and clit. It was a meeting, of sorts. The running commentary in Ava's brain switched off, and every cell in her body was switched on. Divine Damian indeed.

'Let's take a good look at you,' he said, spreading her legs wide open.

Ava suddenly felt vulnerable, but she complied. She extended her legs out and lay spreadeagled, as he gently stroked her inner thighs and then lightly flicked his tongue across her pussy. Ava felt her body tense and excited, aching for release. Damian was not quite looking into her soul, but it was a moment of deep intimacy mixed with pure exhibitionism.

'Touch yourself,' he ordered. 'I want to watch you come.'

Ava did as she was told, closing her eyes and concentrating solely on her own pleasure. She slid her fingers over her wetness, electrified that Damian was watching her, his erection growing bigger and harder. He leaned over and kissed her, then put his finger over hers and took over, rubbing her clit, just as she had. Ava let herself go and gave into the waves of bliss that gushed through her, and she came with a groan.

'Good girl, Ava. That's my girl,' he said as he rolled on top of her.

Ava felt his cock, larger than ever, throbbing on her abdomen.

'I want to plunge my cock deep inside,' he said.

'Sorry, Damian,' murmured Ava, with that tiny fragment of her brain with which she could still register some modicum of reason. 'Anything you want, but not inside.'

'Are you sure? Take a look, Ava. Look at my big, hard cock. Look how much I want you.'

Ava admired Damian's enticing cock and hesitated. She knew exactly where to draw the line: at full penetration. If he did not come inside her, she convinced herself it was not full, 'proper' sex, and she could still think of herself as a 'good girl'. She preferred to dabble at the opening, rather than allow complete, unfettered access. There was no upside whatsoever to engaging any deeper, unless it was a man with potential to become a serious long-term lover.

Delicious as he was, Ava was unable to fool herself into thinking that Damian was a viable proposition. He was a will-o'-the-wisp, impossible to grab hold of; a man who floated through life in a state of ironic detachment. That was part of his appeal, and also, ultimately, his undoing.

They kissed again, and Damian slipped his cock back and forth over her wet pussy. They were both breathless and on the cusp of orgasm. Ava moved on top, and Damian deftly slid under her, licking her clit from underneath. She fondled her nipples as he slid his tongue deep into her vulva, and she watched him pleasure her. He licked her slowly at first, rhythmically, then faster and more relentlessly and she lost all sense of self. She flung her head back and came again noisily, with abandon. She laughed out loud, with the pure joy of being orgasmic and alive. So, this was it: bigger, stronger, enhanced, blended and multiple.

Then Ava took charge and began to lick and massage Damian's balls and then suck his big, slick shaft. She took her time teasing him, focusing on the underside, just below the head. She looked up into his eyes and smiled. She was enjoying this as much as he was. And seeing how turned on she was, Damian was even more turned on.

'You do that so well, baby. You're the best,' Damian moaned as he came in her mouth. 'They don't make them like you anymore.'

Ava lay naked in his arms, blissed out.

'How did you learn to do that? Where did you learn how to move like that? You're so feline, in perfect balance between a Bengal tiger and a pussy cat.' Damian beamed with pleasure as he stroked the length of Ava's curves.

Ava felt like the cat who had licked the tastiest cream. Perhaps because she just had.

'Let's get married now. It doesn't get better than this,' he said.

For one deliriously happy nano-second, Ava imagined Damian was being serious.

~ 14. ~

Justice? What Justice?

'You're our bestest, Mama. I'm so glad you're our Mama,' Khassya said, hugging her mother close.

'You're my bestest girls. I love you both so much. More than anything,' Ava said. 'I live you.' She loved her girls so much, she didn't just love them, she lived them. Living and loving were interchangeable verbs between Ava and her daughters.

Ava was lying on the silky cream carpet in her dressing room, with Sasha wrapped under one arm and Khassya under the other. It was a moment of utter bliss, and she breathed in pure happiness, as she always did when she was with her children. She kissed each girl in turn on the top of the head, inhaling the scent of their sweet essences mixed with fresh shampoo, and she squeezed them tightly. They were already sixteen and seventeen, and yet for all three of them, this was one of the best moments of the day. Laughing, talking, joking, cuddling, trying on their mother's clothes in her extensive walk-in wardrobe. It was a time for girly frivolity and for the deepest of discussions. But mostly, it was a time for love and loving, in a state of heavenly grace.

'How was your evening, my darlings?' Ava asked.

'It was cool,' Sasha said. 'Alex invited me to join him and his family at their place in Provence over the summer. Can I go, please, Mama?'

'Of course. Sounds like things are getting serious between you two.'

'Mmm, yes, I think so,' Sasha replied. 'Alex is great. He's so peng. And he's totally there for me. I can rely on him, you know?'

Ava didn't know what it felt like to have a man to rely on, but she nodded. 'I'm so pleased, my angel. That's just as it should be.'

'You and Alex, I ship it,' Khassya said. The girls were very close, with no trace of competition between them.

'How about you, Khassya?'

'Ilia's parents' housewarming was cool. Best sushi ever,' Khassya said. 'But Ilia's sister's not doing great. She's down to forty-five kilos and back in the Priory. She fell off the wagon and went straight on the coke and booze again.'

Every parent's worst nightmare. Ava shuddered and held her girls more tightly.

'Ilia barely saw his parents when he was growing up; they were never home. He coped okay, but his sister, well, she got in with a bad crowd and went off the rails.'

All three fell silent.

'You know, Mama,' Sasha said, 'Khassya and I are so lucky. We have an incredible life. All thanks to you. We're not even twenty, and you've taken us on the best holidays to the best places. But you know, what we appreciate the most is that you're always here for us.'

'You give us the most important thing of all: love,' Khassya added.

'I love you both so much. I would do anything for you girls. Anything.' Ava never tired of telling her daughters how much she loved them, and the girls never tired of hearing it. There was no need to say more: the circle of love was palpable.

'What about you, Mama?' Sasha asked. 'How was your evening? Quiet night in?'

'Er, no, not exactly,' Ava answered, trying to sound light and airy. 'A friend swung by. It was, er, interesting. Yes, interesting.'

Sasha and Khassya knew by now that meant hot male action.

'Uh-oh. Who was it?' Sasha said.

'Just a guy I met at 5H a few weeks ago. Turns out he was at school with Hugo. A bit older. He's called Damian,' Ava said breezily.

'Is he single? Is he emotionally available?' Khassya asked.

'Is he kind, Mama?' said Sasha.

Ava felt there was something intrinsically wrong here with the direction of the flow of questions. She should be the one worrying about the suitability of her children's boyfriends, not the other way round. 'Well, he's single,' she said. 'That's a good start, I guess. But he's been famously single for twenty years, which isn't a great sign. Who knows, my darlings? It's too early to say. All I know is, he's a tall and smart Etonian with blue eyes.'

'Mama!' both girls cried out in unison, with a groan and a theatrical eye-roll.

'We're worried about you,' Sasha said. 'All those guys. They all look the same. They all sound the same. They even all went to the same school. It's like Groundhog Day: the same thing, over and over again. We don't want you to end up alone.'

There it was again. That word.

Alone.

This was a familiar conversation. They were saved from rehashing it by the ring of the front doorbell. It was Jake, coming to take the girls out.

Ava got up, smoothed her hair and looked out of the window. There he was, with his silver-blue convertible vintage Bentley, handsomer than ever. His Latvian fiancée was sitting in the front seat, pouting and taking selfies of herself from different angles, admiring her new nose job and posting on the Gram.

'What do you see in her, Jake?' Ava asked him.

Aside from them both being female and blonde, Ava could not think of one thing they had in common. Maybe that was it. Jake's new partner was the anti-Ava, as different from Ava as she could possibly be.

'Well, she worships me,' Jake said. 'And I like that.'

It was that simple.

He was still unable to look Ava in the eye and his gaze settled five centimetres above her head.

'I get it, Jake. I really do. Everyone likes to be worshipped.' Ava smiled. 'But tell me,' she added, her eyes narrowing, 'what does your girlfriend actually do all day long?'

'Well, she bakes cakes, and she walks the dog,' Jake said, without a trace of irony.

Ava took a deep breath. Now might be a good time to go into one of those meditative states of extreme relaxation and a Zen manifestation of universal love that she always meant to try: anything so as not to betray a trace of her anguish.

Jake was worshipped and happy. Ava was alone and sad, *still* single.

Where was divine retribution when she needed it most?

15.

The Circle of Enlightenment, Mayfair Style

So much for the paperless new world, Ava thought as she collected her post. There, in among the usual set of bills, the latest *Economist* and a multitude of fliers from overzealous real estate agents, massage therapists and window cleaners, was an intriguing pink envelope. She opened it and read the enclosed pink letter immediately.

Dear ceremony friends,
I am delighted to invite you to Marie-Zephyrine's thirtieth birthday party on 2nd June 2021 @ 7.30 p.m.
    This is a very special occasion, and we would like to share the planning and structure with you.
    Please read the plan and look at the list of things to bring. The aim is for the ceremony to last around two hours, then have food and drinks.

The theme is a birthday celebration of life, with Marie-Zephyrine's close girlfriends gathering to focus on creating a ceremony to bring joy and blessings and to connect to her inner spiritual world.

Items to gather:

- *gong, guitar, drum*
- *everyone bring a mat to lie on*
- *crown or wreath*
- *bowl of rose water*
- *everyone to make a small gift or draw something (separate from the actual present) that represents what you would like to wish Marie as she reaches thirty (love, inner peace, success, healing, etc.)*
- *does anyone have a song or poem or something they would like to creatively share?*
- *candles for room and shrine*
- *petals: real or silk*
- *bring a shaker or rattle instrument for the chanting and singing*

Structure: arrivals 7.30–8 p.m.

- *space set up: chair, throne, bowl, blessed water, petals*
- *Marie goes outdoors, we call her in with a chant and make a bridge-tunnel, symbolising her passing into a new phase that we are greeting her into.*
- *Marie sits on the throne.*

> – *who is willing to give her a foot massage or hand massage?*

We will make a circle around her and chant simple chants. We will throw petals and move in and out of the circle of enlightenment.
Then lying down for gong bath.
Dancing to music, casual socialising, drinks and food.
I look forward to meeting you all.
Many thanks and blessings into your beautiful hearts,

Siri Bhakruvana Singh
P.S. I accept your generous donations to my special children's charity in Malawi. Cash or credit card is good.

At first, Ava wondered if the invitation was a spoof.

She had met Marie-Zephyrine a few years ago at a cocktail party at the French embassy, and she was instantly mesmerised by the perfection of her glacial beauty. They were not particularly close, but they shared a love of French literature and they traded gossip about the hot French men they knew in London. Helpfully, Marie-Zephyrine and Ava liked opposite types. While Ava favoured tall, cool blue-eyed blonds, Marie-Zephyrine, for all her elegance and poise, had a penchant for short, loud and hairy Middle Eastern types who oozed warmth and a vigorous appetite for life. It was fun to go out with her from time to time because she was worldly-wise and beautiful, and they never competed for the same men.

Ava normally dodged these all-female spiritual gatherings. No, she did not need to 'allow vibrational energy to open her heart and germinate the inner seeds of love'. Nor was she particularly keen to 'experience a meditative acoustic experience to explore her inner world'. And did she care to hear 'the healing sounds cascading into an endless, seamless seascape, soothing the body and relaxing the mind'? No, thank you. She knew that these fashionable forays into the metaphysical realm filled a void in the lives of the lunching ladies of Mayfair that a new pair of designer shoes might not. After all, how often can you get your nails and hair done? And how many times a week can you nibble on sushi and feast on chit-chat? Quite a few, as it happened. But a birthday ceremony to honour the flowering of Marie-Zephyrine's inner sacred blossoming as she turned thirty? Again? Ava had already attended her last lavish thirtieth birthday bash, held at her then boyfriend's palatial property in Saint-Jean-Cap-Ferrat in the South of France, a good five years ago.

Nevertheless, Marie-Zephyrine called her and insisted she attend. She promised Ava a 'celebration in grace, joy and pure love with other amazing women'. It would be a 'chance to align herself to her inner truth' and to 'feel the blessings of the universe'. How could Ava resist the irresistible? In a moment of exceptional weakness, she even thought she might volunteer herself to give Marie-Zephyrine a foot massage.

On the day of the birthday blessing, Ava thought she might cry off with suspiciously flu-like symptoms, or perhaps she might have missed the last flight back to London from Timbuktu or some other far-flung location. But no, there was no way out. She showered and psyched herself up for the dark night of her soul to rise up into the light.

She slipped on a pair of navy capri pants, a cream silk shirt and high-heeled Chanel sandals. She imagined she might have to spend most of the evening sitting cross-legged and barefoot, so a dress was most definitely out. Luckily, she had just got her own pedicure: Chanel Rouge Noir, of course.

Ava was usually punctual but somehow, that night, she dawdled and arrived late. Twenty other women were already seated in a circle on an exquisite Persian rug, all facing Siri Bhakruvana Singh. Ava hurried in, flustered, and put her bag and Marie-Zephyrine's present, a copy of *The Art of Happiness*, personally signed by the Dalai Lama himself, down on the onyx side table. The table was carefully crammed with photos of Marie-Zephyrine looking regal in signature grey Dior, towering over Emmanuel Macron; Marie-Zephyrine, immaculate in a black Givenchy halter-neck dress, deep in conversation with Bernard Arnault; and Marie-Zephyrine, smiling in a white one-shoulder Eres swimsuit, draped around a rotund and merry-looking Gérard Depardieu.

Ava squeezed in, apologising profusely and trying to cause as little disruption as possible as she found a space to sit. She took a deep breath and looked around the plush Mayfair room, with its gilded French antiques, Buddha statues and rose-quartz healing crystals. The other women were already in a trance-like state, eyes half closed and holding hands.

Contrary to what her Indian name might suggest, Siri Bhakruvana Singh was a chubby middle-aged Brummie in a pink turban and matching sari. She strummed a guitar and tried to sing, as the women swayed from side to side. Then came the moment they had all been waiting for: she shook her tambourine and started the blessing. The women listened in rapt attention. Ava wondered how she would make it through the evening. Why, oh why, had she not downed a shot or three of vodka before coming out?

'Let me invoke the spirit of goddess Shakti, the sacred essence of womanhood and the primordial cosmic energy of fertility and the doer warrior,' intoned Siri Bhakruvana Singh. 'Shakti. She is the dynamic force. Shshshshsshaaaaaaaktii. The essence of the devotional and the force of the universe herself. Shakti. The forcefield. Shakti the creator. Shaktiiiiiii. Mother Earth. You wonderful goddesses are here in this earthly room with me.'

Siri Bhakruvana Singh looked at each of the women in the room in turn, with a loving gaze. 'You goddesses. We transcend time and space. Let us share some devotional mantras. Let me guide you into the vibrational frequency of Gaia. Our divine and holy juices flowing out of our sacral centres. Feel your vulvas. Feel the divine spirit and the life-giving force. Let us feel and join our oestrogenic powers and come together. The warrior and the devotional. Do you feel the ethereal forces of our sisterhood? Tell me that you feel it. Show me that you feel the vibrations. The whole planet is vibrational. You are vibrational. Let us chant these mantras. Let the world hear our feminine roars. Roaaaaaaaaaaaar. Remember Shakti. Let us be together as one and ascend to the higher being.'

Siri Bhakruvana Singh invited all the women to stand and dance the 'fusion dance'. Ava anxiously looked for a place to hide.

'Feel the healing love. Bountiful and beautiful. Move your centre of creativity. Soften your belly. Keep moving. Aaaaaaaahhhhhh. Just reach up. Aaaaaaaahhhhhh. All together now. Come back to the tree. I am a tree. Floating in the breeze. Rooted in the earth. Come and soften through your shoulder blades and your beautiful body. Breathe and feel the soles of your feet. Reach up from the earth. From the root chakra to the crown. And now swoop down. Aaaaaaaahhhhhh. Bring the earth to heaven. Opening. Softening. Through the stability of the core. Stay close together. Pubic bones forwards. Sway to the music. The vibration of Mother Earth. Shake and thrust your pelvis. Flow with the breath. Forwards. And back. Feel the dynamic, vibrational force field. Everyone together. Let's mingle. Feel every cell in your body dancing in full alignment to the universe.'

Ava wondered if someone had laced her elderflower and rose water drink with acid. Was she tripping? Who were these goggle-eyed women with bouncy curls, weighed down by Cartier love bracelets and hand-of-Hamsa pendants covered in sapphires and diamonds? Why were they waving their arms wildly in the air, chanting, 'Contemplate the divine power of the sun, and may the light illuminate the path to true yonic love'?

Ava suspected she could not spend one more minute in the 'dance to awaken her deepest consciousness and loving spirit'. She made a quick dash for the kitchen, where she managed to locate a proper drink.

'Amaaaaaaaaazing, isn't it? So powerrrrrful? You feeling the love?'

A statuesque woman with piercing purple eyes and a strong Russian accent, who introduced herself as Olga, also thought that a glass of Ruinart might enhance the mind-expanding experience.

'I starrrting underrrrrrstanding my true "Dharma". You agrrrrrrree?'

Ava begged to differ, but she did not care to interrupt Olga's flow of expanded consciousness. In any event, Olga did not pause long enough to give Ava the opportunity to do so.

'I feeling everrrrrrry cell in my body. I opening to love and love in the univerrrrrrrse. The breath work is amaaaaaazing. Like soul cycling class at the KX gym. My vibrrrrational enerrrrgy is so high. I feeling my aurrrrrra five metres high.'

Olga took another gulp of champagne. Ava wondered how many glasses she had already had.

'I is so connection. Connection to verrrry much bigger than me. Siri Bhakruvana Singh, she change my life. Her pranayama save my soul and heal my hearrrt chakrrra. She like gift from universe. She light. She teaching me to stopping everrrything not help me evolving. Is same for you?'

Ava glanced at her limited-edition Rolex, her diamond Bulgari Serpenti necklace and her perfectly cut YSL jeans. There was no point responding.

'We don't have this in Siberrrria, where I from,' Olga continued. 'In Siberrrria is very dark and is very pain.'

Ava was starting to feel the pain too.

Siri Bhakruvana Singh sounded the gong.

That was Ava's cue to slip away quietly, unnoticed. She wondered what the evening of spiritual awakening with Siri Bhakruvana Singh had cost Marie-Zephyrine. Probably enough to save quite a few malnourished Malawi babies. And perhaps save the starved souls of some ladies of Mayfair too.

16.

A First Time for Everything

'Don't we know each other? I keep seeing your face all round Mayfair.'

Ava was bent over her shoelaces, posterior in the air, in her tiniest black running shorts and a tight black tank top. She doubted anyone could see her face right now. She pulled herself up and smoothed her ponytail. Of all the times, in all of town, did this man really have to come over and talk to her now, after a sweaty run, with not a scrap of make-up on and in her trainers, to boot?

Ava recognised his face from around W1 too. It was hard to forget his striking appearance and dashing demeanour. He was the epitome of conventional masculine beauty: tall, dark and handsome. He looked like he was descended from a long line of Greek gods who spent their days basking in the sun in a loincloth, and their nights cavorting with a multitude of fair adoring goddesses. He was precisely the breed Ava actively avoided. The kind of man about whose vanity pop songs are written. A man who changes his women at the same rate as he changes his shirts. A wolf in wolf's clothing, and proudly so.

'My name is Angelos,' he said. 'It's Greek for angel.' He raised his eyebrows and grinned.

Ava wondered if he was being facetious, or if he thought she was just a dumb blonde.

He launched into his potted résumé, though Ava hadn't asked. He was an Ivy League-educated investment banker who now worked for a pukka mergers and acquisitions boutique in the City. He liked to spend his winters skiing in Gstaad and his summers in Mykonos, where his family had a large beach villa and a boat. He looked too languorously predatory, too lazy, to pursue a woman. After all, there was no need: they flocked to him in large numbers. In two minutes, Ava concluded he was a total waste of time for her and for any other sane woman with an ounce of dignity and self-respect. Plus, she guessed he was about eight years younger than her.

She had read somewhere that an acceptable age gap was half your own age plus seven years. On the basis of that rather dubious heuristic, he was okay-ish. But Ava suspected this rule of thumb was only relevant to males and their younger female conquests. It did not seem to apply to cougars and their younger male lovers, a relationship that always gives off a whiff of impropriety, however attractive and youthful-looking the cougar might be.

Caveats aside, Angelos seemed harmless enough. They exchanged phone numbers and he started to message her. He was fun and light, and he was not inordinately focused on taking her to bed, which was a sensible tactic. But he addressed her interchangeably as 'angel', 'beauty' and 'baby'; these intimate and loving terms of endearment formed part of his standard vocabulary. Even though she knew this, Ava was touched when he addressed her so tenderly. However, it was his addition of the possessive pronoun, 'my', that utterly disarmed her. Clearly, she was not his, but like all strong women, she secretly yearned for a man who was stronger than her and to whom she was bonded. It gave her a sense of belonging.

Angelos invited Ava to a party he was hosting at the elegant private members' club Mark's Club. She rocked up unusually late, three hours late in fact, as she had been to a dull dinner party beforehand. She found him almost feverishly awaiting her arrival. She walked onto the garden roof terrace wearing a tight, strapless black Dolce & Gabbana dress and six-inch lace-up gladiator heels and armed with her best smile. This was a duel for which she came fully prepared with all the weapons she could muster.

Angelos immediately swooped in on her and presented her to his friends. They already knew quite a bit about her.

'This is Ava,' he gushed. 'She's a ten out of ten on everything.'

High praise indeed, especially coming from this gorgeous specimen. Ava was taken aback and blushed. They barely knew each other. He grabbed her hand and he continued to hold it as they stood in the middle of the room, chatting.

'You're beautiful,' he said, stroking her neck.

Suddenly, with no preamble, Angelos bent down and kissed her full on the lips, in front of all the party guests. Deeply. Hungrily. Carnivorously. It was a bold, disarming move. But a winning one, somehow. He pulled her closer to him, towering over her. Ava succumbed, wordlessly. She hated kissing in public, and she hated even more that this was how their first kiss played out, in front of all his friends. But nobody was paying attention, and the kiss was so good, she reciprocated passionately.

Angelos lifted her hair and kissed the nape of her neck, running his finger along the length of her bare shoulders. The man could be tender too.

Then he took his phone out. What was he typing? Who could he be texting now, of all moments? Before she knew it, he had ordered a taxi.

He turned to a petite voluptuous blonde, with a short, sleek bob, big kohl-rimmed eyes and full lips. 'Ava, this is Daria, one of my oldest friends. Daria is your exact opposite. She's not a mother. She's not a businesswoman. She's a terrific interior designer. But both of you, hey, you're both super-sexy.' He gestured a curvy figure with a smile.

Daria began to talk to Ava, intrigued. She mentioned that Ava was different to the other women that usually thronged around Angelos; she was more self-contained and aloof. Ava remained quiet as Daria admitted that she and Angelos had been lovers a few years back, and he had broken her heart.

'But is cool now. We friends. Angelos, he good guy. Whoever get him, she lucky lady. He very good lover. Very good,' Daria said with a heavy Greek accent and a broad smile.

Ava was touched at her openness and her warmth. Having got that confession out of the way, the two women gossiped about London, and life as a single woman about town. It was a familiar refrain: how to be a hot girl, and how to get a hot guy. Seamlessly, they moved on to closely related themes.

'My lips. They real,' Daria volunteered proudly. 'And my breasts. They real too,' she added, squeezing her generous bosom.

It was good to know that there were still good-looking women in London who had not succumbed to trout pout or bolt-on boobs.

Angelos motioned that the car had arrived and all three headed out together.

'Oh, hi! Angelos! Sugar-pie,' squealed a pretty young platinum-blonde in a skimpy red satin slip dress. It was more nightie than cocktail gown, but she looked fresh and lovely in it. She leaned over the balustrade and looked down at Angelos, one level down, pushing her breasts together. 'Where've you been hiding all night? I've been looking for you everywhere. Are you guys heading to Annabel's? Guess what? So are we. See you later, alligator.'

'Ingrid, is that you?' answered Angelos, squinting as he looked up.

It was definitely time for him to get his contact lens prescription checked. The many blondes in his life were all beginning to look the same.

'Text me,' he said vaguely.

Angelos, Ava and Daria piled into the back of the waiting midnight-blue BMW, all three giggling and in high spirits. They arrived at Angelos's plush Kensington pad, and Daria and Ava sat on the edge of his buttery black leather Mies van der Rohe daybed.

'You so gorgeous,' Daria said, looking straight into Ava's eyes.

Ava was flattered. Compliments were so much more meaningful coming from another woman, particularly one as stunning as Daria.

'Your eyes, they so green. You got great body and face of angel.'

To Ava's surprise, Daria gently pulled a wisp of her hair back and kissed her softly, a tinge of smoke on her breath.

Ava was thoroughly heterosexual: no fluidity there at all. She loved to be penetrated by a man: the feel of a man's cock driving hard and deep inside her; the weight of his masculinity on top of her soft, yielding female curves; the sweetly tangy smell of his crotch and armpits. But women, that was definitely not her thing. Not at all. Not remotely. Women were not the yin to her yang. There was no powerful thrusting phallus to fill her hole and make her whole.

That said, Daria's kiss was unexpectedly sensual and soft, and Ava found herself tingling in response. In that split second, she decided to go with the flow.

Angelos streamed some Cigarettes After Sex: appropriate for the seductive, sophisticated mood. He shimmied across the room, holding two perfectly chilled crystal flutes of Ruinart Blanc de Blancs and handed them to Ava and Daria. His bachelor pad was 007 sleek and aggressively modern. The space was all smooth marble and reflective surfaces, but the fur throws, the plush velvet sofas and the monogrammed vicuña pillows added warmth and invited lounging. In the dim glow, Ava spotted a signature ultramarine blue Yves Klein, pure abstract colour freed from form, and a searingly powerful Soulages Outrenoir, beyond black. She wished she could spend more time looking at the art, but now was not the time.

Angelos came over and squeezed in between the two women on the couch. He kissed Ava again on the mouth, this time harder and more urgently, and he playfully bit her lower lip. Daria stepped out of her white dress and stripped down to her white lacy thong and high heels. Her body was tanned and curvy, and she smiled, looking back over her shoulder as she peeled off her clothes. She strutted over to the long blue lapis lazuli marble table and lay down, spreading her legs out wide for her audience. She parted her panties to one side and started to touch herself, slowly, absorbed in her own desire.

Ava watched, mesmerised. She took a sip of her Ruinart, and then another, turning to see Angelos watching her, the hint of a smirk on his lips.

It was now or never.

Barely recognising herself, she slipped off her own dress and went over to Daria, as Angelos looked on, drinking his champagne. She kissed Daria again, then licked her small erect nipples, before whipping off her thong and throwing it over in Angelos's direction. She knelt down and began to stroke Daria's hairless pussy with a soft, delicate touch. It felt at once familiar, but also strange and alien. She was on autopilot: sensing, not thinking. Her only emotion was pure unbridled lust laced with adventure and excitement.

Ava continued to tease Daria, then glanced back at Angelos again. His eyes were dark with desire. She turned and opened Daria's pink, fleshy lips. Ava's eyes widened as she felt Daria's hardening clit, her fingers circling it, lightly and slowly at first, then more vigorously. Daria smiled and moaned, her eyes half closed, lost in herself. Ava smiled back and bent down to lick Daria's clit with long, smooth strokes. Daria tasted fresh and clean, and she had a tight, neat, designer-look pussy that definitely looked like it'd had some work done to it, even if her breasts and lips apparently did not. Ava ventured further and inserted one, then two fingers into Daria's pussy, pushing them in and out, in and out. Daria moaned some more, wriggling in ecstasy.

Intuitively, Ava knew exactly what to do. She pleasured Daria as she wanted to be pleasured herself. Going down on her was surprisingly the same as going down on a man: she followed her own line of desire, the direction in which her own lips and tongue led her, but she also sensed Daria, her groans, her shortening breath, the tensing of her muscles, the tightening clench of her hand. She was surprised it was not such an adjustment. After being exclusively with men, in that moment, it felt thrilling to be with a woman and she relished pushing her boundaries. It felt good to go wild. Daria groaned and arched her back, all soft, yielding curves. Ava was giddy with the sheer eroticism of the transgressive scene. The two blondes, both naked and still in their ultra-high heels, looked like they were in the middle of a particularly racy Helmut Newton photoshoot.

Angelos finished his glass and got up to join them. He smacked, then bit Ava's buttocks, as she bent over Daria. Then he leaned down and turned her over to face him. Effortlessly, he lifted her as she wrapped her legs around his torso, and they kissed. She held him tight and rubbed her pussy rhythmically up and down Angelo's smooth abdomen, feeling herself getting even wetter with the stimulating friction.

'You're delicious, Angelos,' said Ava, as she kissed him again.

'I'm here to provide you with much deliciousness, my princess,' he responded.

Daria was right. He was a skilled, experienced lover who knew when and how to be gentle, and when and how to be rough. He laid her back down on the table, stroked her breasts and the curve of her hips and then licked her nipples, teasing them with his tongue. Daria had moved aside to accommodate them, and Ava took her hand and licked and sucked her fingers, while Angelos moved down to Ava's engorged vulva and started to stroke it, and he knew just how. Then he began to lick and suck, patiently feeling her, focused only on satisfying her, surprisingly inattentive to the fire burning in his own loins.

'Angelos,' she whispered breathlessly, 'don't stop. You do that so well. I'm on the edge. I'm about to come.'

She felt herself tense, then explode and melt in waves of pleasure. By now, his cock was rock hard and throbbing urgently. He began to masturbate. Ava lay on her haunches and watched, enthralled. He really was a beautiful specimen. Long, lean and muscular, he had also won in the genetic lottery of cocks: his was long like his body, but wide too, and pointed straight up to true north. He half smiled as he moved his fist up and down his cock with a firm grip, slowly at first, then faster and faster.

He was now ready to penetrate her, but Ava stopped him. She did not want him inside her, not even the famous little two centimetres. If she was going to fuck him, it would be when she knew him properly and without the delicious Daria, however delicious she might be. As it was, there was so much deliciousness all around, it was hard to maintain her self-control. It was certainly hard for Angelos. He continued to masturbate as he watched Ava turn back and straddle Daria's face. Daria parted Ava's soft thighs and licked her relentlessly, savouring every lick. Ava let herself go completely and came again with a loud moan. She kissed Daria and tasted herself on her lips as both women giggled with joy.

At last, they were ready to turn their attention to Angelos. They slid off the table and started licking his cock, together, one blonde on each side, as he looked down at them and stroked their hair. Daria licked and sucked his balls, as Ava focused on the frenulum and his slick shaft. By this point Angelos was incapable of thinking much, but when he did, he wished he had videoed this particularly exciting session on his iPhone.

He guided Daria onto the table, and she eased herself back down. He reached for a brightly coloured condom in a large bowl, conveniently placed on the mahogany sideboard, and he began to fuck Daria hard. As he did so, he held Ava close, and kissed her.

'Kiss me, baby. Kiss me. It's all about you, Ava. Only you. I'm just fuckin' Daria, but I'm imagining I'm inside of you. It's you I want.'

He continued to thrust deep inside Daria, his muscular buttocks like steel pistons, as he kissed Ava. Then, with no warning whatsoever, Daria squirted everywhere. There was no sign of an orgasm, no theatrical cries of pleasure and no tensing of the body, only a torrent of colourless, odourless, non-urine-like liquid that gushed out of her.

Ava was slightly unnerved. It was not, to her, the height of erotica, but everyone else in the room seemed pleased with the proceedings. Daria slid off the table and scuttled off to the kitchen to get a cloth and disinfectant. From the sublime to the less than sublime, with a shot of

Dettol. This was clearly a party trick she had performed in this apartment before, because she knew where the post-squirt cleaning apparatus was stored. It was lucky the table and the floors were all marble. Ava wondered, idly, if squirting stains. Judging by the pristine state of the furniture and the floors, she suspected not.

The night had been sensational: a night of sensations. But it was a one-off and Ava knew she would never want another threesome.

Angelos called her the next day. 'My angel, I think you left your diamond earring at my house last night. If you want it back, you're gonna have to win it.'

'Oh gosh, Angelos, yes,' Ava said. 'I was going to call you to see if you had it. It must have, er, fallen off, in the, er, course of the evening.'

She never lost anything, and she was annoyed with herself for having carelessly let the earring drop off. She knew this was a classic tactic some women used to ensure they would see a man for a second date. Ava was even more irritated at Angelos's cheeky request. She decided to humour him and go along with his little game.

'Tell me, Angelos. What do I need to do to win my earring back?'

'Baby. I'll come over to your place next week. I'll tell you in person.'

When Angelos arrived at Ava's house, she barely recognised him. He was hardly the same flamboyant sex god of last week. He was wearing another immaculately tailored suit, but tonight he looked dishevelled and stressed, and his horn-rimmed glasses obscured his naughty green eyes. His shirt was hanging out the back of his trousers and he was even slimmer, as if he had not eaten a proper meal in days. He reached inside his jacket pocket and handed Ava her diamond earring, then kissed her on the mouth. Ava poured a couple of generous vodkas and they went to sit on the sofa in the living room.

'It's been rough in the office,' he said. 'There's been a new round of redundancies in the bank, and I've had to fire twenty people, including my old boss, a lovely Greek guy who knows my father. He was the man who hired me when I first joined. It was tough, man.'

'I'm sorry to hear that,' Ava said. 'I can imagine that must have been hard for you. It's quite Oedipal, having to fire the man who first employed you.'

'It was.' Angelos downed the vodka in one and looked at her. 'You're quite the psychology expert, aren't you?' he said, smiling for the first time that evening. 'You're so interesting. There's so much more to you than meets the eye. And there's a lot that meets the eye.'

'I was in banking and finance for many years,' Ava replied, too embarrassed to acknowledge the compliment. 'I know that world well. It's cut-throat, ruthless. Dog eat dog; kill or be killed. But still, your colleagues, you spend a lot of time with them. You get close.' She shuffled on the sofa. 'You know, Angelos, my bottom still hurts where you bit it the other night.'

'I'm gonna have to kiss it better. Come here, my angel,' he said, as he pulled her dress up and tenderly kissed her bruised buttock.

Ava sensed he was in no mood to go any further and he gently stroked her bottom as he readjusted the back of her dress. She was relieved. His subdued, thoughtful mood matched hers.

'It's good to see you like this. Just talkin',' Angelos said.

Ava agreed. Angelos was much more interesting as a real person rather than just a sex machine. 'So, tell me a bit about yourself,' she said. It was a classic open question, but not one that one usually asked *after* the kind of night they had just spent together.

Angelos appeared fascinated by the phallic statue of Apollo on the coffee table and didn't immediately register the question. Ava poured him another vodka and couldn't help but blurt out her own assessment.

'From the outside, Angelos, it looks like you glide through life. You waft from one high to the next. Everything falls into your lap. Women, money, success. You've seen it all and you've done it all. What could the ultimate jaded playboy possibly want that he hasn't already had, many times over?'

'Ha,' said Angelos.

Ava was not far off the mark.

'Maybe, well, maybe I am a little bored, to be honest.'

'You're a man of the world, but I suspect that you've never properly connected to a woman. You've never experienced real intimacy. Ever. Women, for you, they're like a transaction: you enjoy the chase, and, er, entering, but you like to exit fast. Like one of your investment banking deals. In and out, as it were. Take your profits and run.'

'Mmm... We don't really know each other, but I think you know me well.'

'I'm not sure about that. But I know your cock,' Ava said with a laugh.

'You don't know my cock nearly as well as I'd like you to.'

'Irresistible as you are, I was restraining myself the other night. I didn't want you to come inside me. I think sex is more interesting when you know each other.'

'I agree with you. I need more than sex. I need a mind-fuck too. I do feel a kind of emptiness sometimes. You know, not many people know this about me, but I used to get panic attacks. It got so bad, I had to see a shrink. In fact, I'm still seeing him.'

Ava stared at the rumpled but beautiful male before her. Angelos? Seeing a shrink? This seasoned womaniser, an Adonis in deepest

Mayfair, suffered from panic attacks? And he cared to share that with her? Wonders will never cease.

'Sure, I can play the game. It's fun. I'm havin' a blast. But I'm not as shallow as I look. It's true, I've had many things in my life, all pretty easily. But I do work hard. I don't need to. My father made sure of that. I'm the only son. My parents adore me, and I love them. I could be goofin' off, havin' a good time. But I could never do that. I've gotta achieve something in life.'

'You're a golden boy, Angelos. I get a strong sense that underneath that seductive playboy exterior of yours, you're actually rather sweet and pure.'

'I'll take that as one of the best compliments someone has ever given me.'

'I mean it,' Ava said.

She also wanted to compliment him as a lover, but she thought better of it. She was sure many women had already praised him on that particular skill set hundreds of times before. It meant nothing to him, like water off a duck's back.

'I'll fall in love with you, babe,' Angelos said, 'you're too lovely.'

Of all the words in all the world, 'love' was the word she most longed to hear. And hearing it casually like that, even in the future tense, was confusing. She made a mental note to unhear it.

Ava did not love Angelos. She liked him, but sexy and charming as he was, she was not drawn to his energetic forcefield. He touched her clit and he made her come, but he did not touch her soul and make her heart sing. Was he too young? Too superficial? Too obviously gorgeous? Who knew? Ava certainly didn't.

Angelos had allowed her to experience something she never thought she would, and for that she was grateful. She was happy that she was still able to surprise herself, especially in the realm of sex.

Never say never.

⌒ 17. ⌒

An Angel's View: Everything, All the Time

Eager for action, hot for the game, Angelos lounged at the best table on the terrace of the Arts Club. He puffed on his fat Cohiba cigar, stretched his long legs out in front of him and coolly scanned the women in the joint. They were busy scanning him. The soft light cast a flattering glow on the glossy crowd, and the canopy of succulent plants and flowers cascaded around like a lush green oasis in deepest Mayfair. It was a Wednesday night, and perhaps he should have gone to Annabel's instead. But he had been there twice already that week and even he needed to mix things up from time to time. As an accomplished banker, he knew that diversification is an important part of any successful investment strategy.

He was sitting with his two closest and oldest friends, Spiros and Pyrrhos, all three in finance, all three transplanted from the turquoise of Athens to the grey of London. Together, they had caroused around town as the three Greek musketeers. But first Spiros, then Pyrrhos got married and Angelos, by far the best-looking of the trio, was the last laughing cavalier, still single.

Angelos winked at three young Lithuanian blondes lined up on the banquette across from him. All three smiled back. Whom to choose? Why choose one, when he could have all three, simultaneously? In any event, he would have been hard-pressed to decide. They looked like triplets: very thin, very blonde, very blue-eyed and very into him. Obviously. Who wouldn't be? With his air of cool invincibility and his penetrating green eyes, he was a babe magnet.

Although he could see the Lithuanians were chatting, he knew what they were really doing was scouring the venue for suitable targets. Their expert eyes darted around the terrace. As a sophisticated man about town who never paid for pussy, at least not directly, Angelos could tell, with a practised eye, a lady of the night from a regular gal. Mayfair was heaving with beautiful women looking for a kind and generous 'sponsor'. They wore cheap dresses, but they always accessorised them with an expensive handbag, purchased by their latest 'boyfriend'. The current bag of choice was the black quilted Chanel calfskin flap bag, with its signature gold-chain shoulder strap and double interlocked Cs. There were an unusually large number of black Chanel calfskin flap bags at the Arts Club that night.

'Man, I love blondes,' said Angelos, though he did not need to. Spiros and Pyrrhos knew his tastes well enough by now. 'I don't think I've ever had sex with a woman who wasn't blonde. Doesn't have to be a natural blonde. And usually, it ain't. But who cares? Bottle blonde is fine by me: dark blonde, peroxide blonde, silky blonde...'

Spiros and Pyrrhos both yawned, one after the other. They had seen Angelos in action a thousand times before. Meeting blondes for him wasn't so much a sport as a foregone conclusion.

'When you gonna grow up, Angie boy?' said Spiros. 'When you gonna get married, have a couple of cute kids, buy a nice house in Fulham with a little backyard? Aren't you tired of chasin' blondes all the time?'

'You're just jealous, man,' answered Angelos. 'I got time for all that other stuff. Hey, I'm livin' the dream, my friend. Why settle down and get married when there are so many beautiful women out there? Why buy the cow when you can get the milk for free? Come on, Spiros. Be honest. When was the last time you got laid?'

'Hmm. You got a point there,' Spiros said sheepishly. 'The baby was up again all last night. Alexandra, she's always too tired for sex.' He grimaced. 'And I'm beat too. Too tired to be horny. It's good to go to the office. Escape. Get some peace and quiet for a change. Have a little snooze.'

'See what I mean?' Angelos said.

He was about to regale his friends with the piquant details of his latest threesome sexploit with two beautiful blondes last weekend, but he thought better of it. What a fantasy session that had been. But they'd heard it all before. It was Angelos's standard MO.

'You're still doin' what we were doin' ten years ago, man. Haven't you moved on by now? What about having, like, a proper relationship, you know? A real connection? I never seen you in love, Angie, in all these years,' Pyrrhos said.

'Oh, come on, guys, give me a break,' Angelos said with a growl. 'Sex is sex. If I wanna connection, I got you two. Or I take my pug Constantine for a walk round the park. Constantine's great. Always happy to see me. Never nags. What's love anyway?' He tapped his hand on the side of his leg and scanned the room again for potential action. 'I don't have to connect to a woman to fuck her. Sex can be two people in a room, just trying to get happy.' He sucked on his cigar. 'Or three people, for that matter,' he added, blowing the smoke out and looking at the Lithuanians again.

Spiros and Pyrrhos barely registered Angelos's throwaway line.

The waitress came to take their drinks order. Her eyes were full of promise as she smiled at Angelos and then batted her long eyelashes at him for good measure. Angelos made a heroic effort not to flirt back; perhaps he might, later, but not now.

'Love? Sure, I know about love. Don't you remember that gorgeous Swedish chick, Ingrid, I sort of dated for a couple of months? You remember her, the tall skinny gorgeous blonde?'

Spiros and Pyrrhos nodded wearily; Ingrid did not particularly stand out from all the other tall, skinny and gorgeous blondes Angelos always dated.

'She's kinda sweet and innocent. Ticks every box. She adores me. And she's always up for sex.'

Spiros and Pyrrhos gave each other a knowing look, exasperated.

'She's so damn hot. All the guys in the room wanna bang her. I know you guys did too.' Momentarily, he looked dreamy with nostalgia, swathed in a swirl of thick white cigar smoke. A dollop of ash fell onto the crotch of his pristine navy trousers. 'And what a butt. I'm usually a tit man, but, hey, her butt's somethin' else. Like that sexy poster my uncle used to have on the wall of his john, you know: the blonde chick in a tiny white tennis skirt, with a tennis racket in one hand, and she's liftin' her skirt with the other hand to scratch her butt and she's not wearin' panties. Ingrid looks just like that, right? Smokin' fuckin' hot.'

The three men's eyes blazed.

'Remember when I took her to the Stones concert? It was lit. They played all their best oldies. The crowd went nuts. We all had those fluorescent lights, and we were dancin' and singin'. But Ingrid, she just stood there. She looked so bored. She didn't know any of the songs. I guess she is only twenty. But still, come on. It was Mick Jagger and the Stones, for Christ's sake! I would have thought she'd've known one or two of the songs. The real deal-breaker was when she asked me who Churchill was. Then I knew I had to dump her. *Kalinixta*. Goodnight and good luck, Ingrid.'

'You know, Angie boy,' Pyrrhos said. 'You gonna get old one day and you gonna be one of those sad old guys, you know, those old playboys that used to be good-looking. The ones who're past it, but they're still chasing tail. Except now they get the girls because they've got the big bucks rather than the hard dicks.'

'My dick's always hard.' Angelos smirked, patting his crotch. It was only then that he noticed the splodge of ash. He scowled and flicked it off. 'I'll settle down one day. Sure, I will. But I got time for that. Plenty of time. Not now. Of course, I wanna fall in love. I gotta meet the perfect one first.'

'Angie. You've met a hundred perfect ones,' Spiros said. 'You spoiled. Too much choice.'

Angelos turned away from the Lithuanian blondes. He'd been there and done that. On repeat.

The waitress wiggled over with a full tray of drinks. Angelos took a long draw of his cigar as he thought about what his friends had said. Maybe they were right. Maybe it was time for him to get serious.

The three musketeers raised their whisky glasses.

Angelos looked his dear friends in the eye and said, 'Here's a toast to our great friendship. I love you guys; you're the best. A toast to love! In whatever form it takes.'

It had been a rough week in the office and even Angelos was tired. He wondered, for half a second, if he would ever meet the perfect one. He wiped the hint of a frown off his face, smiled broadly and started scouring the terrace for fresh blondes.

18.

Three Blondes Waiting for Godot

Only a hundred metres away from Angelos and his buddies, Ava was out drinking with two of her girlfriends.

'The bigger, the better,' Ava said.

The trio were sitting in the gleaming Hall of Mirrors in Oswald's, one of Ava's favourite Mayfair members' clubs – and a haven for wine lovers. Oswald's was a shrine to indulgence; a temple to Bacchus, encased in shimmering, antique glass and burnished gold. The mirrored glass reflected the dance of warm amber lights, and the Venetian chandeliers illuminated the grand Baroque frescos and gilt statuettes to perfection. Ava spotted David Cameron sitting at a corner table, looking trim and happy, so much more handsome in real life, quietly having dinner with his adoring wife, one of the Murdoch sons – hard to tell which one – and a glamorous, busty Elizabeth Hurley. Ava forced herself to stop staring.

Ava's girlfriends, Jeannie and Lizzie, were also single, blonde and brainy like her. All three had 'made it' in a man's world, while preserving the elegant allure of the ladies-who-lunch set, with their immaculately toned Pilates bodies and smooth, ageless faces. Jeannie was a top neuroscientist, and she was working on cutting-edge research linking depression with the trillions of microbiome in the gut. Lizzie was a barrister, one of the most respected and feared in the country, and she was famous for using her steely baby-blues and her peroxide charms to get her clients out of a tight spot.

With all that brain power around the table and fuelled by a rather special Château Cheval Blanc 2011, what were they talking about? The rise of identity politics and the decline of liberal democracy? The technicalities of carbon capture in the battle to reduce global warming? How to harness the power of AI to make the world a better place? Wrong. Completely wrong. They were discussing phalluses, and more precisely, phallus size.

'Of course, bigger is most definitely better,' Ava said. 'Everyone knows that. Any woman who says otherwise is just not being honest. Why do we always think we need to pander to the fragile male ego and lie about the importance of size? Come on, girls. Let's get real here. All that stuff we tell men that "it's not the size of the boat, it's about the motion of the ocean" – it's utter rubbish. Big dicks fill you up. There's something primal about plugging the hole and filling the gap. I'm sure it's biological, right, Jeannie?' she said.

Jeannie cleared her throat. 'Well, scientific studies show that women prefer a large, er, penis, and there are evolutionary benefits to depositing semen to the deepest parts of the, er, vagina, thereby maximising the opportunity for fertilisation.'

'Well, I never. I knew I should have paid more attention in those biology classes,' Lizzie said. 'As for you, Ava, you're impossible. I don't think you can say you prefer a big package in public nowadays. It's just not PC. I'm sure it's size discrimination, or something.'

'Well, lucky we're not in court, Lizzie. We're among friends here and I want to speak my truth freely!' Ava laughed. 'Are you saying that even sexual preference has gone woke?'

'Actually, yes. But in any event, it's so shallow of you,' Lizzie said. 'You're like the female equivalent of those guys who only date leggy young blondes with big tits. You're the same. Except you only date tall posh blokes with blue eyes and huge penises.'

'I know, I know. Tell me about it,' Ava replied. 'It kinda limits my dating pool, that's for sure: the subset of the subset. Don't tell me to change what I like. I can't. It's how I tick.'

'Well, I beg to differ,' Lizzie said, looking ravishing in her perfectly cut navy-blue Alexander McQueen pantsuit. There wasn't an inch of visible flesh, and she looked all the sexier for it. Ava thought she might need to reconsider some of her more revealing wardrobe choices. 'For the record, big penises aren't my thing at all. Men with small ones compensate in other ways. Like being good with their tongue. That's way more important to me. I mean, let's face it. Look at the stats. Fifteen per cent of women can't orgasm. And only fifteen per cent of women can come from penetration alone. That leaves seventy per cent of women who need some form of clitoral stimulation to orgasm.'

At precisely that moment, there was a lull in the conversations across the room. Everyone heard Lizzie's loud barrister's voice, and they all turned to look at her. She smiled back, angelically.

'Well, I'm in Lizzie's camp.' Jeannie nodded. 'My ex-husband was so big; it was a real problem.' She gestured with her hands a good twelve inches.

Ava widened her eyes in disbelief. She wondered if Jeannie was taking a spot of artistic licence. Twelve inches was a problem she had never experienced, but wished she had.

'Yup,' Jeannie said, quite matter-of-fact. 'You may laugh. But my ex, he was hung like a horse. Enormous. More like ginormous. It was awful. Intercourse was so painful. Just getting it in hurt. And then when it was in, when he pushed it deeper inside me, I was in agony! We tried everything: more lube, more foreplay, going super-slowly. Nothing helped. Nothing. Sometimes, I was unable to walk properly for days after we had sex.'

'Yes. I completely agree, Jeannie,' Lizzie said, straightening her back. 'It's not only penetration. It's hard to give a guy a proper blow job when he's too big. One guy I dated had a very long and wide penis. I was gagging when I tried to give him head. I felt like I was going to throw up. His penis kept hitting my tonsils and I had to stop and take breaks so I could breathe properly. And then I kept worrying about scraping my teeth on it. No surprise the poor guy couldn't come. We gave up on that, and we broke up soon after.'

'Hey-ho. Different strokes for different folks.' Ava sighed, still dreaming of twelve inches. 'But I have to say, men with small dicks are usually incredibly insecure. Did you read about that sixty-five-year-old billionaire who died on the operating table, trying to get his penis enlarged?'

'Yeah, shocking. It was on the front page of *The Times*. Must have been a slow news day,' said Lizzie. 'But have you read that woman are getting their nether regions refitted? Totally bonkers. As if it's not enough to have designer handbags and designer shoes. Now we're being shamed into thinking we need designer vaginas too.'

'Yeah, apparently it's a "thing",' Jeannie said. 'Women are getting them tucked and lasered and tightened and rejuvenated and steamed and whatnot.' The good doctor frowned. 'It seems to me we've found new ways to torture ourselves into thinking that even our foofoos need perfecting, and we apparently need yet more plastic surgery, even down there.' She gestured to her crotch area. 'It's like a higher form of self-hatred.'

Ava raised an eyebrow and made a mental note to google 'designer vagina'. She distinctly remembered the look of Daria's perfect vagina, and thought she might do a bit of investigation. It was for research purposes, clearly, not an action point.

'On one level, though, I do think we women have it easier,' Ava said.

'Oh, really?' Lizzie and Jeannie said in unison. 'How?'

'Men's genitals are so much more visible than ours. And if a guy's small, there's not much he can do about it. Going under the knife is clearly a life-threatening no-no. And God forbid if a man can't rise to the occasion; that's pretty rough too. I recently dated a guy and we tried to have sex. Except he just couldn't get it up. I tried everything. It was embarrassing. Eventually, he told me it was because he felt so close and connected to me that his energy went straight to his heart chakra and bypassed his sacrum – you know, the sexual energy chakra. So, he couldn't get a hard-on. A rather imaginative and poetic excuse, I thought.'

The girls laughed.

'Well, that's what that little blue pill's for, isn't it?' Lizzie said. 'I expect all guys over forty are popping Viagra, aren't they?'

The first bottle of Cheval Blanc had been savoured and they decided to order a second.

'So, Ava, tell me, whatever happened to that Etonian chap you were seeing?' Lizzie asked.

Ava's face fell. 'The Etonian? Which one?' she asked, trying to sound casual. 'Oh. You mean Hugo? Yes. Must be Hugo. Mmm... I had a soft spot for him. And I guess he had a hard one for me.'

There was more laughter all round.

'Hugo bit the dust,' Ava said.

'I never understood what you saw in him, aside from the fact that he went to Eton and had a few famous ancestors. He sounded a bit emotionally stunted, if you ask me.'

Ava felt a thump in her chest.

'Wasn't he the one who could never properly commit? A non-boyfriend who was always super wrapped up in himself and his boys, and who never seemed to care about you?' Lizzie's executive summary was harsh but fair. She looked at what men did, rather than what they said, and she saw who they were, rather than who one might want them to be.

'Yeah, but he was also tender and sweet, somehow,' Ava stammered. 'Made me want to take care of him.'

'Really? I thought you wanted an alpha male? Someone to take care of you, for a change?'

'Who knows? Hugo was special. The sex was amazing. Intimate and connected. Well, at least I thought so.' Ava stopped.

'Sounds like Hugo was a friend with benefits, only he wasn't really a friend,' Lizzie said.

Ava sank deeper into her chair.

'I understand, Ava,' said Jeannie, patting Ava's hand. 'I'm sorry things didn't work out for you. I know you liked him a lot.'

'Well, plenty of fish in the sea,' Lizzie said. 'You know what they say. If you can't have the one you love, love the one you're with.'

'That's impossible,' Ava said. 'I could never do that.'

At the thought of Hugo, Ava became dangerously wistful. She wondered what he was doing at the moment. He was probably sprawled out on his beaten-up sofa, trying to focus on the annual report of some company he was looking to invest in. His dog, Nelson, would be nuzzling his crotch. Lucky Nelson. Ava thought of Hugo's crotch. How many hours had she spent drooling over it in real life, versus fantasising about it in the fertile recesses of her own imagination? It was not a good equation. She felt the urge to quickly ping him a smiling photo of herself right now, accompanied by a suitably saucy message. She reached for her iPhone, rearranged her hair and got ready to take a picture, when she remembered that she had, helpfully, deleted his contact details.

She shrugged, put the phone down and looked at her friends. 'We had fun, but it just wasn't meant to be.'

Hugo? Fun? Hardly. He had now stopped texting completely and they hadn't seen each other for months. The last thing Ava wanted to do was chase after a man who didn't want her. Well, that was the idea, at least. But in reality, it never quite felt like she had that level of self-confidence, or self-restraint. If she stopped chasing, would a man ever want her enough to chase her?

'Maybe he'll pop up again at some point,' Jeannie said cheerily. 'Men usually do. And usually at the most inconvenient time. Like, when you don't want them anymore.'

'Or when you've fallen in love with someone else,' Lizzie offered.

Ava nodded, knowing in her heart that she might have to be very, very patient.

Jeannie saw the sad look in Ava's eyes and changed the topic of conversation. 'So, between us girls,' she asked, 'are you swiping? What do you think of those dating apps? I must say, I'm tempted to give it a whirl. Everyone's at it nowadays.'

'Yup. Totally.' Lizzie nodded. 'All the single barristers in my chambers are online. And come to think of it, a few of the non-single ones, too. It's just another platform for meeting men. Like an introduction service. Guys are intrinsically lazy, and they're too busy to go hunting for women in bars, and too afraid to have an affair in the office. So, they're on Tinder because it's so easy. One swipe away from a shag.'

'But what if you're not looking for a one-night stand and you want something more serious?' Jeannie asked.

'I think men want to be in a relationship as much as women. They're not good on their own,' Ava said.

'I guess. Here's hoping,' Jeannie added weakly. 'But, urgh, online dating. It feels surreal, like one of Dante's nine circles of hell. I had a little peek and, honestly, it was like trying to find the least yucky guy you could see on it. It doesn't feel natural. I'd rather meet a man organically.'

'It's the new normal, Jeannie. You've just gotta get with the programme. Did you know that Sharon Stone's on Bumble?' Ava was smiling again now, back to her bubbly self. 'Imagine. Sharon Stone, one of the sexiest, sassiest women on the planet, looking for a partner on Bumble. I saw it in the *Daily Mail*, so it must be true! Apparently Bumble cancelled her profile because they thought it had to be fake.'

'It's a numbers game,' said Lizzie. 'It's like a supermarket for men. More Tesco than Harrods. But plenty of choice.'

'What's that old joke: the odds are good, but the goods are odd,' quipped Ava.

'True, true. You've got to be patient and sift through a truckload of profiles,' Lizzie said.

'You make it sound like a job.'

'Well, in a way it is. It's the most important vacancy of your life: your partner.'

'So, what are the things to watch out for? What are the clues, Miss Marple?' asked Jeannie.

'Well, for starters, you need to be wary of the flattering profile shot taken ten years ago, minus about ten kilos and when the guy still had a full head of hair. And then there's the guy's height. Typically, a man says he's two inches taller than he really is. The worst is when the guy doesn't actually say how tall he is. That means he's really, really short.'

'Oh, Lizzie,' Jeannie said. 'It's a minefield. I'm not sure I can face it. I think I need to find myself first, before I find a guy.'

'It's the way of the world. Forty per cent of couples meet online now,' Ava said.

Jeannie sighed. 'I know I should give it a shot. It doesn't feel much like the way real love works, or at least, the way it used to work.'

'Locking eyes across a crowded room is certainly more romantic,' Ava said, 'but I'm convinced online dating can work. The men on the apps, they're like the men in real life, no better, no worse. Men are men, whether it's in cyberspace or at a party.'

It did not escape Ava's notice that the only man she had ever met on an app was the delectable Hugo. She could just as easily have met him at the school gate, as their children were at the same school. But it hadn't happened that way. In any event, the fact that she had met him through modern technology, rather than in real life, had absolutely no impact on the *dénouement*, or rather, the lack of *dénouement*, of their relationship. Once they had met, they never referred to it, not even once. Probably they were both a bit embarrassed about it. Weren't they supposed to be too sophisticated and too well connected to have to resort to a dating app?

'Okay. Let's get down to specifics here. What are you looking for, Jeannie? Who's your ideal man?' asked Lizzie.

'This man,' Jeannie said, pointing to a picture of Roger Federer smiling on the front cover of the *GQ* magazine that lay on the marble coffee table in front of them. 'He's totally my type. I sat next to him at a charity benefit dinner recently. He's so charming, so understated and one of the nicest men I ever met.'

'Hahaha. I think he's every woman's type, Jeannie,' Ava said. 'Even I would make a special exception for Federer, even if he isn't a blond, blue-eyed Etonian.'

There was more raucous laughter all round and a collective eye-roll. Ava and her type...

'Yep, for once we can all agree: Federer is the perfect male specimen. But you know, Jeannie, you might want to come back down to planet earth before you hit Bumble.'

'Speaking of hot,' Ava said, smiling broadly, 'what do you think of those three guys sitting there in the corner? Not too shabby for a Wednesday night.'

Lizzie looked across at them and held up her wine glass. 'Ladies. I'd like to propose a toast to love. And here's to each of us finding our own dream man. Whether it's on Bumble, or in real life,' she said, winking at the cute guys. 'Bottoms up!'

19.

Mind the Gap

Ava met her next boyfriend, Eren, on his hundred-and-fifty-foot super-yacht moored off the Turquoise Coast in Bodrum, the Turkish Saint-Tropez. The girls were just as alluring as their French counterparts as they danced on tables in the afternoon blaze, in skimpy designer bikinis and gold chains that sparkled around their lithe waists and slender necks. The rosé and the Ruinart flowed liberally and expensively as they celebrated the joy of life.

Ava was on a mission, a mission she accepted with zeal, to forget Hugo, to forget Harry, and to move on, once and for all. Bodrum was the ideal destination for sophisticated but uncomplicated fun, and her glamorous Turkish friends thought a change of scenery would do her the world of good. They kindly took her under their wing and brought her along to Eren's boat party.

It was a warm evening and the sun's rays scattered like streams of gold in a darkening purple sky. The cicadas were chirping, and the air was heavy with the scent of the ocean and oriental perfume. Ava dressed seductively for the occasion. She disguised her sadness by slipping into a long, floaty low-cut black chiffon Yves Saint Laurent number, with a split that ran all the way up her left thigh. She decided to go commando:

a visible panty line was never chic. She wore her hair up for a change, in a loose chignon, and she put on a diamond choker and her lucky heart chakra bracelet, which was supposed to help her get into the right vibrational frequency to attract her soulmate. The results on that were inconclusive, at best. She remembered that the last time she'd worn that dress was with Harry in St Barts. She shook her head at the memory, as though that would stop her from thinking about him.

Ava stepped onto the yacht, head high, heart heavy. The music was pumping on the upper deck, and the guests chatted and shuffled hesitantly around the dance floor. They were already five drinks in, but that was clearly not enough to loosen their inhibitions. Ava was stone-cold sober. She barely knew anyone at the party, and she did not care how ridiculous she looked by starting to dance on her own. Prince's 'Kiss' was playing. The song was over thirty-five years old, but it retained a freshness and an inviting rhythm. Ava moved slowly and languidly at first and all eyes turned on her, male and female. Even Eren's beautiful St Bernard dog began wagging his tail.

Eren stood quietly on the side, smiling, as he observed the spectacle. He felt a rush of desire as he stared at Ava, with her carnal, masculine energy and her inviting female sexuality. He sipped his whisky and crunched the ice cubes with his teeth. He was bald, with big, soft brown eyes and perfect American-style teeth. He was of medium height, but he was clearly a man who worked out, and his muscles bulged under his fitted black shirt. He was a rare breed: a shy tech billionaire whose wealth had not changed his preference for spending time alone, in serene contemplation. But tonight, Eren was in no mood to contemplate.

Ava swayed her hips and flung her head back in abandon, her eyes half closed. She was playing to the gallery and laughing at herself as she did so. It was a moment of pure freedom and unbridled joy.

Shy as he was, Eren could no longer resist. After all, it was his boat, and he was the host. He took another large sip of whisky, swayed over to Ava and started to dance with her. He was a surprisingly sensual dancer, and their bodies melded in perfect sync. He put his hand on her waist and guided her skilfully around the dance floor. She leaned into him and savoured his clean, fresh smell. She immediately recognised his aftershave, Hermès Bel Ami, beautiful friend, one of her favourites.

'Hi,' Eren said, after they had been dancing for several minutes. 'The name's Eren. I'm from Turkey. Sorry about that.' He had a deep, rich voice and a hybrid Turkish-American accent.

Ava laughed. 'Hello, Eren. What a great party! Thank you for the invitation. I'm Ava and I come from Switzerland.'

They both smiled. It was obvious they already knew each other's names, and their place of birth was perfectly irrelevant. They were simply dancing the dance.

'Actually, I love your country,' said Ava. 'I've been visiting for years. Such a rich cultural heritage; such beautiful unspoiled beaches and kind-hearted people. Shame about the government.'

Eren had his own views about the president and the subtleties of Turkish geopolitics, but he was in no mood to dampen the vigorous stirring he felt under his jeans by launching into a discussion on international affairs and realpolitik. 'Yeah, it sure is a beautiful country,' he said. 'I missed it when I lived in the Valley for so many years, but now I spend most of my time here, chillin' on the boat.'

'The Valley?' Ava asked.

'Oh, sorry, yes. Silicon Valley.'

'That must have been quite a change for you, I imagine. From the vibrant blues of Turkey to the white heat of the tech revolution.'

'Yeah, it sure was a leap.' Eren put his hand on the small of her back. 'Why don't we sit down and grab us a glass of champagne?'

They sat close to each other on the beige leather banquette.

'The US was a culture shock,' Eren said. 'I was born in a small village near Antalya, and somehow I managed to get a scholarship to Stanford. I studied engineering and computer sciences and started life as a coder. Boy, I loved it. Couldn't get enough. I used to spend hours messin' around on my computer. There weren't many of us, back in the day. Then after grad school, I started workin' out of a small garage in Silicon Valley with a couple of my college friends. And the rest, as they say, is history.'

'Impressive,' Ava said, 'especially as you must have felt like such an outsider, back then.'

'I guess we're all outsiders, one way or another.' Eren fidgeted with the clasp of his Rolex watch. 'It's part of the human condition. Feelin' alone.' He looked away and out to the ocean. 'Don't they say that love is the only cure for loneliness? That we're all searchin' for our other half: that special person that makes you feel whole, like you belong together? Plato wrote about it over two thousand years ago and Hollywood romcoms are just the modern iteration of the same idea.'

'Mmm,' she said softly, and they sat in comfortable silence.

Eren poured her some more champagne.

Ava loosened her chignon and ran her hand through her long hair. 'Will you excuse me a minute? I need to powder my nose.'

She got up and wandered below deck, looking for the loos. The interior was perfectly balanced between luxury and restraint. The living room was a symphony of whites and creams, like powdery sand, with floor-to-ceiling windows and splashes of colour from the enormous fuchsia orchid display and the Lalique crystal vases bursting with large pink roses. Ava padded down the ivory-coloured carpet and reached one of the glass doors, which opened automatically. Judging by the size of the room, she assumed it was the master suite, Eren's bedroom. The bed was strewn with velvet pillows in different shades of ivory and dressed in inviting silk sheets. Ava wondered when Eren last had a woman in it. She noticed a copy of *How to Make Someone Fall in Love with You* on top of a pile of neatly stacked books, next to a tome entitled *Strings, Conformal Fields, and M-Theory*.

When Ava returned to the upper deck, the mood had shifted, as Ava hoped, and Eren was smiling as he played with his dog, Gates.

'Your yacht is a showstopper, Eren,' Ava gushed. 'Congratulations. You've done it in exquisite taste. The cream colour scheme is so Zen and elegant.'

'Thanks, it's my haven. For many years, I felt guilty about havin' such a fancy boat. But Ömer and I, we hang out on it quite a lot.'

'Ömer?'

'Yes, Ömer, my son. He's eighteen. He's gonna be the next Roger Federer. He trains six hours a day. He's a savage on the tennis courts.'

Ava was impressed. Ambition and discipline clearly ran in the family.

'I never married,' Eren said. 'But I met a woman in Seattle. I'd been there for a few years and things were kickin'. We dated for a couple of weeks, nothing serious. We had a wild night, and I don't know how, but the condom split. You know. One of those crazy freak accidents. The proverbial black swan. A Six Sigma event. Did you know the mathematical probability of a condom breaking is less than two per cent?'

Ava raised her eyebrows. Condoms breaking? With those odds, she wondered how big he would need to be to burst one. She smiled, and Eren, perhaps reading her mind, smiled back.

'I always thought condoms inadvertently splitting was an urban myth,' Ava said. 'More like the oldest female trick in the book for male entrapment. Meal ticket for life.'

Saying that felt like a betrayal of the sisterhood, and yet Ava wondered why more women didn't choose the freedom that comes with making your own money, rather than relying on a man.

'Yeah, it's kinda sketch. I got five guy friends, and they had the exact same thing happen to them. Five! I'd get my tubes tied, but I hear it's deadass painful.' Eren winced and involuntarily touched his crotch. 'Well, it was some curve ball. But that kid, hey, he's the best thing in my life. My son's terrific. We're very tight, Ömer, Gates and me. Three boys on board.'

Eren was surprised how much he had already revealed to Ava about himself, and how easy it was to talk to her. He was usually tight-lipped and reserved.

He knew next to nothing about Ava, and he wanted to change that. A week later, he came to visit her in London. He meticulously planned an evening at the Araki, the city's most extravagant Japanese restaurant. He arrived at Ava's home bearing two dozen long-stemmed white roses, a perfectly chilled bottle of Krug and the latest Haruki Murakami book they had talked about. As Ava welcomed him into her house, she thought how cool he looked. He was not her usual type, but he looked good, with his tanned skin, his open face and his kind eyes. He wore a slouchy burgundy suede Varvatos jacket with a black T-shirt and black jeans, and a couple of suede Tateossian bracelets next to his Audemars Piguet Royal Oak Grand Complication watch. This was no standard-issue black watch with a rubber strap. But Eren carried it off with characteristic modesty.

Ava had sensed his vibe and had dressed to match in a short black leather skirt, knee-high boots and a loose white T-shirt through which you could just about make out the outline of her lacy bra. They made a handsome, well-matched couple as they walked out, hand in hand.

'You mentioned you like Japanese food,' Eren said, 'so I thought I'd take you to the best. It's a real insider's Japanese. Very cool minimalist interiors, simple wooden seats, no artwork. The restaurant only seats twelve people a night. I hope you like it.'

As they chatted, they sampled the omakase sushi tasting menu, with fifteen bite-sized courses. Delicacy followed delicacy: first the Hyogo puffer fish, then the lightly roasted Nagasaki longtooth grouper, one perfectly seared scallop, a morsel of sea urchin and a slither of raw fatty tuna, all meticulously prepared in front of them by *Itamae*, the sushi master himself, and variously accompanied with Ossetra caviar, Périgord black truffle, gold shavings, and even some humble rice. They both felt surprisingly light after such a rich feast and decided to walk back to Ava's house.

'Strange,' Ava said, as she went to open the front door. 'The door's not locked. I'm sure I locked it on our way out.'

Ava went further into the house. Something did not feel right.

'Eren,' she shrieked, as she spotted a pool of broken glass in the atrium. 'I've been burgled!'

'Don't move, Ava. Stay here. Stay right here in the living room,' Eren said, springing into action. He spotted a small white marble statue of the Greek god Apollo on the coffee table and picked it up. Ava wondered if he realised it was a priceless antique, dating from the first century BC, with its perfect phallus remarkably still intact. She was too shocked by the break-in to say anything.

'The burglars might still be here, and I need to have something to whack them with, just in case. I'm gonna go through the whole house, room by room. Whatever you do, don't move. Stay here, Ava, so I know you're safe. Don't worry, babe. I'll be right back.'

He returned five minutes later.

'The house is empty,' he said. 'I've been through every room. Just relax and lie down on the sofa. I'm gonna call the police. Come here, Ava. Baby. You're shakin'. Here. Let me cover you with a blanket.'

Eren enveloped Ava as she lay, distraught, on the couch. She could not bear to think about all the valuables that had been stolen, the safe that had been prised open and the violation of having her home robbed. She shivered under the blanket, even though the night was warm. Eren came to lie down behind her, as they waited for the police to arrive, stroking her neck and shoulders soothingly.

Imperceptibly, the comforting hug shifted. His strokes moved down Ava's back and under her T-shirt. Ava barely registered the change, until she felt Eren's hand on her bare thighs, parting her panties to the side and then gently stimulating her clit. Her body responded immediately to his touch. She was still shaking, too confused and emotional from the burglary to say or do anything. He rubbed her clit slowly, up and down, and then dipped his fingers inside her, one at a time. He withdrew them, licking them in appreciation of her light, sweet taste, then dipped them in again. She arched her back and moaned.

Eren slid off the sofa and knelt in front of her. There he parted her legs and spread them wide. He started to lick her, tantalisingly slowly at first, then harder and stronger. He was tasting her, unhurried, enjoying how wet and turned on she was. She gripped Eren's shoulders and groaned, then gave in to the mounting waves of pleasure that started in her pussy and welled up through her entire body. She came hard in his mouth with one of the strongest multiple orgasms she had ever experienced.

Precisely three seconds later, Ava's front doorbell rang. It was the police.

They say that timing is everything.

'Good evening, gentlemen,' Eren said, wiping his mouth on the back of his hand. 'Thank you for coming.'

Eren continued to court Ava in style. They spent a weekend holed up with room service in the George V in Paris; a week with Ava dressed only in a tiny gold Dior thong on Eren's yacht off the Amalfi coast; a Tuscan touring getaway in his silver open-topped Bentley GTC; and a private tour of the Hermitage Museum in St Petersburg, to coincide with the midnight sun of the Russian White Nights.

Eren was intrinsically kind, and he was motivated by a goodness that Ava had never experienced before. Ava used to think that what she wanted was a tall, charming Etonian, preferably with blue eyes. With Eren, she realised that what she really needed was a man she could admire. A man who could be trusted to 'do the right thing', whatever the circumstances. A man with a moral compass that did not point vaguely in a northerly direction, but one that was set, steadfastly, to true north. A man who would always act with principle and honour, even when no one was watching.

The human body is made of atoms that oscillate in constant motion and it sends off electromagnetic vibrational energy in infrasonic waves. Cocooned in Eren's tenderness, Ava's whole body reverberated on a new, higher frequency. She started to think that perhaps it was okay for her to be treated like a princess. While Ava felt she didn't necessarily deserve to be treated quite so well, she didn't *not* deserve it. She radiated a new light and joy.

Two thousand kilometres away, in Huntington Castle, set in acres and acres of gently undulating green fields, Harry sat in his study, looking out onto his floodlit deer park. He was formally trained as a soldier and a diplomat, and he had survived more than three assassination attempts. But what usually saved his bacon was his impeccable sixth sense. As he drank his customary lapsang souchong tea, he tuned in and felt Ava's luminous vibration beaming out. He sensed there was a new man who might, at this very moment, be supplanting him in Ava's heart and he grabbed his phone.

I'm thinking of you, my A. H. x, he texted Ava, after a year and a half of no contact whatsoever.

There were no additional words, no explanations, no excuses, and no hint that anything had changed in his life. Most of all, Harry said nothing about his wife.

Ava awoke to the buzz of her phone. She looked across the bed. Eren was fast asleep, snoring softly. She leaned across to the night table and saw Harry's message. Her heart started pounding. Maybe the man she still loved also still loved her back? Maybe, after all these months of pining and longing, Harry had finally left Araminta after all.

Ava responded. Of course she responded, immediately.

As Eren made love to her the next morning, Ava gazed into his deep brown eyes and saw only Harry's deep blue eyes. As Eren moved inside her, his body tanned and taut and muscular, she fantasised about Harry's creamy skin. It was not exactly her crowning moment, and she hated herself for it.

Who was she kidding? She wanted Harry. She wanted only Harry, not the anti-Harry. She wanted no one who looked like Harry, nor anyone who reminded her of Harry, nor even Harry minus Harry's flaws, or a new, improved Harry. Only Harry, pure Harry, unadulterated Harry. Harry, exactly as he was, would do just fine. It was Harry's body she yearned for and no other. Love is blind. Love is deaf. And love can definitely be dumb too.

'You okay, baby?' Eren said afterwards, cuddling Ava in bed, as she lay pensively on his chest.

Ava said nothing but nodded and squeezed him in response.

'I'm sorry. That wasn't my best performance. I'm a bit bent out of shape. Got a tough day ahead. A board meeting with that tech start-up. Looks like we're gonna have to get rid of the CEO.' He stroked Ava's hair. 'Are you sure you're okay? You seem a bit distant this morning.'

'I'm fine, Eren,' Ava lied. 'I didn't get much sleep last night. Sounds like you've got a tricky day ahead, darling. Let me go and make you a nice cup of tea while you relax in bed.'

She grabbed her silk robe and went to the kitchen. She stood shaking as she watched the kettle boil.

Ava wanted to fall in love with Eren. More than that, she wanted to fall out of love with Harry. Neither happened. Where was Cupid's arrow when she needed it most?

'Eren, I think we need to talk,' Ava said to Eren that night over dinner. 'I'm sorry. But I'm not over my ex-boyfriend. I think I need to take time out from us. It's not fair on you. It's best we take a break.'

Eren's mouth fell open. 'A break? You mean, you wanna call it a day? Call it quits?'

'Oh, Eren,' Ava said. 'You're such a wonderful man. You've been so good to me. It's definitely not you. It's me. You deserve someone way, way better than me.'

She gulped.

'I just... I need a bit of time and space. Sort my head out. I'm so sorry. You've been nothing but amazing and kind to me.'

'Spare me the platitudes,' Eren said, suddenly brusque. He looked blankly across the room.

They did not stay friends.

20.

Mayfair Marriage: Uncomfortably Numb

'There are only three things a man needs to lead a happy life: a good wife, a good home and a good job.'

Ava sipped a glass of vintage Perrier-Jouet Belle Époque in the grand Mayfair home of Celeste and James, her on-trend hosts. The married couple led lives of utter flawlessness. As fully paid-up members of the metropolitan elite, they were bold and they were beautiful. They lived in the right postcode, dressed in the right clothes, ate in the right restaurants and exercised their just-right bodies with the right personal trainers. James was an uber-successful venture capitalist, who manufactured money the way Toyota manufactures cars. His iron discipline was apparent from both his investment prowess and his well-honed musculature. He had a full head of hair, mysteriously still light brown even in his early fifties, with a touch of distinguished grey at the temples. And he sported New Man's ideal hair pairing: the right amount of sexy designer stubble on his chiselled jaw, matched with an impeccably waxed body, including the less visible parts. Some days, James worried that he was one of those men who had a great future behind him. But a cursory glance at his latest bank statement and at the mega-yacht he was renting this summer to waft around in the Med soon dispelled any trace of self-doubt.

Celeste was his picture-perfect match. She was a tall, pencil-thin Hitchcock peroxide blonde, whose style and immaculate good taste were legendary in all the smart dining rooms of W1 and the Saints: Jean-Cap-Ferrat, Tropez, Moritz and Barts. Come to think of it, and Celeste did, they were all the same people, migrating in reassuring rhythm through the course of the year, year after year. They were like a flock of migrating flamingos: sleek, graceful and permanently in motion, in search of the sun and each other's approval. Celeste's official calling was curating a collection of luxe dog accessories, which she sold exclusively through Harrods and by private appointment. But her real passion was perfection: it was her drug, and there were one or two others too.

Their twenty-year-old son, Tarquin, had just been snapped up by Disney to star as Prince Charming in the live-action remake of *Sleeping Beauty*, and their daughter, Talitha, was an eighteen-year-old influencer with one and a half million followers and a similar annual income. Even their velvet aubergine *devoré* wallpaper in the drawing room was officially perfect and it had its own Instagram entry under #perfectluxehome #timelessclassic #hygge #winner. James and Celeste were admired and envied in equal measure, usually by the same people.

'Yes, indeed. A good wife, a good home and a good job,' James repeated with pride. 'Women are such complex creatures with complex needs, while us men, well, we're pretty simple animals.' He grinned. 'And we've got pretty simple needs too.'

Celeste gave a thin smile. There was nothing simple whatsoever about James.

'Look at Jerry Hall,' the master of the house continued. 'What a gorgeous woman she is, even at, what is she now, sixty-five? And whip smart and funny with it too. You've got to hand it to her. She bagged not one but two billionaires. And what billionaires! Mick Jagger and Rupert Murdoch. Talk about a chameleon. What was it she famously said – that a man needs a maid in the living room, a cook in the kitchen and a whore in the bedroom?'

'Yup, and quite right too,' agreed Alistair, in his smart sapphire cufflinks and matching blue shirt that must have been bought some while back because it was gaping at the belly and was at least a size too small.

Alistair's wife had just left him for a woman, but this in no way detracted from his allure. If anything, it added to his mystique. And his portliness was in no way a bar to his dating triumphs. Women swooped down on this unattached male, new to the singles scene, like hungry vultures on a fresh carcass. Alistair worked for James, and as a favour to him, Celeste imagined he might be interested in Ava, so she sat them together. She did not know that Ava had already been introduced to him at the Cy Twombly vernissage at the Gagosian gallery earlier that week. And in a peculiar twist worthy of a Tom Stoppard farce, and a testament to the bijou world that is the minuscule Mayfair singles scene, Ava heard that Alistair's ex had recently trifled with her own ex. Ava figured she must be bisexual: not a bad plan, as it immediately doubled her dating pool. It was like a game of musical chairs and the race was on to find a new partner before all the chairs/men disappeared. No woman wanted to end up in the existential crisis that was not finding a comfy chair to sit on.

Regrettably, Alistair was not Ava's cup of tea. After a spot of obligatory chit-chat, she turned to Sebastian, the flame-haired bachelor seated to her left. Ava had fond memories of when they had been lovers for a while, back at Cambridge. It had not exactly been a meeting of souls, but their bodies had connected often, and in many interesting ways. She wondered if he remembered that time when they had enjoyed a particularly thrilling session in the crypt of King's College chapel. Their powerful orgasms had echoed under the marble vaulted ceilings and she had come so strongly that she had felt herself tripping with the dancing figures of the luminous medieval stained-glass windows.

'Oh yeah. Jerry Hall. What a woman! She knows her stuff, she does. She knows that a woman should be a woman, and a man should be a man,' Alistair said. 'Call me an old fart, but I don't understand the new dating rules anymore. The natural order is completely buggered up with all that woke stuff. Who the hell knows what gender roles are anymore? I don't think you're even allowed to call them gender roles now. It's neo-fascist, or counter-cultural, or something. Sex used to be about fun but now it's about exploitation, apparently, and men objectifying and oppressing women. And not just by *Guardian*-reading, man-hating feminists with hairy legs and armpits. Now, masculinity is somehow toxic by definition.'

There was a wave of nodding from the dinner guests.

'It's jolly confusing,' Alistair said, his face growing redder. 'If I'm honest, newly single men like me, well, we don't know how to behave anymore. Do you women want us to be strong and tough, or sweet and sensitive? It's a bloody minefield. If you get it wrong, well, you could end up losing your job or locked up behind bars. What's a man supposed to do? It's safest just to be wimpy and wet.'

'Which is a total turn-off, of course. Any real woman, you know, what she really craves,' Ava said with a wink, 'is a *real* man.'

That was Sebastian's cue. Ava felt his hand lightly brush her left knee and she knew instinctively that it was not unintentional.

'I guess the problem is,' she continued, trying to ignore Sebastian, 'that women, well, we want a man to have it all: we want him to be a big strong alpha male, but caring and tender with it too. It's like trying to find a golden unicorn.'

Ava paused; perhaps that was where she was going wrong. There were possibly only about five men in the whole of London who matched her list of ludicrous requirements, who also happened to be single and who might conceivably prefer a thirty-nine-year-old divorcée banker over a twenty-two-year-old lingerie model.

'And by the way, Alistair, don't imagine it's any easier being a woman. In the good old days, women just needed to know how to stuff a mushroom and look passably good. But then came women's lib and my generation of women grew up being told we could be *anything* that we wanted to be. And now, it turns out, we need to be *everything*. We're expected to run a beautiful show home; to break the glass ceiling and be a top boardroom director; to be a tiger mother to our children; to look like we're twenty when we're forty; and to top it all, to perform like a sex goddess in bed, when all we really want is a good night's sleep.'

'Nonsense,' roared Sebastian.

Tall, confident and professionally charming, Sebastian was lionised in all the best addresses in central London. He was the man every man wanted to be, and the man every woman wanted to bed. Sebastian – and it was always Sebastian, never Seb – was the archetypal playboy, straight out of central casting. Fuelled by testosterone and whisky, he was a man with a penchant for fast women and slow horses. Everyone needs a hobby, but what Sebastian excelled at was dabbling. He had been many a debs' delight, and he was secretly flattered to figure on *Tatler's* list of eligible bachelors on a rolling annual basis. He was not just cool, he was ice-cold, if ice-cold was your thing. Regrettably, it was Ava's thing. And try as she might to go for the Alistairs of this world, all soft and cuddly and eager to please, that didn't do it for her. It was the fact that Sebastian was unobtainable that made him so appealing. It had something to do with that cold, unadoring father of hers, maybe. It meant that however hard she tried, however sweet and loving she might be, however amusing, however sexy, such a man would play with her, but he would never love her. She would never be good enough to be loved. Ava must try harder next time. And history, clearly, repeated itself, over and over again.

'None of that Superwoman stuff. That's awfully *déclassé*,' Sebastian said, with his usual blithe airiness and a perfect French accent. 'It's so much simpler than that. If you want to know the three things a man needs, it's good champagne, good pussy and strange pussy.'

He was being his usual spirited self and he enjoyed shocking Celeste with the 'p' word. He could feel her and even the famous aubergine wallpaper throwing him a withering look.

He turned his playful gaze to Ava and smiled. Ava smiled back. It was clear he believed he had another promising night ahead of him, and perhaps he, also, remembered their glorious youthful couplings.

'And while love can be heavenly,' he added for good measure, 'marriage is a nightmare.'

Not that he had ever tried it. Sebastian was a mere bystander, a casual observer of the debris of all those dead and broken marriages around him. And indeed, one or two of those marriages, it was whispered, he had been instrumental in breaking up.

Sebastian looked like a man who had savoured pussy of many varieties, and had not yet, even at forty-two, lost any of his early enthusiasm. With a practised wink and a smile, he had succeeded in bedding many spectacular women. No wonder he could not choose between them: they all merged into one. They were all uniformly slender, well bred and adoring. He had left a trail of broken hearts and dreams in his wake. As to his own dreams, they were hazy. So many of them had already come true: he had inherited the baronetcy and the magnificent Hampshire estate that came with it; he had advised CEOs and at least two prime ministers; and there was even a mini-me Sebastian, little Léo, learning to take his first steps, in considerable style, in a splendid *hôtel particular* on Place Vendôme, right next to the Ritz. As for his heart, it was unclear what it yearned for, or even if he had one.

'I'm not sure I agree with you there, Sebastian. If a man's got good pussy, well, he doesn't want strange pussy,' said Oliver, beaming. He was a freshly minted organic soup millionaire, with thinning hair and a wallet and a belly that had both expanded considerably over the last few years. He was newly and happily remarried. Tatiana, his stunning young wife and his children's former nanny, smiled back at him from across the table. Oh, the joys of fresh love and fresh sex. Ava could practically smell the pheromones bouncing off both of them.

'Absolutely,' said James, pouring himself his fourth glass of wine. 'It's exhausting, juggling a wife and a mistress. And I'm not just talking sexually.' He stopped, realising he had revealed a little more than intended, and added with a forced laugh, 'Or so I imagine.'

'James, darling,' Celeste purred.

James's face fell. His wife's vocabulary, in public at least, was always at its sweetest when she was at her angriest.

'Don't you think, dearest, you've possibly had quite enough *vino*?' Celeste fixed him with her seasoned hostess-with-the-mostest-smile. She felt the onset of a hot flush under her perfect poise.

At the other end of the table, James ignored Celeste and poured his guests and himself some more of his finest Château Mouton Rothschild Pauillac. He opened a great Château d'Yquem Sauternes, to let it breathe a touch in time for the next course. By now, he was too sozzled to worry about the grilling from his wife that awaited him when everyone had gone home.

At least James had managed to avoid the usual endless discussions around the intricacies of Celeste's latest intermittent fasting, meta-vegan, ketotarian, crypto-keto, proto-paleo, pro-biotic, pre-biotic, post-food diet. When it came to hosting dinners at home, James had learnt from bitter experience to put his foot down, and he insisted that the chef lay on real food. Under his careful instructions, Cook had prepared a veritable feast: *coquilles St Jacques grillées et parfumées au safran*; then *filet de boeuf et purée d'épinards poêlés aux champignons* for mains; followed by a selection of carefully chosen French and British farmhouse cheeses; and for pudding, *millefeuille aux framboises*, for those who were not already fit to burst and who dared to veer off-piste from the otherwise cleverly zero-carb feast.

As for the decor, Celeste and her party planner had outdone themselves, it had to be said. The tablescape was an extravaganza straight out of the sumptuous wilds of Amazonia, right in the middle of prime Mayfair, with arched violet orchids, juicy pink bromeliads and opulent cascades of fuchsia roses. Everyone glowed in the flattering shimmer of candlelight and their images were reflected in a rainbow of muted colours that bounced off the Baccarat crystal and the Murano mirrors. Ava admired the gold-trimmed *Carnets d'Equateur* Hermès tableware, with its hand-painted panthers and wild birds of paradise. She knew it was vulgar, but she could not help but calculate over £40,000 worth in plates alone.

'Actually,' Ava said, no longer quite so mesmerised by the plates, 'I think men do have reassuringly simple needs.'

Celeste grew increasingly irritated at the thought of Ava's possibly vast experience of men's needs, however simple. Why had she even invited her tonight? Celeste had only had three boyfriends before settling down to a life of relatively undemanding monogamy with James. In any event, the irony of a simplicity of needs, in a setting overflowing with extravagance, was not lost on the assembled guests.

'Yes. Very simple needs.' Ava smiled and paused. 'Well, it's obvious, isn't it? Men just need to be worshipped and adored.' She winked at Sebastian and tossed her hair back. 'Don't you agree, Sebastian?'

Sebastian smiled back. He really did have the most perfect white teeth. They were never that perfect at Cambridge and Ava wondered if he had succumbed to veneers.

'Too right,' Oliver piped up. His first wife had been replaced because Tatiana was so much better at adoring him than she had been. Gazing lovingly at his beautiful new bride, it was clear to him that there was something to be said for the Russian soul, and the Russian body too, come to think of it.

'Christ, yes. Absolutely,' Alistair chimed in. 'If only I'd known how fun dating life is out there for a single man about town. I wish Louisa had left me sooner. I'm loving all the attention. I never realised how many attractive single women there are in London. And how easy it is to take them to bed.'

Celeste bristled at the other end of the table.

'That said, you've got to watch yourself,' Alistair continued, oblivious. 'I went on a date last week. She was a stunner. But there was something a bit off about her. Anyway, she asked me if I wanted to go back to her place. Hell, yes! How could I resist? She was hot. But she gave off these strange, bunny-boiler vibes. Being the cautious lawyer that I am, I asked her to send me a text confirming her consent to sex. And she did. Apparently, I was not the first man to ask. It's fun out there, but these days, you can't be too careful.'

'Crikey.' James gulped. 'Sounds like a minefield.'

'So, tell us, James. What's the secret to your long marriage?' Oliver asked, switching to safer conversational territory.

James smiled wryly. Strange how no one ever asked the secret to a great marriage, rather than a long one. He was not sure whether longevity was a mark of success or of cowardice, but he answered amiably enough. 'Well, I'm a little bit deaf, and Celeste, she's a little bit blind.'

The guests laughed, even though most of them had heard the joke before.

'And Celeste knows how to mix me the perfect whisky sour when I walk through the front door every night,' James added for good measure.

'Is that a euphemism?' quipped Ava.

There was more laughter. Celeste coughed.

'The secret to a happy marriage? It's the secret to any happy relationship. You just have to keep your, um, pecker up,' said Sebastian.

He was the only person in the room who had never been married. But perhaps he was not too far off the mark. The guests chuckled again. Judging by Sebastian's particularly buoyant mood, Ava suspected that up was precisely where his pecker was right now.

'Oh yes, Sebastian. I agree. Up is always good,' she said, smiling. 'But the secret to a successful marriage? It's like the secret to the elixir of youth. Who knows?'

'The key to a great relationship?' said Oliver. 'That's easy. Keep the fights clean and the sex dirty.'

Ava took a deep breath. 'Well, lucky old you, Ollie, to have figured that out and to actually be doing it.'

Oliver and Tatiana kissed for the gallery. They refrained from using their tongues.

'Before we divorced,' Ava said, 'my former husband and I saw a famous marriage guidance counsellor. She worked with thousands of couples, studying what makes for a healthy, loving long-term relationship. She concluded that there's three things you need.'

Ava paused for effect and looked around the table. Everyone was listening attentively.

'Number one, you need a strong erotic connection. No surprises there, right? You need to have sex with your partner and to connect sexually. And you need to continue to want to have sex with him. Or her, for that matter.'

James shot Celeste a furtive glance. Celeste looked away. She knew, first-hand, the sexual and other ambivalences that made for a 'happy marriage'.

Oliver kissed Tatiana's hand and smiled at her.

Ava continued. 'The second thing is admiration. You need to admire and respect your partner. Our therapist said that the only way to see and appreciate your spouse properly, after many years together, is to step back and look at him with fresh eyes; you know, as though you're seeing him for the first time.'

That was another tricky recommendation. Real life always seemed to get in the way of admiration, somehow.

'And then there's the third ingredient,' Ava said. 'You've got to be on the same journey. You need to support each other. You need to work towards the same goals. And build a real home. Together. As a unit. It needs to feel like your own love bubble.'

Ava's voice faltered slightly. It was no wonder she had divorced. She had barely got one out of three of those elements right in her own marriage. She felt her eyes water and clenched her fists under the tablecloth. Now was certainly not the moment for any public displays of emotion. But as she unclenched her hands, she felt Sebastian give her left hand a little squeeze. He had been watching her and he had spotted her exact moment of anguish. Ava was touched by this unexpected sweetness. Nothing had been said, but everything had been understood.

'That's an interesting list,' said James pensively. 'I'm not sure I have the answers. But I do think you've got to mix things up a bit in a marriage. It's a cliché, but you need to keep it alive, and all that. Or else it's the box-set death march.'

'Yup,' Alistair agreed. 'Too true. Netflix kills sex.'

'I guess it is what it is,' said Celeste pointlessly.

Sebastian started fondling Ava's knee. Tantalisingly, he worked his way up her left thigh with light strokes. The slit of her skirt fell open and Ava sat up straight, her eyes darting from face to face, wondering if they could tell what was happening under the table. Sebastian's fingers ventured to the outside of Ava's knickers and started to caress her through the lace. The thrill of his touch was exquisite, and Ava fought to keep her composure in front of the oblivious guests. She was already wet, even through her panties. Ava turned to look at Sebastian, and he looked straight back at her with a serious expression. Holding her gaze, he worked his way inside her knickers, and began to explore her wetness and her engorged clit. Ava let out a gasp and disguised it by pretending to clear her throat.

'Each marriage is its own mysterious and impenetrable culture,' said Oliver, who had never understood the dynamics of his own marriage, let alone anyone else's. 'I think the death knell for my marriage was the onset of contempt. My ex-wife never spoke to me; she spoke at me. She was constantly interrupting me. She always criticised me. She never stopped nagging. Even in public, she enjoyed humiliating me, in that underhand way she had. Most of the time I could feel her seething with rage, as though what she really wanted to do was smash my face.'

That was almost too much real information for a fashionable dinner party in one of the best houses in Mayfair.

Under the table, Sebastian, who had just found the entrance to Ava's pussy, paused his journey of discovery. He knew to proceed slowly, so that Ava would crave more.

'God help us,' muttered James, under his breath. Then he pulled himself together and said in a cheery tone, 'Anyone for a little digestif?'

'Isn't it ironic,' Ava said, by way of conclusion, 'how all the single people out there are desperate to find a partner, while all the married people are desperate to get rid of theirs?'

Ava felt Celeste looking daggers at her.

As for Sebastian, he wondered if he was losing his touch. Why was Ava still talking, when there was something so much more engaging in hand? He withdrew his fingers from her knickers and slid them over his lips and then into his mouth.

Ava thought she had said way too much for one evening. She took a good look at Sebastian. He was such a stunning physical specimen, so masculine and self-assured. So good with his hands. 'It's playtime,' she murmured softly in Sebastian's ear, lightly brushing his thigh. 'The loos are downstairs, first left by the entrance. See you there in two minutes. We've some unfinished business.'

'You mean, unfinished pleasure,' Sebastian corrected her.

Ava waited a couple of long minutes for Sebastian to disappear and then she too left the dining room. As she walked into the loo, she noticed the sensational Picasso straight ahead, in vivid primary colours, hanging on the black wall. It was eerily prophetic of the fragile mental state of the lady of the house, an early version of *The Weeping Woman*. Celeste had known instinctively that this was the best place to hang the finest piece of art in her home. It was a foolproof way of ensuring that everyone who came to visit would see it. The artist had helpfully signed the work in large, easy-to-read black letters. But now, Ava's mind was not on Cubist art, nor on the arresting depiction of the universality of human suffering.

'Come over here, you,' Sebastian ordered, as he locked the door and grabbed her by the waist. 'I wanted to kiss you all night. You just kept prattling on. Have you any idea how much I want you?'

Judging by the feel of his hard cock, Ava knew all right. She fell to her knees and unzipped his trousers as she looked him straight in the eyes. His large cock flew out and Ava savoured it as she began to suck and lick him while fondling his balls.

'Wow,' Sebastian gasped, catching his breath. 'Forget what I said earlier about good pussy and strange pussy.' He looked down at Ava, stroked her hair and said with a smile, 'What a man really needs is great head.'

Upstairs, Celeste looked at her diamond-encrusted Ballon Bleu de Cartier watch. Sebastian and Ava had both been gone for some time. She wondered, with a slight panic, if Chef had possibly undercooked the scallops.

21.

In Another Time, Another Life

A va could not forget Sami and Sami could not forget Ava. They had said goodbye. But they knew it was not over. A few months later, they said hello again. And they came up with something that they could both live with: a civilised arrangement that satisfied both their needs.

Ava made a point of never sleeping again with men with whom she had ended a relationship. When it was over, it was over and there was never a good reason to go back. Still, she stayed friends with almost all her exes, including her former husband. She wanted to be gracious and kind, even to those who had pulverised her heart into smithereens. The relationships shifted, more or less seamlessly, from one of passionate lovers to platonic friends. They had shared kisses and body fluids, stories and dreams, and at a minimum they had travelled part of life's journey together, however short. Nevertheless, when the romance was over, it was categorically over. On principle.

But Ava made an exception with Sami. She did not care to cease and desist from seeing him. Translation: she did not want to stop fucking him and she had, regrettably, no one else she wanted to break her two-centimetre rule with. She treasured their time together. He was a fabulous lover, and he was a fabulous friend, and she knew he would say the same about her. The key was not to overthink the special hours they spent holed up in Ava's bed. Was this love? Where were they heading? Did they have a future together? There was no need to ponder, let alone answer, some of those big existential questions. It was a time of suspended animation. And very animated it was too. Surreal and yet real. Most of all, it was deep and meaningful, and they cared too much for each other to stop.

Sami's training in the elite Israeli military corps had developed his innate powers of lateral thinking and he was good at cutting to the chase. He came up with a new protocol for when they met. Instead of the tortured cups of tea they used to drink on Ava's grey velvet sofa, as they chatted, wracked with guilt, often for several hours, until neither could take it anymore and they would pounce on top of each other, Sami resolved that they knew each other well enough by now to dispense with the pleasantries. He decided that they should head straight to bed, as soon as he walked through Ava's front door. Ava agreed. After all, it was what they both wanted. Life was too short to spend it exchanging small talk.

Eleven a.m. A cold, rainy autumn day. A day for hiding under the duvet with someone scrumptious. The doorbell rang and Ava opened the door in her black leather dress and her knee-high python boots.

Wordlessly, they kissed, inhaling each other.

'Wow,' Sami said. 'That was some welcome.'

He had been travelling and she had not seen him for a few weeks. He was more tanned than usual, and he sported short, freshly cut hair that made him look ten years younger than he was. She noticed he was slightly nervous, and he trembled a little as he handed her his coat to hang. That alone made her melt. It did not take much, with him, to make her melt. He held her face in his hands and kissed her again as he manoeuvred her up the stairs to her bedroom until they both fell onto the bed. She loved the intensity of his kiss, the feel of his lips and the taste of his mouth. She melted some more. She wondered if there would ever come a time when she would no longer desire him as much as she desired him now, as much as she had always desired him. If anything, her desire grew the more she knew him.

He stripped fast. He had a unique way of removing three layers of T-shirt, shirt and cashmere jumper all at once. Ava had somehow forgotten what a beautiful, lean and hairless body he had. How could she forget? But she did not forget his smell, sweet and lightly musky. He swooped down on Ava, ripped open the poppers of her dress and whipped off her barely-there black thong. She lay naked on the fur blanket except for her python boots and the heavy gold bracelets stacked on each arm. Immediately, he attacked her pussy like a hungry lion devouring his prey. It was as though he had not eaten in months. He licked her relentlessly, as his fingers pounded deep inside her until she came. Ava kept trying to pull him up to her, to kiss him again on the mouth, but he would have none of it and he pushed her back down forcefully. He made her come again, despite herself. She loved to play at being objectified, mainly because she knew that it was a game, and that Sami saw her as so much more than a sex object.

They both spoke sex fluently. It was their language, and they developed their very own dialect. He knew exactly what she loved and how to make her come hard, just as she knew exactly what turned him on. Most of all, they both knew the underlying meaning of their kissing and fucking. It was the perfect expression of how they felt about each other: passionate, connected and naked.

Sami came up from between her thighs and up to her face, held it tenderly between his hands and they kissed again.

'You taste so delicious and fresh. Here, taste,' he said, as he put his fingers in her mouth for her to suck. 'Your beautiful pussy.'

Sami was back on fire, erect and throbbing. He lay on the bed and drew Ava on top of him. She stroked her breasts as she straddled him and looked down at him, smiling. Then she took his big hard cock in her hand and used it to massage her clit. She threw her head back in pleasure, as the waves of desire built up inside her. Slowly, she ground into him, letting him further in, until he plunged deep and hard inside her. She could feel every inch of him as he held her waist and pulled her down, and rhythmically back and forth. Deeper than deep.

'Don't stop, don't stop, darling,' Ava called out.

She felt herself about to come, and Sami waited for her, until they both exploded together, breathless. They rested, panting, for a few minutes, holding each other close. There was no need to say anything. Eternity stretched out. Together in one breath.

Soon, Sami was hard again. He held Ava's hand as he took her over to the large three-way mirror in her dressing room. They both loved mirror sex. Naturally. It was a unique way of seeing themselves, of seeing each other, and of seeing each other together.

Sami positioned Ava on all fours on the soft cream carpet, and he caressed the line of her hips and buttocks. He spread her legs wider apart and licked her slowly from behind, as she arched her back. He clutched her firmly as he plunged his tongue further into her, then reached forward and rubbed her clit with his other hand. Then he drew himself up and started to penetrate her hard. Their bodies melded perfectly together as they moved in perfect sync, almost as one. Almost.

'Look at us,' he said, smiling, as they watched themselves in the mirror, 'look how beautiful we look together.'

It was true. They made a striking couple: Sami with his long limbs and dark, sultry looks, Ava with her voluminous blonde hair and her curves. Watching themselves heightened their sense of oneness, limbs entwined, tongues hungry, as Sami thrust deep into Ava. They both came again, loudly.

'You know, Ava,' Sami said later, as they lay very still on the bed, 'this is the part I really love. The sex is just an excuse to lie close to you.' He stroked her face. 'Actually, I want to see you more than I want to fuck you. I love lying next to you like this. Your nakedness. You're so powerful, with and without clothes.'

They were two paired souls in the universe. Any attempt at rationalisation was futile. It was about feeling, not thinking. Neither wanted to think about what they were doing. Explanations were pointless. And painful.

'So, tell me, Ava, who are you fucking these days, if it's not too personal to ask?'

Ava could not escape the *still* single question, even with Sami. It was a leitmotif in her life. She did not feel like giving him a rundown of her recent sexual encounters. She was embarrassed, even with Sami, that a year on, she was in the same identical place, *still* single.

'It *is* too personal, Sami. But then again, everything with you is personal, darling,' she answered, trying to sound light. 'Let's just say, it's been a while since I last properly fucked anyone but you. You know, full penetration beyond two centimetres,' she continued, her voice suddenly wobbly, as she felt herself choke up. 'That's where, er, you come in, as it were.'

It was where Sami came in, and why Sami came in. She wondered if she would be fucking Sami if she were not *still* single. Probably not. As it was, it had been six months since she had last fucked Hugo in that very bed. She thought momentarily of Hugo, Sami's opposite. Much as Ava adored, maybe even loved, them both, she knew they would loathe each other. Hugo, the blond, blue-eyed airy aristocrat; Sami, the dark, pragmatic lieutenant colonel with his feet firmly planted on the ground. The only thing they had in common was that they both had a perfect large cock that had penetrated Ava and made her come, over and over again.

Ava teared up with shame. She 'had' neither Sami nor Hugo. She was *still* single. She was still alone.

'I'm sorry,' Sami said, 'it must be hard for you. I know how much you love to fuck.' He stroked her hair gently. Sami's kindness made Ava feel even more of a failure.

'When I was married,' Ava said, 'I never so much as touched another man's hand. But towards the end, I used to fantasise about all the sex I'd have once I was divorced. I was planning a fantastic fuckfest. I was going to fuck with impunity. Fuck anyone I wanted. Well, that was the plan.'

She turned her face away, tears running down her cheeks. She was such a loser. Not only couldn't she find a boyfriend; she couldn't even find anyone she wanted to have full penetrative sex with. Beyond shame, she wiped away her tears. She was glad it was only Sami here, by her side. Sami knew her. She did not need to hide who she was from him.

Ava thought, momentarily, and with remorse, of Sami's wife, waiting for him in bed that night. Her tears stopped immediately.

'How about your ex-husband? Does he have someone?' Sami asked.

Ava shuddered involuntarily. 'My ex-husband? Yeah, he's got someone. He's with a girl he met on Tinder. She's twenty-five. I'm sure they'll get married and have a couple of kids.' She tried hard not to sound bitter. 'She's different from me. She used to work in marketing or fashion or something, and now she's learning to be a yoga teacher. She's got a beautiful alligator-covered Smythson journal that my ex bought her, and she writes notes in it about her "yoga journey". She's a nice, sweet girl, I'm sure.'

Sami laughed. He knew full well this was the last thing Ava believed. He pinched her bottom and they giggled together.

'Well, she worships him. He wants that. All men want that. I get it. I didn't worship him. No surprise, really. He wasn't a terribly good husband.'

Ava bit her lower lip. She wondered if she would have worshipped Jake if he hadn't cheated on her for so long. There was no point thinking about counterfactuals. It was over and out. Done and dusted.

'If we were together, I would worship you. And I think you would worship me too,' Sami said.

'Yes, Sami. Of course I would worship you, darling.'

Ava almost said 'my' darling, but she knew Sami did not belong to her. Maybe in another lifetime, when he might be hers, she could think about worshipping Sami. But not in this one.

Why Sami? Why this man she had met in the street? It did not get more random than that. But by the same token, it did not get more predestined than that. It was fate, it was destiny, it was meant to be. He was meant to be. It was so obvious. He was a perfect match for her. And perfectly unavailable too.

Why Sami? It was not his beautiful, athletic body. It was not his warm, dark eyes. It was not the expert way he fucked her. It was not even his sensational phallus. It was because Sami knew Ava, as Ava knew herself. And Ava knew Sami, as he knew himself. He felt her shame and her pain. Their relationship was naked and real. The relationship was wrong, but it felt so right.

As Ava lay in Sami's embrace, she smiled, remembering a line from *Peter Pan*, one of her favourite Disney movies: 'Dreams do come true, if only we wish hard enough.'

22.

Beware Fog

Ava sat at the bar of her favourite Italian brasserie, Cecconi's, sipping a frothy cappuccino and reading *The Economist*, as she scribbled notes in the margin, a habit she had not given up since her university days. She was wearing her full rock-chick uniform of tight black leather trousers, high-heeled ankle boots and a cashmere jumper that was ever so slightly too tight around the bust.

Leandro, her favourite waiter, came over with a plate piled high with freshly baked chocolate brownies. 'For the special lady,' he said with a twinkle in his eye. 'Straight out the oven. For you. You looks so beeeeeautiful today. As usually. *Bellissima*.'

'Oh, Leandro,' Ava replied. 'You're spoiling me. I love those brownies. They're the best. Thank you so much. But not too many. I can't get fat. I still need to find a husband, you know.'

'You no worry. You beeeeeeautiful in the inside,' he said. 'Inside and outside. You like the sunshine. You like fire. You like water. You like all the elements. Great energy.'

Quite aside from his warm Florentine charm and kindness, Leandro was the dispenser of some of the finest dating advice in London. It was usually a riff on, 'Relax! *Si calmi.* You gorgeous. Be patient and your Prince Charming will be coming. I know it. I feel you.'

Ava looked at Leandro, with his blond hair and blue eyes, as he glided elegantly through the room, serving the other diners. He stood up tall, and suddenly she noticed that he bore a striking resemblance to Hugo, if you could imagine a tall, blond, aristocratic Etonian transformed into an Italian waiter. Now Ava knew why she liked him so much. It was the ultimate exercise in transference.

Ava gestured for Leandro to bring her the bill.

'No worry,' he said, smiling. 'Is already done. You don't owe nothing.'

'No, Leandro,' insisted Ava, 'I haven't paid yet.'

Leandro smiled some more.

'The man at the back. He pay for you,' he said with a wink.

Ava narrowed her eagle-eyed gaze. She normally did not miss much, especially when it came to spotting attractive men. How could she have failed to notice him? A six-foot-three dark-blond hunk beamed at her with a dazzling set of what looked like impeccable white American teeth. She knew he had to be American. She didn't know any Englishman whose dentistry achieved that level of perfection, or any Englishman who cared enough about his teeth to do what it takes.

'Well, hello there,' the hunk said, as he swaggered over.

He had an American accent. Of course he did.

'The name's Jack,' he added.

Of course it was.

The light hit his teeth, which gleamed in the morning sunlight. Like his namesake, Jack had something of the young Jack Kennedy about him. He was tanned, he oozed self-confidence and he reeked of sexual conquests. He was categorically Hot Stuff. He looked like a man who was way too busy enjoying life to work and he gave off the air of someone who spent his days lounging around in the sun, stretched out on a sailboat moored off the coast of Nantucket; or après-skiing with a decent whisky, a good Cuban cigar, and a roving but discerning eye, on a sun-soaked terrace in Aspen. Or, as he liked to put it, 'I party like a rock star, I fuck like a porn star, and on a good day, well, I look like a friggin' movie star.' Modesty was not exactly his defining characteristic.

'I saw you from across the bar,' Jack said, 'but I didn't wanna interrupt you. You looked kinda busy there, readin' your *Economist*. D'ya live around here? How 'bout I take you to dinner sometime?'

As he spoke, he smoothly handed Ava his embossed business card with a smile. This was clearly not the first time he was picking up a woman in a restaurant. And it was clearly not the first time that Ava was being picked up in a restaurant. Ava's usual response was to smile back politely, to act flattered, and then to chuck the business card straight into the nearest bin. But Jack had a few rather obvious assets: his self-assurance and his joyful disposition, for starters. It was conceivable he possessed a few other assets that were less immediately apparent. Ava could only hope and imagine that he did. His type usually did.

'Dinner sometime' meant dinner that night. Jack was a man of action, who liked to strike while his iron rod was piping hot. As it happened, Ava was free. In any event, Jack was not a man who took 'no' for an answer. That was part of his frisky, puppy-dog charm. Jack booked a table at Nobu for eight. Ava arrived slightly early, as she usually did, to down a few sips of lychee martini in advance. She was nervous, and she was surprised when Jack entered the dining room, bang on time. He flashed his white teeth as he surveyed the terrain, then prowled over towards her. He looked cool in a distressed tan leather jacket, a tight white T-shirt, perfectly cut cream jeans, and a thick brown leather belt slung low around his hips. Ava had to catch her breath: he was gorgeous. Was he really having dinner with her?

'Awesome you could make it,' Jack said as he sat down. 'This is a terrific place, isn't it? Love the red dress. Anthony Vaccarello for YSL?'

Three lychee martinis in and Jack went in for the kill.

'Babe. You got the most gorgeous green eyes,' he said. 'And those lips. Those legs. You're a real looker.'

Ava smiled. She had heard the same corny lines a hundred times before. But coming from a hunk like Jack, and after enough booze, they somehow acquired more depth of meaning.

He took her hand in his and started to kiss it. Then he looked her straight in the eyes and began to lick her fingers. Before she had time to remove her hand, he was kissing her on the mouth, in full view of the guests trying to chopstick their way through their tuna tataki and baby tiger shrimp tempura lathered in creamy spicy sauce. Luckily they were seated at a corner table and the waiters pretended they hadn't seen anything, After all, this was where Boris Becker impregnated a Russian model in a five-second encounter in a broom cupboard.

The rest of the meal was a perfunctory affair. They barely picked at their miso-marinated black cod and wasabi lobster and they stumbled out before being thrown out. It was a balmy September night. London was at its best, still light and warm under a golden glow. As they crossed Grosvenor Square, Jack flung her against the bronze statue of President Franklin Delano Roosevelt. It was apt: Ava was not the fearful type and, like FDR, with nothing to fear but fear itself, she yielded to Jack as he kissed her again hungrily. Though she was wearing her usual killer heels, she felt small and protected in Jack's embrace. They staggered into Ava's house, limbs entwined, and Jack manoeuvred her onto the dining room table. He tore her panties off urgently, kissed her and penetrated her relentlessly, hard and deep. They were both still fully clothed. They gasped.

'I'm breaking all my rules with you,' Ava stammered.

She wondered if she even had any rules anymore. Rules more honoured in the breach than in the observance, and all that. Her only rule, it seemed, was to do exactly what she wanted to do, when she wanted to do it, on the basis that life is now. That was usually a good enough excuse and it allowed her to behave as naughtily as she wanted. But her cardinal rule was never, ever, to have full penetrative sex on the first date. Not out of any moral consideration that it was somehow 'wrong' to let a man have sex with you immediately. And not because she was a follower of 'The Rules', the idea that you could secure the undying affections of your prospective mate by engaging in a protracted and elaborate courtship, which would fan the flames of desire and lead to a marriage proposal. No. The reason she did not have sex on a first date was that one of the most pleasurable parts of a relationship is the sweet anticipation, the dance of slow, mutual exploration and discovery. She enjoyed taking the time to let her desire grow. She liked the process of getting to know a man. She loathed fast sex as much as she loathed a quick Big Mac and fries. It answered an immediate need and left the soul unfed. But sometimes the soul did not require any feeding. Like tonight with Jack.

'Babe,' Jack said as he thrust deeper inside her. 'You breakin' your rules? Don't ya know? Rules are made for breakin'. Look how much you want me. You're so wet, you're practically squirtin'.'

He yanked her dress to the side and exposed her left breast. Ava was not wearing a bra. He licked her nipple and Ava moaned. Her brain was switched off. All she could feel was his cock sliding deep inside her. He plunged in hard, then almost came out, only to plunge deeper inside her again. Ava's body was taut, on the edge of coming. She held Jack tight and close, and he took her to orgasm despite the three lychee martinis, which normally made coming harder work. Jack came loudly a few seconds later. Ava feared the neighbours heard them even through the thick stone walls. They lay silent for a few minutes, just holding each other.

'Wow,' Jack said eventually, 'that was awesome.'

'Mmm...' Ava said, still floating.

'I wanna see your body. Naked. Strip!'

Ava slid off the table and slowly unbuttoned her dress, looking Jack straight in the eye, then tossed it to the side with a flourish. Her hair was big and wild and it had grown curlier from their sweaty sex. She put her hands on her hips, for Jack to fully take her in, as she stood in her heels, buck-naked apart from a diamond necklace around her neck and a couple of diamond studs in her ears.

'You're lookin' mighty fine, girl,' Jack said approvingly.

Ava laughed. It had been a while since anyone had addressed her as 'girl'. 'Come on. Let's go up to my roof terrace. I want to show you the view. London by night,' she said, taking Jack by the hand.

Ava wiggled her bottom in mock Marilyn Monroe style, and giggled, as they climbed the five flights of stairs to the roof terrace. It was dark, save for a few bright house lights, and the city was quiet. Jack lay down naked on the mound of linen cushions strewn on the wooden bench, and Ava nestled between his legs. She felt his cock stirring again on her buttocks.

'You're a force of nature, Jack. Always up. You're a hard man to keep down.'

'You bet,' Jack said. 'I'm up and I'm hard all right.'

She turned around, straddled him, then took his cock in her hand and slid it into her. 'You feel so good inside me.'

'And you're so wet, babe. My cock needs to feel your wet pussy. I wanna drive my cock deep into you.'

Ava leaned in and kissed him tenderly now, tongue to tongue. Jack sat with his legs wrapped around Ava's back, as she faced him, moving slowly in and out of the lotus position. They took their time, savouring this surprising moment of closeness.

Jack texted her the next day.

Last night was lit. The fuck of the year. We need to repeat. Like, tonight.

It was a good start, Ava texted back. *We can do better.*

Ava opened her front door to Jack the next night. She experienced a rush of desire as she saw him.

'Wow,' he said with his dazzling smile. 'You're lookin' snatched. Did you dress up for me? Look what I've got for you. Look how happy I am to see you.' He gestured at his bulging crotch.

He didn't need to. Ava had already noticed. She could not help but be impressed. He kissed her on the lips and pushed her up against the entrance hall wall, narrowly missing the seventeenth-century Dutch landscape painting that hung there. He hoisted her dress up and turned her round. She was not wearing knickers. He quickly unbuttoned his jeans and penetrated her hard from behind. She was already so wet, he slipped easily inside and pounded into her, as Ava put her hands on the wall for balance.

'You're smokin' hot,' he said as he nuzzled her neck. 'I've been thinkin' about fuckin' you all day long. Couldn't focus on nothing else. Christ, you got me amped.'

Then he sat down on the velvet bench and grabbed Ava by the waist, with her back to him, as he lifted her up and down over his enormous cock. Ava arched her back and felt every inch of him deep inside her until he hit her G-spot and continued to pound her. She exploded with pleasure and laughed out loud as they both came.

Day three, and Ava and Jack managed to make it down one floor to the basement kitchen before anything remotely sexual occurred. Ava poured Jack a double vodka and she went over to the chair where he was sitting with his drink. She took a sip and kissed him, and immediately felt a wave of desire for him as she straddled him. There was something irrepressible about Jack's sexuality. He was always set to 'on', so vibrant and alive. She went on her knees and began to go down on him, savouring every lick, as he stroked her hair and watched.

'Babe. I love the way you do that,' said Jack. 'Where d'ya learn to do that?'

Ava had learnt by feeling and by doing. And mostly because she loved giving a man a blow job. And her enthusiasm for the job in hand was evident. For a start, it was not a job. Did she love it so much because she felt powerful and in control? Because she enjoyed seeing a man's desire for her reflected in his eyes? Because she just loved the taste and feel of cock and sperm? Or because she knew how much men loved it, so perhaps they might, by extension, love her a little bit too?

'Your lips on my cock,' Jack said. 'Wow. Epic, babe.'

Ava came up from between Jack's legs and sat on top of him, driving his cock deep inside her. The chair scraped along the parquet kitchen floor and left a deep white indent on the dark wood.

'The memory of this fuck will be etched on my kitchen floor for decades to come,' she said.

Day four.

Babe. We're gonna do things differently this time, Jack texted Ava. *Or else we'll fuck as soon as I walk through the door. And then we'll never leave the house again. I'm gonna come pick you up, but I'll keep the cab waitin'. We're gonna leave your house immediately and head straight to dinner this time.*

Two hours later, after dinner, they were at it again, like rabbits.

The fantastic fuckfest lasted two months. Then, imperceptibly, something shifted in their relationship. Jack started to stay the night. He asked Ava if she had remembered to make an appointment for her flu jab. He fixed that troublesome bathroom cabinet that kept coming off its hinges. He stopped putting on his lovely Tom Ford aftershave that Ava adored. They began to play Scrabble at home, before going to bed late, too tired to fuck. And Jack's glorious erections started flagging.

'Babe,' he said, looking at her with his big brown puppy-dog eyes, 'this has never happened to me before.'

Ava had not heard that line for a while.

'We lost a truckload of dough in our FX trade this week. We were short cable, and then that darned Turkish lira just kept jumpin' around and we got caught in a dead cat bounce. It's a phase. I'm gonna knuckle down. It's me, babe, it's not you. You're terrific. I'm a little bent out of shape, but I'm a pro and I just gotta get my mojo back.'

'Darling, don't worry. I understand,' Ava said. 'I know you'll do great. I believe in you.'

And for a woman who barely knew her way around her own kitchen, she decided to bake Jack his favourite, a cheesecake, using her grandmother's recipe.

Jack, sweetheart, Ava texted him, *I know you're busy, but come over later. I made a cheesecake for you. I just want to see you and sleep in your arms.*

Sorry, babe, Jack wrote back. *I'm just not feeling the energy tonight. I'll take a rain check.*

Ava was gutted. The last time she had cooked a cheesecake was almost two years ago. It was not food one ate alone. It was not even food. It was love. Who needs the right energy to eat a slice of cheesecake? Jack was a California boy, and his chief appeal was his masterful, sunny

Californication. Now, transplanted to London, what had happened to his explosive, sexual energy? Was he bored of her already? Had he started to see someone else?

Jack began to spend more time at Annabel's or 5 Hertford Street, somehow always late on a Thursday or Friday night. He said he needed to schmooze his investors, though Ava suspected it was more about models and bottles. And instead of texting her throughout the day, as he had always done, his texts became sparser and less saucy. The *Hi, sexy. I wanna be deep inside you and make you come over and over again* turned to, *Sorry. Can't do tonight. Got an investor meet. I'll make it up to you, I promise.*

Ava did not need a degree in semiotics to read the signs. She loathed men who said, 'I promise.' There was no need to promise anything; there was just a need to do the right thing, there and then.

'Let's take a break, Jack,' she suggested, forestalling him suggesting the same thing. 'Why don't you sort yourself out and we'll pick up again when you're ready. Limping along like this isn't my idea of fun.'

They did not see each other for the next six weeks. Ava was distraught. Her body was aching and pining for Jack. She kept replaying their best sex scenes in her mind, over and over again. She could not forget his dangerous dark eyes or that huge cock of his that knew exactly how to make her come.

Then one day, Ava woke up, and she felt fine. Freedom at last. It was as if Jack's fucking curse had lifted. She realised that what she longed for was Jack's cock, not Jack the man. The high-quality sex had impaired her cognitive functions. Once Ava had stopped missing Jack's cock, she did not miss or want Jack the man anymore. Jack had been a false alarm. He had all the bells and whistles, and all the outward trappings, but none of the inner depth that Ava craved. He certainly looked the part, he more or less acted the part, and for sure he fucked the part. But he did not feel the part. There was no emotional connection and Ava could not pretend to herself that Jack was 'it'. He was far from being the Real Thing.

As soon as Ava was no longer interested in him, Jack's texts started coming in thick and fast. Even though there had been no contact between them, it was as though he could sense, telepathically, that Ava was no longer interested in him. The avalanche of messages was accompanied by an assault of selfies: Jack in a slim-cut dark-grey suit heading to a Very Important Meeting with a Very Important Client; Jack pumping iron in the gym, suspiciously sweat-free; Jack fresh from getting his teeth re-whitened, his mouth arranged in a Joker-like rictus; even Jack in a Stanford University baseball cap worn back to front, riding in a lift and staring blankly into the mirror. Jack clearly lived for an audience. He was the embodiment of one of the fundamental principles of quantum physics: that the properties of a subject change based on whether they are observed or not. Unobserved, Jack withered.

As for Ava, she wondered what Jack was trying to achieve. Whatever it was, the deluge of photos failed to elicit much of a reaction. If anything, Jack would have been more successful had he sent one short, sweet message and then given Ava the space for her to reconnect with her desire for him. In Ava's world, more is usually more. But in the topsy-turvy *Alice in Wonderland* world of relationships, less is usually more. The less you do, the more they want. Had Jack maintained radio silence, Ava would have been curious to know what her sexy California boy was up to. And with whom. Now that he was sending her photographic evidence of his every waking moment, the content of his power lunches and random shots of him beside London landmarks as he walked to and from investor meetings, Ava completely lost interest. It takes discipline to maintain mystery. Jack had many qualities, but discipline was not one of them.

Babe, Jack texted, *I just got a $50 million inflow into my fund last week. Let's celebrate. I'll come over tonight and mess up your kitchen. I'm gonna cook you my best seared tuna and that creamed spinach you love. I'll bring some of your favourite Ruinart.*

Sorry. Busy, Ava texted back.

The length of her texts were always in direct proportion to her level of interest in a man.

Okay, Jack persevered. *Let's put a date in the diary. How about Tuesday?*

It was unusual for him to be so precise about when they would see each other next.

Not around, wrote Ava.

Where are you off to? Somewhere naughty?

The 'where?' was irrelevant; what Jack really wanted to know was 'who?' Who would Ava be naughty with?

Paris, Ava answered airily.

She marvelled at how few words she could use and still communicate.

Jack noticed that she had given the location, without any context. He knew that the only reason anyone went to Paris was to have a romantic weekend. He tactically chose to let it pass.

Groovy. See ya Thursday.

Thursday came. Jack rang the bell, as he had so many times before. There was no pouncing and pounding on each other as he strode in, uncharacteristically diffidently. He looked paunchier and paler, like a more hesitant, greyed-out version of himself. It was not a look that suited him.

Jack was off the booze, so they drank jasmine tea and Jack scoffed all the shortbread biscuits. They attempted civilised conversation as they sat demurely on Ava's grey velvet sofa.

If only sofas could talk, Ava thought with nostalgia, noticing a new white splodge on the grey velvet. A few of the more interesting images from her recent past flashed through her mind. She smiled. Luckily, sofas don't talk. But unremovable sofa stains speak volumes.

Jack inched closer to Ava. There were a couple of biscuit crumbs on his chin. The importance of context. In the good old days, Ava would have found it sweet and endearing, and she would have wiped away the crumbs with a kiss. Now, she looked at Jack and found him sloppy. She recoiled. Jack didn't notice and edged closer still. He tried those familiar winning moves. Ava returned his kiss with mild curiosity, to see if it might reawaken her old burning desire for him. No. She did not feel the earth spin on its axis. Jack, oblivious, unzipped his pants and pulled out his large, erect cock. She was surprised to see how hard it was. Truly gravity-defying. Truly situation-defying. Ava tried to will herself into desiring that less than obscure object of desire again, for old time's sake. She felt nothing. It was baffling to remember that a few months back, Ava had thought that Jack might be The Real Deal.

'I'm sorry, Jack,' she said, 'I've met someone else.'

It was true. She had just started seeing Damian. She never dabbled with two men simultaneously. Or at least, she tried not to. In this instance, it was exceptionally easy to be virtuous and resist Jack.

'Well, can we, like, be friends?' Jack said.

Frisky puppy was now looking like a sad puppy. Ava almost felt sorry for him, until she remembered that it was Jack pulling away from her that had brought all this on to start with.

'I don't do "friends with benefits",' Ava said. 'I'm not interested in a fuck-buddy scenario.'

'Mmm. I understand,' said Jack, not understanding at all. 'How about being friends-friends?'

Ava never thought she would ever see Jack begging. Jack the sex god had turned into Jack the beaten dog. How the mighty had fallen. To hand it to him, Jack scored an 'A' for effort, as he pursued her, relentlessly, for the next two months. He chased her up a mountain in Verbier, he tried to entice her with a week's break at his parents' beachside mansion in Palm Beach, he invited her to a fancy see-and-be-seen party at Cliveden. Ava was just not into him anymore. It was not a sliding-doors moment. Now that she knew him better, she did not feel so much as a flicker of attraction towards him anymore. Great sex was a necessary but insufficient condition for a great relationship. The hormones that flooded Ava's body during sex with Jack had clouded her judgement and brought on brain fog.

23.

The California Boy's View: Cosmic Karma

I gotta get my head out my arse.
    Jack stretched all six-foot-three-inches of his prodigious frame out on the black leather and chrome Le Corbusier chaise longue, spilling over the edge. Two years on, he still cursed himself for having caved into his ex-wife Irina's demand for such fashionable but uncomfortable furniture. She was his third ex-wife, though strictly speaking, she did not count, as the marriage was quickly annulled after a disastrous honeymoon in Fiji. It dawned on Jack, regrettably a little late, that perhaps being married to a twenty-two-year-old Ukrainian model with only a smattering of English might not lead to the connubial bliss he had imagined.

'You'll love it, sir,' the seductive blonde saleswoman in the furniture department of Harrods had promised, as the eye-catching couple trudged around the store, looking to furnish their new love nest.

She caressed the top of the chaise longue as though it were a highly desirable man.

'I *know* you will,' she purred.

The woman had known Jack for all of six minutes.

'It's so chic. It's a classic. Truly iconic. The recliner is a manifestation of Modernism: it moulds itself to the body and hangs like sculpture in space. Le Corbusier made his furniture like an extension of people's limbs. Did you know his designs are based on a synthesis of the golden ratio and the Fibonacci sequence?'

As it happened, Jack did not. He didn't even remember what a Fibonacci sequence was. It had been a long time since his last advanced mathematics classes at Stanford.

Two years on, the beautiful Ukrainian had gone but the irritating seating remained, a permanent reminder of an uncharacteristic moment of weakness. He had never got used to it, but he had yet to find the time or the inclination to buy something more cosy.

The doorbell rang. Anastasia, his weekly masseuse, strode in. She was a beautiful Amazonian brunette, and she was exceptionally good with her hands. Jack mumbled a greeting of sorts and took another sip of his Bloody Mary before plonking himself, face down, onto the Gucci massage table. He let his towel drop. He was not wearing any underwear. Anastasia picked the towel up, wordlessly. She had seen it all before, many times, and she carefully repositioned the towel to cover Jack's modesty. Immediately, she sensed that Jack was in a more frenetic frame of mind than usual and she knew he would want a particularly energetic massage.

'It's a clusterfuck and I gotta get out of it. Gotta power through this. Shake that tree,' Jack drawled, through the G-shaped hole in the leather massage table.

Anastasia said nothing. She was used to her clients either falling asleep on her, or babbling in a stream of incoherent consciousness.

'Business has been kinda tough, but I'm the agent of change, man. Just gotta get that last fifty million bucks into my fund. Yeah. Pivot out of crypto and into eco. I was killin' it the last few years. I had one helluva stellar ride. Hey, I'm COO, Anastasia. Know what that is? That's Chief Operating Officer. If anything's operating in the company, I'm the chief of it. That's who I am. But now the shareholders have got my dick in a vice and I gotta take back control. I gotta get a new game plan. Get my jammy groove back.'

Anastasia poured out some almond oil and began to pummel Jack's back with strong, slow strokes, just how he liked it. He was a handsome man, but she noticed he had put on a bit of weight recently. She said nothing, naturally.

'I gotta get back in the game. This is not who I am. Damn. Things are gettin' a bit heavy round here. I'm gonna start by headin' back to the gym and layin' off the booze,' Jack rambled on.

Anastasia spotted the empty vodka bottle on the otherwise immaculate steel kitchen island.

'I gotta stop dickin' around. I know that the only thing that makes me feel better about losin' is winnin'. Jeez. I need to start winnin' again. Yup. Winnin' ain't everything, it's the only thing.'

Jack nodded to himself as he rolled over onto his back. Anastasia attacked his neck and shoulders in a vigorous circular motion and he groaned as she released the agonising tension he felt there. She worked her way down his body to his long legs, and the soles of his feet, and she then kneaded energetically upwards, in the direction of his heart. Finally, Jack was able to relax and he closed his eyes. Anastasia was a little surprised that Jack did not have his usual ginormous erection by this point in the massage.

'You want happy ending, Jack?' she asked nonetheless, as though enquiring if he wanted extra cheese on his pizza.

'Nah, too goddam tired to get hard.'

That was the ultimate indicator that he really had lost his mojo.

Jack slid off the massage table and strode over, nude and still rather splendid-looking, to get his wallet from the vintage Danish oak sideboard. He thanked Anastasia with a lavish tip, then reached for his Bloody Mary, as she slipped out without a word.

Jack sat, slightly dazed, looking around his apartment. It was surprisingly tidy and minimalist, almost as if no one lived there. He barely spent any time at home. He just showered and changed his clothes there. Sometimes, he even slept there. When Irina had left, she had commandeered all the furniture save for the Le Corbusier lounger, the cream leather Jacobsen egg chair, which had a little black pen mark on the arm rest that never came out, and the low Noguchi glass coffee table, which she had always hated and into which, still today, Jack always knocked his shins. She had even taken his favourite Banksy graffiti piece with the words 'From this moment despair ends and tactics begin' scrawled across it. Of everything in his pad, that was what he missed the most, his Banksy. Jack knew it was an ugly piece, with its sad young child begging; it reeked of pain. But he loved it, because it was his daily reminder that winners don't make excuses, ever. Not that he needed reminding. He knew it because the need to win was, to him, like the need to breathe.

He picked up his phone and asked his PA to send a large bouquet of flowers over to Ava. Nothing too crazy: flowers that smelled like flowers, not desperation. Perhaps that might make her a bit more responsive to his advances. She had grown rather cold and distant towards him and he couldn't understand why.

He slapped himself on the thigh and figured he had just enough time to steam and shower before cruising over and shooting the breeze with his investors, back at Annabel's again. He thought he might pop over to Ava's house afterwards and grab dessert there.

'I'm back. I'm gonna get after this,' Jack said out loud, finishing his Bloody Mary. 'I'm a winner. I'm a master of the fuckin' universe. I've got this! Of course I've got this.'

24.

Why Can't Love Be More Like Maths?

'What does the data say?' was one of Ava's favourite questions. She may have struggled to read men, but she was good at reading numbers. Numbers spoke to her in a language that was clear, honest and logical. Men, on the other hand, didn't always say what they mean and didn't always mean what they said. Sometimes, they said nothing at all, and their silence was difficult to decode. Ava had an enduring and rewarding love affair with numbers, but, unfortunately, she could not say the same about her love affairs with men.

It was 7.45 a.m. on a cold, rainy Monday. Ava paced the boardroom of the hedge fund where she had just made partner. The decor was classic hedge-fund chic: obligatory stark minimalism but luxuriously so, with black leather Charles Eames chairs set around a long ebony table, aggressively extravagant fresh flowers on the Bauhaus sideboard and three matching gold Lucio Fontanas hanging on the wall, slashed, ever so tastefully, through the middle. The meticulously violated canvases that were once considered so radical now looked elegant and respectable:

a visual metaphor for man's gilded journey through the existential void. Or something.

Ava came prepared, as usual. She knew, through years of hard work and discipline, that only the paranoid survive. She checked the projector was working, then scanned her spreadsheets one more time and smoothed her hair. The Monday meeting was often gladiatorial: a time when new trading ideas were rigorously debated with the other traders and the rest of the team. Despite her successful track record, Ava always felt her credibility was on the line. Every trade was an opportunity to mess up, so she always worked that little bit harder. She could not afford to get it wrong. She always measured potential returns against the level of risk taken to achieve those returns. And while there was always a cacophony of noisy data, her expertise lay in identifying the real signal.

Men in designer jeans and expensive haircuts started to breeze in, sip coffee and chat about their weekend. Ava was still the only woman in the room, and she sat, quite still, in her sleek black Alaïa dress, waiting for everyone to sit down. She had been trading for ten years now, but still, she felt a rush of adrenaline whenever she wanted to put a new trade on.

All the traders spoke in succession and now it was Ava's turn to explain her latest big idea. She took a sip of water and cleared her throat.

'I'm going to run a large short on Sun4ward,' she said evenly.

'What's a "short"?' asked Wolfgang, the new German intern and the son of the largest investor in the fund. For a young man with more opinions than knowledge, he was remarkably self-assured. That's what an expensive education at Le Rosey buys you: an address book full of useful contacts and plenty of self-confidence, not always warranted.

Fergus, the hedge fund's managing partner, shot him a condescending glance. Not only should Wolfgang have known what a short was by now, but if he didn't, he should at least have had the humility to keep his ignorance well under wraps and google 'short trade' at the end of the meeting.

'A short trade, Wolfgang,' Ava said, 'is when you sell a security before buying it, so you can buy it back at a much lower price. It's about making money by expecting a fall in the value of a stock.'

Wolfgang's father was a cornerstone investor in the fund and not a man one would want to upset in any way. By extension, his son needed careful handling.

'Sun4ward's a clear short,' Ava said. 'It's not just a short, it's a screaming short. It's totally overvalued, and it's a complete fraud.'

There was an expectant hush as she handed out sheets of paper summarising her detailed analysis to her colleagues. Sun4ward was a solar energy start-up and managed to be the darling of both the stock market and climate change activists. With its messianic CEO, the company was universally admired for its vocal stance against fossil fuels and a drive for clean renewable energy. Ava's call was highly contrarian.

'Short Sun4ward? Jesus, Mary and Joseph. Come off it, Ava. That's cat melodeon. Wee bonkers,' said Fergus. He had spent over twenty years in London, but he still spoke with a broad Irish twang, and he usually had a naughty twinkle in his eye. This morning, his eyes were staring hard at Ava. 'Sun4ward's grand, Ava,' he continued. 'The company's saving the planet, one solar panel at a time. It's fierce: sustainable green energy to the masses at affordable prices. Changing the world 'n' all. It's on the side of the angels. What's not to love? Shorting Sun4ward's bleedin' madness; it's like votin' against motherhood and apple pie.'

'I know, Fergus. I love the planet as much as the next person. But the company is a sham,' Ava said. 'I've spent months crunching through the numbers, and they don't stack up. It's all green-washing hype and zero substance. The company's got no real assets and it's burning cash. The stock was completely ramped up by the lead managers at the IPO, and then Sun4ward received generous government subsidies on top. That's obfuscating their dire financial situation. They're running on empty and what's more, they're cooking the books to cover it up.'

Ava coughed and sipped some water. All eyes were on her.

'And yet,' she continued, 'Sun4ward is still valued at just over $15 billion, even though the government subsidies have now ended. It's not even clear if all the solar panels that were supposed to be operational have actually been put up. I've commissioned some drones right now, to check.'

'Aye, but Ava, the company's got market momentum behind it,' said Fergus. He was vigorously chewing the end of his cheap plastic Bic pen. 'Maybe the company's banjaxed, but if your timing's off, it could be curtains for us. We could look like right morons if you're wrong.'

'That's my point,' Ava said. 'Sun4ward's managed to pull the wool over many people's eyes for a long time now. They're hiding in plain sight. But they can only hide for so long. The company's marking its future cash flow to its own spurious models, rather than to market. They're inflating their unrealised earnings into current profits, just like the corporate frauds at Enron and Wirecard. It's an old trick, and a total fraud.' She looked around the room and felt the blood pulsating in her temples. No one looked particularly convinced.

'I'm sure you saw the article in *Fortune* magazine, and the puff piece in the *FT* over the weekend,' said Mukesh, one of the talented quants on the team. 'The company can't do wrong, man. They're hitting all the investment hot buttons: cutting-edge tech, whiz-bang financial wizardry and a green heart to boot. Wasn't the CEO voted, like, one of the hundred most influential people in the world under forty? I mean, he's practically some kind of Jesus figure. Doesn't he, like, meditate for two hours a day?

And he does this intermittent fasting thing where he doesn't eat for sixteen hours at a time, and only showers, like, once a week.'

'Lovely,' quipped one of the junior traders sarcastically. 'So that's why he looks so skeletal and yellow.'

'Guys, you're way too smart to be taken in by the PR fluff,' Ava said. 'Sun4ward's all smoke and mirrors. Take a look at the real cash-flow numbers I put together. I've followed the money, and, well, there is none.'

'No cash is, er, somewhat worrisome,' chipped in one of the quants.

'We all know it's only when the tide goes out that you see who's swimming naked,' said Ava. 'You make the big bucks when the market turns. It's the old market adage: sell at the top and buy at the bottom. No one makes real money in the middle. Like Buffett said, you've got to be greedy when others are fearful, and fearful when others are greedy. Sun4ward's a huge con. We have to short it now, while it's still riding high.'

'Yeah, so bleedin' simple, in theory,' Fergus said. 'But, Ava, Sun4ward's on a roll. It's got market momentum behind it. Shorting could kill us if we're on the wrong side of the trade. We could look like right eejits. You could have the fund in bits if your analysis is off beam.'

Ava turned to Wolfgang. 'You can lose your shirt if you're shorting and the stock goes up. You can end up losing way more than you originally invested because, theoretically, there's no limit to how high the stock can go.' She paused. 'But I know I'm right. Sun4ward is a scam. The numbers don't lie. No one's noticed yet, but this green emperor has no clothes. It's just a question of time.' She pulled up a chart of the stock's performance on the conference room screen. 'Sun4ward's trading at $400. I'm going to start shorting today, at the market opening.'

Ava waited. Two weeks, then three weeks passed. She watched anxiously as the stock rallied and went all the way up to $500 a share. It was the only thing Fergus ever talked about, day in, day out. It was painfully expensive for the firm, and she almost capitulated. The key was to hold her nerve and to be patient. She needed to do nothing. Sometimes, the hardest thing to do was nothing. Her strength in trading was not only an ability to see things in markets that others didn't, but also to recognise when she was wrong and to change tack. But she knew she was right; she simply needed the courage and patience to wait it out.

One morning, Sun4ward's auditors resigned suddenly, claiming 'irregularities' in the figures: $1.3 billion had mysteriously gone missing. It transpired that Sun4ward had built an extensive network of shell companies and created a chain of bogus transactions with third parties to hide what was going on, just as Ava had said. The CEO had wired $500 million into one of his own personal bank accounts in the Philippines, via a bank in Malta and a Liechtenstein foundation with an underlying company incorporated in the Marshall Islands. Shortly thereafter, the CEO, the CFO and the head of sales were arrested and charged with falsifying financial accounts, fraud, breach of trust and market manipulation, which could land them in jail for 225 years each if proven guilty. The share price was in free fall, and it tanked rapidly from $500 to $0.03. The only thing of value left in Sun4ward was the century-old bonsai pine tree that stood at the entrance of their suspiciously grandiose office building in prime Mayfair. The tree turned brown then died, as there was no one to water it anymore.

Ava's trade made a killing. She told no one outside the firm except her daughters. She wanted them to understand the importance of discipline, and of not being afraid to go against the crowd. She made a large anonymous charitable donation to the Friends of the Earth.

25.

Pop Goes the Weasel

It is a truth universally acknowledged that a single woman in possession of a fresh divorce settlement must, naturally, be in want of a new husband. Ava was not quite ready to take the plunge and, in any event, Prince Charming was not exactly beating on her door with an offer of marriage. But it never hurt to check the market out. It was late February, a perfect time to head out to the slopes of Verbier, a mecca for all things pleasurable, discreetly tucked away high up in the Swiss Alps.

She met Callum in the Farm Club, the heaving nightclub whose decor had remained reassuringly unchanged since the seventies. London hedge-fund gazillionaires mingled with Swedish tech entrepreneurs. Young girls buzzed around like bees to a moneypot. It was all good, clean-ish fun, as they boogied to the sound of ABBA and the Bee Gees, sustained by magnums of Bollinger and alternating shots of Grey Goose and Jägermeister. While the music might not be cutting edge, the eye-watering prices were. The hardened skiers and the seasoned après-skiers could forget their serious day jobs and go wild for the night. And though the basement clubs and warehouse techno raves of Shoreditch might be cool in theory, in practice, the one-percenters felt much more at home in the comfort of plush velvet sofas and the music that reminded them of their misspent youth. That was when they had been geeks with NHS glasses and acne. Today, they were titans of finance, with laser eye surgery and monthly HydraFacials. The hairy-chested He-Man look had given way to the full male Brazilian 'back, sack and crack' zero body-hair aesthetic, or some heavy-duty manscaping at the very least. And now, as these alpha males flaunted their gym-honed bodies and oversize designer watches, they were on point, in the money and in demand. How the mighty had risen.

Ava spotted Callum immediately. He was difficult to miss. Six foot, slim, with tousled dark-blond hair and blue eyes, which she noticed even in a dark nightclub. She was in her element, dancing with abandon to the seventies music, in a tight white T-shirt and white jeans that glowed in the fluorescent light. She knew that white, though not altogether slimming, was the colour of choice if you wanted to stand out here. She smiled at Callum and, as if by magic, he shimmied over and started to dance with her.

He was a decent dancer for a Brit, though strictly speaking he was Scottish. His ancestral home was a neo-classical Robert Adam masterpiece set in ten thousand acres of wild grouse moors. His family had been making whisky there for the last five hundred years, until Bernard Arnault came with an offer that even they could not refuse. Callum was sent off to board at Eton, naturally, followed by a stint at Christ Church, Oxford, and then Harvard Business School, and he now lived a life of discreet, cosseted splendour in the heart of Mayfair. Where else? The path was well trodden by his father, his grandfather and even his great-grandfather before him. But rather than dabble with the LVMH clan in the upper echelons of the firm or sit at table with the serious grown-ups in venture capital, private equity or hedge funds, Callum decided to branch out solo. He set up a company that did something frightfully clever, and with impeccable environmental, social and green credentials, in biotech. It was hard to hear the precise details above the pounding of 'Dancing Queen'.

He wore the classic uniform of his breed and class: jeans, no-brand trainers, a yellow cashmere jumper with holes in it and a tailor-made, pale blue Turnbull & Asser shirt that was noticeably frayed at the collar and cuffs. The only clue to his illustrious lineage was his gold pinkie signet ring, which had been handed down from his great-great-grandfather and bore the family coat of arms. As he moved closer, Ava could smell the sensual top notes of Hermès Vetiver Tonka cologne on his neck. It was one of her favourites, and an unusual choice for a man like him, verging as it was on the Euro metrosexual. Ava felt a lurch in her stomach. She knew she wanted him.

They danced the night away, and inexorably, Callum cornered Ava outside the loos. He pinned her up against the wall, pressed his pelvis into hers and kissed her. It was electrifying. Ava was not sure if it was the fact that Callum was exactly her physical type, or that their bodies moved so in tune with each other on the dance floor, or that they had both consumed vast quantities of champagne; perhaps a heady mix of all three. There were fireworks. Luckily, Ava had arranged to meet her friends at eight o'clock sharp the next morning to go heli-skiing, which was only five hours away, or else the fireworks would have continued back in her hotel suite.

They agreed to meet the next night over a cosy fireside raclette dinner. Melted cheese is not usually the food of romance, but when in Verbier... Sober, Callum was less bold and more nuanced. There was a sensitivity and diffidence to him that had not been immediately apparent under the pulsating strobe lights of the Farm Club. It made him even more attractive. Newly separated, Callum's priority was the well-being of his young son and daughter, whom he adored, and he was focused on finalising his complex divorce settlement. He had just come out of a ten-year marriage to his third cousin once removed, whose own distinguished family owned the Highland estate right next to his. Ava did a double-take: the similarities between Callum and Hugo were striking, and she had an uncomfortable hunch that they must know each other well.

Ava smiled to herself as she remembered the words of Harry's sister, who had married four times herself.

'Where there's one, there's two,' she had said. Or four, as the case may be.

It was a comforting thought. Perhaps she was right. Maybe Ava could feel for another man what she had felt for Harry, and then Hugo. If Ava could not have Hugo, maybe Callum would do? After all, on the surface, they were practically identical. Looking at Callum and thinking about Hugo was like an exercise in human 'spot the ball': hard to tell them apart. The main difference between them was how they smelled: Callum, of vetiver with velvety hazelnut and a woody mellowness, and Hugo, of tenderness and sensuality with a tinge of pain.

Inevitably, they chatted about their respective marriages and subsequent break-ups.

'Why do you think it's so hard to find a partner?' Ava asked. It was one of her favourite questions to which she had been trying to find an answer for all her adult life.

'Gosh, I don't know,' Callum said, twisting his signet ring. 'I suppose it's because there are so many variables: physical attraction, emotional connection, an overlap in values, matching intellect, compatible families, timing, et cetera, et cetera.'

'Mmm, yes, it's complicated,' Ava sighed. 'It feels like such a slog. It's a miracle anyone ever finds anyone.'

'Yes, it is,' Callum murmured, smiling.

Ava took another sip of wine. Emboldened, she asked her second favourite question. 'Why do you think we fall in love with the people we do?'

Callum fidgeted with his ring again. 'Well, I think the answer to that is multi-layered too.'

Ava suddenly regretted asking the question. It was as though she was asking him what she would need to do for him to fall in love with her. Why did she keep asking inappropriate questions that made her look so desperate?

'They say love is blind,' Callum said, 'but I don't think so. I think we fall for people that are culturally, intellectually and socio-economically similar. We tessellate. We're attracted to people with shared interests and a similar world view.'

'I agree with that,' Ava said. 'But I don't think that's enough, or not enough for me at least. There's got to be some emotional hook. I found that the men I loved all had early childhood experiences that mirrored my own. It's uncanny. Like we speak the same emotional language and we share a similar psychological DNA.'

'I suppose there's more to falling in love than just thinking, "She's hot."'

Ava laughed. How often had she been beguiled by beautiful blue eyes? It was happening right now. 'Well, finding someone you find physically irresistible is not a bad place to start,' she said with a wink. 'Sounds shallow, but we're animals after all. And all those pheromones we release, they serve an important biological function, right? Wasn't it scientifically proven that our sense of smell makes us attracted to reproducing with the people who have the exact opposite immune system to our own? Love doesn't get more Darwinian than that.'

'Follow your nose! The ultimate natural selection.'

'Yes, nature is wondrous, isn't it? Complex and yet so perfectly ordered.'

'Scientists say that falling in love is just a set of powerful hormones: testosterone and dopamine and oxytocin swilling around in our brains and bodies. So, attraction has a chemical explanation.'

'I'm sure that's partly true,' Ava said, 'but being the soppy romantic that I am, I hate the idea of reducing love to a few signalling molecules made of amino acids and peptides and steroids. It's a bit like dissecting a butterfly's wings to try to understand their ethereal beauty and the magic of flight.'

'I guess evolutionary biology is only a small part of love,' said Callum, fidgeting with his ring again. 'They say opposites attract, but I think that differences can become a source of irritation and conflict over time.'

'So, if I may ask, how come your marriage didn't work? I thought you and your wife were like two peas in a pod?'

'Yes, we were.' Callum looked away as he spoke. 'But my wife, well, my soon-to-be ex-wife, she never wanted to have sex with me. It was like she was permanently rejecting me. And then I stopped asking. Eventually, I, er, looked elsewhere.'

'Oh, I see. I'm sorry.' Ava bit her lip. 'Rejection is so very painful.'

'It was like having the stuffing knocked out of me. I lost all sense of self.' Callum reached for more wine.

They both fell silent.

'Perhaps that great cynic George Bernard Shaw was right when he said that "Love is a gross exaggeration of the difference between one person and everybody else."'

'Only someone who's never been truly in love could say something like that,' Ava said. She thought about why she had loved Harry and Hugo, but not Roger or Eren, who were intrinsically 'nicer' men. Maybe it was because neither Harry nor Hugo wanted her, so it made her want them more. She tossed her hair. Now was not the time to look back. She stared at the gorgeous Callum seated in front of her and her hormones responded appropriately.

Back in London there followed another cosy candlelit dinner. Ava and Callum went back to Ava's house for a proverbial night cap. And then, the moment they were both waiting for. They sat on Ava's bed and kissed. Callum gently pulled her hair back and unhooked her bra. He caressed her shoulder, fondled her breasts and moved his hand down her body. He lightly brushed her thighs and between her legs. He was soft and tender. Almost too tender. Ava could barely feel his touch She longed to feel his X-factor, his raw masculinity. There was none. Perhaps his bite would kick in later. There were plenty of compensations in the meantime: his beautiful, athletic body, his refined pre-Raphaelite face, and his blue, blue eyes.

He came on top, looked meaningfully into her eyes and penetrated her. Ava felt nothing. She resisted the overwhelming urge to ask Callum if he was in. Instead, she adjusted the angle and moved positions, but still, she could not feel him. His cock was on the small side, but not completely tiny. Of all the fatal flaws, not being able to feel his cock was more than a little disturbing. Maybe for another woman, it might not be the mother of all deal-breakers. After all, there was always the tongue. But for Ava, feeling, and feeling cock, was everything. In any event, Ava knew that Callum was way too interesting on all other counts to give up on. And she was not a woman to give up easily.

She swung into action. She came on top, cowgirl style, and lowered herself on to him, then began to grind back and forth. No, that did not improve matters. Then reverse cowgirl: this was not usually her favourite position as there was no eye contact and just a view of her bottom, which Callum certainly enjoyed, but she was looking at his feet, which was rather less interesting for her. But no. Still nothing. She tried the eagle, as in spreadeagled. The visuals were arousing: her pink pussy was invitingly wet and wide open, and they were both mesmerised as they watched his cock thrusting in and out of her. Even that didn't work. Ava wrapped her legs around his shoulders and made a very special effort to contract her Kegel muscles extra tight. No better. And her pleasure was considerably diminished by worrying that it made her look like she had a double chin. It gave her an uncomfortable neck strain to boot. Then she tried the usual winner, doggie style. He penetrated her as hard as he could from behind. It was still a resounding no. Ava could not feel him at all. She masturbated herself to orgasm, taking her time, as he kissed her and watched, spellbound. As she lay breathless next to him, she put his less-than-rousing performance down to first-night nerves. It happens to the best of us. Everyone is allowed an off-night and Ava was sure she had had plenty of those.

Curiously, Callum had a rather different view. He came strongly with a groan.

'Wow. You feel incredible,' he said. 'You're so intense. I've never met such a passionate woman.'

Passionate? Ava had gone through the motions, and she thought her own performance had been somewhat lacklustre.

Callum came back to Ava's house a couple of nights later. He looked cool in a tight black turtleneck jumper and black jeans. Ava put on the only long floaty dress she owned. She thought that looking less va-va-voom might be helpful. She set the lights low, plumped up the cushions on her sofa and put on some sexy fifties jazz. She arranged a simple but tasty sushi dinner, accompanied by a crisp, dry Montrachet. They chatted playfully as they fed each other dainty morsels with chopsticks. But they were not hungry and the spread lay largely uneaten.

After dinner, they went to lie on Ava's grey velvet sofa, scene of many a happy assignation. They started to kiss. Callum went through the exact same moves as before: he stroked Ava's shoulders, fondled her breasts, moved his hand down her body and then briefly between her legs. Then he came on top. That, at least, was a good sign. It looked like his masculinity was in the ascendant and he might now be taking charge. He gazed into her eyes meaningfully and penetrated her.

'Darling, yes. That's great. Harder. I want to feel you,' Ava said.

Callum plunged deeper. Ava thought that perhaps now she registered a little micro-sensation, the semblance of something firm moving inside her.

'Harder, Callum, harder, darling, deeper. I want to really feel you hard inside me.'

Callum thrust harder and deeper.

'Yes, darling, yes,' Ava said. 'That's it. Yes. Don't stop. Yes. Harder.'

She heard a strange crack that was eerily like the sound of a breaking bone. A sort of pop. An ominous pop. Callum howled and spun off her, his face crimson.

Something had gone horribly wrong.

Yikes, thought Ava, *this could be serious*. She sprang into action, immediately called an Uber and comforted Callum, still writhing in pain and bent over double, as they drove to the nearest A&E hospital unit. It was not the easiest of situations to explain to the army of paramedics, nurses and doctors who came in to take a closer look at this medical rarity. Callum was in too much pain to be embarrassed. The medics listened, aghast, as he described, in excruciating detail, what had happened.

'I was having sex with my girlfriend. Well, here she is.'

They all turned, open-mouthed, to look at Ava.

'We were in the missionary position, and I was, er, thrusting quite forcefully inside her, when I felt my penis bend, almost like it was buckling, even though I was rock hard, harder than I've ever been. I felt a terrific shock of pain, a bit like a tear, and then I wasn't erect anymore. It was like a thousand needles running through my penis. And then a searing thump of pulsating pain, as though all the blood vessels in my penis had snapped. My penis still feels like a locus of serious agony,' Callum said.

Ava was astonished at how articulate Callum sounded, even *in extremis*.

The medics peered at Callum's swollen purple penis. Ava noticed one of the doctors involuntarily grab his own crotch to check his apparatus was still intact. After an emergency MRI, Callum was diagnosed with a tear in the *tunica albuginea*, commonly known as a penile fracture. There are no bones in the penis. It had just sounded as if there were. Callum was lucky he narrowly escaped the need for reconstructive surgery.

Ava had fractured a man's penis. She was wracked with guilt for having encouraged Callum to thrust deeper and harder inside her. But secretly she was relieved that the fracture had not happened when she was the one who had been on top and in control. There but for the grace of God...

Callum's penis turned purple and then black from the swelling, a bit like an undersized, misshapen aubergine. Ava was terrified it might shrivel up and fall off completely. He refused to talk about it, and the topic was strictly taboo. Injury stopped all form of play for three weeks, as he walked around with a miserable hangdog expression. Understandably, Callum was incapable of rising to any occasion.

Without sex to stoke the fires of desire, the sizzling red heat of the burgeoning romance subsided. It soon became apparent that aside from a strong physical attraction, Ava and Callum did not have that much in common. He was a country boy; she was an uptown girl. He was partial to deep house; she adored opera. He loved all things traditional and institutional; she loved to challenge established practices and she fervently supported anything that promoted equality of opportunity and meritocracy. He was a man who need never worry about anything, let alone buy his own furniture; she'd had to fight for everything she ever had and there were no family heirlooms to get all nostalgic about. He was an aristocrat who loved to go back to what he ironically referred to as his 'gaff': the ornate, turreted castle that featured prominently in *Historic Castles of Great Britain*; she came from nowhere and never, ever wanted to go back there. He was the 'Right Honourable' in waiting; she waited for nothing, and she made things happen.

More disconcerting than their differences, some of which were, to an extent, surmountable, Ava wondered if Callum had the capacity to feel her. How could he? He was so detached, he could barely feel himself. Ava was attracted to how he wafted through life so effortlessly. But the flip side was that he had no bite. After all, how could someone like him have any bite? His family's name was emblazoned in gold on whisky bottles consumed around the world and engraved on marble plaques in art galleries and museum wings. There was even a small family bank that bore his hallowed name.

The main thing Ava and Callum did share was that they were both damaged goods. His fractured penis was an apt metaphor for all that was broken in him. It was as though he was so shut off from his own feelings that he did not recognise how fractured he was. In that sense, Callum and Ava were similar. They had similar issues, but they expressed them differently. While Ava tried to exorcise her inner demons, Callum pretended they didn't exist. That was not how they did things on the grouse moors and in the draughty castles. It was so much easier to simply glide through life and carry on. After all, Callum glided so beautifully.

Happily, Callum made a speedy physical recovery, and play, of sorts, resumed. Unhappily, not much happened to write home about. His appetites failed to match Ava's, either in bed or in life. Callum could not reach deep inside Ava and touch her soul. And try as she might, Ava could certainly not reach Callum. While a little Highland fling might pass the time pleasantly enough, what Ava wanted was so much more than a fling, Highland or not. And the bagpipes needed to be in full working order.

⌒ 26. ⌒

View from the Grouse Moors: What's Under the Kilt?

Callum flinched in anticipation of pain as he washed his penis in the shower. There was no pain. Not anymore. His penis was now operational, and mercifully back to how it had looked, *ex-ante*. There was no scarring. He was back from the brink. It had been the most terrifying experience of his life. He thought of how he might have lost his precious member. It was a thought he did not care to entertain for one second longer.

As he lathered himself, he thought of Ava. The saucy minx. And he grew hard. He was definitely back. Ava had sparked a boyish intensity in him. She was so different from the women he usually went for. It was a Verbier fling. He decided to stick to a Highland fling next time. So much safer.

27.

Don't You Want Me, Baby?

It was a fresh spring evening and Ava was having dinner at Annabel's with her closest and dearest male friend, Bruce. They were sitting under the stars in the Garden Room, where the roof had been retracted and the lush foliage swayed in the welcome breeze. Tall, elegant, smooth ebony skin, bitingly clever, highly principled and brutally honest, Bruce and Ava were cut from the same cloth. If he were not gay, they would, by now, be happily married, with three children. They would walk down the street together, laughing, arm in arm, and pass a handsome man who would smile at them. But they were never quite sure if the man was smiling at Bruce or at Ava. Quite possibly both.

They did not see each other that often now. Bruce, a man who used to enjoy living in the fast lane, had sought a more peaceful existence up in the Shetland Islands, where he'd opened an organic bakery. Nevertheless, the bond between them was unbreakable and they were always there for each other, through thick and thin.

They sat eating chocolates. Ava barely registered the fascinating people running amok, even though the crowd was unusually alluring tonight. There were stunning socialites and 'models' with large breasts and tiny bodies, sheathed in wisps of sparkly dresses, and with cascading mountains of freshly blow-dried hair, real and fake. Charismatic plutocrats and dashing captains of industry hatched their latest plans to take over the universe, while investing, ostentatiously, with a social and environmental conscience. And there was even the odd mere mortal. Everyone was in a state of high alert, ready for action. Their heads were on swivel sticks, moving left and right, as a procession of gorgeous people paraded by, tummies sucked in, and bosoms thrust out. It was business as usual; and the business that went on in this pleasure palace took many different shapes and sizes. Much as she loved Bruce, Ava was not in the mood for the carnival of the animals tonight, and she couldn't help but wish she had stayed home listening to BBC Radio 4.

'The light up in the Shetlands is spectacular, especially in the summer. You and the girls must come up and stay. You'll love it,' Bruce said. 'Anyway, enough about me and spelt grains, gluten-free bread, and my non-existent love life among the sheep farmers. What's happening in *your* love life?' He cast her a penetrating look.

The muscles of Ava's temples started to twitch. 'Oh, Bruce,' she said with a little sigh, 'it's been interesting times.'

'Uh-oh. You mean, like the ancient Chinese curse for troubled times?'

'Yeah, something like that,' Ava said listlessly. 'I feel like I've got one hand in the freezer and one hand in the oven, so on average, I should be feeling okay. But somehow, it doesn't quite work that way.'

Bruce laughed. 'You? Average? There's nothing average about you.'

'You know, at this point, I'm yearning for average. A life that's predictable and safe. After all those highs and lows, and all that "excitement", average and normal sound like a pretty good option.'

'Oh, come on. The Ava I know doesn't do average and normal. You thrive on the thrills. You need them. They make you feel alive.'

Ava knew Bruce was right. She tossed her blonde mane and smiled. And as she did so, she locked eyes with a rather attractive man sitting alone at the bar, straight in her line of vision, right behind Bruce. Ava recognised the type immediately. Refined and aloof, he exuded a restrained sexuality that needed to be unleashed. Or at least, that was what Ava thought. And she wanted to unleash him, on sight.

Suddenly, the evening was more promising. Now Ava regretted having dressed in black leather trousers and a plain black T-shirt, rather than her usual night-on-the-tiles uniform of short, tight minidress.

Mr Gorgeous at the bar was pretending to read his *Financial Times*. Every time he looked up and smiled at her, Ava caught a glimpse of his dazzling, swimming-pool-blue eyes. Ava took a quick look behind her. She wanted to make sure he was smiling at her, not at a more beautiful woman behind her. No, there was no one behind her, just the gold, floral and leopard de Gournay wallpaper and a few succulent pink rhododendrons.

'So, come on, spill the beans. What's happening with Hugo?' Bruce asked.

'Hugo?' Ava said faintly. 'He skedaddled. It's over, whatever "it" was. Not a lot, as it turned out.' She fiddled with her earring. 'Except that, for the record, in case you were remotely interested, he was irresistible in the sack.'

'Duh,' said Bruce with a smile. 'Of course he was great in the sack, or you would never have been interested in him. I know you, Ava. I've known you for twenty years, remember? I know how important mind-blowing sex is to you.'

'Sometimes I wish it wasn't. The sex kind of swung it. Because we were good in bed together, I thought we'd be good in life too. But I guess it doesn't work that way. Hugo said he couldn't offer me anything until he felt a bit more stable in himself, until his divorce was finalised, until his kids stopped acting up, until he found himself a new house. Blah, blah, bloody blah. It sounded like he was working on the best set of schoolboy excuses since he was at Eton and the dog ate his homework.'

'Ava, darling, you're over-analysing and over-thinking,' Bruce said. 'Look at it from Hugo's perspective. He just got out of a marriage, he wrote a rather large cheque to his ex-wife and he's feeling bruised. You're so hard-core and full-on. Any man needs to be on top form to be with you. You don't tolerate anything less. Hugo probably didn't feel up to the job. I love you, you know that. But you're a handful. No man can coast through a relationship with you, and he needs loads of self-confidence to take you on.'

Ava clenched her jaw. Why couldn't Bruce find a way to make Hugo want her? Talking about Hugo, Ava went off into a mini daydream about his phallus. Was it really only men who thought about sex twenty times a day?

'You know, Ava, women are often looking for hidden depths in a man. Men are not that deep. What you see is what you get. If he says he's not ready for a relationship, he's not ready. End of. Move on. It's not personal.'

'Of course it's personal.' Ava ground her teeth. 'Hugo decided it was *me* he didn't want to be in a relationship with.'

Bruce shook his head. 'You need a little time to lick your wounds. You'll get over it. Believe me, when a man is genuinely interested in you, you'll know it. He'll be constantly texting you and he'll want to see you all the time. If he's not interested, he won't text and he won't ask you out. It's that simple. If you're confused about a guy's behaviour and his mixed signals, it means he's just not that into you.'

Ava stopped scoffing the chocolates. She looked up and smiled. Bruce smiled back. Straight behind Bruce, Mr Gorgeous also smiled back. It was a circle of smiling. How conveniently they were all seated. Ava did not even have to adjust her position to take a good look at him. She looked him straight in the eyes. Brazenly.

Bruce continued to diagnose Ava's man problems, thinking of ways to help her out of her funk. But somehow, Mr Gorgeous, smiling at her, was like a balm for her soul.

'Sometimes, Ava, you emasculate men, you know that?' Bruce went on. 'Let the man be the man. You're always complaining that men aren't masculine enough for you. But they can't be male with you, because you're always competing with them. That's not attractive to any man, let alone an alpha male. Let your feminine side shine through. Be softer, more vulnerable. No man wants a man in a woman's body. Men want a woman in a woman's body.'

Ava was only half listening to Bruce's wise words. She knew exactly what she needed to do. She was just not very good at doing it. What she wanted at this point was to find a way to get to know Mr Gorgeous. He flashed her another smile and winked. Then he slid off the bar stool and walked off in the direction of the loos. That was her cue.

'Bruce, will you excuse me for a couple of minutes? I need the loo,' Ava said.

She adjusted her cleavage and fluffed up her hair as she sauntered off. As expected, Mr Gorgeous was waiting for her in the corridor in front of the ladies'.

'Hi,' he said, smiling broadly. 'I was wondering if you'd come out here. I hoped you would.'

'Oh, hello,' Ava said, trying to sound cool. 'Actually, I needed to use the loo,' she improvised.

'I couldn't help but notice you. You've got such a great smile,' Mr Gorgeous said.

'You too,' said Ava.

It was astonishing how pulse-quickening such a banal exchange with a beautiful stranger could be.

'My name is Leonard,' His Gorgeousness said.

'I'm Ava,' she replied, detecting a charming South African, Americanised lilt. 'Are you from here? You've got an interesting accent. I can't quite place it.'

'I live round the corner, but I'm originally from Jo'burg.'

'Oh, we're neighbours then. I live around the corner too.'

'Of course you do,' said Leonard. 'I could have predicted that.'

'Why, don't tell me you're a brain surgeon too.' Ava shook her head and smiled at his self-confidence.

'Actually, I am.' Leonard paused to let that sink in. 'How about a neighbourly drink sometime?'

Brains as well as beauty.

Ava looked into Leonard's blue eyes. 'Sure.' She tried to sound as casual as possible, but her voice went up a little and her heart rate too.

'I don't have a business card on me,' he said. 'Why don't you give me your number and I'll text you.'

As compelling as Leonard was, Ava was not in the habit of giving random strangers her phone number, even those professing to be brain surgeons. But she registered the Patek Philippe Nautilus Chronograph and the Belstaff leather jacket and she decided that Leonard was not an axe murderer and he warranted further investigation. She gave him her number and sashayed off, wiggling her bottom more than strictly necessary. She looked back over her shoulder and winked at Leonard. Leonard winked back. He noticed she had forgotten to use the loo.

'Are you okay?' asked Bruce. 'You were gone for quite a long time.'

'All good,' responded Ava brightly as she sat back down. 'I was admiring the interior design in this joint. The loos have pink hand-carved sinks made of onyx, with gold swan taps. The whole thing is completely over the top, but somehow it works.'

She felt the vibration of a message from her phone in her back pocket. Discreetly, she pulled out her phone and noticed that Leonard had just messaged her. She smiled. It had been a good decision to come out tonight after all.

Over the next few days, Leonard and Ava exchanged the usual flurry of texts. Good news: Leonard was sexy and successful. Bad news: he was getting married next week.

I know we shouldn't, Leonard texted, *but you're irresistible.*

Familiar words. They elicited in Ava a boringly familiar response.

I don't touch married men, she wrote. Strictly speaking, this was more an expression of intention than reality. *Though I guess, technically, you're not married quite yet.*

Are you naughty? Leonard asked.

What do you think?

Leonard sent her an emoji of a blushing, smiling face with hands stretched out, whose meaning was indecipherable. It could mean anything she wanted it to mean. Leonard clearly didn't know her well enough yet to never, ever use emojis with her. Words were what turned her on.

I'm naughty, Ava texted, *but I'm very nice too.*

She was not sure if niceness was a desirable quality to a man like Leonard. But she did know exactly what she needed to do to get the text conversation straight on to 'hard' and 'wet' territory. She decided that it was not territory she wished to visit with Leonard. Showing heroic discipline, she thought it best to cut all contact with him immediately.

Sorry, Leonard, tempting as you are, I don't think it makes sense to stay in touch. Good luck for the future. Text me if you ever get divorced.

Ava had a flash of déjà vu from when she broke up with Harry. Finally, it seemed she might be learning something from her past mistakes. Better late than never.

A couple of months later, Ava was at the Jan van Eyck private viewing at the National Gallery. A familiar brunette walked over to her. Ah, yes. Now she remembered where she had seen her before. She had spotted her out and about in Mayfair, laughing and smiling, with a tall man with piercing blue eyes. It was Leonard's wife. She had long, rather fake-looking hair extensions and matching long, rather fake-looking eyelash extensions. She wore a black Louis Vuitton dress with the familiar logo stamped all over it, to alert the casual onlooker that it was a Very Expensive Piece. And no one could fail to notice her enormous pear-cut diamond engagement ring and the matching diamond eternity band, as they sparkled in the light.

'I keep seeing you everywhere in Mayfair,' said the brunette to Ava. 'We seem to like the same places. You look so interesting. I thought I would come over and introduce myself. My name's Debbie.'

Ava thought that Debbie was interesting too. But for different reasons. She was keen to know what woman had managed to capture Leonard's heart.

It transpired that Ava and Debbie had a bit more in common than a fancy for tall, successful, blue-eyed South African brain surgeons. They both came from underprivileged backgrounds, and they had both worked their way up and out of their own rat holes. They were both pin-thin and obsessed with maintaining their bodies hard through daily exercise and a high-protein, low-carb diet. And they both had a passion for Flemish Old Masters. But while Debbie had married spectacularly well, and Leonard was her second husband, Ava had slogged her way to financial freedom. It made for a rather different world view. Nonetheless, within a couple of weeks of meeting, they began to hang out together. Ava got to know an awful lot about Debbie, and, in particular, about the state of Debbie's marriage.

Debbie was one happy bunny.

'Lennie's amazing,' Debbie gushed. 'I'm so blessed. The universe totally delivers, you know. We're going to the Cheval Blanc in the Maldives for Christmas.'

Ava shrunk. It was her favourite hotel in the world, in her favourite beach spot. She imagined Leonard making love to Debbie on a deserted beach at sunset or bending her over on the balustrade of their water villa, as the stingrays and sea turtles glided past. The dream.

One month later, Debbie's demeanour changed. She was distinctly less glossy, and the logo dresses were replaced with leggings and scruffy trainers. There appeared a new poodle, Queenie, who was always by her side. Instead of the beautiful Hermès Birkins that Lennie liked to lavish on Debbie, she now carried a dog lead and a plastic poop bag. Something was most definitely up.

'Lennie's behaving a bit erratically,' Debbie told Ava over coffee in Cecconi's. 'I think he must be really stressed out. Poor baby. You know, he's not just a top brain surgeon. He also owns forty hospitals around the world. All that responsibility. All those lives. Anyway, he's got some private equity outfits vying to buy his hospitals. It's going to make a' – she cleared her throat – 'substantial difference to our lifestyle.'

Debbie sounded upbeat, but Ava noticed that her usually flawless olive skin was not quite as unblemished as it used to be.

A couple of weeks later, over emergency drinks at the Blue Bar in the Berkeley hotel, came more revelations.

'Lennie and I have stopped having sex,' Debbie announced.

She attacked the maraschino cherry perched at the top of her long glass and took a large, noisy gulp of her third piña colada. Then she shovelled three large handfuls of salted almonds into her mouth in rapid succession. Ava had never seen Debbie eat so much.

'Lennie hasn't touched me since the honeymoon,' Debbie confessed. 'No sex in three months. I don't know what the hell's going on. I had a bit of a nose around and I found some Viagra in the drawer of his night table. Maybe he can't get it up. Perhaps he's embarrassed, so he doesn't want to have sex with me anymore. He's working round the clock. I barely see him.'

Ava was surprised to learn how fast Debbie's life in paradise had unravelled. Obviously, Leonard was stressed, but she wasn't sure she agreed with Debbie's line of reasoning. Surely Leonard bought the Viagra because he wanted to have sex?

'I wouldn't say anything to him now, Debbie,' she advised. 'He's probably focused on closing the hospitals deal. You know, when men are stressed out, they retreat back into their man-cave. They don't like to talk about it, not like us women. His sex drive will come back. Just be patient. I wouldn't add to his stress if I were you.'

'I bought some gorgeous new Agent Provocateur lingerie,' Debbie said, munching more almonds. 'I tried to, you know, get it on with him, but he turned me down flat. Do you have any idea how humiliating that is? It's never happened to me before. Ever. I'm beginning to wonder, maybe he's gay? I mean, he's forty-nine, and this is his first marriage. That's a bit of a red flag, isn't it?'

Ava cocked her eyebrow. Leonard didn't seem remotely gay when they had met at Annabel's.

A month later, Debbie confided in Ava, somewhat tearfully, 'Lennie's moved out of the house. I'm utterly devastated. It's only been five months! We've only been married five months and Lennie's left. It's insane. I can't believe this is happening to me. Lennie won't even talk to me anymore. He told me he's moving out by WhatsApp. What man does that?'

'I'm so sorry, Debbie,' Ava said.

It was hard to know what to say. Leonard's behaviour was cowardly at best. At least, that's how it appeared, from Debbie's side of the story.

'When I think back,' Debbie said, 'we had the most incredible wedding reception in Harry's Bar. Alain Ducasse did the food. The champagne and the wines were all vintage, and they were whizzed in direct from France. You know, Lennie's super close to Lord You-Know-Who, and he's got some of the best vineyards in the world. So we got a special deal after Lennie performed that tricky op on him. And we had ten thousand refrigerated white roses flown in from Ecuador. It was amazing. Maybe you saw the pictures in *Tatler*? And now this? The man is a psycho. He's not normal. He suffers from narcissistic personality disorder.'

Later that night, Ava had dinner at George with one of her beaus. As she went to the loos to double-check she didn't have any of that lovely creamed spinach stuck to her teeth, she heard a familiar voice coming from behind her. It was a deep, sexy voice with a faintly South African, Americanised lilt.

'I'd recognise that pert derrière and those beautiful long legs anywhere.'

'Leonard!' Ava squealed.

She tried to sound cool, but she was breathless, even though she was standing perfectly still. She had known it was only a matter of time before she would bump into him again in Mayfair.

'I moved out,' he announced. 'I'm sure Debbie told you. We're getting a divorce. Life with her was unbearable. What the hell was I thinking? Debbie's gorgeous, but she's impossible. She's a psycho. She's not normal. She suffers from narcissistic personality disorder.'

Ava smiled at the identical words she had heard that very day coming out of the mouth of his soon-to-be ex-wife.

'Boy, did I get it wrong,' Leonard said. 'That's what happens when you let your pecker do the picking.' He looked Ava up and down. 'You know what, you and I should have got it on as soon as we met. You would have saved me the pain, and expense, of my disastrous five-month marriage. I knew, deep down, that I was making a mistake. But I didn't have the balls to call the wedding off at the last minute.'

Ava smiled sympathetically. 'Don't be so hard on yourself. We all make mistakes. At least you realised it and you got out fast.'

'It's come at such a bad time. I'm in the middle of trying to sell my hospitals group. This is quite a blow for me. I feel like such a failure. It's going to take some time for me to be myself again. I've lost all my self-confidence.'

Ava found it hard to believe that a man like Leonard – successful, handsome, clever, life-saving – might ever lack self-confidence.

'You'll be fine, Leonard,' she said. 'You need a bit of time. You know, it's a cliché, but time is a great healer.'

It was such a banal statement. Couldn't she think of anything more original to say?

'Yup, you're right, I guess.' Leonard looked at her more closely. 'Be honest with me. Did you get to know Debbie as a way of getting closer to me?'

Ava's mouth fell open. It was an arrogant observation, particularly coming from a man who had just said he had lost his self-confidence. But as it happened, Leonard was right. Ava was mesmerised by the intimate details of Debbie and Leonard's relationship. It gave her a privileged insight into Leonard. And somehow, it was awkward to tell Debbie that she had met her fiancé a week before her marriage, let alone that he'd tried to pursue her. Once they got to know each other better, it was too late to say anything.

'Hey, you look like dynamite,' Leonard said. 'I'm so glad I bumped into you. After I got married, I deleted your number. I wanted to be a good boy. But once I knew I was leaving Debbie, I thought about the beautiful blonde that I met in Annabel's. I walked past your house quite a few times, hoping I'd bump into you.'

Had Leonard been stalking her? Ava's mind boggled. All he had to do was whistle and she would have come running, fast.

That night, Leonard reverted to type and sent Ava the customary *I want to fuck you* texts, accompanied by a series of photographs that grew progressively more risqué as the night went on.

Leonard, Ava texted back, *you can't send semi-nude photos. It's reckless. What if a journalist got hold of them? Or maybe Debbie installed spyware on your phone.*

Ava knew that big, powerful men had big, powerful egos. They thought they could get away with whatever they wanted to get away with. But this was downright irresponsible.

You're right. I don't trust Debbie, or her Rottweiler divorce lawyers, Leonard agreed.

Then he totally ignored what he had written only two seconds before and sent Ava three full-blown, erect dick pics. He still had his socks on.

Don't you want to see my big, hard cock, he texted. It wasn't a question.

As it happened, Ava preferred to see Leonard's cock in person, at the appropriate time and place. She did not need a preview.

I trust you, Leonard wrote.

I'm trustworthy, Leonard, but not everyone is, typed Ava. *Be careful. Your whole career could blow up at the click of an iPhone camera.*

I know. You're right. I'm just letting off steam, he texted back.

Ava imagined Leonard wanted to let off something a little more liquid than steam. And she could think of a hundred and one better ways in which she might assist him, in the flesh, but she said nothing.

A couple of nights later, Leonard messaged Ava again.

You look smoking hot in your new WhatsApp photo. You have no idea how much I want to fuck you. I get hard just thinking about you.

Rather than being turned on, Ava was mildly irritated at the stream of randy late-night text messages. Where was it all going? The last thing she needed was a naughty pen pal.

Erotic messages aside, Leonard regaled Ava with the intimate details of his proposed divorce settlement. He ignored the counsel of London's finest and most expensive divorce lawyers and bowed graciously to every single one of Debbie's extravagant financial demands. This included Debbie appropriating his magnificent white stucco-fronted Mayfair townhouse, overlooking one of London's most beautiful gardens. Naturally, Debbie demanded that the exquisite back-lit onyx table that seated twelve, a spiralling three-metre-high Bohemian crystal chandelier and the Ron Arad stainless-steel sofa, that had once been displayed at the Museum of Modern Art in New York, be thrown in too. After all, they had all been tailormade for the house. She also made sure to include the circular wall-mounted Anish Kapoor mirror artwork that Leonard adored, together with the Olafur Eliasson monochromatic, immersive light installation. She loved how that beam of orange light helped her achieve an 'experience that transcended space and time', and how the 'boundless reality of light and truth was conditioned by the elemental perception of it', as she liked to explain to those house guests who cared to ask. Debbie even remembered to add the umbrella stand, which also figured as its own line item in the official divorce papers. Well, it was an Armani Casa umbrella stand, after all.

You had to hand it to Debbie. It was nice work for a five-month marriage. Little wonder Leonard lost his sparkle.

Finally, he invited Ava to dinner. It had been seven months since they had first met. In that time, Leonard had been engaged, married, separated and divorced, and he was now officially single. In that time, Ava had tried to get over Hugo, she had dated Roger and then Eren, and dabbled with a few other men, and she was now, also, officially single. Again.

Leonard knew Ava was a fan of good red meat, so he thoughtfully picked CUT, London's finest steak restaurant, for their dinner date.

'You look like a goddess,' Leonard said, as Ava strode punctually into the restaurant where he was already waiting for her.

They perched side by side at the bar, swivelling with anticipation on the leather bar stools. After several weeks of feverish sexting, during which Leonard had told her the hundred ways he wanted to fuck her and lick her, and precisely how she should suck him and lick every drop, Ava sat smiling demurely, practically a virgin queen.

She dressed relatively modestly. Leonard was a sophisticated animal, and she knew he would prefer her elegant and refined, rather than trussed up like Jessica Rabbit. She picked a feminine red Alaïa dress, not too short, not too low cut, which allowed for a trace of nipple, and she slipped on a pair of nude Louboutin heels with matching red soles. She spent twenty minutes arranging her hair into an artful chignon, to make it look as though she had barely spent two seconds putting her hair up in a bun. She had read in one of the glossy magazines at the hairdresser's that afternoon that it was scientifically proven that men were attracted to women who smiled a lot and who wore red. She already smiled a lot naturally. And now, in her red dress, she was all set for a great night.

Leonard looked sleek in black pants and a slim-cut black Tom Ford shirt, and he wore a Lange & Söhne Tourbograph Pour Le Mérite watch. To the untrained eye, it looked like an ordinary watch with a brown crocodile strap; but it was one of only five in the world. The surgeon in Leonard was fascinated by its intricate oscillating mechanism, like a beating heart.

He was, by nature, an attentive and generous host, and tonight Leonard pulled out all the stops. They started with a vintage Roederer champagne, which was a perfect match for the hamachi yellowtail sashimi, and they both ordered the Kobe beef, which she was able to cut with her fork, accompanied by a fine 2013 Château Petrus Pomerol.

The conversation flowed, as did the alcohol. Ava was too nervous to eat much, but she had no trouble drinking. She smiled and laughed at Leonard's jokes and anecdotes. She tried to make eye contact, but she noticed Leonard was not particularly good at holding her gaze. She knew he was a bit shy, but it was disconcerting for such a successful man. When Ava did catch a glimpse of his eyes, she noticed again how blue they were. She wanted to dive into those eyes, but Leonard looked away.

'I want to tell you something, Ava,' Leonard said, suddenly serious. 'I want you to know that you have a boy round the corner from you, who's here for you, day and night. Whatever you need, I'm here for you.'

Ava was confused. She thought, at first, that Leonard was referring to the concierge in his building. Then it dawned on her that the 'boy' was him. She'd clearly had too much to drink, because she felt a little tear slip out of her right eye. One of the busiest men in London was here for her, day and night? That was one of the kindest things anyone had ever said to her.

'Thank you, Leonard,' she said, choking up. 'Thank you. That really touches me.'

'Totally,' Leonard said, 'I mean it.' At last, he looked straight into Ava's eyes.

For a few magical seconds, they were connected: the sun and the moon and the stars were in perfect alignment, and time stretched out to infinity.

But then the waiter arrived with the wild field mushrooms, and Leonard adjusted the back of his collar. The magical interplanetary moment passed. They discussed Debbie and the divorce, the impending sale of Leonard's hospitals and his plans for a long summer vacation in his favourite watering holes in the South of France.

By now, Ava had had enough light banter. She had seen pictures of Leonard naked and yet, she didn't know much about what lay beneath. The time seemed right to delve below the surface.

'You're a riddle wrapped in a mystery inside an enigma. You're so tightly wrapped, Leonard,' she said. 'It's tough to know what you're thinking, and it's even tougher to know what you're feeling.'

'Yup,' Leonard agreed. 'I'm beyond tight.'

Trust him to use a sexual simile.

'Do you want to stay that way?'

'It's not a priority to change right now, to be honest. I've got so much on my mind. The sale of my hospitals, it's a big deal. It'll take real work to pull it off.'

'I understand, Leonard. Really, I do. I used to be closed up, like you. But I was missing out, and you are too. You could be so much happier if you let your guard down and opened up emotionally. For one thing, sex is better when you have a real connection. You told me you've never had that. And I think, deep down, you're curious and you want it.'

'Maybe.' Leonard was delicately cutting his knife into the tablecloth, like he might wield his scalpel to cut into brain matter in the operating theatre. 'But I'm good. It would be a complicated journey for me to change. And I've got enough complexity at work.'

'But you know, Leonard,' Ava said softly, 'connected sex is electrifying.'

What had gotten into her? Couldn't she give it a rest? Trying to explain the bliss of intimacy to a man like Leonard was like trying to get a square peg into a round hole, as it were.

'I know it's complicated to open up. It's hard to be vulnerable,' Ava murmured. She decided to practise precisely what she preached, and to be open with Leonard right now. 'After my divorce, I realised I wanted a different kind of relationship. I was craving connection and depth. It's not an easy journey. But I think the ultimate strength is being vulnerable, isn't it? It takes courage to show who you really are.'

Leonard knew Ava had his best interests at heart. But the search for meaning, closeness and intimacy were not on his agenda. Not now anyway. Maybe not ever.

'You're beyond lovely to me, Ava. You've always been kind to me. You've been a great friend. I'm not sure what I did to deserve it. But you should know' – his voice faltered – 'I would disappoint you in the sack.'

Ava was confused. Was this the same man who had told her how much he wanted her to come hard, not just in his mouth, but dripping her wetness all over his mouth?

'Why, Leonard?' Ava asked gently. 'Why do you think you would disappoint me in bed?'

'Because I would want to have sex and then leave,' Leonard stammered. 'I always leave after I come. And you would not want that. As you shouldn't. But it's me.'

Ava gulped. So much for deep intimacy. She had never met a man who did not want to stay the night with her after sex. That was often the best part, when they were both naked, and the real conversation could begin.

At this critical point in the discussion, Mayfair being Mayfair, one of the American investment bankers working on Leonard's deal sauntered over to say hello. Leonard put his work face back on and straightened the back of his shirt collar, even though it was still perfectly straight.

'Well, hello, John,' Leonard said. He was back to his extrovert public persona. 'What a surprise to see you here! London's quite the global village, isn't it? This is Ava. She's not only beautiful, right? She's clever too and she works with money, like you.'

Ava blushed.

'Well, aren't you a dark horse, Lennie,' John said. After a few obligatory pleasantries, they discussed the hospitals deal. 'I think I can leverage some buy-in for a paradigm shift around the valuation, but I'll need to action a deep dive and some thought-leadership around that and then mobilise buy-in from our lead investors in Jeddah. I'll circle back once I've reached out to them. We can take this to the next level, Lennie.'

Ava was barely listening, still confused by what Leonard had just told her.

Leonard called for his driver to take them back to Ava's place. When they arrived at her house, he leapt out and accompanied her to the front door. Ava felt her heart beat faster. She noticed that the chauffeur kept the engine running.

'It's been such a wonderful evening,' Leonard said. 'Thank you for agreeing to have dinner with me. You're such great company. I really enjoyed our time together.'

His words bore an uncanny resemblance to a polite thank you that might be extended by a maiden aunt after a cup of tea and cream scones.

'Leonard, it's for me to thank you,' said Ava, struggling to get her keys into the lock. 'It was a lovely evening. You're such a thoughtful and kind host. I had a great time too.'

She hovered expectantly. She had heard, loud and clear, what Leonard had said in the restaurant, and yet she waited for him to grab her by the waist, haul her inside and ravish her, just as he had told her he wanted to do, many, many times. Instead, Leonard pecked her on the cheek, turned on his heels and walked back to the purring Mercedes.

Ava sat slumped on the velvet ottoman in the entrance hall. She knew from her own experience what it was like to have men around her whom she was fond of, but whom she did not desire sexually. Quite possibly, they had also been confused by her behaviour. Maybe this was the universe punishing her? A maelstrom of bad karma? The inevitability of fate? What goes around comes around?

This was different. Ava knew that Leonard desired her. He had told her many times how much he wanted her. She could feel it. She also knew that Leonard was a busy man who would not waste his time with anyone unless he wanted to. His time was strictly accounted for and he would be perfectly happy having dinner on his own.

Maybe she should make the first move? Perhaps it was time to cast her scruples aside and jump Leonard's bones. After all, he had told her he was shy, hadn't he?

No. Definitely no. Ava was never, ever going to make the first move on a man. Ava loved an alpha male; she was not about to become one. Still, she was baffled. Now that he could have Ava, why didn't Leonard want her? She was unsure whether to laugh or cry.

Neither nor, as it happened. She felt a sudden queasiness in the pit of her stomach and a strange gagging sensation in her throat. She made a hurried dash to the loo and vomited up the contents of her entire dinner.

Once the retching and heaving subsided, Ava wondered if this was symbolic of the current state of her life.

28.

The Hero's View: The Delicate Dance of Mortality

'Scalpel,' Leonard said to the scrub nurse without looking up.

His rangy frame stooped over the inanimate mound on the operating table. The body was completely covered in a thin blue sheet, and it was impossible to know there was a real live human being underneath. Only a gelatinous, semi-oval, little grey heap with blood swilling all over it was visible.

'The number twelve, please,' he added.

It was a pointed, crescent-shaped blade used to make small, precise incisions. Leonard, for one, knew that the first cut is not always the deepest, contrary to popular opinion.

He stood tall, towering and omnipotent in his green scrubs. He stretched his arms up and moved his stiff neck from side to side. He resisted the overwhelming urge to run his gloved hand to the back of his head to relieve the tension. It was only then, two hours into the operation, that he noticed how much his back was hurting. His face mask covered the lower half of his face and his eyes shone brilliant blue in the dazzling white light of the operating theatre. Today, it was a craniotomy, and it was a rather unusual case. An eighteen-year-old girl, a non-smoker who categorically did not do drugs and barely drank alcohol, had suffered a near-fatal aneurysmal sub-arachnoid haemorrhage. What had started as a bad headache had turned into a massive bleed in the brain, with weakness running all the way down her left side, violent convulsions and loss of consciousness. She was lucky to have been rushed to the emergency unit of one of Leonard's hospitals in record time.

Leonard bent back over the operating table. He had made a tiny incision into the scalp and then created a small bone flap in the skull. The next part was always the hardest, even though he had performed it maybe five thousand times before: cutting into the brain. It did not require any special technical expertise. But even now, after all these years, Leonard found it emotionally challenging and intellectually baffling. To think he was cleaving through a human being's thoughts and dreams, emotions and memories, loves and desires, with the tip of his steel scalpel. All of consciousness and identity reduced to a tangle of veins, arteries, lobes, membranes, neurones and cerebrospinal fluid.

He asked for a pair of diathermy forceps and carefully picked through the spaghetti heap of intricate red blood vessels and the glistening white lump that was the brain. How like a jumbled clump they looked to the naked eye, and yet how delicate they appeared under the beam of the operating microscope. Leonard, who had been a neurosurgeon for almost twenty years, was keenly aware of the precarious balance between life and death. He was both the agent of life and the potential instrument of death. Meticulously, he cut through the soft white jelly of the cerebrum, and the thin arachnoid membrane. He used one of the retractors under the patient's frontal lobe and slowly pulled the brain up from the base of the skull. This was the most complex part of the operation and, psychosomatically, he felt the thud of his own pulse at the back of his head.

'Almost done. It's almost ready to be clipped,' Leonard said to the surgical technologist.

He began to relax. All he needed to do was place a small titanium clip at the neck of the aneurysm, where it branched out from the main artery, to prevent it from rupturing again, and then close the skull and stitch up the scalp. Easy. He was already thinking about the long hot shower he would enjoy when all this was over.

All at once, the brain began to swell, inexplicably. The aneurysm burst again, and dark red arterial blood shot upwards. Through the microscope, all Leonard could see was a swamp of bright red blood. The patient was seconds away from another catastrophic haemorrhage, and death.

Leonard froze. A single bead of sweat trickled down his back, even though the operating room was freezing cold.

'What the fucking fuck? Fucking hell. Fuck. Focus. Fuck. Keep the brain alive,' Leonard muttered to himself. 'Keep the brain alive.'

The room was quiet except for the soft bleep of the anaesthesia machine and the blood pressure and pulse monitors. Leonard knew he had to stop the bleeding and keep the brain oxygenated. He took a deep breath and closed his eyes. He visualised the vast expanse of arid African bush, and he felt the blazing sun powering through his body. It took him straight back to his childhood in the savannah.

The sun.

Life force.

Leonard's finely tuned reflexes kicked in. He knew he could not panic, nor could he be seen to panic. His alarm would spread like contagion to the operating team, and it would prevent them from functioning effectively.

All this happened in three seconds, tops. Leonard looked at the mass of blood, expanding and contracting rhythmically, and then down the microscope again and back to the spurting aneurysm.

'Four millimetre, short-angled clip,' he shouted. 'Now!'

It was unusual for Leonard to raise his voice.

The nurse had already anticipated his request and handed him the correct titanium clip. He quickly loaded it onto the applicator tip and pressed the springs of the handle together so that the clip blades sealed the gushing artery. The fountain of blood stopped immediately. Leonard had saved a life, another life, seconds away from the greedy clutches of death. He wiped his brow with the back of his hand and then exhaled deeply with gratitude. Everyone in the room breathed a sigh of collective relief.

'Guys,' Leonard said, looking up in turn to the anaesthesiologist, the nurse, the surgeon's assistant and the surgical technician. 'You all did great. Thank you. None of this would have been possible without real teamwork. Good job. Well done.'

It was typical of Leonard to share the fruits of his own mental and physical agility and his accomplishments with the whole team.

The perfect cadences of Bach's 'Brandenburg Concerto' that had been playing softly in the background gave way to the pounding beat of Foreigner's 'I Want To Know What Love Is'. Leonard always liked to end his operations on a high note, and the nurse had turned the volume up. He tapped his foot to the music as he finished the operating marathon, neatly stitching up the back of the patient's cranium.

Leonard laughed out loud. The operation was, in the end, a resounding success. But he was forty-nine years old and he didn't know what love was.

A few hours later, Leonard was trying to relax at the Connaught Bar. He looked perfect, as usual, in his dark jeans that were neither too tight nor too loose, and his smart black leather Loro Piana jacket. He flipped through his leather agenda, with its pristine cover and neat handwriting all in the same colour ink. For a man who loved to be at the cutting edge of technology, he still kept a paper diary, for the sheer pleasure of being able to use one of the limited-edition pens he loved to collect.

'Good evening, sir,' said the waiter, smiling. 'It's nice to see you again. What can I get you to drink?'

Leonard looked up. Every day, he made agonising decisions that could bring a person back to life or hasten their death, and here he was, struggling to decide what he wanted to drink. He stared blankly at the waiter.

'Shall I bring you your usual tequila, sir? No ice?' the waiter suggested. 'With a large bottle of Evian, room temperature?'

Leonard nodded. That was exactly what he needed.

Today had been a victory, and his blood was still pumping with residual exhilaration, but it had been a close shave. He wondered how he could have averted the near disaster. What could he have foreseen? What should he have done better? How could he enhance his performance next time?

The reality was that sometimes bad stuff happens. Leonard knew that surgeons have to play at being God. He was definitely not God. Some days, he barely felt human.

Leonard was tired. He rubbed his eyes, then looked out of the window absently. Just at that moment he spotted Debbie, elegant in a black mink coat, the one he had bought her last Christmas. Leonard was not surprised to see her. After all, she lived around the corner, in his beautiful old home. She was laughing and she looked happy, hand-in-hand with a grey-haired older man in a camel-coloured overcoat. For a fraction of a second, he forgot they were divorced, and he was about to tap on the window to draw her attention and invite her in for a drink. Then he remembered. How could he have forgotten that Debbie was no longer his wife? He was dog-tired. He laughed at himself, sat back in the velvet armchair and straightened the collar of his shirt. He called his assistant.

'Hi, Susan. How's the best executive assistant in London?' he said, trying to sound upbeat but feeling drained. 'Tell me, when am I supposed to be where this week?'

Leonard knew all right. His agenda was right there in front of him. But he had been out of the office a lot, and he wanted Susan to feel like she was needed and appreciated.

'Hi, Leonard,' Susan said. 'I heard the op was tough but successful. Congratulations.'

Leonard flinched. He knew that a few extra seconds' prevarication would have been catastrophic.

'Well, as I'm sure you know, you've got a busy few days coming up,' Susan continued. 'There's that interview with the *FT* tomorrow over lunch. You remember, they're doing that "Person in the News" profile on you. I booked you the corner table at Harry's Bar, the one at the back you like. One o'clock.'

Leonard sipped the tequila and closed his eyes, savouring it.

'After that, Ahmed will pick you up and take you straight to the airport. You're on your usual overnight flight to New York. As soon as you land, I scheduled your next meeting with Jack Blaine at The Mark hotel. They confirmed your usual corner suite.'

Leonard was annoyed with himself for having invested in Jack's hedge fund. For a man with a meticulous eye for detail, how did he fail to spot the signs? His performance had gone completely off the boil. He was a cocky Californian, and he had seemed pretty switched on when they had first met. Leonard was not an easy man to impress, but Jack dazzled him with his financial wizardry. Money, finance: that was not his world. The jargon and the fancy graphs had bamboozled him. Soon after, it seemed Jack had suffered some sort of personal crisis and his fund performance had dived. Leonard had never let his personal affairs impact his professional life, ever. He wanted to meet Jack and the rest of the team in Manhattan again, and decide if it was time to liquidate his position. 'Then there's that keynote address you're giving to the Academy of Neurology at their black-tie benefit dinner at the Plaza,' Susan said. 'I told Conchita to pack your tux and to remember your onyx dress-shirt studs and Cartier cufflinks.'

Leonard thought his speech needed finessing. He would have time to work on it on the plane. He wanted to sound a more optimistic note about the exciting new technological advances, rather than bemoan the spiralling costs and the spectre of litigation that loomed over all medical practitioners, especially in the US.

'Then you've got that breakfast meeting the next morning with Blackstone, also at The Mark, and lunch at The Grill with Oaktree. David Solomon confirmed he's joining too.'

Leonard drank some more tequila and gave a ghost of a smile. Negotiations with the two rival firms for his hospital chain had reached a critical point, and both had given their best and final offers in the bidding war. They were talking a very chunky figure in the ten digits. It was smallish change for the private equity houses, but for him, it would be a total game-changer. Monopoly money. He was brought up Catholic, and though he had lapsed in his late teens, he welcomed divine intervention in whatever shape. He was glad he had chosen Goldman's to advise him on the deal. Thanks to Debbie, head honcho Da-So, as he liked to be called, aka CEO David Solomon, was going to attend the meeting in person. That was a bit of a coup. His personal presence alone helped raise the offer price. Leonard smiled again as he thought how clever it had been of Debbie to invite him to their wedding.

'And then you fly to London straight after lunch. Back home for the weekend, as you wanted. I hope you have a great trip, Leonard. And try to catch some sleep on the plane. You're going to need it.'

'Thank you, Susan,' Leonard said. 'I don't know what I would do without you.'

It was Susan's birthday in a couple of days and Leonard had already arranged to send her a massive bouquet of flowers and a special bottle of Krug in his absence.

He was exhausted and he needed to get an early night. His brain was whirling with disparate thoughts. There was so much complexity in his life right now: the hospitals sale, the operating he wanted to continue, the media spotlight, his philanthropy. He was used to it by now, but he needed to bring it all together and stay on top of it. At least the divorce was finalised in record time. That was one less thing to think about.

It had been quite a ride from the shack in Jo'burg, before he got that scholarship to Harvard med school. People looked at him, elegant and refined, and they imagined he had spent his childhood riding thoroughbred stallions on a lavish reserve in the African bush, like something from *Out of Africa*. But his life back then was outside toilets and baked beans for tea.

He thought about his dinner date with Ava the other night, and how much he'd enjoyed it. He had not had sex for five months now and he wondered if that was bad. Somehow, he was too busy to think about sex these days. He was surprised how close he had grown to Ava, even though they had never slept together. She looked like she would be good in bed.

But he worried that he would disappoint her, that he would come too quickly and fail to satisfy her. She looked like she had had many men in her life. A man-eater. He was curious to know what Ava thought of his dick pics. She never said anything. Just thinking about her, he felt something coming up...

Leonard finished his tequila and headed out into the cold, dark night. He shuffled back to his brand-new limestone and marble penthouse, with its sensational views overlooking Hyde Park. He was alone again. As usual. The way he liked it. He was a hero. He healed thousands with his life-saving brain surgery. He wrote bestsellers on the mysteries of consciousness and the complexities of the electrochemical impulses between the brain, the mind and the soul. It was a shame he was so afraid of baring his own soul.

29.

Now You See Me, Now You Don't

Ava always believed she had a type: a tall, ice-cool alpha male with blue eyes. Her spectrum of attraction was, in her mind, narrow, but very, very deep. But in reality, she had been enthralled by a rainbow of many diverse colours. There was Harry, charming and urbane in his dark grey Savile Row suits; Hugo, charming and self-deprecating in his faded GAP jeans and white Uniqlo T-shirts; Sami, charming and hungry for life in his tan suede Tom Ford bomber jacket. Different as these men were, there was one thing they had in common: they all had a dog. And they all used a picture of their four-legged friend as their WhatsApp profile photo. Ava learnt to recognise each and every one of them. There was Harry, with Sherlock and Watson, his beloved twin whippets, elegant and racy like himself; Nelson, Hugo's adorable, sad-eyed beagle; and Sami with his golden retriever, Solomon, as clever as his namesake and his master. She wondered if men chose dogs in their image, or if the dogs came to look like their owners over time.

Ava thought of how much she had loved all these different men. She had spent hours longing and aching for each of them. Sure enough, after a while, the pain of living without them faded, and there remained a sweet, sentimental tenderness. She remembered all the good parts, and the bad bits were somehow forgotten, more or less. Real life moves forwards. Desire renews itself. Love lives to see another day.

But every one of Ava's former lovers, every single one of them, always came back to her, always, like homing pigeons. They did not like to be ignored, they did not appreciate being neglected and, most of all, they did not want to be forgotten. If ever there was a tactic designed to reawaken in them fresh lust and new appetites, it was ZERO CONTACT. That was precisely when they all sprung back to life, like magic, just when Ava stopped pining for them.

Ava was in the office. It was a slow trading day, and she was studying a request from one of the doctors she'd met on a recent trip to India, for the establishment of a basic medical centre in deepest rural Rajasthan. She had experienced first-hand the mystic soul of the Mughal Empire, all shimmering pinks and oranges, but also the stench of the slums, black and blacker. What interested her was less airy philanthropy, more making a real difference between life and death. She pulled out her iPhone to make a bank transfer when up popped a familiar photo. She did a double-take. It was a shot of Sherlock and Watson frolicking on a vast expanse of green lawn.

My darling A, I've just flown in from the Middle East. How about a spot of lunch? H x

It was vintage Harry. No preamble, no context. Just like the Queen, Harry's guiding precept was 'Don't complain, don't explain'. It had been six months since Ava had last heard from Harry, with that one short text, just when she thought she might, possibly, be falling in love with Eren.

Ava reread the message and looked for the part that said he had finally left his wife, that he loved her more than ever, and that he was now coming to whisk her off into the sunset. There were no such words. No matter. For sure, Harry wanted to tell her all this in person. Evidently, it was not protocol to declare this on a WhatsApp message.

Hello H, she texted back, her heart beating faster, *I'm free. A x*

Free? Of course she was free. Nothing would ever stop her from being free for a date with Harry. She hastily cried off her lunch date with Mr Nice-But-Not-Quite-Right, and tried to steady her nerves.

Mark's Club. Ava and Harry dined there often, back in the day. A quietly luxurious Mayfair gem, tastefully curated in swathes of muted gold and burgundy velvets and silk damasks, the venue was suitably exclusive and ultra-discreet. Harry could, almost, feel as if he were dining at Huntington, except his own Old Masters were real and priceless. Mark's staff were attentive and well trained. They knew their Château Lafite from their Château Margaux, and the bread knife from the fish knife. Given how hard it was to become a member of the club without languishing for several years on the waiting list, it was remarkable how much more polished the waiters were than most of the guests. The fact that they served carb-laden comfort food of the kind that could only be found in British boarding schools circa 1970 was a welcome added bonus.

Ava stepped inside. She was wearing a tight Givenchy dress with more than a suspicion of cleavage, a white gold and diamond necklace and vertiginous Vuitton sandals. Timeless. Sexy, but not Too Much. Perfectly *comme il faut*. Harry would approve, she hoped. She was early, and she ordered a glass of champagne in an attempt to compose herself. Twice in three minutes she checked her pocket mirror for signs of runny mascara. Harry, also a stickler for punctuality, arrived a few seconds later. Ava's heart stopped as she caught a glimpse of him out of the corner of her eye. She pretended not to notice him, but he was hard to miss. He was suntanned, wearing his usual uniform of double-breasted grey suit and pale blue shirt, whose carefully chosen shade brought out the blue of his eyes to perfection. He kept his sunglasses on, momentarily, as he strode in. He looked older and more lined, but as elegant as ever. Ava felt a familiar rush of desire for him, and she took a deep breath.

Harry held her waist tightly as they kissed, lingeringly, on the cheek. She lost herself in the scent of his distinctive cologne mixed with the heavenly smell of his body, and she restrained herself from the overwhelming urge to kiss him full on the mouth. Harry, inhaling Ava's fragrant odours, repressed a similar impulse to do the same.

'You look well, my A,' he said smiling, as he stepped back to take a good look at her.

It was his usual greeting. He always used the possessive, even when it was not remotely warranted. Ava thought it must be some feudal relic, *droit du seigneur* and all that, which coursed through Harry's veins, just as it had done through his ancestors'. The power of pedigree.

'Thank you. So do you, Harry. Dashing as ever.'

'Dashing around, more like,' Harry answered. 'I haven't slept in days. Those government planes, you know. It's not exactly like sleeping in the comfort of one's own four-poster bed.'

No, Ava did not know.

They sat down, side by side on the banquette, so that their bodies touched, even if their lips could not.

'I've got a present for you,' he said, taking out a small pale blue box from his jacket pocket with a flourish.

Ava's heart beat faster.

Harry held out a Smythson Nile-blue box, rather than the distinctively more desirable Eau de Nil-blue Tiffany box. She forced herself to smile graciously as she opened the package.

'Oh,' she said, her eyes widening at the crocodile notebook with the words 'YES, YES, YES' embossed in gold on the front. 'Oh.' She gulped. 'Thank you.'

She had waited so long for Harry to pop the question: the only question that mattered. The question to which the only answer was, of course, 'YES, YES, YES'. She smiled more broadly, eyes shining, as she waited for him to speak.

'I haven't stopped thinking about you, my darling,' Harry said. 'The last few months have been so terribly troublesome. Life at Huntington has become utterly intolerable. Araminta is more beastly than ever. She attacked me with a kitchen knife last week. Her drinking is now completely out of control.'

Ava nodded. She had heard these courtly tales of domestic abuse in the castle many times before. It was all familiar territory, and she made a heroic effort to stop her eyes from rolling. She waited, with a fixed smile, to hear the significance of the 'YES, YES, YES'.

'You have no idea, my darling, how much I've missed you. I think about you every second of every day.'

Harry stared at her with his intense deep-blue gaze. The words that Ava was so used to hearing tripped off his tongue, yet Ava still felt her heart thumping in her chest, as though she was hearing them for the first time.

'I've decided the time is right to embark on a spot of property development. It's been in the works for years,' Harry said. 'My trustees have agreed to sell some of our family's estate to Her Majesty's Government. We're going build a whole new town, several schools and a big extension to the M1 motorway. It's not going to be an insignificant project.'

Ava nodded. He always spoke in litotes; a mark of his impeccable breeding, no doubt. If Harry said it was 'not going to be an insignificant project', that meant it would be a massive stonker of a deal.

'I need to make a move, my sweet. I need to leave Araminta before I sign off on the venture. It really is now or never,' Harry said as he looked deep into Ava's eyes.

'Yes,' said Ava, waiting with bated breath.

Her head was spinning, and she was struggling to think. All she could do was feel. She felt Harry and her deep love for him. She prayed that it be now, not never. Please, please. She returned Harry's gaze, searching for clues as to what he might decide to do. Harry was always doing another mega-deal, and it was always mega-crunch time. It was baffling how crunchy his life seemed to be.

The waiter arrived and took their order. Salmon tartare, no onion, for Ava, and beef tartare, the dieters' favourite, for Harry. He asked for a bottle of chilled Krug, as one had to cave into decadent pleasures sometimes. It was simply a question of choosing which ones.

'I love your sunglasses,' said the heavily made-up blonde with garish red lips sitting next to them. She took advantage of Harry's upward gaze at the waiter to start chatting to him, and she totally blanked Ava. 'They're Maui Jims, aren't they? They're great. I lost my last pair on Elton's yacht in Mustique last Christmas. What a nuisance!'

What a nuisance indeed, thought Ava. *What a nerve, to interrupt us like that.*

She was stunned that another woman had the gall to try to pick Harry up with Ava sitting right there next to him. The wonderful world of Mayfair... And while Ava usually had some tolerance for discussing the merits of various sunglasses brands, Elton's yacht or even Mustique with random restaurant neighbours, now was not the time. She concealed her irritation and smiled sweetly. She knew Harry hated red lipstick, especially when it had, rather regrettably, spread onto Ms Red Lips's front teeth. But Ava also knew that any female attention, for Harry, like for her father, was always welcome, irrespective of where it came from.

Harry nodded, smiled faintly and turned back to Ava. 'Enough about me. How have you been, my darling?'

Harry's question as to her well-being felt a bit like the journalist who asked Mrs Abraham Lincoln if she had enjoyed the play, after the bullet had struck her husband. Eton and what passed for family life at Huntington had not exactly equipped Harry to speak with any eloquence about emotions. Life was best managed like a civilised game of croquet: keep calm and carry on. Anything else was simply *infra dig*. In any event, Ava was not wildly keen to share the searing pain of her broken heart and the pummelling to her soul with Harry himself. It was bad enough to have lived through it. Revisiting that pain with its sole perpetrator was the height of bad taste.

'I'm fine,' she murmured, with only a slight wobble. The inability to express any real emotion was contagious. Now, finally, she was fine. But how she had struggled to be fine. How hard it had been to find her way forward. She had wasted a long time getting to feeling 'fine'.

'It's been, um, interesting. I've learnt a lot,' she added.

Harry did not care to ask her what she had learnt. If he had, he might have heard that she had learnt to trust actions a whole lot more than words. Especially when it came to Harry's words.

'I can't get over how well you look, darling. You look better than ever. You look younger every time I see you,' he said.

A familiar deep voice disturbed the hushed ambiance of the room, followed by raucous laughter. Without even seeing him, Ava immediately recognised Damian, and she steeled herself for the gorgeous blonde with legs starting at her armpits that he would naturally have by his side. No. It was not leggy Ms Russia. It was not even a beautiful aristocratic young English rose. Damian sauntered into the courtyard with Harry's wife Número Uno, beaming with pride to be seen in such a public place on the arm of one of the most eligible men in London. Damian caught Ava's eye, winked conspiratorially and wondered, for a brief second, if they should swap lunch partners. He thought better of it and prepared to set off rapidly in the opposite direction. It was too late. Número Uno saw her Número Uno and bounded over towards him.

'Harry, darling, what a divine surprise,' Número Uno fawned. 'You look terrific.' Her loud American-accented voice registered with all the diners, as did the latest round of her rather disquieting cheek and lip filler. 'You're so thin. And so suntanned. But darling, someone needs to tell you. You must apply moisturiser. Your skin looks so dry. They do a marvellous one at Harrods. Don't be so bloody English and go get some moisturiser! Men must moisturise too, you know.' She turned to Ava and beamed a smile of pure venom. 'Who's this?'

It must have been the fourth time that Ava had been introduced to Número Uno. Every time they met, she had made an extravagant fuss of her, complimenting Ava on the glow of her skin or her stunning earrings, only to make an extravagant show of not remembering who she was the next time they bumped into each other.

Happily, Damian cut the (un)pleasantries short. He intuited the potentially explosive nature of the chance encounter, and swiftly manoeuvred Número Uno far away, to a table on the other side of the room. It was not a case of cosmic coincidence. More like the usual suspects gathering in the usual hotspots to enjoy the usual scene.

'Handsome fellow, that Damian,' said Harry, with a half-smile. 'Looks rather *simpatico*, don't you think?'

Harry always had an uncanny sixth sense.

'Mmm,' Ava said, feeling herself blush at the memory of a naked Damian with a huge erection, lying on her grey velvet sofa, performing cunnilingus on her. Rather well, she remembered.

'Well, I must say, I'm relieved they left,' Harry said. 'I'm not sure I can cope with my first ex-wife in such close proximity. Not today, at least. I'm awfully jet-lagged. But I do worry about her. I really do. I think she's been so dreadfully lonely since I left her. It was a long time ago. Still, it must be so very hard for her.'

Ava smiled at his patronising words. Bless him: Harry couldn't help it. It must indeed have been the jet lag that accounted for Harry forgetting, temporarily, that Número Uno was a lot less lonely now she had several tens of his millions to cuddle up to. In any event, that appealed to Número Uno more than cuddling up to her real-live flesh-and-blood husband, back in the day. And Harry also appeared to have forgotten that he had regaled Ava with amusing tales of their rather peculiar sex life. Recollections vary through time, clearly. It was not a sexual pairing made in heaven. Número Uno was considerably more interested in vigorous hoovering than vigorous fornication, even though they kept an army of servants up at Huntington. And when fornication did take place, rarely, it was always anal rather than vaginal. She hated eye contact during intercourse, plus anal sex was considerably less messy than vaginal sex, in her opinion. In any event, Número Uno's preferred and principal preoccupation was rearranging her sock drawer by colour and in perfect alignment.

'Ava, darling. Now tell me. What's been happening in your life? The girls well?' Harry asked. He still didn't remember their names. Before Ava had a chance to answer, he looked very serious and added, 'You know, I really think I have to leave Araminta this time. I don't think I can take any more of her antics. She's grown more feral than ever.' He took a sip of the perfectly chilled Krug. 'I think a lot about what that Buddhist monk in Yangon said to me. Do you remember? He said that he could see you, bouncing down the street, swinging your bag, like you always do. He said we would be married.'

Married. How could Ava forget? It was the word Ava had been waiting for Harry to pronounce for so long. But this was not, strictly speaking, the right context. It never was, with Harry.

'If I leave Araminta, will you come and live with me at Huntington? Could you bear to leave your beloved Mayfair and live in the country with me? You're such a clever, clever thing, you. Do you think you could bear my lifestyle, my official duties, all my obligations?'

Ava paused. Harry had already asked her that question a hundred times before. Every time, Ava's answer had been the same: a very consistent, emphatic and unequivocal, 'YES, YES, YES.'

'Are you absolutely sure, Ava, that you would really want to be with me?'

'Harry,' Ava said evenly, 'when I say YES, it's YES.'

She stared into Harry's blue eyes and felt that familiar pull into his cosmic force field. The room faded and all she could see, all she could feel, was Harry.

'I love you,' she whispered, and squeezed his hand under the tablecloth.

It had been so long since she had said those words to a man. The last time was when she had told Harry how much she loved him, and then left him. Ava loved Harry. She would always love Harry. But today, for the first time, she looked dispassionately at him. As she listened to the usual monologue, without the feel of his magnificent cock inside her, or the taste of his delicious sperm on her tongue, or the overwhelming sensation that he touched her soul, she wondered if, during all this time, what she saw before her was Harry as the man could be, Harry as she wanted him to be, rather than Harry the man, as he really was. The truth was, she knew exactly who he was. And even with all his faults, and despite all the pain he had caused her, she still loved him deeply, to his core.

'Let me get the bill. I'll walk you home, my sweet,' he said, suddenly impatient to leave.

Ava knew what that meant.

It was a short stroll back to her house. She unlocked the front door and they kissed urgently. Harry tasted like home. Ava fell to her knees and unbuttoned his flies. His large cock was rock hard and Ava started to lick and suck him hungrily. Harry looked down at her, into her eyes, as she devoured him. He came, fast and strong in her mouth, with a loud groan. It felt like he had not come in a very long time. He drew her back up to his face and kissed her, then unzipped her dress. She was braless.

'I love your breasts, darling. You know, you have quite the most perfect breasts I've ever seen,' he said.

Ava knew that was some compliment. Harry had seen quite a few sets of breasts in his time. He licked her nipples and stroked her clit through her nude silk panties. Then he pulled her knickers to the side and rubbed her clit, up and down, slowly, then round and round, faster. She was on the edge of orgasm.

'Do I satisfy you? Do I satisfy you sexually?' Harry whispered as he caressed her. 'It's important to me that I do. I know what a high libido you have, darling. I want to know that I can make you happy in bed.'

Ava was surprised at Harry's need for validation. Had he not seen her orgasm a thousand times, with either a laugh or a sob, or a shudder or a gasp? Had he not felt the intensity of their closeness when they would lie entwined, ecstatic in each other's arms? Still, Harry needed and wanted to hear the words.

'Yes, my love. You're the best,' Ava said.

Harry bent down and flicked his tongue lightly over her clit, then stronger, and he plunged his fingers inside her wet pussy and pounded her.

'You know you're the best, darling,' she gasped. 'I love you, Harry,' she said, breathlessly, as she came in Harry's mouth.

He held his throbbing cock, hard again, and ready to penetrate her. 'I love you too, my darling. I want you. I need you. I want to feel you. I want to be deep inside you,' Harry said, 'and I want to stay there forever. Forever. YES.'

YES. The word was like an electric shock and it jolted Ava out of her dreamy post-orgasmic bliss. At once, she could see this very scene being replayed over and over again through the years. Harry would never leave his wife. It would be a life with Harry and a life without Harry. A world of beautiful words and no actions. In that turbo-charged blast of clarity, Ava made a decision: she chose not to be drawn into Harry's magnetic orbit anymore. Her therapist was right: she could choose what to do and how to feel.

She pulled on her dress and stood with her hands on her waist.

'No, Harry. No. You know how much I love you. I want you. I want to feel you, deep inside me. More than anything. But not until you leave Araminta. We've been through this so many times. I want all of you, or nothing.'

Harry sighed. 'I understand, my love,' he said, 'and I respect that.'

He buttoned up his trousers and carefully tucked his shirt in.

That night, Harry called her and told her how beautiful she had looked that afternoon and how close he felt to her. He repeated how much he loved her, how much he wanted to feel her, to be inside her, beside her, always by her side. He told her that he was waiting for the right time to leave. That the time was not quite right, not now, but it would be, very, very soon.

Ava knew the drill. Waiting for Harry needed a constant renewal of faith and love. It required a particular state of mind that suspended reality. Harry Zen: an ability to view time as infinite and unbounded. A belief that time's wingéd chariot might be kept at bay forever and that Ava would remain on permanent standby, always patient, always loving.

But Ava had waited long enough. The carefully balanced electrical wiring that Harry had been so skilled at servicing went into overload and her fuse blew. At last. She knew she couldn't wait one second longer.

Ava wanted more than a Smythson notebook with the words 'YES, YES, YES' embossed on it. She wanted a life of 'YES, YES, YES'. In the fog of love, far from being a window to truth, her mind was a mega-delusion generator. Finally, she believed that, maybe, she deserved a little more. If she didn't respect herself, how could she possibly expect Harry, or any other man, to respect her? The only way forwards was to say 'NO, NO, NO' to Harry and to start believing that she was worthy of a full, real, complete love.

Ava would start by trying to love herself for a change.

'Cheerio, Harry,' Ava was now able to say.

And this time, it was goodbye for good. And that, as it happens, was that.

In the vast green plains of deepest fragrant Bagan, nestled amid the sacred stupas, and beside the mighty sweep of the Ayeyarwady River, there is a Buddhist monk, chuckling quietly in his golden-domed, candlelit temple.

30.

Life: Don't Cock It Up

'The "we" is so much stronger than the "I",' Ava said slowly. She paused for the audience to absorb the full significance of her words. She was at the Natural History Museum, standing at the podium, in a bare-backed champagne-coloured sheath, giving the opening address at a charity fundraising dinner focused on education for disadvantaged children.

'Together, with your help, we can make a real difference. Together, each one of us here can give poor children an equal start in life. Every child deserves access to equal opportunity. It's shocking how many children leave school without the basic numeracy and literacy skills to get on in life; and they end up in the same poorly paid jobs, just like their fathers and mothers before them, and so will their sons and daughters after them. Together, through education at all levels, we can break the cycle of underprivilege. We can change lives for the better. Ladies and gentlemen, I want to thank you all for coming tonight. Thank you for your support and thank you for your ongoing generosity. And most of all, thank you for making a real difference.'

As the audience clapped, Ava smiled and glided back to her table, shaking a few hands along the way. Many years had passed since she herself had been one of those disadvantaged young kids who had won a scholarship to a private school and then university. Yet she had never forgotten how lucky she was to have had that opportunity, and she was honoured that she was now in a position to help others.

'Great speech,' said Hayden, one of the country's top venture capitalists, as he pulled out her chair and helped her sit back down. 'Good point you made about the direct impact the charity has on people's lives. I also like minimal overheads and no red tape. It's an ethos I instil in all my start-ups.'

He took a sip of water. Ava noticed he did not touch his champagne or his wine.

'I've been looking at different charities over the last few months. Looks like I've met you at the right time, Ava. I want to get involved. I'll get my people to get in touch with your people on Monday.'

Ava was thrilled. Hayden was no pushover, and his personal endorsement would be enough to persuade others like him to join.

'Thank you,' Ava said. She hesitated, then added, 'I know you've come from a challenging background yourself. You know how hard it is when you start off on the wrong side of the tracks.'

'Yup. I see you've done your homework,' said Hayden. 'My mum was a hairdresser, and my dad, well, I never knew him. He took off before I was born.' He cleared his throat. 'I'm aware you didn't have the easiest of starts yourself, Ava.'

Ava blushed and looked away. She hated talking about her past and she wondered how Hayden knew. As she cast her eye over the crowded dining room, she saw a beautiful young woman, with long dark hair down to her waist, hovering behind her.

'Ava, I'm Tracey. Remember me? Sorry to disturb you. I just had to come over and say hello.'

Ava stared at Tracey. She barely recognised her. How different she looked from the shy, ungainly teenager she had met some three years back, when Ava agreed to fund her higher education and living expenses. She even sounded different. Her broad Northern Irish accent was now replaced with the Queen's English.

'Ava,' Tracey continued, smiling, 'you transformed my life. I am so grateful for everything you've done for me. I finished my studies in biochemistry and I'm now working at a start-up at Oxford University.'

'That's amazing!' Ava beamed. 'Well done. I'm so pleased for you, Tracey.'

'Yes, we're working on a cure for Hodgkin's disease. We're on the cusp of some great things.' Tracey looked down. 'You know, my brother died of Hodgkin's five years ago; he was only sixteen. So young, still a child. But thanks to you, I'm working. I'm doing something I believe in, and now I'm sending money back to my ma and my three sisters back in Belfast. I'm building a successful career and a meaningful life. None of this would have been possible without you. I'll always be thankful for your support. You believed in me.'

Ava hugged Tracey again and said, 'You don't know how happy this makes me. Women have a lot to navigate, particularly where you're from. I know it's a tough journey. It's a privilege to be able to help. Really, it is.'

Tracey squeezed Ava more tightly, and whispered, 'I felt so alone.'

Ava felt her eyes water. She knew all about being alone, back then and still now.

'Then I heard about the charity. It was life-changing. And knowing that you had my back, well, that made all the difference.'

'Please keep in touch,' Ava said, as she wiped away the tear under her eye. 'I want to know how you get on. And tell your sisters about the charity. Maybe they also want to go to Oxford to study, like you.'

Ava took a deep breath, smoothed her dress and sat back down. Hayden edged his chair closer to hers and stretched his arm out onto the back of her chair. Ava thought she felt her hair being lightly stroked, but it must have been her imagination.

'So, tell me, how come a beautiful woman like you is still single?' he asked. 'You must have so many admirers. I guess it must be because you don't want to be tied down.'

There it was. The *still* single question. Ava crumpled inside. Was it that obvious that she was *still* single, or had Hayden asked around?

'Well, perhaps I want to be tied up, rather than tied down.' Ava had finally learnt that the only way to tackle the dreaded *still* single question was to deflect it with humour.

But why was she flirting with Hayden? It was the habit of a lifetime.

'Tied up? Well, that can be arranged,' Hayden said, now tracing a finger gently down the back of Ava's naked spine.

Ava turned to look at him. He was the quintessential plutocrat. Very tall, sexy bald, with piercing blue eyes, perfect Hollywood-white teeth that had clearly been capped, immaculate grooming and an air of confidence that comes with being a highly successful self-made man. It was only then that she spotted his wedding ring, a platinum band that matched his platinum Richard Mille Grand Complication.

'Actually, I'm between husbands,' she said.

She thought that was probably one of the unsexiest remarks any woman could make. She wanted to discourage his pincer manoeuvre of attack. She knew she would find it hard, and hard to resist too.

Hayden smiled and his teeth glinted in the light. Ava could practically see the hungry tiger under the claret-coloured velvet Kingsman tux, waiting to be unleashed.

'So, what, exactly, are you looking for in your next husband?'

'Why, that's easy,' Ava said with a laugh. 'A man to worship and adore. Oh, and a man with a strong moral compass.'

'I see.' Hayden inched further towards her. 'Every man dreams of being worshipped and adored. Especially if the woman doing the worshipping is you. But tell me, what do you mean by a "strong moral compass"?'

'Oh, I think you know, Hayden. A man who acts with honour and honesty and courage. A man who does the right thing. No messing around.'

'Well, it's never black and white, is it?' Hayden flinched ever so slightly. 'My wife is beautiful. She's an amazing woman. She's a great mother. She runs a great home. Well, four homes, in fact. She works out a lot and she stays in shape. But, well, she never wants to have sex with me. What's a red-blooded male supposed to do?'

Ava had heard that comment so many times before, she felt both her eyeballs do a double pirouette to the back of her head. It was all so predictable.

'I see,' she said dryly. 'I know that sometimes a candlelit bath with your wife and a glass of bubbly doesn't quite cut it. You need a bit more ... er, excitement?'

The word had tripped out of her mouth, and she regretted saying it. She knew exactly which Pavlovian response it would trigger in Hayden.

'Excitement?' said Hayden, pouncing on the word. 'Why, yes. Excitement. How did you know? That's exactly what I'm missing.'

'Excitement, Hayden, like magic, is something you make.'

'Really? I'm not sure excitement can be manufactured.' It was a surprising comment, coming from a man like Hayden, who was used to making anything he wanted happen.

Ava winked at him. 'Just use your imagination. You look like a man who's got plenty of that.'

Hayden started gently caressing Ava's shoulders.

'Not that kind of excitement.' Ava laughed, shifting away from his touch. 'Excitement with Mrs Hayden... Obviously.'

The very last thing Ava needed was to get involved with another married man. Hayden was indisputably an alpha, and an 'H' to boot, but a married 'H'. In any event, in the wake of Harry, Hugo, et al., Ava had decided to stop looking for her Mr H. And this time was no different to the other married men she had fallen for. It was like asking for pain and rejection, and she'd had enough of that by now. Maybe she had learnt something after all. It was not exactly a giant leap, but perhaps a little shuffle forwards.

'You know, for a woman, especially a beautiful woman, ageing can be an awful thing,' she said. 'It can almost feel like a personal failing, like something to be ashamed of. Maybe your wife could do with a little more of your time and attention? Perhaps you could rediscover her all over again? That could be exciting for both of you.'

Hayden raised his right eyebrow, almost imperceptibly, and an ironic smile formed on his lips. The dining hall grew quiet, and the throng of people in it faded to grey. They were the only two people in the room, floating in an infinite continuum of time and space. Ava and Hayden looked at each other, their blue and green eyes penetrating, searching, feeling each other.

'Hayden? Now there's a man I wouldn't kick out of bed for eating crackers.'

Ava could hear a woman on the adjacent table gossiping about him.

'Did you see him on the *Sunday Times Rich List*? He's married, of course. All the good ones are. Story of my bloody life. I think he's either on his second or third wife. Can't quite remember.'

'Yeah, whatever,' said another female voice. 'But these married guys, they're all detachable. You just gotta be there at the right time and know how to detach them. Right? The truth is, no man ever leaves his wife without having a warm bed to fall into.'

The two women guffawed loudly.

The spell between Ava and Hayden was broken, and Ava suppressed a giggle. She knew from Hayden's grin that he had heard the snippet of conversation too.

'For the record, she's my third wife,' Hayden said.

'Hey, who's counting?' Ava laughed. Her face turned serious, and she added, almost inaudible above the din in the vast vaulted space, 'Oh, the things we do for love. We live for love. We die for love.'

Hayden heard her perfectly, but he pretended he hadn't, and he leaned in closer. 'Do you mean the things we do for love, or the things we do for sex?'

Ava trembled, remembering all the things she had done for love. She rubbed her bare shoulders, suddenly feeling a chill. 'Well, Hayden, don't you think the best sex is an expression of real love?'

'Maybe. Who knows? I certainly don't,' said Hayden. 'Real love? It never lasts. Sometimes love feels like a story we tell ourselves to explain why we desire the people we do. To make that person seem more special than they really are.'

'Ah, come on, Hayden, now you're sounding like a real cynic,' Ava said, now smiling. 'If a woman said what you just did, she'd be accused of being a miserable old bag. But coming from a man like you, well, it almost invites one to prove you wrong.' She winked.

'You could always try me.' Hayden winked back and flashed his white teeth. 'You look like a woman who likes a hard challenge.'

Hayden placed particular emphasis on the word 'hard' and Ava couldn't stop herself laughing again. She could see where all this was leading. It was a road she had taken one time too many. The journey had always ultimately hurt her, and the destination had never been where she wanted to end up.

'Love,' she said. 'It's the elixir of life. It's what makes us human. Love makes life worth living. It's the only thing that matters. Love is the only thing that remains, when everything else has disappeared.'

'Sounds like you're one of the last great romantics left in Mayfair.'

'I'll take that as a big compliment,' Ava said. 'I'm a believer. Somehow. Despite all the evidence to the contrary. Love is the ultimate triumph of hope over experience, isn't it? After all, what's a life without love but blinks of desolation?'

31.

The Course of True Love Never Did Run Smooth

S omewhere in a faraway land, the goddess of winter sprinkled snow crystals with a bountiful and loving hand. The full moon glowed in the velvet sky. The mountains, resplendent between heaven and earth, surveyed the human dance of love and seduction far below. There was magic in the air.

Ava looked out at the wintry wonderland with a dreamy look in her eye. She was *still* single, but she was no longer lonely. She had stopped searching for her Prince Charming. Finally, she understood that she didn't need to chase love; love would, at the right time, in the right place, chase her. She began to believe that maybe, just maybe, she was worthy of love.

It was a snowy New Year's Eve in a beautiful chalet filled with beautiful people. A time to celebrate; out with the old, in with the new. It could have been a scene in Mayfair, Antibes, Courchevel, St Barts or the Hamptons, but it happened to be Verbier. Again. Blondes with plumped-up breasts and lips, sculpted bodies and hungry eyes mingled with perfectly mannered men perfumed with the scent of money and effortless superiority. The room buzzed with the beau monde in high spirits, living the dream. Everyone looked 'simply divine, dahrling'.

Ava gave both her daughters a big kiss as they headed out. How blessed she was to have such loving girls.

'It's going to be the best year ever, Mama,' Khassya said.

'Totally epic. I can feel it,' Sasha added.

She went to sit with some of her old friends around the large oak dining table, overflowing with a mouth-watering spread of dressed lobster halves, Russian caviar, foie gras and other lavish delights. There were Oliver and Tatiana, now six months pregnant and expecting twins, still looking adoringly at each other. Celeste, impeccable in her coiffed iciness, was throwing daggers at James, who was deep in conversation with the long-limbed Ethiopian chalet girl, the soul of Africa burning warm and bright in her amber eyes. Damian, debonair as ever, was stretched out on a lounger on the terrace, puffing on a cigar and chatting with an aspiring actress who had, perhaps strategically, skied right into him on one of the baby slopes. Oh, and there was Jeannie, lustrous with love, arm in arm with her fiancé, Eren, whom she'd met while waiting for her Caramel Ribbon Crunch Frappuccino blended concoction, as he stood waiting for his double espresso in a Mayfair Starbucks. Ava hadn't thought to introduce them, but they were destined to meet.

'Men are hunters, by nature. They need to chase you.' Ava was sitting next to Lizzie. They were discussing men. Again. 'If it's too easy, it's boring and they don't think you're a prize.'

'Nah,' said Lizzie, gorgeous as usual in slim-cut cream Ralph Lauren trousers and a matching cream turtleneck jumper. 'It's the twenty-first century, Ava. Those old rules don't apply anymore.'

'I wish I could agree. I think if you want a Real Man, you need to let him behave like a Real Man. And that means letting him run after you.'

'Oh gawd. I'm not sure I know what a Real Man is anymore, let alone if I want one. I just want a hot guy who's also a great shag. I need regular sex. Flush out the pipes and clean away the cobwebs.'

'I get that. Can't be too difficult to source. Simply swipe right on Tinder, I guess.'

'And why not?' Lizzie grinned. 'It's the new gig economy. Reminds me of that stupid joke men tell about why bother to buy the cow when you can get the milk for free. Well, the female variant is why buy the entire pig when all you get is a little sausage?'

Ava threw her head back and laughed. 'Why indeed? No little sausage for me, thank you very much. Perhaps I'm old-fashioned. But I like to be chased. Sometimes it's frustrating, that's for sure. I just find it demeaning to run after a man.'

Lizzie wondered if Ava had already had too much to drink and it was making her soft in the head. What happened to the kick-ass girl she knew from before, the fierce woman who took no prisoners and who went for who and what she wanted?

'I dunno anymore. I give up. It's too bloody hard, this search for a bloke.' Lizzie sighed. 'I only got to where I did in life by having balls. I've got more balls than most of the guys I know. I can't pretend to take a back seat; it feels so phoney.'

'I understand, believe me I do. And I don't have all the answers. But I think all the skills that you need to get ahead in your work life – like you, as a barrister, you know, being strong and tough and in control – well, men don't want that in their girlfriend. Men like it when women are sweet and feminine and vulnerable, and then they can be your hero.'

'Christ, you're sounding like my grandmother.' Lizzie gave a mock yawn. 'No, not my grandmother. My grandmother's grandmother.'

Ava ignored the joke. 'Maybe it's just a question of range and knowing when to be hard and when to be soft.'

'Team Tits always gets such a raw deal.'

'I know,' Ava said. 'I spent most of my life looking for love in all the wrong places and I made so many mistakes. And guess what? I'm *still* single. But recently I realised, after a lot of screw-ups, that whether you're hard or soft, tough or sweet, you've got to love yourself first.'

'Screw-ups, or screws?'

'Both.' Ava chuckled, then looked serious. 'I learnt the hard way, through years of pain and rejection and getting it wrong. If you want the King of Hearts, you need to be the Queen of Hearts. If you don't love yourself first, you're going to spend all your time running after men who don't love you either. Trust me, I know all about that. I could write a book on it.'

'No offence, Ava, but I'm not in the mood for those psycho-babbly clichés. All that woo-woo spirituality.' Lizzie frowned. 'All that "Love yourself. Accept yourself. Awaken your feminine inner goddess beauty". Blah, blah, blah. Feels like a Mindful Mac meditation. So corny.' She picked up her champagne glass and downed it in one. 'What did I learn during my years of being single? I learnt that the only language men really understand is when you behave like a bitch. Men want you if they think they can't have you. Then they want you more. There's only one strategy with men that works every time: make them beg.'

'Mmm...' said Ava. 'Maybe that works in the short term. But I'm not sure it works long term, not if you want a proper relationship. Take a look at our Jeannie; she looks so happy, doesn't she? She stayed true to herself and look how naturally she met Eren, in Starbucks of all places.'

Lizzie closed her eyes. She thought of all those hours she'd wasted on Tinder and Bumble and Inner Circle and Hinge and Raya, always hoping for bigger, brighter, better. Perhaps her dream man was under her nose too?

'Make men beg? I don't think so. I don't like myself much when I'm being a bitch.'

'Oh, come off it, Ava. Men love a tough broad.'

'I prefer to be hard to get, yes, but easy to be with.'

Lizzie rolled her eyes at the tedious mantra.

'Sounds boring, right? But tell me, Lizzie, how's the "treat 'em mean to keep 'em keen" approach working for you?'

'I'm working on it,' Lizzie snapped.

'I understand your frustration.' Ava spoke more softly now. 'Believe me, I tried every strategy in the book until I realised there's no magic silver bullet. Finding the man of your dreams is not a twelve-step programme. It's one of the hardest things in life.'

'Yeah. Hard to think straight when you're desperate, that's for sure.'

'And if there's one thing I know for sure, it's that desperation smells.'

Both women laughed in recognition.

'Anyway, I'm so over all that man-hunting thing,' Ava said. 'Always looking, looking, looking. It's exhausting. It's not how I want to spend my time. For me, now, the only way forward is to be the sunniest, happiest and best version of myself that I can possibly be. That's what I've changed: my relationship with myself. I'm trying to loathe myself a little less, and to like myself a little more. I'm trying to be the person I want to be, rather than the one I'm doomed to be.'

The last few months had been 'not boring'. Ava had so much hope and longing for true love, and so little to show for it. Love? What love? It was a parody of love. She was in a Feydeau farce, with none of the funny bits. She saw, in a flash, a tableau of the libidinous men who had frolicked in and out of her life: Harry, Hugo, Sami, Roger, Eren, Callum and all the other minor characters. They all blurred into one. A cortège of joyous highs and crashing lows. A game of snakes and ladders, but with no clothes on. The dance of the hokey-cokey: in, out, in, out, shake it all about. It made for relatively amusing dinner party anecdotes, but after a while, it was just same old, same old.

Ava had received plenty of punches, but what was the punchline? Her 'I fuck, therefore I am' mantra had not exactly led to the happiness and intimacy she yearned for. That is, until she decided to give herself that love. Only by being at peace with herself, on her own, could she hope to attract her dream man. After all, don't they say that fabulous loves fabulous?

Ava looked around the room. The dinner party was kicking. All the men with their perfectly groomed designer stubble were speaking with loud elongated vowels and drinking shaken, not stirred, dry vodka martinis. The stunning partners who accompanied them defined themselves, with absolutely no intended irony, in relation to their man, be it as wife, second wife or wife in waiting, rather than by what they actually did, which was looking after their husband, second husband or potential husband. It made for the usual dinner party chatter: the summer holiday brag; the direction of house prices in Mayfair; how to make the perfect sourdough; where to source the best squat-proof yoga leggings; clever little Johnnie's progress through Eton. How much more thrilling could the conversation get?

The dancing started and the music grew louder and unashamedly retro. Ava went to dance. It was U2's iconic 'I Still Haven't Found What

'I'm Looking For' and she couldn't help but smile at the irony. Only now, for the first time in her life, Ava had finally stopped looking.

Oblivious to the other people in the room, she began to move slowly at first, too sensuous and completely inappropriate for the buoyant rock beat. As she felt the rhythm pulsate through her, she moved faster and wilder, tossing her long hair back. She threw her arms up in the air, rolled her shoulders, one at a time, and swayed her hips, smiling. All she could feel were the waves of happiness surging through her, as she abandoned herself to a moment of pure elation: the sheer bliss of being alive and in the moment. She was flying. Flying solo, but flying nonetheless.

The midnight hour rang.

'Five, four, three, two, one ... Happy New Year!' the revellers cheered in unison and kissed each other. They stood on the balcony, watching the impressive fireworks display bursting through the night sky. Ava stood awkwardly at the side. Still, she felt strangely exhilarated. She was putting the past behind her. After all, it was never too late for new beginnings.

As her friends staggered over to the local nightclub, she could legitimately cry off and head to bed, alone but happy. It had snowed all day. Tomorrow was forecast to be a sunny day with fresh powder snow. Ava could think of no better way to ring in the new year. She wanted to be up on the first lift at 8 a.m. January 1st was always the best day to ski, as the slopes were guaranteed to be empty.

Ava slept deeply and woke up feeling joyful, despite the alcoholic excesses of the night before. She stepped out onto the balcony, naked save for a furry blanket wrapped around her. The sky was dark purple and there was the whisper of a golden sunrise in the east. The moon receded and the sun took its place, rising majestically, and turning the sky dusty crimson and then deep orange, like dragon fire. It was a dance to the flow of the universe; a marvel so beautiful Ava thought her heart might break. Dawn: an everyday miracle.

Ava felt very, very small and yet free and empowered. How lucky she was to be part of this beautiful world. She felt more alive than ever, and simultaneously, she felt a pang for her own mortality. Like Keats and his nightingale, she felt the painful beauty of this world and its finiteness. Nothing lasts forever. She had read somewhere that even the sun would burn out and die in seven billion years. She calculated that she herself had another forty, perhaps fifty years to live, if she was lucky. It was a sobering thought, and it strengthened her resolve. She had better live those minutes and hours and days and years well. Life is now and now is all we have.

At last. Ava smiled with a new sense of understanding. She took a deep breath and thanked the universe, the cosmos and its wondrous known and unknown planets, exoplanets, galaxies and multiverses for her happiness. After all, we all know that it's always darkest before dawn.

Now was Ava's dawn. Now was her time and she never wanted to go back to the dark side. She had spent so much time looking for a man, looking for love, looking for answers, looking for meaning, looking to be saved, always looking and never finding, when all along the answer was inside of her. She was going to save herself. She was going to be her own knight in shining armour.

That was quite enough spirituality for one day.

It was time to hit the slopes. Ava shivered and jumped back inside. She reached for her sleek black jumpsuit that squeezed her tight in all the right places, and she grabbed her mirror sunglasses. She was ready for a thrilling morning, a thrilling new year and a thrilling new life, with or without a man.

She breakfasted like a queen, with gusto. Two servings of creamy scrambled eggs; warm olive bread, straight out of the oven, with a thick layer of salted butter; smoked salmon and a large slice of apple crumble. She scraped her hair back into a ponytail, lathered on the sunscreen and spritzed some Guerlain scent behind her ears.

Ava stood in the empty cable car as it floated up the mountain. She beamed with exhilaration, taking in the beauty of the valley below, shimmering with white fairy dust. The air was crisp and fresh, and she inhaled deeply, filling her lungs with its purity. The snow muffled all sounds and there was a stillness and a serenity that seeped, by osmosis, from nature into her mind and body.

Ava thought of the psychic she had seen almost three years ago. All her predictions about her beautiful daughters, her trading successes, her friends, they had been totally spot on. Every single one of them. Except for what she had said about men. There, she had been completely off base.

The psychic had spoken with such conviction, and she had been so certain that Ava would soon meet the man of her dreams. Her 'H' man. 'H' for 'heavenly husband'. 'H' for 'ha ha ha' more like. Ava had met quite a few 'H's, but none of them had been right. She wondered if she would have paid them so much attention if their initial had not started with the letter 'H'. The importance of being 'H'. Ava believed in Harry, then she believed in Hugo, because she wanted to believe that the psychic was right. But it was simply wishful thinking.

Still, on such a sensational morning, even the psychic's misjudgements were irrelevant. Ava wanted to spend the day communing with nature and skiing like a Bond girl, or at least trying to. She leapt out of the cable car, grabbed her skis and strode across to the next chairlift. She felt the buzz of a new text message from the phone in her jacket and she fumbled to get it out.

Merry Kissmas and Happy New Year. You and your sensational kisses are missed. I've been a bloody fool. H xx

The power of a nineteen-word text message hurtling through cyberspace and straight into her inbox.

Ava felt her whole body shift. She could barely breathe, and she unzipped the top of her ski-suit. She slipped on the icy walkway and only managed to stay standing by clutching the metal rail in the nick of time. She reread the text, precariously balancing her phone in one hand and her skis, batons, ski gloves and sunglasses in the other. She only knew one man who wrote with such a tortured syntax. It mirrored his tortured soul. It was Hugo: who else? What could he possibly want now, just when she had started to forget him? It had been a year and a half since she had last heard from him. Sod's law and all that. She felt a familiar mix of elation and annoyance. The universe was definitely teasing and testing her. But what was the test? And what on earth did she need to do to pass?

Wrapped up in her thoughts, she vaguely sensed a tall person walking towards her. He came to sit next to her on the open-air chairlift. The mountain was totally empty. They were the only two people on it. She was mildly irritated. Could he not sit somewhere else? She wanted her own space, with no one encroaching in on her.

'Happy New Year,' the tall man greeted her. 'Splendid morning, isn't it? Aren't we lucky! Looks like we've got the whole mountain to ourselves.'

Ava nodded, frowning. There was no 'we'.

The man shuffled across and settled into the chairlift, so close she got a whiff of his after-shave, Tom Ford's Fucking Fabulous. Ava was lost in thought about how to respond to Hugo's message.

Eventually, she registered the man's deep voice and his English accent. Ava squinted in the dazzling light and shifted her gaze away from the sun. She turned towards the man. He took off his sunglasses and she found herself looking up into a pair of irresistible blue eyes. They were the exact same colour as the sky.

'How do you do?' he said, smiling. 'My name is Hunter.'

THE END
(THE BEGINNING, ACTUALLY)